Bewitched by the Boss

Mixing business with pleasure
has never been so good

In February 2006, By Request brings back two collections containing three favourite romances by our bestselling Mills & Boon authors:

MILLIONAIRE'S MISTRESS

The Sicilian's Mistress
by Lynne Graham
The Rich Man's Mistress
by Cathy Williams
Marriage at His Convenience
by Jacqueline Baird

BEWITCHED BY THE BOSS

The Boss's Virgin by Charlotte Lamb
The Corporate Wife by Leigh Michaels
The Boss's Secret Mistress
by Alison Fraser

Bewitched by the Boss

THE BOSS'S VIRGIN

by

Charlotte Lamb

THE CORPORATE WIFE

by

Leigh Michaels

THE BOSS'S SECRET MISTRESS

by

Alison Fraser

MILLS & BOON®

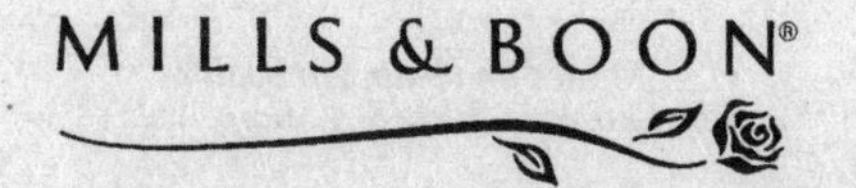

All the characters in this book have no existence outside the imagination of the author, and have no relation whatsoever to anyone bearing the same name or names. They are not even distantly inspired by any individual known or unknown to the author, and all the incidents are pure invention.

Harlequin Mills & Boon Limited,
Eton House, 18-24 Paradise Road, Richmond, Surrey, TW9 1SR

The Boss's Virgin, The Corporate Wife and *The Boss's Secret Mistress* were first published in Great Britain by Harlequin Mills & Boon Limited in separate, single volumes.

ISBN 0 263 84657 1

158-0206

Printed and bound in Spain
by Litografia Rosés S.A., Barcelona

THE BOSS'S VIRGIN

by

Charlotte Lamb

Charlotte Lamb passed away on 8th October 2000 at her home on the Isle of Man, surrounded by her family. Charlotte Lamb started writing for Mills & Boon® in 1971, and published one hundred and sixteen novels. More than one hundred million copies of her stories were sold worldwide. THE BOSS'S VIRGIN was completed just before her death. Charlotte Lamb will be missed by millions of readers around the globe.

CHAPTER ONE

THE party was going to go on for hours, but Pippa was tired; it was almost midnight and she normally went to bed before eleven. When she was younger she'd been able to stay up all night at parties, but her body didn't have the late-night habit any more since she'd had to be at work by eight every weekday morning. She had been forced to realise that burning the candle at both ends was crazy.

She kept yawning, which wasn't surprising since the flat was packed with people and oxygen was scarce. She was beginning to feel quite dizzy as she shuffled around, dancing with Tom under flashing strobe lighting.

'Can we go soon? Would you mind?' she whispered in Tom's ear, and he blinked down at her, looking half asleep himself before he smiled that slow, sweet smile of his.

'I don't mind at all. I'm dead on my feet. Let's go and find Leonie and make our excuses.'

They found her in the kitchen making more bites on sticks: bacon-wrapped dates, bits of cheese sandwiched with pineapple, like the other finger food she had been circulating earlier. She hadn't had any help organising her party; she must have been working very hard all day.

'Sorry, Leonie, we have to get moving,' Pippa said apologetically, kissing her. They had worked together for some years now and Pippa was fond of her. 'We have a long drive back. It was a lovely party; we had a great time. Thanks for inviting us.'

Leonie pushed back her long blonde hair then hugged Pippa. 'Thanks for coming. People seem to be enjoying themselves, don't they?'

'They certainly do. Great food and great music. Where did you get that lighting from?'

'Hired it—it didn't give you migraine, did it? I know it triggers migraines in some people.'

'No, it didn't give me migraine.' But she had hated it all the same; the constant, blinding flashes of bright light combined with the loud music had made her head ache.

'Have some cheese,' Leonie offered, and Pippa took a piece, bit it.

'Delicious, thanks,' she said. 'Sorry to have to go. I hope you'll be very happy, Leonie. You've got a great guy there; I'm sure you will be.'

Leonie glowed, eyes happy. 'He is gorgeous, isn't he? And so is Tom!'

He laughed and she kissed him. 'I mean it! You are. I'm really looking forward to your wedding.'

'So are we,' Tom said, holding Pippa tighter. 'We seem to have been planning it for years. I can't believe it's going to happen at last next week. You'll be planning yours now. Believe me, it's a mistake to hurry. There's so much to work out.'

Tom was good at planning, drawing up lists, double-checking every little detail. He had masterminded their wedding; Pippa had simply attended to the details.

'Well, must go,' he said, and she followed him out of the flat into the faint chill of a spring night. She took his arm, snuggling close to him for warmth. The flat had been so crowded and overheated; the fresh air hit them with a blow that woke them up.

His car was parked down the road. All around them London glowed and buzzed although it was nearly midnight. On a Saturday most young people went out or had parties. The central city streets would be heaving with people drinking and laughing, spilling out of pubs and restaurants to stand in the road, talking, reluctant to go home yet.

Tom hadn't drunk much—he never did; he was a very careful abstemious man—but he had to concentrate to keep his wits about him as they drove through the busy streets which led through the West End and the grey, crowded streets of the much poorer East End into the eastern suburbs. At last, though, they came to the road leading to rural Essex, and within twenty minutes were a short distance from Whitstall, where they both lived.

A small Essex town with a busy market once a week, it had once been a remote village, a cluster of small cottages around a pond, where cattle had stood up to their knees, drinking, a medieval church with a white-painted wooden spire, and a couple of traditional pubs. They drank at The Goat, whose new sign suggested devil worship, although the name actually related to the goats which had once been kept on the common. The King's Head had a very old sign: a mournful Charles the First swung to and fro in the wind above the door.

During this century the village had grown into a town as the railway, and then the advent of the motor car, encouraged people from inner London to move out into the country. With new people had come more houses, circling and doubling the old village centre.

Tom had arrived first and bought a new house on a small modern estate which had been built. Pippa had come to his house-warming party and fallen in love with Whitstall, so she had bought herself a cottage there, too.

'We'll be home soon now,' Tom murmured.

Pippa yawned beside him, her chestnut hair windblown around her oval face and her slanting green eyes drowsy. 'Thank goodness! Mind you, I enjoyed the party. It's great to see our colleagues letting their hair down now and then. They're usually concentrating too hard to smile much.'

'It was fun,' he agreed. 'Leonie and Andy seemed to be on top of the world—she's very happy, isn't she? Getting engaged suits her.'

'Suits me, too,' Pippa said, chuckling.

He laughed, reaching a hand across to touch one of hers, the hand which bore his ring, a circle of little diamonds around a larger emerald. 'Glad to hear it. It certainly suits me. Being married will be even better.'

'Yes,' she said. At last she would be part of a family; she couldn't wait.

The street lamps had ended. They were driving along narrow, dark country roads between hawthorn hedges beyond which lay fields full of black and white cows which had a ghostly look as they moved, flickering and dappled, over the grass they grazed on. Here and there one saw a frilly-leaved oak tree, or an elm vaguely outlined against the night sky.

Pippa sleepily thought about her wedding dress, which would soon be finished. The village dressmaker was hardly what you could call rapid—indeed she worked at a sloth's pace, whenever she felt like it,

Pippa had decided—but the dress was exquisite, a vision of silk and pearls and cloudy fullness. Pippa had a final fitting tomorrow morning. She couldn't take time off work; her fittings had to happen at weekends. Of course, Tom had never glimpsed the dress; everyone insisted that that would mean bad luck.

She already had her veil, but she had yet to buy the coronet she would wear to hold her veil down. She had been looking for exactly what she wanted for weeks, without success. Then on Friday evening, as she'd walked to the tube station, she had seen a coronet of pearls and amazingly lifelike white roses in a wedding shop in Bond Street. Unluckily the shop had shut at six o'clock, so she hadn't been able to buy it. She would go back on Monday, during her lunch hour.

It had taken months to plan everything. She had often wished she had a mother to help her, but, being an orphan without any relatives, she had had to manage alone. The wedding had eaten up half her savings as she had no family to pay the costs. Tom had generously insisted on paying half, making himself responsible for the reception, the white wedding cars and the flower arrangements in the church.

Her green eyes slid to his profile, half in shadow, half lit now and then by moonlight, showing her a straight nose, floppy fair hair, a still boyish face. He was a wonderful man: tender, caring, warm-hearted. She had known him for four years and the more she learnt about him the more she liked him.

And yet... She sighed. And yet, she was still uncertain, troubled. He had first proposed two years ago, but she had gently refused that time, and the next two times he had asked her to marry him. Marriage was an important step; it meant far more than living together, or sharing a bed. She hadn't had a family or a home as a child. She had been brought up in foster care, never feeling she belonged to anyone, or anywhere, envying other children who had parents who loved them.

She had no idea who her parents had been, in fact. She had been left outside a hospital one rainy spring night. Nobody had ever come forward with information about her background. Enviously she had watched other children at school who had a family, a home, something she was never to know.

In consequence she took marriage and family very seriously. To her, marriage meant committing to spending the rest of your lives together, and she wasn't sure she could face that with Tom.

Oh, she liked Tom a lot, found him very attractive, knew him well. He was her boss. They had worked together every day in the same London office for four years, and had always had a good working relationship. Pippa enjoyed his company; he was a good-looking man, and when he kissed her or touched her she wasn't repulsed. If they had not slept together it was because Tom had never insisted. Oh, they had come close to it, yet he had always drawn back, saying he wanted to wait until they were married. He wanted their marriage to mean something deeply important, and she was impressed by his personal integrity. She saw marriage in the same light. Sex was easy. A life commitment was hard.

And yet... She gave another sigh. And yet, something was lacking between them. She knew very well what it was: that vital ingredient. She had been honest with Tom from the beginning, telling him the truth about how she felt. She was not in love with him, even though she liked him so much, and to Pippa it was vitally important to love the man you married.

He had said he understood, accepted that, but he believed she would begin to love him once she was his wife, once they shared their lives fully, and maybe she would. She hoped so.

The car put on more speed. They were coming closer to the little cottage where Pippa lived. Tom came very fast round the final corner just as another car came out of a narrow lane to the right.

Pippa gasped, sitting upright, as tyres screamed on the road surface. Tom put on his brakes and tried to spin the wheel to avoid the other car, but it was too late. The cars hit each other with a violence that threw Pippa forward; she would have gone through the windscreen if her seat belt had not held, and if the airbag had not ballooned outward to cushion her fall.

For a moment or so she was too shocked to move or think, could not remember what had happened. Then she dazedly began to fight her way out of the billowing folds of the airbag, to sit up and take stock. At her side, Tom had also been cushioned by his own airbag, but he had already recovered enough to undo his seat belt and open the car door.

'Are you okay?' she shakily asked him.

'I think so. Stay here,' he muttered.

The other car, a long red sports car, was skewed across the road, its nose buried in the hedge.

Had the driver been killed? she anxiously wondered, as Tom began unsteadily to walk towards it, but then the sports car's door opened and the driver emerged, a tall, lean man, whose immaculate evening dress seemed incongruous in this situation.

Pippa stared, her body pulsing with shock, her heart beating too fast inside her ribcage, her skin cold, her limbs trembling.

The two men faced each other, inches apart. 'Are you hurt?' Tom asked.

A deep voice answered curtly. 'Just cuts and bruises. No thanks to you. What the hell were you doing, driving at that speed?'

Defensively, Tom countered, 'Why did you pull out like that, without looking?'

'I stopped to make the turn. When I looked left the road was empty. I started to come out, then you appeared at about seventy miles an hour. I had no chance to avoid you.'

It was true. Tom had been driving too fast; he should have slowed as he approached the junction. That was what he normally did, but at this time of night he hadn't been expecting to see another vehicle turning out. It was pure luck that the accident hadn't had worse consequences. They could all have been killed.

Tom didn't argue; no doubt he realised he wasn't entirely blameless. He was usually such a careful driver; it wasn't in character for him to take risks.

Glancing past the other man at his red car, he asked, 'Is there much damage to your car?'

They stood with their backs to Pippa, who huddled down inside her black velvet evening jacket, shivering, but not taking her eyes from them. Tom bent down to peer at the sports car's long, sleek bonnet.

'I'm afraid there are a lot of scratches on here.'

'Yes,' the other man agreed angrily. 'It will cost the earth to have the paintwork renewed and the car is new. What about your car? Is that badly damaged?'

He was over six foot, with a long, supple back and even longer legs. As he half turned to glance back at Tom's car she saw his strong features: hard, sardonic, an imperious nose, a generously cut mouth, heavy-lidded eyes, and the way his dark hair curled behind his ears.

He glanced at Tom's car. 'I see you have a passenger,' he murmured. 'An eye witness. A woman? I hope she'll tell the truth if we have to go to court.'

'Don't be offensive,' Tom snapped. 'I admit, I was driving too fast, but I was on the main road. You were coming out of a small lane; you should have waited, let me go past. I'll pay your garage bills; there will be no need to involve the police, or go to court. But if we did my fiancée would tell the absolute truth; I wouldn't ask her to lie.'

The other laughed curtly, his manner making it plain that he did not believe that.

Tom was bristling. Pippa saw his hands screw into fists, but he kept his voice level. 'We had better exchange addresses and the names of our insurance companies. By the way, I work for mine, so you need have no fear they won't pay.'

He turned away to walk back towards his own car. 'I'll get my documents.'

The other man leaned into the red sports car and emerged again with some papers in his hand. He began to follow Tom and Pippa turned her head away, face hidden by the high collar of her velvet jacket.

She sensed the other driver bending to stare at her and closed her eyes, hoping he couldn't see her clearly.

'Is your companion hurt?' he asked Tom, who was

looking into his glove compartment for his documents.

'What?' Tom looked at her. 'Are you okay, Pippa?'

'Just tired,' she whispered huskily, not turning or lifting her head.

But she still felt the probe of the other man's grey eyes and her heart beat like a metronome.

'I'll get you home as soon as I can, darling,' Tom murmured, brushing a strand of her rich chestnut hair back from her forehead.

He turned towards the other driver, proffering the documents he held. The two of them used the bonnet of Tom's car to write down the information each needed. Still keeping her eyes almost closed, Pippa watched through her lashes, breathing unsteadily, hearing the deep, cool voice talking, hoping he wouldn't ask for her address or demand she speak to him.

If she could only get away, escape; she felt doom threaten her, a fate she was not strong enough to withstand. Hurry up, Tom, she thought. Don't stand there talking.

She knew that soothing voice he was using; he was trying to calm the other driver, placate him, talk him round. It was a technique Tom used in business every day; he was an expert at persuading people to do what he wanted.

They worked for an insurance company in central London. Tom was one of the executives who dealt with large claims. He needed all his tact, diplomacy, cool patience, to negotiate with claimants and lawyers. He was doing that now.

Stop talking, Tom, she thought desperately. Get

back in the car and let's drive away. Take me home. Take me safely home.

The two men shook hands—a typically polite English gesture. They had come to an agreement.

'Goodnight, Mr Harding. I'll be in touch.'

The other murmured a reply, less clearly, shot another look into the car. Pippa tensed in dread, but he turned to walk away and she could relax a little, letting out her held breath. He was going.

Tom got back into the car beside her, groaning.

'Well, that was bad luck. My own stupid fault, driving too fast.' He started the engine; it flared, raced, while he listened to it anxiously. 'Let's hope there isn't too much damage.'

'Did you notice much?'

'One wing has crumpled, that will have to be replaced, and my door is badly scratched, but it could have been worse.'

'We could have been killed,' she agreed, her eyes fixed on the man sliding his long legs back into the red sports car. The night wind lifted his thick, silky black hair, winnowing it like caressing fingers.

Yes, it could have been much worse; it could have been disastrous. Her entire body was limp, as if she had barely escaped with her life. All the adrenalin had drained out of her. She yearned to be alone, in her cottage, to think, to recover from this.

Tom parked outside her cottage a few moments later and turned to kiss her. 'Goodnight, darling. I'm sorry about the accident.' He looked down at her, frowning. 'You're very quiet—are you angry with me?'

'No, of course not. I'm very tired, that's all.'

'And having an accident didn't help,' he wryly

said, grimacing. 'Sleep well, anyway. I'll see you on Monday.'

She got out of the car, waved to him as he drove off, and let herself into her cottage, switching on the light. Before she could shut the door again a furry black shape brushed past her and ran gracefully through the hall into the kitchen.

Groaning, she closed the door and followed. 'You're a nuisance, you stupid cat. I want to go to bed, not hang around here feeding you.'

Samson ignored her, nose in the air, his elegant black body seated pointedly beside the fridge. He knew there were the remains of a chicken in there, left over from the dinner she had cooked for Tom last night, and although he would eat tinned cat food if nothing else was available his favourite food was roast chicken.

Pippa knew she would get no peace until she had given in, so she got out the chicken and sliced some into Samson's bowl, added crushed biscuit, poured fresh water into another bowl, and put them down. The cat immediately started eating.

Pippa left the kitchen, turning off the light, and went upstairs, stripped, put on a brief green cotton nightdress. In the bathroom she cleaned off her make-up and washed. In the mirror her face was oddly grey, her eyes dilated, black pupils glowing like strange fruit.

Shock, she thought, looking away hurriedly. Returning to her bedroom, she got between the sheets and switched off the light.

The cottage only had two bedrooms and a bathroom; downstairs there was a comfortable sitting room and the kitchen, with its small dining nook at one end. Her firm had helped her with the purchase; the price had been very low because the place had needed so much work. It had been occupied for years by an eccentric old man.

He had left the cottage more or less as it had been when he'd inherited it from his father forty years earlier, she'd been told by the estate agent. He had done no repairs, no redecoration. By the time he died himself, the place had been in a parlous state. But—the agent had beamed—it wouldn't take much trouble to modernise.

She should never have believed him. Even though the price had been low, the mortgage was more than she would have wished to pay. She had very little left over once she had paid it each month. Despite that, she loved this little house; it was the first real home she had ever had.

In her childhood she had passed from one "family" to another. Some foster mothers had only liked small children and hadn't been able to cope with older girls. Once her foster family had split up in divorce and she had been parcelled off to another one. She had yearned for stability, for a sense of belonging, a real home—and at last she had one. No price could be too high for that.

She could do without expensive clothes, make-up, visits to beauty parlours, holidays abroad. She had a home of her own; that was all that mattered.

She had had to minimise the expense of conversion, though. So she had done all the redecorating herself, even painted the outside walls, standing on a rather rickety ladder she had bought for a song in an auction, but she had had to pay a local builder to repair the roof and instal a new bathroom. Those jobs were beyond her.

But when she and Tom were married they would be living here; she wouldn't have to move again. Tom had grown to dislike his own house; living on a housing estate meant living with noisy children running around all day, kicking balls, shouting, riding far too fast on their bicycles along pavements, and his neighbours played their radios and televisions too loudly.

Life would be easier for them if they lived in her cottage. Tom insisted on taking over her mortgage and she meant to pay for all the food they bought. Their joint income would be comfortable. They would even take holidays in the sun in exotic places.

Lying in the dark, staring up at the ceiling, Pippa smiled at that thought. She hadn't been abroad much; she was dying to go to foreign places, enjoy better weather.

An image flashed through her mind with a strangely vivid sensation, as if it was happening now, right now, and she started, shuddering.

The car crash, those terrifying sounds of tyres screaming on tarmac, the airbag ballooning into her face, the red sports car skewed into the hawthorn hedge, the moment when the driver got out.

Her heart beat painfully, her ears drumming with agitated blood. She shut her eyes. She wouldn't think about it. She had to forget; she must clear her head.

Oh, why had it happened? Why now? Fate had a strange sense of humour. Only one more week and she would be Tom's wife. Why had they had the accident, crashed into the man's car, at this particular time?

She tried to sleep, but was awake most of the night.

The flashback kept coming. Her brain was her enemy and would not let her forget. As the hours wore on, her head began to ache. She was first hot, then cold, twisting and turning in the bed, hearing the tick-tick of the clock on her bedside table as though it beat in her blood.

Eventually she did fall into a heavy, stupefied sleep from which she woke abruptly when her alarm went off at nine o'clock. She felt like death as she stumbled out of bed.

After a shower she dressed in jeans and a clean white T-shirt, then went downstairs to make coffee.

Samson gave her an angry greeting. She was usually up well before this time, and like all cats he had a good sense of the time, especially where meals were concerned. While she moved about he kept brushing against her, slithering between her legs, making his demand calls. Miaow. Miaow. Where's my breakfast? Where's my food?

After giving him a saucer of milk and cereal, she let him out of the back door, watched him streak through the little garden, then she poured herself orange juice and sat down to sip it. After contemplating the idea of some toast, she decided against it—she really wasn't hungry.

The dressmaker arrived half an hour later, bright and cheerful in a neat grey skirt and blue blouse. 'Lovely morning, isn't it?' She said as Pippa opened the front door.

'Lovely.' In fact Pippa hadn't noticed; she had been too preoccupied. Now she glanced around, absorbing the bright spring sunshine, the blue sky, the tassels of catkins on a hazel tree in her garden, the frilly yellow daffodils and deep purplish blue of hyacinth. She had planted them last year; this year they had come up without her help.

'Yes, lovely,' she agreed. Another one of Fate's little jokes, this wonderful weather, the beauty of the morning. It should have been stormy, threatening, not full of light and hope. The weather did not fit her mood at all. 'Can I get you some coffee, Mrs Lucas?' she asked, stepping back to let the dressmaker into the hall.

'Thanks, I'd love some later, but I'd like to get on with the fitting first; I have a busy day ahead.' Mrs Lucas considered her, frowning. 'Aren't you well, dear? You're very pale.'

'We went to a party last night, and on the way home we had a bit of an accident.'

'No! Was it serious? Anyone hurt?'

'Thank heavens, no, and the car wasn't badly damaged, but it was a shock.'

'Of course it was. Bound to be. No wonder you're pale. Well, I won't take up too much of your time. There isn't much to do; the dress is nearly finished. I just want to check that it fits perfectly. Have you got everything else, now?'

'Almost everything.'

'Good girl. Well, get your jeans and T-shirt off, stand on that chair, and I'll slip the dress over your head.' Mrs Lucas stood waiting while Pippa obeyed her. The silk and lace dress was carefully held between her two hands and once Pippa was in position she delicately lifted her hands and the dress dropped over Pippa's head and rustled softly as it fell to her feet. There was a small mirror on the wall opposite her; Pippa could see a partial reflection of herself, looking strange and unfamiliar in that dream dress. What was it about a bride that left a romantic glow?

Mrs Lucas got busy with pins, tucking in her waist a fraction, clicking her tongue. 'You've lost weight again! Another pound, I'd say.'

'Sorry. I'm not dieting, honestly. I can't think why I'm losing weight.'

'Oh, it often happens to brides. Wedding nerves, rushing around, forgetting to eat; they always seem to lose weight. Don't worry, I can cope.'

Her mouth full of pins, she adjusted the set of the lacy bodice from which Pippa's head rose so vividly, with that frame of bright chestnut hair lit by morning sunlight. Pippa watched her mirrored image with uneasy green eyes. Everything seemed surreal, unlikely—was that really her?

And if she seemed strange to herself now, she was going to feel much stranger in a week, after her wedding.

Looking at her watch with a groan, Mrs Lucas got up from her knees. 'I must go; I've got so much to do today. I'll just take the dress off, Pippa, before you get down. Next time you see it, it will fit you perfectly, I promise. You're going to be a lovely bride.'

The silk and lace softly, sibilantly, lifted over her head. Mrs Lucas inserted the dress back onto a hanger inside the plastic carrier in which she had brought it, and zipped up the carrier.

'Have you got time for that coffee?'

'Sorry, no, not really. See you soon.'

She was gone a moment later. Pippa put her clothes back on and made herself black coffee, sat sipping it, trying to shake off her disturbed and uneasy mood.

In a week's time…just a week now…she would be

Tom's wife. She should be radiant, over the moon. A woman's wedding day was supposed to be the happiest of her life—so why didn't she feel happy?

Maybe all brides felt this sense of doom, the fear, the sinking in the pit of the stomach close to nausea? Far from being happy, she had a strong feeling that she was about to make the worst mistake of her life.

She must stop thinking like that! What was the matter with her? She was going to be happy. She wouldn't let herself think negative thoughts.

She went to bed early that evening and was up in good time to get to work. Tom was always there early, and expected her to be early too. Working in an insurance company wasn't exactly thrilling, but the job paid well and the work was never complicated or difficult.

Monday was always a calm day; the postbag was light and their workload was easy enough to deal with as they always tried to clear their desks by Friday afternoon, so she was able to go to lunch a little early that day, to give herself time to get to Bond Street, and then hopefully grab a snack before she went back to the office.

She caught a bus, then walked anxiously, hurriedly, to the bridal shop, relieved to see that the pearl and rose coronet was still in the window. The assistant sat her in a chair in front of a mirror, brought a wedding veil and the coronet for her to try on.

Pippa gazed at herself, smiling; it really was perfect, just what she wanted.

'You look lovely,' the assistant told her, and Pippa thought she looked pretty good, too.

'It's exactly what I've been looking for,' she confessed. 'I'll take it.'

Then the smile went and her eyes widened in horror as she saw a reflection of the street outside behind her shoulders.

A man stood there, staring at her: tall, elegantly dressed, his black hair brushed and immaculate.

In the mirror their eyes met. His were fixed and glittering, bright and hot as burning stars. Pippa stared into them, her stomach turning over, grew icy cold and fainted.

CHAPTER TWO

SHE recovered consciousness slowly, not quite sure what had happened, her lids flickering, then rising; she looked up, her green eyes dazed, not focusing properly.

Two faces bent over her. The assistant looked anxious, upset. The other…

Pippa took one look at him and promptly shut her eyes again. She did not want to believe he was real. Surely she wasn't imagining things, dreaming him up in the oddest places, at the oddest times? Her head buzzed with distressed questions. What was he doing here? Come to that, what had he been doing outside the bridal shop? What was going on? First the accident; now he'd turned up while she was trying on her bridal coronet. What was Fate up to?

'She's fainted again,' the assistant said. 'Oh, dear. Do you think she's really ill? She's very pale. Should I ring for an ambulance? Or a doctor?'

'No, I don't think she's ill; she's just playing dead,' said the deep, cool voice she remembered so well.

How dared he? What right did he have to read her so accurately? Angrily she opened her eyes once more and glared at him, beginning to get up.

It didn't make her any less furious that he helped, as effortlessly as if she weighed no more than a child, lifting her with one arm around her waist, his warm hand just below her breast, the intimacy of the contact making her heart thud painfully.

'Oh...perhaps we shouldn't move her yet,' the assistant nervously murmured. 'She may still be groggy.'

'Oh, she'll be okay. Would you run out and stop that taxi going past? Thanks.'

Pippa was still being held close to that long, lean body; the proximity was doing drastic things to her, especially when she looked up and sideways at the hard-edged, smooth-skinned, masculine face.

She heard the other girl's high heels clipping across the shop and knew she was alone with him. Panic streaked through her; she pushed him away and his arm dropped.

Those bright eyes gleamed with what she grimly recognised as mockery. So he was finding the situation funny, was he? Her teeth met.

'Feeling better now?' he enquired softly.

'Yes, thank you.' Her voice was cold and remote, hiding the rage she felt although she suspected he wasn't missing it; his argument was open, unhidden.

The shop assistant rushed back, breathlessly said, 'The taxi's waiting.'

'Thank you.' He looked at Pippa. 'Maybe you should take the veil off before we go?'

'We' go? she thought. She wasn't going anywhere with him.

But the assistant came to help her. 'So, did you want the coronet?'

'Yes, please.' Pippa fumbled in her bag, found her credit card and held it out.

The assistant offered her the payment slip a moment later and she signed it, then took back her card and put it away, very slowly and carefully, deliberately delaying in the hope that he might go outside to talk to the taxi driver.

She might then have a chance to escape, run off down the road, but he waited beside her, perhaps anticipating her intention. Finally she had to leave the shop, as they walked out on to the pavement he held her elbow lightly, propelled her towards the taxi.

'I don't want to…' she breathed.

'You might faint again; we can't have that.' He smiled, lifting her into the back of the taxi.

She couldn't quite catch what he said to the driver before climbing in beside her, but before she could ask him the taxi set off with a jerk which almost made her tumble forward on to the floor.

'Do up your seat belt,' she was ordered, and her companion leaned over to drag the belt across her shoulder and down to her waist, clip it into place, his long fingers brushing her thigh. He had a fresh, outdoor scent: pine, she decided, inhaling it. She wished he would stop invading her body space. It was far too disturbing.

'Where did you tell the driver to go?' she asked huskily as he sat back, not meeting the eyes that watched her as if he could read her every thought.

'I feel it's time we had a private chat. I told him to take us to my hotel. Have you had lunch?'

Agitated, she protested, 'I'm not going to your hotel! I have to get back to work.'

'You can ring and tell them you've been taken ill,' he dismissed. 'Have you had lunch?'

'Yes,' she lied, and received one of his dry, mocking glances.

'Where? You came out of your office, caught a bus

and went straight to that shop. Where could you have had lunch?'

'You've been following me? Spying on me? How dare you? You had no right,' she spluttered, very flushed now. 'Were you on the bus? I didn't see you.'

'No, I followed in a taxi, then walked behind you along Bond Street.'

She thought harder, forehead wrinkled. 'How did you know where I worked?'

'Your fiancé told me where he worked, so I rang up and asked the switchboard if you worked there, too.'

Simple when you know how, she thought; she should have guessed he would track her down if he wanted to, but she hadn't thought he would want to.

'They tried to put me through, but someone in your office said you had just left, were going shopping in your lunch hour. I was ringing on my mobile from the foyer of the building. A minute later I saw you come out of the lift so I followed.'

She was speechless. He made it sound perfectly normal to follow people around, spy on them—nothing to get excited about. But she was so furious she couldn't even get a word out.

He gave her a wry grin, eyes teasing. 'Stop glaring at me. I had to see you. You knew that, from the minute his car crashed into mine. You knew we had to meet again, that we have a lot to talk about.'

'We have nothing to talk about! I don't want to talk to you at all. I just want to get back to my office and forget you exist.'

But she was so nervous that she put up a shaky hand to brush stray strands of bright hair away from her cheek, aware that he watched the tiny movement with those intent, glittering eyes.

'And you think you can do that, Pippa?' he drawled, moving even closer so that their bodies touched.

She couldn't bear the contact, shifted away into the corner, body tense and shuddering.

'Yes.' But her eyes didn't meet his and she felt him staring at the telltale pulse beating hard in her throat.

He reached out a hand; one long finger slid down her cheek then down her neck, awaking pulses everywhere it rested, until it pressed down into that pulse in her throat. 'What's the point of lying? You're not convincing me; you're only lying to yourself.'

'Don't touch me!' she muttered, knocking his hand away.

The taxi turned into a hotel entrance, set back from the road. She looked up at the grand façade, ornate and baroque, with ironwork balconies outside every other widow, flags flying on the steep roof. She had heard of the hotel but never been inside it; it was far too expensive. Normally she would have loved to go there for lunch, but not with him.

'You get out here; I'll go on to my office!' she insisted, holding on to the seat with both hands.

To her relief and surprise, he got out without replying and paid the driver. Only then did he turn back towards Pippa. 'Out you get!' He reached over and undid her seat belt before she had notice of his intention.

She wanted to yell, scream, hit him, but the hotel doorman had appeared behind him, magnificent in livery dripping with gold braid, smiling an obsequious welcome, and she was too embarrassed to make a scene in front of such an audience.

'I can't. Let me go,' she said instead, very quietly, still hanging on to the seat.

'Let me help you,' he blandly murmured, and the next second he had taken her by the waist and was lifting her out of the taxi. Keeping his arm around her, he guided her up the steps into the hotel foyer while the doorman closed the taxi door and followed them. A moment later Pippa found herself being propelled into a lift; the door shut and the lift began to rise.

There was nobody else in the lift with them; she felt free to break away from him, using every ounce of her strength, looking at him with angry hostility as she reeled against the lift wall.

'How dare you manhandle me like this? And if you think you can get me up to your bedroom…'

'Suite,' he coolly corrected. 'There's a sitting room; we can have lunch there.'

'I am not going with you! Bedroom or suite, I am not going anywhere alone with you!'

'You're alone with me now,' he pointed out in silky tones, leaning over her in what she interpreted as menace, despite the laughter gleaming in his eyes. His proximity was threat enough, even when he didn't touch her.

'Stop it! Keep away from me!' she whispered, trembling.

His face was inches away from her own. 'What are you so afraid of, Pippa? Me? Or yourself?'

Confused, she muttered, 'Don't be stupid. How can I be afraid of myself?'

'Of what you really want,' he enlarged, eyes watching her intently. 'Of your own instinct and desires. You're so terrified of how you feel that you need to shelter behind a pretence of hating me. You can't risk so much as a look at me, can you?'

Face burning, eyes flickering nervously, she said, 'I don't know what you're talking about. Do I have to remind you that I'm getting married in a week's time?'

The lift stopped and the doors opened. Nobody was waiting on that floor; there was no one in view at all. He stepped out, grabbed her hand and jerked her out after him.

'I am not going with you! Let go of me!' She struggled to get away, flailing at him with one hand, managed to land a blow on his cheek, and gave a little cry of pain as she hurt herself on the hard edge of his bone structure.

'Serves you right! You shouldn't be so violent!' He ran an exploring hand over his cheek where a red mark burnt. 'That hurt me almost as much as it probably hurt you.'

'Good!'

A room door nearby opened and an old lady in a pink linen suit, wearing a small black hat with a black lace veil which fell over her eyes, came out, gave them a startled, uneasy look.

'Is anything wrong?' she quavered.

Pippa hesitated fatally; he answered before she could. 'She's shy, that's all. Honeymoon nerves! You know how women get on these occasions.'

The old lady blushed and then smiled; Pippa glared at him. He was maddening; he always had been.

'I should carry you over the threshold, darling,' he said, and suddenly grabbed Pippa off her feet before she could stop him, lifted her up into his arms and strode off with her while the old lady gazed after them with a romantic smile.

Pippa knew she should call his bluff, struggle, hit him again, but with that happy, wide-eyed audience she simply couldn't. In any case a moment later he paused in front of double doors, produced a key and unlocked the suite, carried Pippa inside, into a small hallway, and closed the door behind them with his elbow.

'Put me down!' she hoarsely demanded. 'Put me down at once!'

He carried her into a bedroom and dropped her on the large, white-and silver-draped bed.

Her heart beat wildly in her throat. Surely he didn't intend… She rolled over to the far edge of the bed and shakily stood up, looking around for a weapon to use if he tried to come anywhere near her. The table lamp looked heavy; it had a bronze cast base and could probably kill someone.

But he was turning back towards the door. Over his shoulder he casually said, 'Use the bathroom, if you wish. Your hair could certainly do with some attention.'

The door closed behind him. She was alone and safe, for the moment. Her gaze wandered round the room, absorbing the luxury of the furnishings: high French windows covered with lace and floor-length curtains that matched the white and silver satin bed-cover, the bronze-based lamps with their wide silver satin shades, walnut-veneered furniture that was probably reproduction, not genuinely antique, a chest, a wardrobe whose doors were set with mirrors, a dressing table on which stood a vase of white carnations and roses.

She began to walk towards the door of the *en-suite* bathroom, paused to bend over the flowers, inhaling their faint scent then hurried on, in case he came back.

The bathroom was entirely white, with nineteen-twenties-style fittings, elegant fluted chrome taps. In a cupboard above the vanity unit she found his toiletries: aftershave, an electric razor, shower gel, shampoo. Somehow it was too intimate to stare at them. She quickly shut the door on them and opened her bag.

She found a comb and ran it through her hair, renewed her make-up, considered her reflection, disturbed by the feverish brightness of her eyes, the faint tremble of her mouth, the fast beating of that pulse in her neck.

It was crazy to let him do this to her. She had to pull herself together and somehow talk her way out of this suite. She had given him time to calm down, to think—maybe now he would realise he had to let her leave?

Turning away, she picked up her bag and left the bathroom, quietly opened the door of the bedroom. If he wasn't in earshot she might be able to get away now.

She couldn't hear a sound so she began tiptoeing back along the little hall towards the outer door. Before she reached it, however, a voice spoke softly behind her.

'Don't even think about it.'

She froze, looking round.

He was leaning on the open doorway into what she glimpsed to be a sitting room, his arms crossed, his body lounging with casual grace, those long legs relaxed, making her forcibly aware of his intense sexual allure, the gleaming display of the peacock. And he knew it, too; he was watching her with that infuriating mockery, knowing what she was feeling, amused and sure of himself.

She probably still had time to make a run for it, but he would only take a few seconds to catch up with her and her self-respect wouldn't allow her to make a fight of this. In any case, she knew she would only lose. She had to use other weapons against him.

'I have to get back to work.'

'I've already rung your office and told them you fainted and would be going home to rest instead of going to work.'

She furiously broke out, 'You had no business to do that!'

He ignored her angry splutter. 'I've ordered lunch, too—something simple. I thought you wouldn't want anything elaborate. Salad, some cheese, cold beef and chicken, some wholemeal bread, pickles, some fruit, yogurt, and a pot of coffee.'

'I'm not hungry. You eat lunch; I'll get back to my office.' She turned towards the door of the suite.

'Do I have to carry you in here?' his voice silkily enquired, and she froze.

'Why are you doing this?' she burst out. 'What's the point? You're married; I'm getting married—we have nothing to say to each other.'

Four years ago she had joined his firm after the company she had been working for had gone into liquidation. Pippa had been shocked by the news that everyone was being made redundant, but by sheer good luck she had got a new job the same day. During her lunch hour she had gone into an employment agency to register and had been given an immediate interview with a nearby office.

She had walked down the road, very nervous, a little shaky, and been shown up to the personnel officer, who had tested her various secretarial skills and spent half an hour questioning her.

Pippa hadn't expected to be given a job there and then, but the personnel officer had leaned back at last and said, 'When can you start?'

Heart lifting, Pippa whispered, 'Do you mean I've got a job here? You're taking me on?'

The woman smiled, eyes amused. 'That's what I mean. So when can you start?'

She didn't need to think about it; she knew she would be out of a job by the end of that week and would need to be earning again as soon as possible. She had no one to help her with her rent and the cost of living. She only had herself to rely on.

'On Monday?' Relief and delight were filling her.

'Wonderful. Report to me at nine o'clock and I'll have someone show you to your desk. You'll be working in the managing director's office. His private assistant will be in charge; she'll tell you what she wants you to do. It isn't a difficult job, but it's vital that everything runs smoothly in that office and Miss Dalton is a tough organiser. Be careful not to annoy her. The MD insists on a smooth-running office.'

It sounded rather nerve-racking to Pippa, but the salary was good and the work not too onerous. She left there walking on air, and got back to find everyone else in her office gloomily contemplating living on social security until they found work elsewhere.

'What about you, Pippa?' asked the girl whose desk was opposite hers. 'What will you do?'

'Oh, I've got a new job. I start there next Monday,' Pippa airily told her, and everyone else stared in disbelief.

'How on earth did you manage that?'

'Just luck.' She told them what had happened and they were envious and incredulous.

'I'm going there as soon as I've finished work,' one of them said, and others nodded their heads.

By the end of the week at least half of them had managed to find new jobs—some just about adequate, although one of them had got a much better job. There was a much more cheerful atmosphere in the office. They had a big party in a local Chinese restaurant on the Friday evening, knowing that they would probably not see each other again, although some close friends would keep in touch. Working together was a matter of propinquity. Once they all split up their friendships would begin to fade.

It had been Pippa's first job. She had only been sixteen when she started work there and now she was twenty but felt older because ever since she'd left her last foster home she had been living alone, in one room, managing a tight budget, always struggling to make ends meet. That had made her grow up fast, had taught her a discipline she relied on to help her through each day. She couldn't allow herself to buy anything she could do without; thrift was essential on such a small amount of money.

Her clothes had to last and look good in the office so she bought inexpensive but well-made skirts and blouses which she could vary daily, and wash again and again. She ate little, bought cheaply in street markets, mostly vegetables and fruit, pasta, some fish now and again, or more rarely, chicken. She only had one electric ring to cook on; she had to choose easily cooked food.

She had never been able to afford to entertain so she didn't accept invitations from other people, since she couldn't reciprocate. Once or twice she had had a date with one of the young men in the office, but none of them had attracted her much and the dates had been rather dull.

She felt a little sad, saying goodbye to people she had worked with for four years, though. She was going to miss them. All the same, she was deeply relieved to have another job to go to immediately. She couldn't imagine how she would have paid the rent otherwise. The life of the street people, homeless and hopeless, gave her nightmares for a while. Being made redundant like that had destabilised her life, made her feel threatened, even after she'd got that new job.

On the following Monday she nervously made her way to the office block where she would be working, was taken up in the lift from the personnel office by one of the girls who worked there.

'You know who you'll be working for? Mr Harding, the managing director.' Her voice had a reverent note. 'You're so lucky. He's gorgeous. And nice. But he's married, worse luck! His wife is really lovely; she's a model. You often see her in glossy magazines. They make a stunning couple.'

'What exactly will my job entail?' Pippa asked. 'I was never told.' That was what interested her, not the sexiness or availability of the boss.

The other girl shrugged. 'Working on a word processor, sending out letters, sorting mail, taking phone calls—the usual office routine. There are half a dozen girls working in the office and Mr Harding's PA is a dragon lady. Miss Dalton.'

'The personnel officer warned me to be very careful with her.'

'She wasn't kidding. She bites!'

She hadn't exaggerated, Pippa discovered a few minutes later, contemplating the tall, cold-eyed woman who ran the office.

Felicity Dalton wasn't beautiful, but she was striking—very thin and elegant, with long, straight black hair she wore drawn off her face and held with a large black clip. In her beautifully shaped ears she wore diamond studs. Her white blouse was immaculate, her black jersey skirt emphasised the sleek lines of her body. She looked as if she had been sculpted out of ice. A snow queen who clearly did not like people much, especially those of her own sex, whom she treated with hostility and contempt.

She gave Pippa brusque instructions, left her seated at a desk and went back to her own private office.

The other girls all grinned at Pippa once Felicity Dalton had gone. 'Scary, isn't she?' one whispered. 'I'm Judy, by the way.'

She was the same age as Pippa, and immediately likeable, a short, rather plump girl with curly brown hair and bright brown eyes, the pupils circled by golden rays which made her look like a lion.

'Hi. I'm Pippa.'

'Lovely name. Mine's so ordinary.' Judy sighed, then went on, 'If you need any help, just ask. It's not so long since I was new here; I know how it feels.'

Over that first week Pippa had to go to Judy for

help more than once. Some of the letters they had to send were automatic replies to particular types of complaint; she wasn't always sure which reply to send but Judy knew the office routine by heart.

The managing director himself was away, Pippa discovered, so their workload was not as heavy as it would be when he was working there.

'What's he like?' she asked Judy, whose brown-gold eyes turned dreamy.

'Very sexy. The Dalton's crazy about him, but she'll never get anywhere. He's married to a really stunning woman; he never notices the Dalton at all. That's what burns her up, why she's so frozen and nasty. She's hurting, so she makes sure we all feel the same.'

'Poor Miss Dalton,' Pippa said, with the first real sympathy she had felt for the older woman, who was never pleasant to her.

'Don't feel sorry for her! Just because her heart's breaking is no reason why she should make our lives hell, is it?' Judy was made of sterner stuff; her brown eyes glinted crossly.

Pippa grinned at her. 'No reason at all, no! Anyway, you didn't say what he was like to work for!'

'He's quite tough, too, actually, but in a different way. He expects us to work very hard, and he won't tolerate mistakes, but he isn't nasty, like Dalton. So long as you work hard he's decent to you. Half the girls in the office are nuts about him, but he never encourages them. He's a happily married man.'

'Has he got children?'

'One, a boy, around four years old, called Johnny. Randal has a big silver-framed photo of him on his desk. And another photo of his wife in evening dress—she really is fantastic. Wait until you see her!'

She was not to see Mrs Harding for some months, but Randal Harding was back at work thc following Monday. Pippa had got in early to give herself a head start; she was only just able to keep up with the work as yet, and Miss Dalton was watching her like a hawk, pouncing on her every mistake. Pippa could not afford to lose this job, so she'd got an earlier bus that morning.

It was a fresh, blustery day; her curly chestnut hair had got blown about as she'd walked along the road, and her skin was flushed with exercise and cool air.

Nobody else was in her office; she sat down in front of her word processor and switched on, arranged her pens beside a pad next to the phone and was about to start work when the door opened. Looking round with a smile, Pippa was startled to see a man entering the office. She got an immediate impression of height and dark, brooding good looks.

He looked surprised too, staring at her. 'Who are you?'

She didn't like his curt tone. Coldly, she answered, 'I work here. Who are you?'

'I'm the managing director.'

She gulped. Oh, no! She should have guessed. She had known he would be back at work today.

'Would you make me some coffee and bring it through to my office?' he asked. 'Bring a pad, too. I want you to take dictation.'

The door shut again; he was gone, leaving Pippa breathless. Well, that hadn't been a good beginning, had it? She wouldn't have left a very favourable impression on *him*. And she had been so keen to impress him!

Hurriedly she made him coffee, got a few biscuits from the tin kept in the cupboard where the coffee-making equipment was stored, laid a tray, collected her pad and several pens, and went through to his office.

That first session with Randal was tense and anxious; she was terrified of making a mistake. He was clearly in a temper; she sensed he would have gone into hyper-rage for any reason, however slight. So she concentrated hard, listening intently, her pen moving fast and fluently over the pad while he dictated several memos to staff, letters to clients.

Miss Dalton arrived just as he finished. Pippa incredulously saw that the snow queen looked flustered, her skin flushed, apologising as she hurried into the room, still wearing her smart black raincoat.

'I am so sorry, Mr Harding; I left early so that I would be here when you arrived, but there was some sort of hold-up on the buses; I had to wait for ages before I could get one.'

He nodded impatiently. 'Never mind, Miss Dalton. Pippa was here early and has taken dictation.' He looked at Pippa. 'Get those ready to sign as soon as possible, would you? Thank you.'

Pippa retreated, still shaky, and felt Miss Dalton's icy eyes on her all the way.

Judy was just hanging up her coat. 'Where have you been?' she asked, and Pippa told her in a whisper. Judy whistled. 'She won't forgive you for that for a long time! The boss is her property; she'll hate you for being here when she wasn't.'

She was absolutely right. Miss Dalton was on

Pippa's case all day, snapping at her, complaining about her work, criticising her for wearing eye make-up, not to mention vivid red varnish on her fingernails in the office.

'You look like a tart! Mr Harding doesn't like his employees to wear that much make-up! Don't come to work like that again!'

Pippa mumbled an apology; the other girls discreetly averted their heads.

Later that morning Miss Dalton struck again accusing her of gossiping to Judy when she should be working.

'I've finished the work Mr Harding asked me to do—shall I take the letters to him to sign?'

'No,' snapped Miss Dalton. 'I'll do it!' She came over to Pippa's desk, picked up the perfectly typed letters and went out with them.

'Brrr…icy weather,' Judy whispered. 'I told you so. She hates you now. Take another step near Mr Harding and she'll kill you.'

'It isn't fair. He asked me to take dictation, and I did—it wasn't my fault she wasn't here.'

Miss Dalton came briskly back and loaded Pippa with more work, telling her to hurry up and finish it.

All that day, Pippa couldn't do anything right.

It was huge relief when Miss Dalton finally departed, leaving Pippa to finish a new pile of work she had been given to do.

'I'll be here for hours—she wants all this done by the morning,' Pippa moaned once the door had shut on the older woman.'

'That will teach you,' Judy teased before she left. 'In future try not to be seen with the boss! Remember, you are a lowly slave and she is the queen!'

It was another hour before Pippa finally got to the bottom of the pile and could switch off her machine and clear her desk. Everyone else had gone; the offices were empty and silent. As she got up to leave the door opened and to her dismay there was Randal Harding again.

Glancing at him, she felt her heart flip over—he was intensely sexy, in his three-piece dark suit, a smooth-fitting waistcoat over his white shirt. He leaned against the doorframe, re-knotting his maroon silk tie.

'Still here? You work long hours, very conscientious,' he said with a faintly teasing smile. 'Everyone else gone?'

She nodded dumbly, unable to speak because he made her so self-conscious.

'Come on, then; the cleaners will be here in a minute.' He switched off the lights, plunging the room into darkness, and she hurried towards the door, stumbling into him and feeling something like an electric shock at the contact.

'Have you got far to go? Where do you live?' he asked.

'West Hackham. Twenty minutes by bus,' she whispered, keeping her eyes down. She was terrified in case Miss Dalton should still be somewhere around, or heard they had left together. Her life wouldn't be worth living if that happened.

'Same direction as me. I'll give you a lift. My car's parked just down here; come along.'

She hung back, 'No, really, it doesn't matter.'

He gave her a wry, amused look. 'Don't look so scared. I don't bite and I won't make a pass.'

She flushed in horror. 'No, I didn't mean…didn't think…'

He took her elbow and propelled her onwards. 'Do you live at home, or have you got your own place?'

Why was he asking that? she wondered, still pink and uncertain. The other girls hadn't said anything about him making passes. Indeed, they'd said he was happily married. Maybe her imagination was working overtime.

They left the building and turned down into the underground car park. Pippa's eyes widened as they halted beside a long, sleek black Jaguar saloon. She had never driven in a car like that before.

He unlocked the car and put her into the front passenger seat. Pippa stroked the cream leather upholstery, gazed at the polished walnut dashboard, equipped with all sorts of gadgets, including a CD player. It must have cost the earth; he must be very wealthy.

As he started the engine he asked her, 'Where did you work before you joined us, and why did you leave?'

She told him the name of her old firm. 'They went into liquidation. We were all made redundant.'

He gave her a sidelong smile of sympathy. 'Tough luck—were you out of work long before you came to us?'

'No, I only left them the week before I joined you.'

'That must have been a relief; no joke being unemployed. I hope you're going to be happy with us.'

'I'm sure I will be,' she said, suppressing all memory of Miss Dalton. 'I already feel at home in the office.'

He flashed her that warm, sideways smile that

changed his face entirely. 'Good. The work you did for me this morning was excellent. If you keep that standard up, we'll feel we were lucky to get you.'

Out of the corner of her eye she watched his long-fingered hands on the wheel, his dark jacket sleeves shooting back to show his immaculate white shirt cuffs. She couldn't blame Miss Dalton for being crazy about him; it would be easy to get that way. His hard profile had a power and masculinity that would have made a strong impact even if he had not been very good-looking, and now that he was no longer in a temper she began to see a charm and warmth that had not been visible when they'd first met.

She hoped he would be like this most of the time, not in that stormy, brooding state. Why had he come to work in that mood today? Had he had a row with his wife?

He drew up outside her address and shot a look up at the shabby Victorian house, the woodwork cracked and peeling, the front door needing new paint. The garden was neglected and overgrown, full of uncut grass and rambling bushes.

'Is this your family home?' he asked slowly.

'No, it's let out by the room—I rent one room here.'

He grimaced. 'If I were you, I'd move. It looks as if cockroaches and rats live here, too.'

'No cockroaches or rats, but there is the odd mouse,' she admitted. 'I don't like to kill the one in my room; like me, it has to live somewhere! But this place is cheap, and the room is quite spacious. I'm used to it.' And she couldn't afford anywhere better.

'Where do your family live?'

She hesitated, hating to talk about her background, then defiantly told him, 'I haven't got one.'

He shot her a sharp look. 'No parents?' He sounded incredulous, disbelieving.

'No family at all.'

His grey eyes searched her face; she looked away from their penetrating probe, feeling like someone under searchlights.

'How long have you been alone?'

'Always.' She paused, hesitating about saying any more, then plunged on, 'I was found as a baby. I've no idea who I really am or who my mother was.'

There was a little silence, then he said gently, 'I'm sorry. You can't have had a very happy childhood. I'm lucky. I have a sister, although both my parents are dead now. And I'm married, of course, with a child. Having a family roots you in life.'

'Yes,' she muttered, because she, of all people, knew that. She dreamt of marrying one day, having children, having a family of her own at last.

She didn't want to talk to him any more; she hurriedly got out of the car, whispering, 'Thanks for the lift, Mr Harding. Goodnight.'

He sat watching her as she fled up the path and unlocked the front door. Pippa was aware of his gaze, but didn't look back. She was a very down-to-earth person; she knew she must not let herself think about him too much. He was her boss; that was all. Just that, nothing else, ever.

Yet whenever she forgot to keep a guard on her mind she thought about him that evening, sitting in her lonely room, listening to her second-hand radio. She couldn't afford a television but radio was some sort of companion: another voice in her room, music, plays.

She had never been in love, never thought much about other people. Now she couldn't stop thinking about Randal Harding, remembering his vivid grey eyes, the charm of his smile, the grace and beauty of his male body.

She was filled with curiosity about him. Was his home as beautiful as his car? Elegant, luxurious, comfortable? He wouldn't be alone tonight, like her—he would have his wife and child for company. Did he know how lucky he was?

That was the beginning. Over the weeks that followed she saw him most days, and each time he gave her that smile, sending her temperature sky-high. Occasionally she had to work for him, and tried hard to stay calm and collected, but it wasn't easy when it made her heart race dangerously whenever he smiled or his hand brushed hers.

One day he called her into his office while Miss Dalton was having coffee in a café across the street with some friends—a birthday celebration, Judy had told Pippa. Judy knew all the office gossip: what was going on and who was dating who.

'They make these wonderful cakes,' she'd said enviously. 'Coffee-iced walnut cakes, chocolate eclairs that melt in your mouth. It's the place to go, if you can afford it. I've been once and still dream about it.'

'Sounds blissful,' Pippa had agreed; she could never have afforded food like that. Her budget was far too restricted.

Mr Harding had put his head round the door at that minute. 'Come through,' he told Pippa, who had got up, flushed and anxious, while Judy whistled under her breath.

'Let's hope Dalton doesn't get back while you're with him! Or your head will roll. Come to that, I'm suspicious, too—why does he always ask for you? Why never me?'

Pippa hadn't even tired to answer that; she couldn't. Randal had taken some sort of interest in her from the beginning—was it because of what he had found out about her background? Was he sorry for her? She didn't like that idea.

When she went into the other room and found Randal Harding standing with his back to her, staring out of the window at the blue, cloudless sky, she began to breathe rapidly, shallowly. While she gazed at that long, supple back, those even longer legs, he turned his head to smile at her, making her heart roll over in a now familiar, disturbing fashion.

'I want to ask a favour of you—this isn't work, so feel free to refuse if you're not happy about it—but I'm very busy today and I can't spare the time to do it myself. My son is five tomorrow and I haven't bought him a birthday present yet. Do you think you could go shopping and choose something for him?'

Taken aback, since she hadn't expected that request, she stammered, 'Well, of course, but...I don't know what toys he already has or what he likes...'

'He hasn't got any big vehicles—trucks, farm vehicles, fire engines, that sort of thing. He loves toy cars, so that would probably be the best bet.'

'Right, then; okay, I'll do my best. When did you want me to go?'

'Take an extra hour for lunch.' He pulled out a sheaf of bank notes from a wallet in his jacket, and counted some out into her hand. 'That should be enough. And would you buy a birthday card, too?'

His fingers brushed hers, making her legs turn weak, but she nodded, smiling, and hurriedly retreated.

She managed to do her shopping in a world-famous toyshop. It only took a few minutes to choose and pay for a huge bright red fire engine with expanding ladders and tiny firemen in yellow helmets, coiled water hoses, all the equipment a boy would need to play firemen. In another shop she bought a card which she thought quite funny, with a big gold number five on it and a line of pink elephants dancing and playing the trumpet.

She had lunch nearby, before returning to work at the usual time. Miss Dalton was at lunch when Pippa got back.

'She was looking for you,' Judy warned. 'Asking why you had gone to lunch early and who gave you permission. I played dumb, said I didn't know. Where have you been, anyway?'

'Shopping,' Pippa said, rushing into Randal Harding's office and laying the package she had bought on his desk, then hurrying back before Miss Dalton caught her. The last thing she needed was trouble.

'I worry about you,' Judy said. 'What's going on between you and Randal?'

'Nothing! Don't be silly.' Pippa buried herself in her work.

She got into trouble when Miss Dalton returned ten minutes later and demanded to know why Pippa had gone to lunch early.

'I had some urgent shopping to do,' Pippa said, eyes lowered.

'I don't believe my ears! So you just went off to do it without a word!'

Pippa thought of telling her Randal Harding had given her permission to go, but decided that might merely make matters worse, so said nothing.

'How dare you walk out of here without permission? You will go to lunch at the time allotted to you in future.' Miss Dalton's voice was acid. 'One more trick like that and you're out of a job!'

Pippa shivered. She needed this job; there was no guarantee she would get another. Without an income she would find life very hard. 'I'm sorry,' she whispered.

'You'll be even more sorry if you keep annoying me like this!' the older woman snapped.

Judy rolled her eyes at Pippa behind Miss Dalton's back and mouthed, 'I told you so!'

As the time to stop work came closer Miss Dalton came over to look at Pippa's desk and gave her an icy, triumphant smile.

'You've fallen behind again, I see. Your work is far from satisfactory. Well, I want all those letters finished when I come into work tomorrow—understood?'

'Yes, Miss Dalton,' Pippa wearily said; she seemed to spend her life running on the spot just to keep up. She had never had this trouble before.

When everyone had gone she put her head down on the desk, tears welling up into her eyes. Day after day Miss Dalton attacked her, overloaded her with work, watched her like a hawk, and Pippa was exhausted by the strain of it. She had enjoyed her last job; everyone had been friendly, she had been able to keep up with her work. But now she didn't know if she could keep on going; she might have to resign—was that what Miss Dalton wanted? Was she trying to drive her out?

'What's wrong?'

The voice made her stiffen, instinctively wiping her wet eyes with the back of her hard before she sat up.

'Nothing…sorry…just tired,' she mumbled, avoiding Randal Harding's eyes.

He came over to her desk, put an imperative hand under her chin and tilted her face, stared down at it, his grey eyes moving from her wide, wet green eyes to the tremulous curve of her pink mouth.

'You've been crying.'

'Just tired,' she stupidly repeated, staring up at him, conscious of a now familiar turmoil in her body . Her heart was beating so hard it deafened her; she couldn't breathe properly, couldn't focus on his face, which loomed far too close to her own.

'Nonsense, something else is wrong—tell me!'

She shook her head, her mouth dry and her blood running like fire. Never in her life had she felt like this; it was terrifying. Was she falling in love with him? That would be folly, but she had no idea how to stop herself.

His face seemed to be coming closer all the time. She gazed into those brilliant grey eyes, so dazed and confused she couldn't think straight, then her stare dropped to focus on his hard, male mouth, and panic rushed through her.

Was she imagining it, simply because she hungered for it so much, or was he about to kiss her? A second later his mouth touched hers and she shuddered, eyes closing.

His kiss was light and cool for a second or two, then it took fire and his arms went round her, pulling her up from her chair, dragging her so close to him that she felt the pressure of his thighs, the warmth of his body under his elegant clothes, the fierce beating of his heart.

Pippa had never been kissed, touched, like that before. She didn't know what to do, how to feel. Eyes shut tight, plunged into deep, velvety blackness, she swayed helplessly in his arms, her lips parting to give him access to her mouth, entirely given up to him in unconscious surrender.

Only when he lifted his mouth and broke the spell holding her did she begin to think again, and then shame and shock made her turn first red, then white.

'No, you mustn't! You're married!' she broke out.

He looked down at her, his face a battleground of conflicting feelings, gave a long groan. 'Yes. I'm sorry, I shouldn't have touched you. I didn't intend to kiss you. I just couldn't help it.' He ran a caressing hand down her face, trailed his fingers over her mouth, awakening all her pulses again.

'Don't,' she whispered, dying to have him kiss her again.

'God, if only you weren't so young!' he muttered. 'Practically a child. I have no right to come anywhere near you; don't think I'm not ashamed of myself. I just don't seem able to stop thinking about you. I've been wanting to kiss you for a very long time.'

'Randal,' she moaned, shuddering. 'But we can't...shouldn't... You're married.' A pang of jealousy wrenched her. 'And your wife is beautiful.'

His face hardened, darkened. 'Oh, yes, she's beautiful. But our marriage is a sham. We rarely even see each other. She has been having an affair for a year; she's often away—why do you think I asked you to buy the present for Johnny? My wife isn't at home; she has probably forgotten his birthday.'

Startled and distressed, Pippa said, 'Oh…I'm sorry. Really, very sorry. That's very sad. I thought you were happily married; everyone said so.' Then she bit her lip, frowning, as a new idea came to her. 'But I don't want you to use me to get your own back on your wife, or to boost your ego. I'm not a consolation prize, Mr Harding.'

His mouth twisted bitterly. 'I wasn't using you that way, Pippa. Believe me. I kissed you because the temptation was irresistible, that's all. The minute I saw you I wanted to kiss you. It has nothing to do with my wife. I fell out of love with her long ago. Our marriage is over in everything but name. Her current affair is about the third. They never last long, but while they last they're all she cares about. I haven't divorced her yet because of Johnny. I don't care a damn if I never see her again, but I love my son and I don't want him made unhappy.'

'No, poor little boy. He must miss his mother when she's away,' Pippa said, sighing. 'My childhood was pretty grim. I'd have given anything to have a family, even just one parent, anyone who cared about me. I'm sure Johnny loves you very much. He needs you.'

'I'm the only parent he has, most of the time. He's used to his mother vanishing for weeks on end.'

'But she does come back, surely?' Pippa took a deep breath, 'And it won't help if you start having affairs too.'

Randal Harding gave her a wry smile. 'You're older than you look, aren't you? Wiser, too. Of course you're right. I don't want to do anything that might hurt my boy.' He smoothed back a tousled strand of hair from her face, his fingers caressing. 'Or you, Pippa, I don't want to hurt you, either. But I think I'm falling in love with you.'

He knew she was in love with him, and felt a quiver of warning.

'You're so sweet and gentle,' he whispered. 'I can't help wanting you.' He leant his head to kiss her again, but she drew back sharply, shaking her head.

'No! You mustn't,' she hoarsely said, and he looked at her with a new possessiveness.

'You want me, too, don't you, Pippa?'

There was a passionate curve to his mouth that made her afraid—afraid she wouldn't be able to go on rejecting him for long. She wanted him too much. The beat of desire in her blood warned her that sooner or later, if he kept kissing her, she would give in to him. She couldn't bear the idea of becoming his secret mistress; it would make her so ashamed.

She gave her notice to Miss Dalton the following Friday. It was accepted with a triumphant smile. Miss Dalton thought she had won. Her hostile tactics had scored a victory. Pippa allowed her to think whatever she chose. She didn't care. All that mattered now was to get away from Randal before it was too late.

He had left the day before, to spend a week at a business conference in the States. By the time he returned Pippa had left the firm. She had left the area, too—given up her room, moved into central London, got a job in the insurance company for which she now worked, and had found another one-room flat in

Islington, where she'd stayed until she had saved enough to buy her own home in Whitstall with the company's help. She hadn't kept in touch with anyone at Randal's firm; she didn't want him to know where she had gone, so she had had no news of him.

Until now…

Four years had made few changes in him, although his face seemed harder, more sardonic. That brooding look she remembered seemed darker, more stormy. Was his wife still having affairs? Maybe Randal had had some too, now. He couldn't have been without a woman for four years.

She felt much older, much more in control of herself as she told him, 'You're married and I'm getting married next week!'

'I'm not married any more,' he said, and her stomach seemed to drop out of her in shock.

CHAPTER THREE

EYES open wide, she stared at him in disbelief. 'You're not married any more? What do you mean?'

He smiled dryly. 'Renata left me two years ago, ran off with a golf champion she met in Scotland. She's always had an obsession with golf. Having landed a champion at the peak of his earning capacity, she wanted to hang on to him for good. She didn't just want to have an affair; she was determined to marry him. She asked me for a divorce, I gave her one, and she married him the minute it was final.'

She absorbed that, watching him intently. How had he really felt when his wife asked for a divorce? He hadn't wanted to divorce her, she remembered. That had never been in his mind. Had it been a shock to him when Renata asked him to let her go?

'I didn't hear about it,' she said. 'I suppose it was mentioned in the newspapers, but I rarely read gossip columns. What about your son?'

'She left him with me.'

That shocked Pippa. What sort of mother could abandon her child without a backward glance? Of course, Mrs Harding had spent very little time with her son, according to Randal—had she preferred to leave the boy behind, or had Randal made that a condition of agreeing to the divorce?

He added a little contemptuously, 'Renata told me her new husband didn't want a child around, cramping his style. They lead a very busy social life off the gold course; children aren't part of their scene. But then Renata was never a devoted mother, anyway.'

That, too, she remembered. 'So he lives with you now,' she thought aloud.

Randal grimaced. 'That would be difficult to manage unless I hired someone to take care of him. I have to go away so much. No, he's at boarding school in Buckinghamshire, and he likes it, thank heavens.'

'Poor little boy, he must have been upset.' The trauma of divorce always hurt the children most, didn't it?

Randal shook his head. 'I don't think he was that bothered, as far as his mother was concerned. It didn't mean he saw her less—how could he? She was rarely at home anyway. He had the stability of knowing I'd always be there for him. If he had preferred to be at home I'd have got him a full-time nanny, but he wanted to go to boarding school. One of his friends had been at his place for a year and Johnny thought it sounded great. He has lots of friends around day and night, all the things kids love—computers, sport, a swimming pool—and he's doing well in class. Oddly enough, his new stepfather has a sort of cachet, too. Sports heroes in the family are assets. The other boys envy him. Renata and her new husband visited the school and Johnny was thrilled. I'm going to visit him, myself, this weekend. I'm allowed to take him out of school at weekends; I try to do that at least once a month.'

'Well, give him my love.' She went pink. 'Not that he'll remember me, of course.' She had often thought about Johnny; strange to think that he had never even met her.

'No, you never saw him, did you? It's time you did. You must come with me at the weekend.'

She stiffened, eyes hurriedly moving away from him. 'Well, I would have loved to, he sounds a lovely little boy, but this Saturday is my wedding day, you know.'

'Ah, yes,' he drawled. 'Your wedding day. I'd forgotten that. And you're going to marry that insurance man? You can't be serious!'

She resented the ironic note in his voice, the mocking smile curling his lip. Flushed and angry, she bit back, 'Perfectly serious! You don't know Tom. Don't talk about him that way.'

'I met him, remember? I have a very shrewd idea what he's like.'

She didn't like the way he said that; he was coldly dismissive of Tom. 'He wasn't himself. The accident upset him.' She turned towards the door. 'Look, I really must be going.'

She started to walk away, but at that second somebody knocked at the outer door of the suite, calling, 'Room Service!'

'Come in,' Randal replied, and she heard a key turn then the door opened and a waiter pushed a loaded trolley into the sitting room, gave both of them a polite smile.

'Where shall I set the table up, sir?'

'Over by the window,' Randal told him, and the man wheeled the trolley over there, lifted the flaps which formed a table, began moving food around on the table surface, placed two chairs.

'Leave it. We'll help ourselves, thanks,' Randal said.

'Would you sign this for me, sir?' the waiter asked, presenting him with a pen and the bill.

Randal signed, tipped him, and the man departed. Pippa began drifting after him but didn't get very far. Randal's long fingers took her arm, held her firmly.

'No, you don't. You're staying. We have a lot to talk about yet.'

'We don't have anything to talk about!'

'I'm not married any more,' he reminded her, still holding her arm with all the potential force of those long, sinewy fingers, reminding her that if she tried to break free he was capable of resisting any effort she made.

'That has nothing to do with me!' she denied, trying not to sound too disturbed by that contact. 'Please let go of me!'

Instead, he swung her round, closer to him, his long leg touching hers. 'You were enchanting when you were twenty,' he managed, his grey eyes sliding over her in slow, sensual appraisal. 'You're gorgeous now. I just can't imagine you with the insurance salesman—how does he handle all that fire? With tongs, at arm's length?'

She didn't like the intimacy of the questions, and especially she didn't want him analysing her relationship with Tom.

To silence him she pulled free and sat down at the table. 'This looks good, all of it. What are you going to have? Some of this beef, or some cheese?'

He laughed softly. 'Trying to distract me, Pippa?' Bending, he brushed his lips along the curve of her throat, sending a shiver through her whole body. 'You're easy to read, you know.'

Was she? The remark was alarming. She must defend herself better, refuse to let him pick up her reactions. It was dangerous to let him know… She shut her eyes in dismay, refusing to continue with that line of thought, refusing to admit what it was she did not want him to know.

He stayed there for a moment, their profiles almost touching, watching her sideways, trying to gauge her expression, then at last he straightened, walked to the chair at the other side of the table and sat down opposite her.

'You help yourself, while I inspect what we have here.'

Eyes lowered, still trembling after the touch of his mouth on her skin, the scent of his body, she took more salad, a little cheese, a slice of chicken breast, a little mayonnaise, then a piece of the wholewheat bread. When she offered Randal the glass salad bowl, without looking at him, he took it, saying, 'I haven't eaten all day. All I had for breakfast was coffee and orange juice.'

'They say you should always have breakfast. Have you been staying here long?'

'No, I've been at another long conference. I seem to spend a lot of time at them.' He helped himself to wholegrain mustard. 'I don't spend much time in my own home.'

'Do you still live in the same house?' Making polite small talk helped to pass the time and she hoped it would lighten the atmosphere, making her nerves less tense, the situation seem less threatening. After all, what threat did he pose to her. He might make a pass, but she only had to reject him; he wasn't the type to turn dangerous.

Was he?

What did she know about him, though? She had known him for a few weeks, five years ago. How did she really know what sort of man he was?

'No, I moved to a flat; it made life simpler. Someone comes in twice a week to clean. I eat out a lot, or have a salad, or scrambled eggs—something I can cook myself. Johnny has a room of his own in the flat, of course, but he's only there during the school holidays. He seems to like it, though.'

'Have you actually asked him if he minded moving home, as well as going away to school?'

He shot her a wry glance. 'No, I haven't—you think I should?'

Pippa shrugged. 'It's a bit late now; you've presented him with a *fait accompli*. But next time you take a major decision that will affect him, I'd certainly ask him first.'

He leaned back in his chair, surveying her with half-lowered lids. 'If I wanted to get married again, for instance?'

Her eyes opened wide. 'Well…yes…' Her heart skipped a beat; her skin turned cold. 'Is that on the cards? Are you thinking of marrying again?' Not Miss Dalton? She thought, aware of a sense of shock. No, it must be someone new.

'Maybe,' he drawled. 'Do you think I should consult my son before committing myself?'

'Does he know her?'

'Not yet.'

'Well, I should make sure they get on well before you make any definite decision.'

She concentrated on her food, angrily conscious of a burning pain inside her stomach whenever she thought of Randal marrying again. It was stupid to be jealous—she had no right to care what he did. She was getting married herself. It was four years since she had worked in his office, four years since she had seen him, talked to him, been crazy enough to let him kiss her. A lot had happened to her in the years since then. She had grown up, learnt a lot more about the world. She had been a romantic, wide-eyed, innocent child four years ago. Now she was a woman and Randal Harding was nothing to her.

'How long have you known your insurance salesman?' he asked, and she looked up, her heart crashing like an exploding plane as she met those brilliant grey eyes.

How could she keep telling herself he was nothing to her if her body kept betraying her every time she met his eyes? The minute she'd seen him again, the night of the accident, she had been instantly overwhelmed by those old feelings. She had tried to convince herself she had forgotten him, but she had been lying.

'Four years,' she said curtly.

'Since you ran away from me, in other words?'

'I didn't run away!' she crossly denied, resenting the way he put it.

'You walked?' he dryly mocked.

'I just decided to get another job,' she corrected, her green eyes defying him. How dared he talk to her like that when he was planning to get married again himself? 'And I found this job with the insurance company, and started working for Tom.'

'How long before you went out with him?'

She bristled, her face hot, her nerves jumping. 'Why do you keep on at me like the Inquisition? My private life is nothing to do with you at all.' It had, in fact, been a very long time before she accepted a date with Tom, but she knew what Randal would make of that confession, so she was not going to admit it.

'Are you in love with him?'

'I'm not answering any more questions!' She leaned over and picked up the coffee pot. 'I'm going to have some coffee—would you like some?'

'Please. Black, no sugar.'

She poured the coffee and gave him his cup, took her own cup over to the couch. As she sat down and put her cup on the coffee table in front of her she realised she should have sat down in a chair, but it was too late. Randal had followed her and was sitting down beside her, his long legs stretched out, one thigh touching hers. She would have felt stupid if she had got up and moved to a chair; it would have been some sort of betrayal.

'If you aren't in love with him, why are you marrying him?' he murmured.

'I didn't say I wasn't in love with him!'

'Ah, but you didn't say you were! And that was as good as an admission.'

'I didn't answer because you had no right to ask the question!'

'If you were in love, why wouldn't you want to admit it?'

Conversation with him was like trying to make your way through a minefield. She was terrified of every step. Furiously, she looked round at him, glaring. 'Will you stop asking me questions?' But that was a mistake, too, because he was closer than she had realised. She found herself looking into grey eyes which were just inches away, and swallowed convulsively.

'What's the matter, Pippa?' he silkily asked.

'Nothing! I don't know what you mean!' she blustered.

'Oh, yes, you do,' he whispered, and before she could back away his head swooped down; his mouth took hers with fierce demand.

She struggled in a desperate effort to get away, but his body shifted to hold her back against the couch, his wide shoulders pinning her down. She pushed him away without making any impact on him at all. He was far too powerful and she was shaking too much to be able to make him shift.

The heat of his mouth was burning her up. Her lips parted, her eyes closed, her pulses beating wildly.

It was like rushing back through time to the day when he last kissed her; she couldn't think, could only feel, given up entirely to the pleasure and intense sweetness of his mouth on hers, his body lying across her. Her hands went round his neck and closed in his thick, dark hair. The pressure of his chest, his thighs, deepened; his fingers caressed and stroked, moving from her shoulders to her breasts, awakening her body to sensations she had never felt before. She wanted to be naked in his arms, to feel his touch with even more intensity.

From time to time in the last four years she had had dreams like this, woken from deep sleep drowsily, still trembling from the passion of his kiss, lain there crying, aching. She had suppressed the memory of those dreams, refused to think about them, or him, and gradually they had come less often—but they had not stopped entirely, and now they were visiting her again, but this time the dream was reality. This time she was in his arms, giving in to the temptation to kiss him back, to yield.

Randal lifted his mouth slowly to look down at her. Pippa kept her own eyes shut, trembling violently. She dared not meet his stare. She knew what he would be seeing, how she must look to him—weak, flushed, her mouth still parted and swollen from his kisses, still drowning in the desire pulsing through her.

'Now tell me you love him,' he huskily challenged.

She forced her eyes open, their pupils distended with passion. 'I'm going to marry him!'

'You must be insane. You won't be happy, either of you. He'll soon realise you don't love him and then he's going to hate you. He'll feel conned, trapped, and your lives together will be hell.'

'You don't know enough about us to make a prophesy like that!'

'I know about bad marriages,' he said flatly, and she winced.

'Just because you had a bad marriage doesn't mean Tom and I will. We're very different people. Tom's sweet and kind and caring, and I wouldn't hurt him for worlds. I certainly won't have affairs with other men. I'm not the type.'

'I could have an affair with you,' he said huskily, his mouth brushing the soft lobe of her ear, and she shuddered.

'Don't kid yourself! You may be vain enough to think you only have to snap your fingers to get any woman you want, but you wouldn't get me!'

'I just did,' he whispered. 'A minute ago you were in my arms and you weren't struggling. I could have got your clothes off and had you, don't deny it. It was me who called a halt, not you.'

'That's not true!' But she knew it was, and that made her even angrier, with herself as well as him. She had briefly tried to push him away, but once his mouth touched hers she had collapsed, shaking and in near delirium, kissing him back with all the passion of her dreams.

She had never felt like that about Tom. She liked Tom, admired and respected Tom, but she didn't burn with desire for him and if she was strictly honest she knew she never would. But she wasn't telling Randal that; it was no business of his how she felt about the man she meant to marry. Who did he think he was?

He smiled at her, and her head swam. 'You know it's true, Pippa. After I stopped kissing you, you just lay there with your eyes shut—what were you doing? Waiting for me to kiss you again?'

'I was too horrified to move!'

His eyes narrowed, hardened. 'What?'

'You'd scared me stiff! I was terrified of what you might do next.'

His mouth was tense with rage. 'You little liar! You weren't scared; you loved having me kiss you!'

'I hated it!' she flung back recklessly, too angry with him now to care what she said, beginning to get up, intending to make a dash for it, escape from the hotel suite.

Randal's arms closed round her and dragged her back down on the couch. 'We'll see about that,' he softly murmured, and began to kiss her again, his mouth sensually coaxing, sending waves of heat and dangerous pleasure through her.

Afraid of losing control, she gasped out, 'You're

hurting me!' and grabbed a fistful of his black hair, yanking it violently. 'Stop it!'

His lips lifted and he grimaced down at her. 'No, you're hurting me! Let go of my hair before you pull half of it out!'

'Serves you right!' she muttered, her fingers releasing the thick strands she was gripping.

They stared at each other, faces very close, breathing thickly.

'I want to leave,' she said shakily, looking away because being so close to him made her physically weak. 'Stop this, Randal. Let me go.'

He leaned down and gently, lightly, brushed his mouth over hers. 'Very well. I'll drive you home.'

'There's no need to! I can take a train.' The very prospect of having him drive her made her nerves jump violently. She had to get away from him; she couldn't take much more.

'I'm driving you,' he insisted. 'I'm curious. I want to see where you've been living. I hope it's better than that place you had when you worked for me. That wasn't fit for human habitation. Do you still live in one room?'

'No, I have a cottage,' she said with pride. She loved her home. What would he think of it? She had to admit she would rather like him to see it.

His brows rose. 'Do you rent it?'

Her chin lifted. 'No, I'm buying it on a mortgage.'

'Really? Your salary must be good.'

'I'm earning far more money now, and the insurance company helped me buy my cottage. It's company policy to assist staff to buy their own property; they feel it makes us more contented, so they give us low-interest loans.'

'And it ties you to the company?' he cynically suggested. 'So, what happens if you change jobs, move to another firm?'

'The interest goes up to the average rate and you can't blame them for that. After all, why should they continue to help you if you've left them? But you can continue with the mortgage, just like anyone else.'

'Where will you live, after the wedding?'

'At the cottage. Tom lives on an estate; his place isn't as nice as mine.'

He stood up. 'Well, let's go. Sure you don't want any of that fruit? You could take some with you.'

She shook her head. 'No, thanks. I ate more than enough.'

They left the suite and took the lift down to an underground car park. She saw Randal's car immediately: sleek and red with a long bonnet and streamlined curves. The last time she'd seen it there had been scratches and bumps all over the front, but there were none there now.

'It looks as good as new. I hope it didn't cost too much to have it repaired.'

'It had some bumps hammered out, but it didn't cost the earth.' He opened the passenger door and helped her into it, walked round and slid in beside her, behind the wheel.

The journey took nearly an hour. Traffic was heavy at this time of day through the city; they kept getting trapped in crowded streets with lines of other vehicles. Randal didn't say much. She tried not to look at him, but was deeply conscious of him beside her, those long slim legs stretched out, his elegant hands moving on the wheel. Pippa had to shrink down into her own seat to avoid any contact with him; the car was small and he was very close.

Eventually, though, they emerged in flat Essex countryside and through the open window beside her she felt cool, fresh air on her hot face, blowing her chestnut hair about. She stared out at the hedges of hawthorn, just coming into leaf, which in a month or so would be thick with white flowers, at the green fields and trees, the villages through which they passed, some with ancient timbered cottages or white-frame wooden churches in tidy churchyards where old yew trees stood, bearing testimony to the long-forgotten tradition of planting yew in churchyards so that bows could be made from it, at old pubs with swinging signs.

Everything looked so normal and familiar. Only she was altered; she did not know herself. Deep inside her panic surged. Her life was in confusion, like a landscape after an earthquake, the earth blown apart, wrecked, destroyed.

'Which road do I take now?' Randal asked and, pulling herself together, she gave him directions.

'It isn't far; we should be there in ten minutes.'

'Do you like living in the country?'

'I love it.'

He was driving slowly as they passed the junction where the accident had happened the other night. His sideways glance told her he remembered the place.

'Where had you been?' she asked. 'That night?'

'I had been having dinner with a business associate. I got lost; I don't know this part of the country.'

They drove on and a few moments later were parking outside her cottage. He turned his head to stare at it.

'Well, thank you for driving me home,' she huskily said, opening the passenger door.

He got out and came round to help her, his hand firmly gripping her arm. 'It's a pretty place. Have you redecorated since you bought it?'

'Yes,' she said. Afraid her neighbours might see him, be curious about him.

'I'd love a guided tour.'

In agitation she shook her head. 'I'd rather not ask you in! I expect Tom will call in on his way home from work; he'll be anxious about why I came home early. I usually come home with him. He lives quite nearby.'

Randal locked his car with a remote control, still holding her arm, then guided her towards the cottage. 'It's only half past four. He won't arrive yet, will he? He looked the type to keep long hours at work. You've got time to show me round.'

'Why are you so maddening?' she fumed. 'Why do you always have to turn everything into a battle, and win?'

He laughed softly. 'Why do you? What is your problem? Whatever I ask you to do, you argue!'

She unlocked her front door, choked with irritation. 'I just want you to go away! You know that!' Samson appeared from the flowerbeds and brushed past both of them, heading for the kitchen and, he hoped, food.

Randal smiled an amused taunt. 'Oh, I know that, but I'm not going, Pippa. I intend to save you from yourself.'

She swallowed, face disturbed. She didn't like the sound of that. What was he plotting? There was a brightness, a mischief in his eyes, that made her feel threatened. Did he intend to stay here, confront Tom, perhaps tell Tom...? Tell him what, though? They had never been lovers. There was nothing to tell. A kiss or two, that was all. She had fled before any affair could start.

And of course that was an admission in itself, because if she had not been afraid of what might develop between them she would never have been driven to flight. Would Tom realise that?

He would if Randal drew him pictures, she grimly admitted, and no doubt that was precisely what Randal intended to do. Would Tom be shocked when he discovered she had been in love before they met?

She had never lied to him, yet she had never told him anything about Randal; she had never even mentioned his name.

He looked around at the black wood beams. 'How old is the cottage?'

'The deeds date form the eighteenth century, but there was a dwelling here before that, judging by old maps of the area.' She looked at the green glass clock on the mantelpiece which she had bought in a local antiques shop. 'Tom will be here before long. Would you mind going? I want to have a shower and change before Tom gets here.'

He took no notice, wandered around the room, looking at ornaments, books, taking them out of the white-painted shelves and flipping through them, went to the window, stared out at the back garden, then walked through into the kitchen. Crossly she followed and found him opening cupboards, inspecting the inside of the fridge. Samson excitedly cavorted around him.

'Nice cat,' Randal said, scratching behind Samson's ear. 'I like the way your kitchen is laid out;

the colour scheme is very cheerful. It must be a pleasure to come in here on winter mornings.'

'You aren't planning to make me an offer for the place, are you?' she tartly enquired, and he gave her a teasing grin.

'I'm just curious about how you live. I'm trying to imagine you here. Are you always alone, or does the fiancé spend some nights here with you?'

Hot blood ran up her face. 'I told you, I'm not discussing Tom or our relationship with you!'

His grey eyes probed her face. 'You don't sleep with him, do you?' He sounded cool enough, yet something in the way he stood, body tense and alert, made her nervous. She wished she knew what he was thinking, what he was planning.

'None of your business!'

He took a step towards her and suddenly she was terrified. Turning on her heel, she ran out, up the stairs, into her bedroom and bolted the door. Sinking down on her bed, she listened; would he come up here or leave?

There wasn't a sound. No footsteps on the stairs, no movement in the passage outside the door.

He must still be downstairs. Or he could have gone, let himself out of the front door soundlessly.

She swivelled to pick up a hairbrush from her dressing table and brushed her gleaming chestnut hair; it was in disarray after the drive, with the wind blowing through the open window. Getting up, she looked in her wardrobe for something to change into when she had had her shower and chose a pale green tunic dress which ended at the knees. Simple but stylish, it was one of Tom's favourites among her clothes.

She opened drawers, found clean lingerie, laid it all

on her bedside cabinet, then went to the door and listened with her ear against the panel.

Still silence. She carefully opened the door and froze in shock, finding Randal leaning there; in a second he was halfway into the room and she fell back, breathless.

'Go away!'

His gaze ran round the room, absorbing the delicate pastel colours of the walls, the pretty curtains which matched exactly the cover over her bed, the pink carpet and the white and gilt furniture.

'Charming. Did you say you decorated it all yourself?'

'Go away,' she repeated, her heart in her mouth. 'I don't want you here.' He was taller than she remembered, his head towering over her in this little room, the masculine force of his physical presence disturbing.

'Why did you come upstairs, if you didn't want me to follow you? You knew I would.'

She gave him an icy, resentful look. 'I was hoping you would take the hint and leave my house.'

'You aren't a very convincing liar, Pippa,' he mocked, coming nearer, his grey eyes wandering possessively over her. 'Were you going to take your clothes off? Don't let me stop you.' Leaning over, he picked up a filmy white slip from the cabinet. 'I can't wait to see you wearing this.'

'No,' she whispered, shuddering at the way he was looking at her.

'Yes,' he silkily said, dropping the slip and reaching for her at the same moment.

She couldn't breathe, her throat painful, making a sound somewhere between a sob and a groan. She wanted him and at the same time was afraid of him. Inside her desire and fear fought, but desire was winning and she knew it.

'Don't,' she begged, her legs giving way under her, and he picked her up bodily and carried her to the bed.

Her eyes closed, she arched helplessly towards him as he kissed her with sensuous insistence, his hands exploring, caressing. She lost all consciousness of what he was doing, her own instincts driving her. She needed to touch him, open his shirt and discover the power of his naked flesh and muscle, clasp his nape and stroke his hair. She had dreamt of doing this, over and over again, and now she was doing it.

Above her she felt the ragged beating of his heart, his skin on hers.

Confusion flooded her mind—how could she feel his skin on hers? Opening her eyes, she looked down and realised he had undressed her somehow; she was naked, her slip, her bra and panties all gone. While she had been preoccupied with touching him he had been stripping her.

'Pippa,' he moaned, burying his head between her breasts, kissing the deep cleft.

He was naked, too, she realised in shock. He must have taken off his own clothes as well as hers—how had he done that without her knowing what was happening?

Or hadn't she wanted to know?

His mouth closed over her breast, drawing a nipple inside the warm wetness, sucking softly.

Pleasure overwhelmed her; her arms went round him, holding him closer; she stroked his long, naked back and felt his knees nudging her thighs apart, his body sliding between them.

'I want you badly,' Randal groaned, and at that instant she heard a muffled sound from the door.

Stiffening, she raised herself to look past Randal. He turned his head, too.

Tom stood in the open doorway, face rigid, grey, staring.

CHAPTER FOUR

THE silence seemed endless. Pippa wished she would fall through the floor; she couldn't meet Tom's eyes. She was icy cold, shivering and sick in spite of the warmth of Randal's body lying on top of her, hiding much of her nakedness.

What could she say to him?

Even worse, what was Tom going to say to her?

In fact, he said nothing, simply turned on his heel and walked out without a word, although his body language was very vocal: the stiffness of his back, the way his head was carried, the way his arms were held, his hands clenched at his sides.

Randal whistled softly. 'Oh, dear. I suppose he has a key? And let himself in? If he'd had the good manners to ring the bell first we'd have had time to get our clothes on again before he walked in here. He didn't even call out, just came upstairs without warning, so he only has himself to blame for what he saw.'

Rage and resentment filled her. 'Don't you dare try to shift the blame to him! I've no doubt Tom was trying to be thoughtful. He'd been told I was ill—he didn't want to force me to get out of bed and come downstairs to let him in!'

She roughly pushed him off and scrambled out of bed, pulled on her clothes with hands that trembled while Randal watched her lazily, lying on his side, the afternoon sun gleaming on his smooth, naked shoulders, his lids half lowered.

She tried to ignore him but even now her stupid body went on reacting to his, her mouth dry, her pulses hammering. Why was it that she never felt like this about Tom? Tom was physically attractive, he was a wonderful companion, she liked him—but she couldn't pretend he made her as aware as Randal could just by being there in the same room.

'At least you won't have to work out how to tell him!' he drawled.

It didn't help that he was right. She snapped back, 'There's nothing to tell!'

'Oh, come on, Pippa! It's time to stop lying—to him or yourself. He'll expect some sort of explanation! After all, as far as he knows you and I have never met. You hadn't told him about me, had you? He didn't react to my name when I gave it to him that night so I knew you hadn't told him about me. Yet when he walked in here five minutes ago he caught us making love! How are you going to talk your way out of that?'

She had no idea. 'I hate you!' she whispered before hurrying out of the room and running downstairs.

She found Tom on the point of going, his back to her, the front door wide open.

'Don't just go, Tom,' she said shakily. 'We must talk. I'm very sorry. I know how angry you must be, but…'

He turned to stare at her as if he had never seen her before. 'Angry?' he repeated in a low voice. 'Shattered, Pippa. I'm absolutely shattered. You, of all people, behaving like…like that.' His mouth writhed in distaste. 'I'd have taken an oath on it that you weren't capable of being promiscuous. If I hadn't seen it with my own eyes I'd never have believed it.'

She bit down on her lower lip, said in a smothered sob, 'I know, I'm sorry.'

Tom looked down at the floor, face tense, then walked past her into the sitting room. Pippa closed the front door and followed him. As she appeared he turned on her and grated, 'Who is he?'

She was startled—hadn't he recognised Randal? She had been certain he must have done, but of course Tom had only seen him briefly, in the dark, and he had been in shock, himself, after the accident.

'Randal Harding,' she prompted, but Tom's face remained blank.

Then he said slowly, 'I've heard that name before somewhere. Does he work at the office?'

She shook her head. 'No. The car crash the other night, remember?'

Tom stared, eyes widening. 'The car crash? My God, yes, you're right—that was the name of the fellow whose car hit ours.' He brushed his pale hair back, forehead creased, visibly thinking back. 'But...I don't understand... You didn't even speak to him that night; you stayed in the car. Don't tell me he came here today and talked his way in?' His voice deepened. 'Did he attack you? Is that what was happening just now? Was he trying to...? Pippa, what did he do to you?'

She shook her head, close to hysterical tears as it dawned on her that he was handing her the perfect alibi, making up a story for her to use. But she couldn't lie to him or put all the blame on Randal, even though he might deserve it.

She had asked him to go away and leave her alone but he wouldn't go. Briefly she was tempted to tell Tom what he clearly wanted to hear—that she was innocent, that Randal had been forcing her. But, no, she had to tell Tom the truth, however painful and embarrassing. She had lied to him by omission for the past four years, hiding a very important piece of her life from him. She had to tell the whole truth now.

'No, Tom. I know him. I knew him before the accident. I worked for him before I came to work with you.' She swallowed, very pale, holding herself rigid. 'I…we…' What should she tell him? How should she explain? She and Randal had not been lovers, but they might have been, if she hadn't left.

Tom leapt to the obvious conclusion, face grim. She had always thought of him as boyish. That young, cheerful look had gone now. 'He was your lover?'

'No!' She hesitated, making herself expound on the flat denial, because he had to understand how it had been. 'Well…no, but…he might have been. That was why I left. He was married with a child. I couldn't break that up, but I wasn't prepared to be his mistress, so I resigned and left the firm. I haven't seen him since.'

Tom ran a hand over his face, as if to expunge all trace of emotion from it before he spoke. When he did, he sounded almost calm, his voice flat, toneless. 'Why didn't you tell me the other night? You must have recognised him.'

'Yes, of course, at once.'

It had been a blinding trauma, the instant when Randal had got out of his car and she'd seen those long legs, the windblown black hair, the strong, sardonic face. Time had rushed backwards at an alarming pace. She had felt like a girl again, trembling and breathless.

'Then why didn't you tell me you knew him?'

'I couldn't bear to. I didn't know what to say. And I thought it wasn't necessary. After all, nothing had really happened. We were attracted to each other, and might have become lovers, but I went away, so it didn't happen. There was nothing to tell. And I didn't think I'd ever see him again after that night.'

'But today you did.'

'Yes.'

She knew what he must be thinking—and she couldn't blame him. She hadn't set eyes on Randal for four years until the accident, and today they had ended up naked in bed together within hours. Tom was justified in being shocked. She was shocked herself. She had thought she knew herself pretty well, could predict how she would behave in any given situation. She had had to learn that there were depths of her nature she hadn't had any idea about. But, after all, how well did anyone know themselves?

'I really am sorry, Tom. I never guessed what would happen,' she stammered, very flushed.

'Are you saying he did force you?'

She wished she could say yes, but shook her head. 'No, he didn't use force—he's devious and scheming, but never violent.'

Randal had had no need to use force. He had used her own feelings and desires against her and had a walk-over because she was too weak to defend herself. Whatever she might say to him, however fiercely she rejected him, Randal had some way of seeing past all that and realising his power over her.

Tom took a long, rough breath. 'What exactly are you telling me, Pippa? That you're in love with him?'

She bit her lip, staring back in helpless silence.

Tom slowly nodded. 'And not with me. You've

always said so and that's the truth, isn't it? You'll never be in love with me.'

Pippa still couldn't find the words to answer him. She could not lie, and yet how could she tell the honest to God truth without hurting him even more?

'Well, say something!' Tom shouted, his face white. 'Surely you can say something! Aren't I entitled to that, at least?'

Moistening her lip with the tip of her tongue, she took a deep breath, whispered, 'Tom…I'm so sorry…I don't know what to say. But it isn't love, that isn't what I feel for him, I don't even know what it is I do feel. Only that I don't seem able to control it.'

He laughed mirthlessly. 'And all this time I've been putting you on a pedestal. I was waiting until we were married before I laid a finger on you, because I thought you were a virgin, pure as driven snow. And now, less than a week before our wedding, I find you in bed with a stranger!'

'I'm s…' she began, and Tom suddenly shouted at her.

'Don't keep saying that!'

For a second she felt danger in him, a rage surging under his pale skin, making his body tense. She even thought he was going to hit her, and as their eyes met she knew she was thinking that too, but in the end Tom's basic decency won out and his shoulders sagged. He turned away from her to stare out of the window.

After a minute's silence that felt more like hours, he said, 'So what now? The wedding's off, I presume? Do you want me to deal with all the cancellations and phone calls? It would be better coming from me.'

'What…what will you say?'

'I'll tell the truth. We've changed our minds at the eleventh hour.' There was another pause, then he said abruptly, 'Will you be okay?'

She was touched by his concern. 'Yes,' she whispered.

'Goodbye, then.'

Spinning on his heel, he walked out of the room. She stood there, listening to him going, feeling limp and exhausted. The front door quietly closed.

It was so sudden, this ending—a week ago they had been busy planning the last details of their wedding, yet now there would be no wedding.

Her brows knit. What about her job? Tom had said goodbye—had he meant she no longer had a job? His words had sounded so final and she wouldn't be surprised if he had been firing her by implication.

How could they work together after this? The office gossip was going to be horrendous. Humiliating for Tom. The girls were going to be sorry for him, and, worst of all, show it, which he would hate. And if she went back, it would be embarrassing for her, too. People would whisper behind their backs, stare whenever they met them; some would drop hints, even have the cheek to ask direct questions.

Why? Why call the wedding off? Is there someone else? Have you met another guy? Or has Tom found another woman?

She shuddered, imagining it. No, she couldn't bear to go back and face Tom's hurt eyes, his wounded bride, or one of those curious, insolent interrogations.

Tomorrow she would have to write, resigning, and

then she would put her cottage on the market and move again. A sigh wrenched her. Last time there had been no problem moving home, that shabby little room hadn't mattered to her, but this time she was bitterly reluctant to leave her home, the cottage she had spent so much time and energy and money on improving. It had been the very first real home she had ever had. She did not want to leave it. But she knew she couldn't stay here, not now.

Standing at the window into the back garden, she watched sunlight sparkling on spring flowers: the few last white narcissi, pale, frail flowers, purple hyacinth, whose fragrance made them hypnotic for insects which buzzed between them, making deep splashes of colour against the green of the lawn, newly budding bluebells under the apple tree not yet in blossom. She would probably never see another spring here.

Tears filled her eyes. She leaned on the window frame, put her hands over her eyes, weeping.

The first she knew of Randal's arrival was when he took hold of her shoulders and turned her towards him, one hand behind her head, pushing her face into his chest. She was too miserable to protest or struggle; she desperately needed comfort. Weakly, she lay against him, sobbing.

His fingers stroked her hair, rubbing her scalp in a sensuous rhythm she found hypnotic. 'Was he very unpleasant?'

She drew breath, said shakily, 'Not at all. I almost wish he had been. He was hurt, which was far worse. I feel so guilty.'

Randal put a finger under her chin and lifted her head, stared down into her tear-wet green eyes. 'You didn't love him and he'd have realised it eventually, after you married him, and then he'd have been a damn sight more hurt. Surely you see that?'

She didn't answer, her mouth trembling. Randal put his thumb on it and traced the weak curve, caressed her upper lip, watching her like a cat watching a mouse. To her, his grey eyes seemed cruel, predatory.

'I think you'd better go now,' she said, eyes flaring with hostility.

His arms tightened round her and he bent his head to take her mouth fiercely. The heat of the kiss melted her anger, made her knees give way under her, but she didn't mean to let him do this to her again. She had to get control of herself—and him.

She grabbed his shoulders to push him away but couldn't move him. It was like trying to push over a rock.

Abandoning the attempt, she meant to let her hands fall, but his kiss deepened, invading her parted mouth. A groan broke from her. Her fingers curled instinctively and she found herself holding on as if she was clinging to the only thing that would stop her collapsing on the floor.

Randal murmured thickly, pulling her even closer, and lifted her off her feet. A second later she was lying on the couch, still held in his arms, her body on top of his, his hand grasping her head, holding it still, while he went on kissing her with a devouring passion that turned her blood to fire.

When he lifted his head she couldn't move, her green eyes drowsy and half closed, breathing thickly as she stared down at him, her body aching with pleasure.

'You see? You're mine,' he whispered. 'It would

have been a crime if you had married that poor fellow. He deserves a wife who loves him. It was kinder for him to find out, even if the shock did hurt him. He'll get over it and find somebody else, and be happier with her than he could ever have been with you.'

She closed her eyes and let her head fall on to his chest, feeling the deep reverberations of his heart under her face, the rise and fall of his breathing.

'I take it the wedding is definitely off?' he quietly asked, and she nodded.

'Yes, Tom said he would see to the cancellation of all the arrangements.' A wry, painful smile twisted her lips. 'He's a bit of a control freak; he doesn't trust me to take care of it myself.'

'Why were you crying?'

She sighed. 'For Tom…'

'You never loved him! Admit it!'

'No, but he loved me and I've hurt him. Also, I've realised I have to sell this cottage, and I love it so much. But I'll have to resign from the firm, I couldn't go on working with Tom after this, and I can't stay here once I've given up my job. I'd have to rearrange the mortgage, and I might not be able to afford a much higher mortgage.'

'You worry too much; that's your problem.'

She looked at him angrily. 'That's typical. You just brush my worries aside with a shrug. The fact is my whole life is being torn apart, for the second time, and it's all your fault again. Last time I was only living in that room, but this time I'm going to lose the first real home I've ever had.'

'Come and live with me.'

She started, drew a long, sharp breath. 'I'd rather die!'

Maddeningly, he laughed. 'I don't think you would, when it came to the moment of choice. Think about it. Die, or live with me? Now, which do you think you'd choose?'

'Oh, you think you're so funny!' She struggled, fuming. 'Will you let me up, please? I think you should be going.'

He sat up, brushing back his tousled black hair. 'Is there anywhere around here to have dinner?'

'Drive back into London,' she curtly said, getting up and tidying her clothes, her hair.

'I want to have dinner with you.'

She turned on him, eyes blazing. 'Haven't you done enough to me today? I got up this morning feeling fine, with my wedding a week away and my life arranged in front of me. Then you came along and blew it all to pieces. And now you want me to have dinner with you? The answer is no! I won't have dinner. I never want to see you again. Is that clear enough?'

He looked into her eyes and her bones turned to water inside her. 'You don't mean it. You want me as much as I want you. Why pretend you don't? We're both free now.'

She hesitated, looking down. He wasn't going to give up and go away, but she wasn't giving up, either. He had walked back into her life and broken her world apart, without caring if he hurt her, or Tom, only interested in getting his own way. He kept saying he wanted her. He hadn't said he loved her. If he loved her he wouldn't have pursued her ruthlessly when he knew she was getting married in a few days.

He hadn't even seen her for four years. He could

have had no idea whether she loved Tom or not. No idea, either, what she felt, or wanted, or thought.

That didn't matter to him. He had no respect for her, no interest in what went on inside her head, or her heart. All he cared about was her body. He was determined to have it.

That wasn't love, was it?

And she wasn't going to let him have his own way.

'Pippa,' he softly said. 'What do I have to do? Beg? Have dinner with me. We have a lot to talk about.'

They seemed to have been talking all day, getting nowhere. How could they when they weren't talking about the same thing? She had to persuade him to go away, but how? There was only one way. She must let him think he had won, must pretend to give in, then he would leave the cottage and she could escape.

'There is a country club a couple of miles away,' she murmured, and felt him smiling to himself. He thought he had won; she was going to be easy.

'Do they have a good restaurant?'

'It's quite good. English and French cooking.'

'Should I book a table? Or can we just turn up?'

'I should book.' Out of the corner of her eye she shot a look at the clock on her mantelpiece. It was half past six.

'What's it called?'

'Little Whitstall Country Club. You'll find it in the telephone book by the telephone. Or would you like me to book it?'

'No, I will.' He walked over to the phone and began flicking through the pages. She was thinking feverishly. How was she going to persuade him to leave for a while?

He made the call, put down the phone and turned to her, his gaze wandering down over her.

'I suppose you'll want to change into something more formal?'

She pretended surprise, looked down at her clothes. 'Oh…if you like…'

'There isn't time for me to go back to London to change; what I'm wearing will have to do. But I must buy some petrol. I'm not sure I'll have enough to get back to town later tonight, and all the garages will be shut by then, I suppose. Where's the nearest garage?'

'I don't know one on the way to the country club, but there is one a mile away, in the first village back from here. While you get your petrol I'll change into something more suitable.'

He smiled at her and she ached with a strange mixture of pleasure and anger. He was charming, far too charming. She didn't trust him. He meant to sleep with her tonight, after dinner. No doubt he would get her to drink a lot of wine, then he would bring her back here and talk his way into the cottage, upstairs into her bedroom, then into her bed.

Pippa wasn't even sure she had the strength of will to resist him, but if she did surrender tonight she was going to despise herself tomorrow.

'Okay, I won't be long.'

She stood there, listening to his departing footsteps, the front door closing, his car door opening and slamming again, the engine firing and then the sound of his car moving away, before she moved herself.

First she ran upstairs, found a suitcase and packed in a hurry, then she changed into jeans and sweater, carried her suitcase downstairs and put on a warm sheepskin jacket hanging in the hall. She had no idea where she was going, but she had to rush, to get away before he got back.

She knew a small hotel in Maldon, on the Thomas estuary; she had been there before. She looked up the number, rang them, booked a single room, then after hanging up she put down water and a saucer full of dried food for Samson, who had vanished again, through his catflap in the kitchen door. He could come and go as he chose, so he would be okay for a couple of days. In any case, she knew he visited several other houses nearby, where he got fed and cosseted. Cats were self-sufficient and independent.

Before leaving she carefully turned off all the lights, checked she had her credit cards and cheque-book, everything she might need. Fifteen minutes later she was in her car, driving away, being careful to take a route which would make sure she did not pass Randal's car returning.

CHAPTER FIVE

THE weather had turned chill and misty by the time she reached the little estuary town of Maldon. The weather rolled in from the sea and was funnelled up the river. She parked in the car park behind the hotel and carried her case through the bar to check in. There were a few people drinking in the bar; they mostly seemed to know each other, which meant they were either local residents who drank here or they kept a yacht at Maldon, as many people did from London and the south of the country. As Pippa passed they all turned their heads to inspect her, some murmuring comment to companions. In the summer Maldon had many visitors, but at this time of year there were far fewer.

While she was filling in the card handed to her by the small, trim receptionist, she was asked, 'Will you be having dinner tonight, madam?'

'Yes, please,' Pippa said, handing the woman the registration card.

'What time?'

Pippa glanced at her watch and was surprised by how quickly she had driven there, but then she knew the way through the winding marsh roads. She hadn't had to consult a map or slow down to check sign-posts.

'Eight-thirty?'

'Certainly, madam. The dining room is on the left

through the bar. Jim will take your bag upstairs for you.'

A white-bearded old man popped up from an inner office and seized Pippa's case, carried it up the wide, ancient, creaking staircase with Pippa following him, feeling guilty.

He looked old enough to be her father. She hoped the case wasn't too heavy for him.

'This was an old pub, miss, till it was modernised and turned into a hotel,' he told her. 'Hundreds of years old. There was a pub here in the Middle Ages, I'm told. A lot of local people still treat it as their pub.' He put her case down outside a door at the end of a short corridor and produced a key. 'Here you are, miss. I hope you'll be very comfortable in here.'

She looked around curiously while the porter carried her bag inside. 'TV, with remote control,' he pointed out. 'Hospitality tray, with tea and coffee, and if you want fresh milk contact Reception. The bathroom is on your right.'

She smiled. 'Thank you.' And tipped him.

He saluted and was gone, leaving her alone. She was pleased with the room; it was spacious and a little old-fashioned, all chintz and oak furniture, which she found comforting. She unpacked, put her clothes away, found the hospitality tray, which bore a kettle, tea and coffee sachets and a cup, and made herself a cup of coffee.

She drank it standing next to the window, which looked down through mist on to a quayside lined with rows of small boats. Now and again a figure moved through the mist, grey, wavering, insubstantial, like a living etching. There was the faint sound of footsteps and then the silence came back and nothing stirred except the gentle lapping of water at the quay steps.

She had half an hour before her dinner. After that long drive she felt like a walk so she put on her jacket and went downstairs, crossing the bar again to go out on to the quay. The people drinking all watched her with the same unblinking curiosity.

As she walked out of the hotel the mist swallowed her. From somewhere nearby she heard a church clock chime. That might be eight o'clock. She couldn't go far or she would be late for dinner. Wandering along the quayside, she read the names of boats. The mist was thickening; she could barely see a hand in front of her face. Shivering, she drove her hands down into her jacket pockets. There was nobody else around; she could have been marooned on a desert island, or the last person alive on earth.

A moment later, though, she heard footsteps behind her and glanced round. A tall shape loomed through the mist. She couldn't see his face but she instinctively felt him staring at her, felt a strange prickle of threat. He began to walk faster, and panic flared inside her. She quickened her steps, too, almost running, and tripped over a lobster pot someone had left on the quay.

Pippa sprawled headlong. The man behind ran to catch up and knelt down beside her. 'Did you hurt yourself?'

Shock made her speechless. She turned her head to look up at him incredulously as she recognised the voice and face. Drops of pearly mist dewed his hair and brow and he was wearing a leather jacket zipped up to the neck.

'What are you doing here?' she burst out. There

was something of black magic about his appearance out of the mist when she had thought him safely miles away.

Randal stood up, pulled her up beside him, his strong hands clasped around her waist. 'Thought you'd given me the slip, did you?' Dry mockery in his smile made her bristle.

'How did you know where I'd gone?' She was still having difficulty believing he was here. She tried to work out how he had followed her. 'Did you see me leaving when you came back from getting petrol?'

'I didn't go to get petrol,' he wryly admitted. 'I was a bit suspicious about your sudden agreement to have dinner with me. I had the feeling you were planning something so I parked just down the road, behind some trees, where I could watch your cottage without you seeing me. I had a suspicion you would try to cheat, and I was right, wasn't I? I saw you come out of your cottage and get into your car. When you drove out I followed at a discreet distance.'

It was the same trick he had played when he waited for her to come out of her office and followed her to the bridal shop. She might have guessed he wouldn't just go off to get petrol, leaving her the opportunity to escape before he returned.

It dawned on her that he was still holding on to her. She slapped his hands down and took a step back.

'Careful! You don't want to end up in the water, do you?' he said as she toppled on the edge. He took her wrists and pulled her towards him to safety.

She broke free again. 'Who do you think you are? James Bond? Why can't you leave me alone?' she broke out, trembling with rage. 'The fact that I left like that should tell you I don't want to see you. Ever again. Why don't you take the hint, and stop harassing me!'

'I'm not harassing you,' he smoothly said. 'I was worried about you, driving off in that state. You were upset over your ex-fiancé. And it was misty. You might have had a crash.'

'But I didn't!'

He shrugged his wide shoulders gracefully. 'No, you didn't. But what on earth made you chose to come to a dead and alive hole like this?'

'I like it. It's peaceful.' Shooting him a resentful look, she added pointedly, 'Normally.'

He smiled. 'Have you booked into your hotel for dinner?'

'Yes, and I must get back for it at once,' she said curtly, and began to walk fast.

Randal kept pace with her. 'I'm staying there too.'

Her heart sank, although she should have guessed. Where else?

'We can have dinner together, after all,' he triumphantly added.

She considered refusing, for a moment, but knew he would somehow make sure he won the argument and felt too tired to fight him any more. He was the most maddening man she had ever met. He wouldn't listen to her. If she ran he pursued her. He had ruined her life twice, and she had fled, but here he was again. She had a terrible suspicion that she was never going to be able to shake him off. Was she going to spend the rest of her life running away from him and being pursued?

Inside the cosy warmth of the old hotel she hurried upstairs to take off her jacket and do something about her appearance, brushed her hair, renewed her make-up, staring at her reflection and horrified at the feverish brightness of her green eyes, the tremor in her mouth.

He always had this effect on her. Could he see that? How could he fail to notice the way she was shaking?

She turned away, shivering, then went downstairs again and found the dining-room.

Randal was already seated at a table by the window overlooking the quay, a bottle of white wine chilling in an ice bucket beside him. He had shed his leather jacket and was wearing a dark jacket, a crisp white shirt and a blue silk tie. Her breath caught. Did he have to be so good-looking, so distinguished?

He rose as she joined him. 'There you are! I was beginning to think you had run off again.'

She sat down opposite him and glanced through the menu, which was not extensive but sounded good; she decided to have melon followed by grilled sole with a salad. The waiter came to take their order, wrote down what she wanted first, then turned to Randal, who chose melon, steak and chips.

When the waiter had gone Randal poured wine into her glass. 'How long do you plan to stay here?'

'I haven't decided yet.' She sipped the golden wine and felt a little warmth come back into her veins. 'Not long. I must go back soon and start planning. I have to write to the insurance firm, resigning, put my cottage on the market and start looking for another job.'

'I'll give you one.'

She gave him a dry look. 'No, thank you. I don't think that would be a good idea.'

'Why not?'

Flushed, she looked down into her wine glass, playing with the stem. 'Don't they say, ''Never go back''?' She wished he would stop asking her these pointed questions; she didn't want to think about the reasons for the way she felt. She didn't know herself why she had these strong impulses, this desire to run from him and keep running.

'Who's they, anyway?' he asked, watching her across the table with narrowed, searching eyes.

She shrugged, looking up briefly, then down again, because she could not meet his lance-like gaze. 'Oh...people.'

'People with minds like train tracks. You should never make rules for life. Life is for living, spontaneously, on instinct. You don't need rules. You're not a machine, you're a human being, a living organism.'

She sipped more wine. 'Talking about living spontaneously, I've been thinking I might get a job aboard—Paris, say.'

There was a pause, then he asked flatly, 'Is your French good enough for that?'

'I speak a little, and if I'm living there I'd soon learn a lot more. And I've always loved the idea of living in Paris; it's such a beautiful, exciting city.'

Gravely, Randal said, 'But you'd be a foreigner, far away from home—it wouldn't be an easy life and you would have to speak French all the time. It can be difficult to be accepted into the local community. I'd think very carefully about going to work there.'

The waiter returned with their first course: a whole ogen melon, with a lid carved out like petals, golden and ripe, chilled from the fridge, filled with a medley of soft fruit—cherries, peach, strawberries steeped in liqueur. Was it Kirsch? she wondered, rolling it round her mouth.

'I wasn't expecting it to be this good,' Randal said, tasting it too.

'Neither was I,' she admitted.

'But you said you knew this place pretty well, had been here a few times.'

'That's true, but the food wasn't this good when I ate here before. Maybe they have a new chef.' She ate a cherry. 'These must be imported; you won't be able to get fresh cherries here for a couple of months. Tom and I picked cherries in Kent last June when we were staying at a farm. Of course, Kent cherries are pink and cream, not dark red, like these.'

Randal's face tightened, a frown drawing his brows together. 'You know, what I can't understand is why on earth you let yourself come so close to marrying him. Surely your common sense warned you it would be the biggest mistake of your life if you went ahead with it?'

Defiantly, she retorted, 'We could have been very happy! What do you know?'

'You weren't in love with him, and I suspect he wasn't really in love with you, either! I didn't get the impression he was sick with passion.'

She looked daggers at him. 'You don't know Tom; he's a good man.'

'Good, but boring. Oh, come on, Pippa, you know he would never set the world on fire. How could you have been happy with him? Unless all you were looking for was a nice, quiet, comfortable life with a man who wouldn't ask for too much from you.'

She finished her melon and sat back, glowering. 'Will you please stop talking about it?'

'Maybe that really is what you want? A man who won't expect too much?'

Her skin was burning; she resented his comments. 'Look, thanks to you, my marriage is off so there's no point in discussing it any further, is there?'

'I'm just trying to work out your motivation,' he calmly told her, and she clenched her hands into fists on her lap, wanting to punch him.

'Mind your own business, will you? If I need a psychiatrist, I'll go and see one. I don't want you doing amateur work on my head.'

'You need to do some thinking! You're one of the most mixed-up women I've ever met! You have no idea about what goes on inside you, do you?'

She was about to snap back at him when the waiter appeared to take their plates away, so she closed her mouth and looked down while the man refilled their glasses. Pippa was startled to see she had drunk most of the white wine she had had in her glass. She had drunk it without realising what she was doing. It was strange; she had rarely before drunk much wine.

Maybe it was another way of running, fleeing from Randal Harding. She needed to muffle her senses, dull her nerve-ends. Escape.

She didn't want to think about what she needed to escape from.

As the waiter went away again Randal's supple, powerful hand stretched across the table to move the low vase of flowers between them so that he could see her more clearly.

'I'd like you to come with me to see my son—will you?'

Surprised, she looked up, green eyes wide, hesitated. 'I'm sure he would rather be alone with you. He must miss you, even if he does like the school.'

'I want him to know you, and I want you to know him.'

She stared at him, biting her inner lip. 'Oh. But…why…?'

'Johnny rarely if ever sees his mother. I think he needs women in his life; I don't want him to grow up in an all-male world. It isn't healthy.'

She couldn't argue with that. She believed children needed two parents—she knew she had needed, longed for that. 'But surely you have a sister? Or another female relative?'

She knew so little about him; his marriage had been a towering wall between them, and she had seen nothing beyond that.

Impatiently, he said, 'Why don't you want to meet my boy?'

'I didn't say I didn't it's just that I…' Her voice trailed off. How could she tell him she was afraid to meet his son in case she grew fond of him? The child had already lost his mother; it would be cruel to let him get used to her, herself, only for her to vanish too one day.

'What?' he demanded relentlessly, those grey eyes boring into her like lasers. He wasn't giving up, and she didn't have the energy for another fight, so with a sigh she gave in.

'Oh, very well.' It was easier to agree now and make some excuse when the time came than to go on arguing.

He gave her that warm, charming, triumphant smile. She regarded him dryly, understanding the triumph. He loved to win. That much she did know about him.

'Good girl,' he approved. 'I'm sure you'll like him.'

'You've never told me much about him. What's he like?'

'Me,' he said, with self-satisfaction. 'He's very like me.'

Sarcastically she murmured, 'Oh, well, I'm sure he's gorgeous, then.'

Randal looked at her through his lashes with an intimate, mocking amusement, making her heart knock at her ribcage; she expected him to make some tart come-back, but at that moment their main course arrived and they began to eat.

They spoke very little; she wondered if he was silent because he had achieved his objective in getting her to agree to meet his son, and no longer had much to say. That would be typical of him; he was a very focused man, concentrated on getting his own way.

When they had finished their main course Randal asked if she would like a pudding, but she shook her head.

'If I eat any more I'll never be able to sleep tonight.'

He nodded. 'I won't have anything else, either. Coffee?'

'No, that might keep me awake, too.' It was half past ten by then, and she couldn't stop yawning, so she was sure she would sleep, but coffee might be a mistake.

'Tired?'

She yawned again, nodded. 'Sorry. It has been a fraught day. I've used up all my energy.' She rose. 'I must get some sleep; I'll have a lot to do tomorrow. I'll go home, write to the insurance company and resign, and tell them I'm selling my home, then I must talk to an estate agent and put the cottage on the market.'

They walked up the wide, creaking stairs together a few minutes later. 'What time shall we have breakfast?' he asked, and she looked at him impatiently.

'You have it whenever you like!'

'I want to have it with you,' he said in a coaxing voice, giving her that smile.

'How do I know what time I'll wake up? I didn't ask for a wake-up call. I may sleep late.' They arrived at her door. Her key in her hand, she faced him, chin up. 'Goodnight.'

'Goodnight,' he said, turning away.

She breathed a little easier; she had had an uneasy feeling he might not go too readily and had been nerving herself for a fight. He turned the corner in the corridor and his footsteps faded. Putting the key in the lock, she opened the door and began to go into her room. A second later Randal was inside too and the door was shut. She hadn't even heard him coming.

Angrily, she blazed at him. 'Get out! How dare you? Do I have to scream the place down?'

Randal grabbed her by the shoulders and kissed her hungrily, his mouth a sensual temptation. Head swimming, eyes closed, she swayed in his arms, trying desperately not to go under, struggling not to surrender to the physical glamour of his kiss, his touch, his body pressing against hers.

The trouble was, she could never fight her attraction to him. She might stay cool and collected when he was talking to her—she could fight her feelings so long as he didn't touch her. But as soon as she was in his arms she felt herself weakening, yielding to the powerful erotic sensations he awoke in her. Her mind could not control her body. She felt as though her brain was submerged beneath some level of consciousness her waking mind could not reach. She was helpless in the grip of a desire that beat inside her, deep and harsh and driven, sending wild vibrations through her and silencing all rational thought.

Slowly, Randal pulled his head back and looked down at her, and Pippa opened her eyes to stare back at him, shuddering.

'You kiss me like that, and yet you keep pretending you don't want me?' he whispered. 'What's going on inside that head of yours? We're both free now, there's nothing to keep us apart—so why are you still fighting it?'

CHAPTER SIX

SHE had asked herself the same question, ever since they'd met again, and she still wasn't sure of the answer. They were both free now, as he said. She wanted him, she couldn't deny it—and yet…

And yet for some reason she found herself backing away every time they came too close, and she didn't know why.

'You're moving too fast,' she guessed aloud without real conviction, pushing at his shoulders and taking a step back. 'We only met again less than twelve hours ago and a lot has happened since then. My marriage is off, I'm leaving my job and selling my home—the last few hours have been an emotional avalanche. I'm still reeling. The last thing I need is you trying to force the pace.'

He let go of her slowly, frowning. 'Maybe that's it. But I'm afraid you'll run away again. It's a habit of yours. And you're deceitful, Pippa. I left you getting ready to have lunch with me earlier today and what did you do? You ran away here, to Maldon. Why did you do that? Maybe that's what you're intending to do again. Maybe tomorrow morning I'll find you've skipped the hotel and gone before I get up for breakfast.'

Soberly, she said, 'I promise I won't. I give you my word.'

He studied her face intently. 'You'll meet me downstairs for breakfast? You swear?'

'I swear. What time?'

'Eight-thirty?'

She nodded. 'Eight-thirty. I'll be there. Then I'm checking out and going home to write letters and make phone calls.'

He moved towards the door. 'Okay, see you at breakfast, then.'

She followed so that she could bolt the door as soon as he had left and Randal looked down at her mockingly.

'Goodnight.' Bending briefly, he dropped a light kiss on the tip of her nose, then he was gone, and Pippa bolted the door after him. That tiny, intimate caress left a warm feeling inside her, though, while she was undressing, taking off her make-up, washing, getting into bed.

There was something special between them; there had been from the beginning. She had never felt anything like that for anyone else. Oh, she liked Tom, but ruefully she had to admit that if she had married him it would have been a disastrous mistake. She would never have loved him, really loved him.

Switching off her bedside lamp, she lay in the darkness listening to the slow lap-lap of water on the quayside, an occasional footfall out there in the damp grey mist. Above her the ancient floors creaked as someone walked across another bedroom. Pipes hummed as water ran. But otherwise the hotel was quiet, nobody seemed to be listening to television or talking, and it didn't take her long to get to sleep.

The room was full of sunlight when she woke up; the mist had obviously cleared. Slipping out of bed, she parted the curtains to peer out. The quay bristled with masts; brightly painted little boats moored in rows, bobbing against each other as the water rose and fell.

She read their names, smiling. The *True Love*; *Scrumpy Joe*; *Heggarty Peggarty*; *Sue-Anne*. Some of them had men working on them, unpacking sails, scrubbing decks, painting, coiling ropes. Along the quay sat men drinking mugs of tea or coffee. After the grey damp silence of yesterday, the quay had come alive and was full of people.

Sunshine made you feel happier. Smiling, Pippa walked into the bathroom and took a shower before getting dressed to go down to breakfast. Although she had eaten that large dinner last night, she was now hungry again, perhaps because the sunshine had lifted her spirits and she felt more positive.

She put on jeans and a bright turquoise sweater, did her make-up, then quickly packed her case before leaving the room. As she came down the ancient stairs she saw Randal sitting in a chair below, reading a newspaper and looking up every so often to check if she was on her way.

'Why are you waiting there? Why not in the dining room?' she asked him as he stood up to greet her.

'To make sure you didn't creep away without breakfast,' he coolly admitted, flicking a glance over her from head to foot before following her into the dining room.

'I promised I wouldn't!' A little flush flowed into her face at the way he had looked at her. He didn't miss a thing, from the peaks of her breasts inside the sweater to her trim waist and long legs in the tight jeans. And that look, the glitter of desire in his grey eyes, made her pulses leap and race.

He shrugged. 'I wasn't entirely sure I could trust you.'

She couldn't honestly resent that; she knew she deserved it.

They were shown to the same table they had occupied last night, and given menus. 'Tea or coffee?' asked a young waitress. 'White or brown toast?'

'Coffee,' they both chose.

'And mixed toast?' suggested Pippa. Randal nodded, and the waitress vanished to fill their order.

Breakfast didn't take up much of their time; Pippa just had a bowl of fresh fruit followed by a boiled egg with toast. Randal had porridge and a kipper. By nine o'clock they had finished, and left the dining room together.

Pippa paid her bill and asked for her suitcase to be brought down. While she was waiting for the porter Randal quietly asked, 'You're going straight to your cottage now?'

'Yes.' She took a deep breath. 'And, please, don't come there too. I have a lot to do and I would rather be alone.'

His face impassive, he turned away. 'I'd better pay my own bill; I still have to pack. You'll probably leave before I do. Drive safely.'

He hadn't promised he wouldn't come to the cottage. She looked crossly at his back as he began paying his bill. Then the porter appeared with her case. With him on her heels, Pippa walked out to the car park and a few minutes later was driving away.

This morning the marsh looked quite different; with the mist gone the horizon was bright and the fields shimmered under the sun. She drove slowly, enjoying the landscape and the sound of birds. A heron flew low, its grey profile memorable, legs trailing, fixedly gazing down at the silvery estuary in search of prey.

It was twenty past ten when she arrived home, and as she parked she saw with a jolt of shock that Tom's car was parked a few feet away. Dismay filled her. He must be in the cottage; he still had a key. Questions buzzed inside her—why was he here? At this time of day he should be at work. What did he want? He had been surprisingly low-key yesterday in his reaction, but he had had time to think about it. Had he come back to make an angry scene?

Her teeth gritted. Whether she wanted to or not, she had to face Tom; she wasn't running away, not any more. She had done too much of that with Randal. So she lifted her chin and walked towards the front door, which opened as she approached.

Tom confronted her in his dark city suit, like a grim avenging angel.

'Where have you been?' he asked with belligerence. 'It looks as if you've been out all night. Your bed wasn't slept in and everything is spotless.' He paused, then asked tersely, 'I suppose you've been with *him*?'

She walked past into the cottage, sighing. 'No, I haven't!' It wasn't exactly a lie, because Tom was really asking if she had slept with Randal, and she hadn't had she? 'I don't want a row, Tom. No inquisition, please. Why are you here?'

'I realised I had to see you to sort things out. We didn't talk properly yesterday, did we? So I took a day off work.' He followed her into the kitchen and watched her put on a kettle and start laying out cups and saucers, put teabags into the teapot.

'I thought we'd said everything, Tom.'

'We were both in shock,' he said roughly. 'Now we've calmed down and I've had time to think. Look, if you want to stay in your job, you can. There's no need to feel you have to leave. People have broken off engagements before. I'm big enough to cope with a few jokes and snide remarks. You can take time to stay on, look for another job if you still want to move, but walking out right now you wouldn't have a salary until you started work elsewhere, and I don't want you to get into financial difficulties because of me.'

She looked at him incredulously, her green eyes swimming in tears. 'Oh, Tom, that is so sweet!'

He shuffled his feet, very flushed. 'Just common sense. A broken engagement isn't the end of the world. We'll get over it. So—do you want to stay on?'

She shook her head. 'Thank you for offering, Tom, but, no, I would rather leave. You're braver than I am. I don't think I could face those jokes. I'm sure I shall get another job even if it isn't as well paid.'

'With him?'

Her eyes dropped to the floor. 'No.'

'You used to work for him, you said.'

'Yes, I did.'

With an angry bite, Tom demanded, 'But he didn't offer you a job? What a bastard. When it's his fault you need a job.'

Pippa groaned. 'Oh, Tom. Yes, he did, actually. He said I could have a job with his firm, but I'm not taking up the offer.'

Tom thought about that. 'But you and he are… getting together?'

'No! I've no intention of… No!'

He ran a hand through his hair, his face confused. 'I don't understand. I thought that was the whole point? That you were in love with him, that that was why you weren't going to marry me? If you aren't going to him, then why is it off between us?'

The kettle boiled; she made the tea, her back to him. 'It isn't that simple, Tom. Try to understand. I know it's hard, but try. Seeing him again made me realise I was not in love with you, and never would be. And I couldn't go ahead with the marriage when I knew it wouldn't work for us. Do you see?'

'No, I don't! You say you aren't going back to him, which I suppose means you aren't in love with him—so how did that make you realise you weren't in love with me, either?'

'Tom…' She fumbled for the right words, helpless to make it clear without hurting his feelings. 'Tom, I was in love with him four years ago. Desperately in love. I got badly hurt, but at least I knew I was doing the right thing in going away, in not breaking up his marriage. When you and I started seeing each other I thought I was over all that. I'd forgotten how I felt about Randal. I didn't try to compare the way I felt about you with the way I had felt about him. I honestly believed we could be happy together.'

'I still think we could be!' Tom said eagerly, coming closer. 'If you aren't in love with him, we still have a chance, Pippa.'

She picked up the teapot and poured the tea, shaking her head. 'I'm sorry, Tom, but, no, we don't have a chance. I know now that it was wrong of me to think I could make you happy.'

He put a hand on her back, gently stroking her spine, and leaned his face against her thick chestnut hair, murmuring into it, 'How can you be so sure? Two days ago, everything was fine. Then you bump into this chap and suddenly the wedding is off and you tell me we don't have a chance. But you still haven't made it clear. If you aren't in love with him either, why can't you marry me?'

She closed her eyes, groaning. 'Because I remember how I felt about him! And when I do marry, I want to feel that way again.'

He turned her round, still holding her, and softly kissed her. 'You could learn to feel that way about me, Pippa.'

She shook her head regretfully, hating to hurt him, but knowing it was kinder in the long run. 'I'm sorry, Tom. I'm very fond of you, and I like you a lot, but I know now that I could never love you the way I loved him.'

He groaned and kissed her again, harder, with pleading. 'Pippa… I don't want to lose you. I think we could be very happy together. We have been, haven't we? I always believed we were a perfect match. Are you sure you aren't chasing some impossible star? Looking for the perfect man? What if you never find him? Are you going to spend the rest of your life alone?'

The doorbell rang sharply and they both started. The noise went on, getting louder, more peremptory.

'Is that *him*? It sounds like him,' Tom said angrily. 'I'll deal with this. You stay here.'

'No, Tom,' she anxiously said, trying to stop him, but he was already on his way to the front door like an advancing army, bristling with war-like intent. Pippa ran after him, caught up just as he yanked the door open and glared at Randal standing outside.

'Clear off. You're not wanted. By either of us!' Tom barked.

'Pippa can talk for herself. She doesn't need you talking for her!' Randal drawled with an infuriating look of superiority.

'She's engaged to me!'

'That doesn't make her a deaf mute! Even if you'd like her to be one!'

'How dare you?' fumed Tom.

Pippa suddenly sensed they had an audience; across the road a curtain twitched, eyes peered at them, and a woman coming down the road had halted to stare, fascinated.

Angrily, Pippa hissed. 'Come inside. People are watching!'

'Not until this fellow has left!' Tom said with a sullen glare at Randal.

'I'm not going anywhere.' Randal shrugged.

Flushed and distressed, Pippa pulled Tom back inside the cottage and Randal coolly followed, closing the front door behind him.

'Tell him to go away,' Tom urged, giving her that pleading look again, making her feel guilty and very sorry for him. 'What's he doing here, anyway? You said you were never going to see him again, so why's he here?'

Randal gave her a narrowed, dangerous look. 'Did you say that? Did he ask you to promise not to see me again? And did you agree?'

'I asked you not to come here,' she reminded him, chin lifted and green eyes angry.

'And now I see why,' he said through his teeth. 'You'd arranged to meet him here and I would have been very much *de trop*.'

'No! I hadn't arranged to meet him. He arrived out of the blue.'

'And talked you into going ahead with the wedding? He's got your lipstick on his mouth, so don't tell me he hasn't been kissing you!'

'What if I have? It's no business of yours!' erupted Tom. 'Our wedding is no business of yours. You aren't wanted here; she just told you. You see? I knew how she felt. She's no deaf mute. She's saying what I said she would say. So, why don't you just clear off? And don't come back.'

'I'll do whatever I damned well please!' Randal bit out.

Pippa's mouth went dry; she had never seen him look so angry. He scared her.

But she wouldn't let him see that; she pushed between him and Tom, staring angrily at Randal.

'Go away! I told you not to come here, and I meant it. And stop threatening Tom. Or I'll hit you with the nearest heavy object!'

He looked down at her, his face softening, relaxing, his mouth curling at the edges with amusement and his grey eyes dancing.

'I'm really scared!'

'I mean it!'

He held his hands up, palms towards her. 'Okay, okay, I'll be good. Promise, miss.'

She studied his features, hoping he meant it, but not assured by the amused mockery in his eyes, then turned to Tom. 'I think you'd better go now, Tom.'

Tom was still in a belligerent mood. 'Why should I leave? Tell him to go.'

'I will,' she told him firmly. 'But first I want you to go. I don't want you both leaving at the same time.

I don't want a fight starting up outside the cottage; the neighbours have had enough excitement for today. Once you've driven off, he can go.'

'Tell him to go first, then I'll leave. Why should I be the first to go?' Tom stubbornly said.

She put her hand on his arm, her eyes pleading. 'Don't be difficult, Tom, don't go on arguing. Just leave, please.'

He hesitated, clearly very reluctant to climb down, especially in front of Randal, but eventually shrugged. 'Oh, very well, but only for you.' Averting his eyes from Randal, he marched out of the room towards the front door. Pippa followed, ruefully wondering why men were always so obsessed with their pride, their sense of themselves.

She had the strong feeling that Tom was more concerned with defeating Randal than he was with her.

Tom opened the front door, then paused, looked at her. 'Will you be staying on here, in the cottage?'

'No. I'm going to sell it. I'll contact an estate agent later today, or tomorrow.'

'Don't do that. I'll buy it. You know I've always loved it. It will save you the agent's percentage to sell it direct to me.'

She was taken aback. 'Are you sure you really want to live here?'

'Certain. I'll get the house valued to make sure I'm paying the market price; I don't want you to feel I'm cheating you. Or you can get an agent to value it, if you prefer. Once we've agreed the price, we can complete the deal through our solicitors.'

Slowly, she nodded. 'Okay, Tom. You have the house valued. I trust you. Get in touch with someone. He can ring me to make an appointment to view the cottage.' She smiled at him. 'It will save me a lot of money to cut out an agent.'

He nodded, then shot a look past her into the hall. 'Are you sure you can deal with him? I'll sit in my car, if you like, until he goes.'

'There's no need, Tom. I'll be okay.'

He shrugged, smoothing down his fair hair. 'Very well, if you're sure. But don't let him talk you into seeing him again.'

'I won't, don't worry.'

Tom bent and kissed her lightly on her lips, said huskily, 'I'm going to miss you.' Then he walked away, got into his car, and drove off.

Sighing, Pippa slowly closed the front door and turned back, starting as she found Randal only a few feet behind her, his graceful body leaning against the wall in a casual manner which did not, disguise his poised capacity to be difficult.

'Were you eavesdropping?' she angrily demanded.

He raised one brow mockingly. 'I wanted to make sure he left without making any more trouble.'

'It was you who made the trouble!' She opened the front door again. 'Now, will you go, please?'

He sauntered back towards the kitchen, saying over his shoulder, 'Not yet.'

She let the door slam again and ran after him. 'I don't want you here! We've got nothing to say to each other. We've said it all.'

He swung, and the tension in his long, powerful body sent her heart into her throat. 'I haven't. Why did you let him kiss you?'

'I didn't let him. It just happened! But it's not your business, anyway.'

'Oh, yes, it is,' he said, and she looked up again

to find his grey eyes focused on her mouth with an intensity that made her pulses race.

She didn't want to respond like that. She wanted him to go away and leave her alone. But when he looked at her with such desire she felt her own passion leap up to meet his, and that terrified her.

'Leave me alone!' she whispered, her heart beating worryingly fast.

He pushed the chair aside and took her shoulders in his strong, supple hands. 'You belong to me, Pippa, you know that, even though you keep trying to pretend you don't. From the minute we met we both knew we were meant for each other. If I'd been free then, we'd have been together all these years, but by bad luck I wasn't free, so you ran away, and you're still running. Why?'

'I told you. You've ruined my life twice—I'm not going to let you do it again!'

'You love me,' he whispered, his hand going down to her waist, pulling her closer. 'I love you, too. Stop wasting any more of our time.' His cheek descended against her face, their skin brushing softly. She wanted to resist, push him away, but she was paralysed, her whole being intent on her awareness of his heart beating against her own, his arm round her waist, his thigh pressing into hers, his mouth sliding over her cheek to her mouth. However hard she tried, she could not fight his physical power over her.

His kiss parted her lips. The warm tip of his tongue slid through into her mouth, his other hand went up the back of her head and cradled it, his fingers in her hair, softly pulling her head back as his kiss drove into her.

'No, don't,' she muttered under that fierce, possessive mouth.

He kissed her harder, more demandingly, and she groaned, her lips trembling, burning. Eyes shut, she clung to him in spite of her warning brain, in spite of all her reasons for fighting him off. It was the same every time—the instant he touched her she melted like candle wax in his hands.

Suddenly, she was floating, like a leaf in the wind. She fought to force her eyes open, dazedly looked up at him, her body still shuddering with pleasure. He had picked her up bodily and was carrying her in his arms, a hand under her legs, the other around her shoulders.

'What…what are you doing?' she whispered, but he didn't answer.

She found out what his intentions were a second later as he lowered her to the couch in the sitting room. Angrily, she tried to get up again, but he was beside her, fencing her in, a little heap of cushions behind her and his long, lean body stretching out in front.

'I hate you!' she breathed, trembling with an explosive mixture of rage and helpless desire. He was dangerously close, their bodies touching at every point from her shoulders to her feet, and she was on fire, wanting him so much it felt like dying. Yet at the same time a warning voice inside her head told her it was dangerous, lethal; he would only hurt her again. She must not let herself surrender.

'Do you, Pippa?' he asked silkily, smiling as he stared down into her bitter green eyes.

'Yes! I hate the sight of you,' she insisted, staring back at him with such fixed intensity that for a moment she wasn't even conscious of what his lean fingers were doing, until she abruptly realised he had pushed up her turquoise sweater and undone her bra, and begun stroking and caressing her naked breasts.

Her heart thudded against her ribcage; she gasped, 'No! Stop that!'

Randal's head came down; his lips opened on one of her hot, swollen nipples, drew it inside the moist warmth of his mouth, and sucked.

Pippa moaned, pushing at his head, but it was immovable and she was helpless in the grip of pleasure. Her body was arching towards his, even while she tried to push him off. She despised herself for finding it impossible to resist him, but the ecstasy of his sucking mouth made her ache and shudder. She wanted him badly, badly. It would be so easy to give in, open her body to him and hold him inside herself, merge with him until they were one person, even if it was just for a few moments.

But the instant satisfaction he could give her wouldn't last; she would come out of it and have to face herself afterwards. This need she felt was purely physical, sheer sensuality, a wild, beating urge deep in her body. Her mind warned her not to give in to it.

'I'm not sleeping with you!' she broke out, struggling.

His head lifted, his face darkly flushed, his eyes sensuous, drowsy. A wry smile curled his mouth. 'Stop fighting the way you feel, Pippa. You want me to make love to you, even if you're determined to insist you don't.'

He looked down at her body again, bent and ran the tip of his warm tongue softly over the nipple he had been sucking, and she couldn't keep back a cry of intense pleasure.

'You see?' he said. 'You want it, just as much as I do. What I don't understand is why you keep protesting that you don't.'

CHAPTER SEVEN

'YES, okay,' she broke out hoarsely. 'I go out of my head when you make love to me. I don't deny it.' Angrily, she saw him smile, his grey eyes glittering in triumph, and went on in a hurry, 'But I still don't want to get involved with you again. Last time I got hurt and I don't want to get hurt again. I keep telling you that. Why can't you get the point?'

He grimaced impatiently. 'Not again! We keep having the same circular argument! But if you insist, we'll go round again. Sooner or later maybe I'll make you listen. Four years ago, I was married. Now I'm free. We both know that. I'm in love with you, I want you, you just admitted you feel the same—so where's the problem?'

While he was talking in that brusque, impatient tone, she was discreetly clipping her bra together again, pulling down her sweater, smoothing her tangled chestnut hair. When he'd finished, she got up in a quick movement, before he could stop her, walked to the window, stood there with her back to him, speaking quietly. 'The problem is simple, Randal. I don't want to get hurt again. You know I was abandoned as a child—four years ago I felt I was being dumped again, when you chose your marriage and your child over me.'

He started to protest. 'For heaven's sake! What else could I do? He was only little; I couldn't walk out on him...'

She interrupted. 'Randal, listen! I'm not saying you were wrong. I understand. Your little boy needed you and had the right to expect that you would be there for him, protect him, make sure he was happy.'

'I'm his father; I had to look after him. Renata was far too selfish to bother about a child, even her own. All she wanted was to have a good time, and looking after a little boy didn't come into her scheme of things.'

'I know Johnny needed you to take care of him. I see that. I know you had no real choice. You felt you had to stay with your wife for his sake. But that doesn't change the fact that I felt you didn't really care about me. And, however good your reasons, I want a man who'll really care about me.'

He got up from the couch impatiently, his voice rising. 'Of course I cared about you, Pippa! How can you think I didn't? It was a terrible choice I was forced to make! Do you think I found it easy? I agonised over it for a long time.'

She swung round to face him, her face pale and grave. 'I just said, I know why you had to put your son first. But understanding doesn't alter anything. When it came to it, you chose your marriage and your child, not me, and I know you always would.'

He ran his hands through his hair in restless frustration. 'I had to then! What else could I do? You keep saying you understand, but do you? I had to choose Johnny four years ago, but it's different now. Everything's sorted. My marriage is legally over. Johnny's at boarding school. I've had a private detective looking for you ever since my divorce was finalised. You've been on my mind all this time. I love you, Pippa, and now we can get married. There's nothing in the way of us being together.'

'There's me, Randal.'

He stopped a few feet away and stared at her, eyes glittering, sharp, probing her face. 'What does that mean?'

'I won't let it happen to me again. I know now that you'll always put your son first and me second.'

'Pippa, it isn't a contest. You're being ridiculous! You sound as if you're jealous of Johnny, jealous of a little boy; that's crazy.'

'No, of course not. I'm not jealous of him. But I'm still afraid of getting hurt. You say you love me, but I'd never feel I was really important in your life.'

'Pippa…' He reached for her and she backed away, shaking her head.

'No! Please go, Randal, don't drag this out. I'm serious. I mean what I say, and it won't make any difference in the long run for you to make love to me. We both know I'd find it hard to say no at the time, but afterwards I'd still feel the same. I got hurt last time; I don't want to be hurt again. I've thought long and hard about this. There's no future for us.'

He raked back his tousled hair, grimly staring at her. 'I don't accept that! You're making a stupid fuss about nothing.'

She shrugged. 'If you think that, you just aren't listening or trying to understand. There's no point in talking. I'm not going to change my mind and you're refusing to see my point of view.'

'Okay, I'll leave—but you promised to come with me to see Johnny. Will you at least keep your word about that?'

She made a weary gesture. 'What good would it

do? I'm not going to be part of your life. There's no point in my meeting him.'

Randal was as serious as she was now, his grey eyes level and silvery, like cooling metal, hardening and losing colour as if all the passion had drained out of him, leaving him icy cold. 'I think there is. I'd like him to know you. The two of you matter more to me than anyone else in my life. I want you to know each other.'

She bit her lower lip, frowning. 'Why? What's the point?'

'I just told you. I want you to meet, even if it's only once. And you promised you would. A few hours of your time, that's all I'm asking you—surely you can spare a few hours?'

Pippa groaned. 'Why are you so obstinate. You never give up, do you?'

He shook his head. 'Not when something really matters to me.'

She sighed deeply, thinking. 'Oh, very well, I'll come, just once. And then…that's it, okay? You understand? You accept that I do not want to see you ever again after that?'

He nodded. 'I hear what you say. I'll pick you up on Friday, mid-morning, around eleven. Bring a change of clothes and a nightie. We'll be spending the weekend at a hotel.'

'Oh, will we?' she bit out, body tensing in immediate alarm and distrust.

He caught her quick sideways, suspicious look and laughed in light mockery. 'Oh, don't worry, I'm not planning a seduction scene. Johnny will be sharing my room; you'll have one of your own. You'll be quite safe.'

She had never been safe with him; since the beginning he had made her desperately happy, then bitterly unhappy, and she was determined never to let him risk her happiness again. Next time she fell in love she wanted it to be with someone who loved her the way she needed to be loved, who put her first.

She walked away from him to the front door, opened it. Randal came after her, looked down at her searchingly. 'By the way, did I hear you agreeing to sell this cottage to Tom?'

'I knew you were eavesdropping! You have no shame at all, do you? When you're after your own way you'll do anything to get it.' She shrugged contemptuously. 'But, yes, Tom asked me to sell it directly to him instead of putting it on the market. We were going to live here together, you know, once we were married; he likes the cottage.'

'I hope you're going to have it professionally valued!'

'Of course, but it's going to make selling it much easier. It will save me the ten per cent the agent would charge, and I trust Tom.'

'I can't say I do!' Randal snorted.

'You don't know him! He's a good man.'

'So he isn't buying the cottage just to stay in constant contact with you?'

She resented the dry, ironic note in his voice. 'No, certainly not. He's buying it because he loves it, he always has—and after all, I was going to sell it anyway. The sale will be handled through our solicitors; we won't need to be in contact.

'I was jealous,' he coolly retorted. 'He had your lipstick on his mouth, it was obvious he'd been kissing you, and I was jealous.'

She felt hot colour burn along her throat and face, and looked down, taken aback. The fierceness of his voice made her melt internally, made her legs weak.

He watched her briefly, his face unreadable, then said, 'See you on Friday.'

He walked down the short drive, got into his car and drove off. Pippa watched him vanish, then went in and shut the front door before going upstairs to have a cooling shower and put on a thin cotton shirt and a pair of cream linen trousers. Love was altogether too exhausting. She could not bear many more scenes like that. Fighting Randal had left scars on her heart and mind. She felt mauled, as if she had been in a cage with a tiger and barely escaped with her life.

She sat down to write her letter of resignation to the insurance company. Before she started looking for another job, it might be a good idea to have a long holiday. She felt she needed one.

She spent the warm spring afternoon in her garden, mowing the lawn, pruning and weeding; it was a peaceful occupation, and she didn't need to think too hard, but her body used up a lot of the buzzing energy inside her. The weather stayed fine and bright; it was pleasant in the sun. By the time she had eaten a salad and watched TV for an hour or so she was tired enough to go to bed and sleep without difficulty, keeping thoughts of Randal at bay when she was awake but finding him invading her dreams when she slept.

On Thursday Tom came round with a surveyor to price the cottage. While the man wandered around, measuring rooms and testing various parts of the building for signs of woodworm or damp, or other problems, Pippa and Tom sat outside in the garden with coffee and biscuits.

'You should make quite a bit of money on the deal,' Tom said in his calm, practical way. 'You got the place very cheaply and you did the bulk of the redecoration yourself so you didn't really spend too much on it. It was a very good investment. You'll finish up with a considerable profit. Will you buy another place at once, or invest the money and rent somewhere for the moment?'

'First I've decided to have a holiday.' That reminded her of something she had forgotten. 'Did you manage to cancel the honeymoon?'

'It was far too late for that. I've decided to go alone.'

She bit her lip. 'Oh. I'm sorry, Tom…'

'I'm sure I'll enjoy it. I was due a holiday anyway. Where were you thinking of going?'

'I haven't thought about it yet. When I come back, though, I'll have to get another job, then I'll see what property values are like wherever I move. I sent my resignation in, by the way. They should have it by now.'

Tom nodded, staring at two robins squabbling over some nesting material, a few scraps of twine Pippa had used to tie up lupins months ago, in the summer. They had frayed and broken, were hanging loose; the robins each had hold of one of them and were pulling and squawking crossly at each other.

'What about…him? Are you seeing him? Going on holiday with him?'

She sighed. 'Tom, don't keep asking about Randal, please. I don't want to talk about him.' She shaded her eyes to look up at the sky. 'It's such a lovely morning; don't waste it.'

Tom looked sulky, then said, 'What will you do with your wedding dress? Keep it for next time? When you marry him?'

She winced at the sting of the question. She couldn't blame him for feeling bitter, though. She hadn't broken Tom's heart, she didn't think he was madly in love with her, but she had damaged his ego, his sense of himself, and to the sort of man Tom was that would be very painful. His dignity was very important to him.

'I've talked to the dressmaker and paid her. I'll put the dress away for the moment.' She put a hand on his arm tentatively. 'I'm sorry, Tom. I've made a mess of your life, I know that, but I never intended to. It was just bad luck that we had that crash and I met…him…again. But although it was bad luck in one way, I do think it was just as well in another. How could we have been happy when I didn't really love you the way you should be loved? Sooner or later you would have realised something was missing and then it would have been ten times worse for both of us.'

He grunted, head turned away. She couldn't tell what he was thinking from the grim profile which was all she could see.

'You'll meet someone else, Tom,' she offered uncertainly. 'And this time it will be love on both sides.'

The surveyor, a thin young man with horn-rimmed spectacles and a very serious expression, came out to join them, looking around the garden. 'Very pretty out here, isn't it? This is a really charming property, in fact. I'll have to measure the land too, before we go. But you've done a very good job with the cottage. I gather it was in a pretty poor condition when you bought it, and you did most of the decorating yourself?'

'All of it, apart from the retiling of the roof and the plumbing. I even put in most of the kitchen myself, modernised it all. The old man who lived here hadn't touched the place for years and years.'

'Well, I'm impressed. You're very clever.'

'Thank you. Coffee?' She picked up the vacuum jug of coffee; it would still be hot.

'Black, no sugar,' he said, smiling at her, his blue eyes twinkling behind the heavy spectacles. 'Do you do the garden yourself, too?'

'Mostly, yes. I can't afford to pay people to do things for me. I enjoy gardening, anyway. In fact, I like doing things well; it gives me a buzz.'

He sipped his coffee. 'I know what you mean. I suppose most of us like doing things well. And you make good coffee, by the way.'

She laughed. 'Thanks.'

Tom shifted impatiently in his chair, irritated by this light-hearted conversation. 'Have you talked to your solicitor yet, Pippa? About selling the cottage?'

'I alerted him to the prospect. He didn't seem to foresee any problems.'

'Good. I expect you want to finalise the deal as soon as possible. I've put my own place on the market, but if it doesn't sell at once the firm will help me with a temporary mortgage on the cottage.'

'That will be helpful and should speed the deal.'

The surveyor finished his coffee and got up. 'I'll get on with measuring the garden and the rest of the area on which the cottage stands, then I can draw up a map to go with the deeds.'

As he walked away Tom looked at his watch. 'Half past eleven. Nearly lunchtime. Will you have lunch with me, Pippa?'

'Sorry, I'm too busy,' she quickly said. The sooner she stopped seeing Tom the better, for both of them. There was no point whatever in continuing to see him. His restless impatience with the surveyor just now made it obvious that he did not see her in any simply friendly light. He hadn't yet cut the strings that had bound them together. If he didn't set eyes on her for months, he would finally forget they had ever been about to marry, especially as she was quite certain he was not in love with her. Theirs had been an affair of proximity. Tom had wanted to marry her because she was the sort of wife he had always meant to pick. She was competent, sensible, good with money and a home-maker—he had felt he could trust her.

Now they both knew he had been wrong. She hadn't been the wife for him, any more than he was the man for her. Tom was possessive, but he was not passionate; that was why he had been happy to wait to sleep with her. Pippa had been forced to realise that she was very definitely passionate—she burned with desire whenever Randal touched her. She wanted to feel that way about the man she did eventually marry.

But it would not be Randal himself. He didn't love her enough. He loved his child more, and although she admired him for his fidelity to the little boy it still hurt her feelings.

The truth was, Randal didn't love her the way she needed to be loved. That was the root reason why she would not marry him. She wanted a man who would love her more than anyone else in his life, always put her first. The emptiness and loneliness of her childhood had left her aching. How often she had envied friends their homes, their parents, brothers and sisters—the affection and caring of those they lived with.

How often she had wished she had those things, too. She had always yearned for love, to be the centre of somebody's world, to know she was beloved and cherished. She would never have that with Randal. Oh, she believed him when he said he loved her, she knew he desired her, but the strong, protective love she had hungered for as a child would never come to her from Randal. He gave that to his son, which was only natural.

When Tom and the surveyor had left she sat on in the sunshine, facing facts about herself. It was childish and immature, no doubt, to want to come first with Randal—she knew people would see it that way, and maybe they were right, but she couldn't help her own instinctive reactions. She had dreamt for too long of finding someone who would love her the way she needed to be loved. She couldn't abandon her dream now.

The following morning she was up early, having slept badly. First, she packed a light weekend case, taking the bare minimum of clothes.

Then she had a shower before getting dressed in a simple green silk tunic which cut off just above her knee. With it she wore white high-heeled sandals and carried a white shoulder bag. The impression left by her reflection in her dressing table was one of cool elegance. She was satisfied by that. The last thing she wanted was to encourage Randal to think she might be an easy target.

She forced herself to eat some fruit and a slice of toast, then filled in the time before Randal arrived by checking that the cottage was scrupulously tidy, locking all the windows and doors apart from the front door. As she finished Randal drove up in his gleaming sports car.

Pippa's heart missed a beat, she suddenly couldn't breathe, but somehow she managed to pick up her weekend case and go out to meet him, locking the cottage door behind her. Randal got out of his car and took her case, put it in the boot, while, legs weak under her, she walked round to the passenger door and got into the front seat.

Randal slid in beside her, stretched those long, long legs of his, and started the engine again. She glanced sidelong at his lightweight pale blue linen jacket, the even paler trousers, exquisitely tailored, the smooth dark blue leather shoes which shrieked money. Randal was a luxury item from head to foot; he looked gorgeous. She looked at the supple, powerful hands on the wheel and had a heart-stopping flash of memory; those hands touching her as they had on the couch in the cottage, stroking her breasts while his mouth moved possessively on her bare skin.

She wrenched her gaze away and stared fixedly out of the window, shuddering.

She mustn't let herself remember. She had to get over him, stop wanting him, stop loving him.

But how did she do that when every bone in her body melted at the thought of being in his arms?

She had to make herself think about something else.

'How long will it take to reach this school?' She tried to sound calm and relaxed, hard though it was when she was so deeply conscious of being alone with him in this tiny space, their shoulders, their legs only inches apart.

'An hour and a half. I've said we'll pick up Johnny for lunch. I booked a table at the hotel; it isn't far from the school, and the cooking is extremely good. They have a top-class chef.'

'Does Johnny know I'm coming with you?'

'Yes, I talked to him on the phone last night. He was very excited about spending the weekend out of school—although he loves the school, going away is a stimulating experience for him. There's a riding stable near the hotel; he wants to spend a couple of hours there tomorrow. Would you like to ride?'

'Well, I have ridden a horse a few times, Tom thought it would be fun to go—but I'm strictly a beginner and I haven't brought any suitable clothes. I don't have any jodhpurs or boots or a hard hat, and it's dangerous to ride without a hat, at least.'

'Maybe they hire the gear out?'

'You know the place, I suppose. You've been there before with your son? Do they?'

'I've no idea, I've never asked, but if we can hire what you need do you want to ride?'

'It could be fun—are you going to ride?'

'I will, if you will. There's a qualified riding instructor who can look after Johnny, if we don't ride, but I'd like to go just to keep an eye on him.'

'And you have got the right gear with you?'

He nodded. 'After Johnny said he wanted to ride, I looked out some boots and jodhpurs, and I found a rather old hat which will do. There was no point in ringing you though, because the shops were shut by then, and I thought the stable might be able to find you some gear.'

'Well, if they don't hire clothes I'll watch. Don't worry about me.' She leaned back in her seat, watching the green English countryside flash past.

As they turned a corner another car tore towards them at a dangerous speed and Randal braked to avoid a crash, skewing his car closer to the hedge, as he had that night he and Tom crashed.

The other car screeched past. Randal came to a full stop, the bonnet of the sports car mere inches from the hedge. Silence fell on them like the dust of this quiet, narrow country lane.

Pippa only then realised that she had screamed. The echo of her cry of fear went on and on inside her head, and beside her she heard Randal angrily swearing.

After a minute, he turned towards her, releasing his seat belt, his face full of concern.

'Are you okay? I'm sorry about that. He was doing about eighty miles an hour—we're lucky I wasn't driving fast myself and we came out of it unscathed.'

She laughed unsteadily, tears of fear and wild humour in her green eyes. '*Déjà vu.* That was pure *déjà vu*. Just like the night you and Tom crashed into each other.'

He smiled wryly. 'I suppose it was. My heart is going like a steamhammer. Feel it.'

He took her hand and carried it to his chest, laid in on his shirt above where his heart beat violently. The warmth of his body lay under her palm; she pressed down on it, wanting desperately to undo his blue shirt and feel his skin against hers.

Randal watched her face closely and must have read the leap of hunger in her eyes because he suddenly leant over, his body above hers, coming down on her, holding her down. She knew she should push him away, refuse to let him kiss her, but the shock of the near accident was still inside her; she felt reckless, abandoned. She met his mouth with passion, her lips parting. His hands caressed her, and she felt desire tear through her like a hurricane, destroying everything in its path.

If they had not been sitting in a car at that moment, heaven knew what might have happened next, but they were parked on a public road and visible to anyone driving past. They could not go too far.

Randal groaned, slowly lifting his mouth. 'I would kill to have you now. Do you know what you do to me?'

Dazedly she lay there, eyes half closed, breathing thickly. She knew what he did to her—did he feel like this?

Her senses rioted: heart beating dangerously fast, pulses throbbing with fever, heat burning deep inside her. She hadn't wanted him to stop, had needed him to go on, to take her, satisfy this terrible need.

'We'd better get on or we'll be late arriving at the school, and even later for lunch,' Randal said, running a hand over his deeply flushed face. 'Sit up, Pippa. Stop tempting me.'

He clipped his seat belt together, started the engine again and slowly moved off, and she closed her eyes, fighting to get back to normal.

The rest of the drive was uneventful; they didn't talk any more. She pretended to be asleep and, indeed, did doze a little, drifting in and out of daydreams, fragments of memory, of him kissing her, touching her.

They reached the school just as many other cars were leaving, loaded with boys being taken off for the weekend by their parents. Randal parked on the wide gravel driveway, left her in her seat and walked into the school to find his son.

Pippa curiously gazed up at the building, built rather like a Scottish castle, with four storeys of stone walls draped with Virginia creeper, rows of arched windows and, at each end, turreted towers. She hoped it had central heating or it must be an icebox in winter.

A few minutes later Randal returned with his son, who was carrying in one hand a leather overnight bag. Johnny was taller than she had expected, a healthy-looking boy with his father's dark hair and slim build, but as they came closer she saw that he had sensitive features, wide blue eyes, a fine nose and wide mouth, a mobile face that reflected his emotions as he talked to his father.

She slid out of her seat to greet him, smiling.

'Johnny, this is Pippa,' Randal told him, taking his overnight bag and putting it into the boot of the car, and the boy held out his hand, staring at her.

'Hello.'

'Hi, Johnny,' she said, holding his small, slim fingers warmly. How much did he take after his mother? Physically he was very like Randal, but what about his nature, his personality? Was that inherited from Randal, too, or from his mother?

'We have to hurry,' Randal told them. 'We mustn't be late for lunch at the hotel. Hop in, Johnny.'

They drove off a moment later and were soon at

the hotel, a white Georgian building in spacious gardens. Randal manoeuvred his way through the arched gateway into the car park behind the hotel.

'This was once a coaching inn, in the eighteenth century,' he told her and Johnny. 'The coaches came through that arch and their horses were stabled overnight in those boxes, groomed, fed and watered, to rest until early next morning.'

The old stables had been painted pristine white and were used as outbuildings. Hanging baskets of flowers swung along the walls, spilling geraniums and nasturtiums, pink and white and vivid orange, giving colour to the ancient stone-cobbled floor. They all got out. Randal carried their bags through a door marked 'Reception'; Pippa and Johnny followed him into the low-ceilinged lobby and found him signing them all in while a pretty receptionist watched him, smiling.

A porter collected their luggage, to take it to their rooms, while they walked through the hotel to the dining room for lunch.

As the head waiter showed them to their table Johnny gave a little gasp and stopped dead, staring across the room at another table where a ravishing blonde was half rising, staring too.

'Mummy!'

Pippa's heart burned over in sick dismay.

CHAPTER EIGHT

SO THAT was Renata, Randal's ex-wife! And she was every bit as beautiful as everyone had ever said she was. Her figure was full and curvy, high, beautifully shaped breasts emphasised by the lilac shirt she wore, the lapels open and deep, revealing the smooth golden flesh, a trim waist, slim hips and long, long legs in white, tight-fitting jeans. Her hair was the colour of summer corn, ripe and golden, falling in rich waves around her lovely face.

Every man in the place was staring avidly, coveting her. Pippa gave Randal a quick, searching look, and found him staring too.

He must have been in love with her once. Perhaps he still was under his talk of hating her? It wouldn't be surprising. Pippa knew she, herself, was attractive, but she had no illusions. She couldn't hold a candle to Renata. The other woman was one of the best-looking women she had ever seen.

She was smiling now, at her son, and Johnny ran to her, was gathered up in her open arms and kissed.

'Surprise, surprise!' she cooed at him.

Randal walked over there, too, as if drawn by invisible ropes, said curtly, 'Why didn't you let us know you were coming?'

'I did say I'd try, didn't I? But I wasn't sure I'd make it. I didn't want to disappoint him if I couldn't get here.' Still holding her son's hand, she smiled up at Randal lazily, her blue eyes sultry. 'How are you, Randal? You look terrific.'

'I'm fine.' Randal shot a glance at the man seated at the table, gave him an unfriendly nod. 'Hello, Alex.'

'Hi, how're you?' the other man drawled in a strong Australian accent. He was tall, bronzed, blond, with a clean-cut profile, and wore a tan linen suit, jacket open to show a lemon shirt.

'Fine thanks.' Randal held his hand out to his son. 'But we'd better have our lunch now—see you later, no doubt. We're staying here. Are you?'

'For tonight, at least,' Renata said. 'Maybe we could have dinner?' She glanced past Randal at where Pippa was standing beside their table. 'Is that your girlfriend? You didn't say there was someone special. We must meet her—could we make up a foursome tonight?' Her gaze coolly slipped over Pippa in her simple green silk tunic, one pencilled brow lifting in silent, unfavourable comment. 'Pretty,' she murmured in tones that made it clear she did not really think Pippa was anything of the kind, and Pippa stiffened in resentment. Who did she think she was?

'Give us a ring later,' Randal said remotely, walking away, bringing Johnny with him.

As the little boy sat down he looked at Pippa and said, 'That's my mummy.'

'Yes,' Pippa said with a forced, bright smile, picking up the menu and pretending to study it with interest.

Johnny copied her, following the words with his finger.

'Can I have this melon filled with fresh fruit?' he

asked his father. 'Sorbet's a kind of ice cream, isn't it?'

'Yes, and this is raspberry sorbet. Good choice. I think I'll have the same.'

'Steak with peaches? That sounds nice. I never ate steak with fruit before.'

'Excellent,' Randal said, as if not quite listening. His forehead was lined; he looked abstracted.

Watching him from behind lowered lashes, Pippa caught the frowning look he threw across the room at his wife and wished she knew precisely what was going on inside his head. Clearly it had thrown him to see Renata here—but just what sort of shock had it been? There was a streak of dark red across his strong cheekbones, a little tic under one eye. Randal was trying to seem calm and in control, but obviously he was nothing of the kind.

The waiter came and took their order. She had melon, too, with fruit and the raspberry sorbet, followed by halibut in a light orange sauce.

Johnny talked excitedly about an adventure trip he had been taken on by the school the previous week. 'We camped in the woods and did canoeing and climbed trees—I climbed to the top of one, and I didn't fall out, but Jamie fell and broke his wrist so he can't do games or swim and can only write one-handed. And we ran races. I got a blister as big as this…' He measured an improbable size with his fingers. 'It burst and pink stuff came out…'

'Thank you, very interesting, but no medical details while we're eating,' his father said. 'I'm glad you had a great time. But be careful climbing trees. You don't want to break your wrist, do you?'

'No. Jamie screamed,' Johnny said thoughtfully.

'Screamed and screamed. And now he's got plaster on his wrist and can't do anything. We all wrote our names on the plaster and drew cartoons.'

As they were drinking their coffee Renata and the blond Australian came past and paused. She gave a dazzling smile to Randal and purred, 'We'd like to take Johnny for a drive to have tea somewhere—would that be okay? It's ages since I saw him. Please, Randal?'

Randal considered her dispassionately, his grey eyes remote, then looked at his son. 'Up to you, Johnny. Do you want to go for a drive with Mummy and Alex?'

Pippa read his uneasy hesitation, the uncertainty in his eyes. He sneaked a look at the blond golf champion. Was Alex a hero to him? wondered Pippa as he slowly said, 'Well, okay, then, if you don't mind, Dad.'

'Whatever you want to do is okay with me, Johnny,' Randal reassured firmly, and the boy's face lightened.

'Come on,' Renata said, offering her hand, and he got up from the table and went with her. Over her shoulder she said to Randal, 'See you at dinner.'

When they had gone Randal let out a long, rough sigh. 'There wasn't any choice, was there? I couldn't refuse to let him go while he was there, listening. I don't want him blaming me because he never sees her.'

'I'm sure he wouldn't. You seem to have a great relationship, the two of you.'

He smiled at her. 'Do you think so? Well, I hope so. It isn't that I want to stop her seeing him—I wish she visited him more often—but Renata is given to arbitrary fits of spite. She might suddenly decide to take off with him, not bring him back—only to get bored with the game after a day or two and dump him, and Johnny could get hurt.'

Dryly, Pippa said, 'I don't think she'll run off with him. I think she's looking forward to playing a very different game tonight, at dinner.'

He gave her a shrewd, sharp look. 'What are you talking about?'

Pippa lifted a shoulder in a shrug. 'She may enjoy having a succession of men, but I got the impression she was still interested in you. Maybe she's the type to want to keep any man she's owned once on a leash, and she resents the fact that you got away.'

'Do you think so?' he asked, finishing his coffee.

Pippa did not add that she also suspected that his ex-wife had not been pleased to see him with another woman, especially one who was a good ten years younger.

'If you're ready, shall we check out our rooms and unpack?' he suggested, rising, and she agreed, following him out to the reception area. They collected their keys and took the lift upstairs to the first floor.

Pippa let herself into her own room; Randal stood at the door, staring round, frowning. The room was small but comfortable, with a single bed. On a luggage rack against the wall stood Johnny's overnight bag.

'They obviously thought Johnny was going to be using this room,' Pippa said, seeing a connecting door open, leading into another room.

Randal walked over there and went through into what turned out to be a sitting room. Pippa followed him across that into a third room, a spacious double bedroom with twin beds covered in blue silk brocade that matched the floor-length curtains. It was a charming room, with elegant eighteenth-century furniture. On the luggage rack were her suitcase and Randal's side by side.

She turned on him. 'You can't have made it clear that this room was for you and Johnny! They obviously thought you and I would be sharing this room, while the smaller room was for the child.'

'I didn't discuss the sleeping arrangements with the booking staff!' he said irritably. 'I just asked for a double suite and one single room. I'll ring down now and get you a better room.'

'No, don't bother—that room is fine.' She picked up her own case. 'I'll unpack. Would you collect Johnny's case and unpack for him?'

He took her case from her. 'Look, I'm sorry, Pippa. I didn't realise they would give you such a tiny room.'

'It doesn't matter; it's only for a couple of days.'

'You can use the sitting room as much as you like!' he offered in placation, carrying her case into her small bedroom.

She deliberately checked that there was a bolt on the inside of her bedroom door. 'Thank you.'

'Will you mind having dinner with Renata and Alex tonight?' he asked, removing Johnny's case from the luggage rack.

'No, why should I?' She put her case on the bed and unlocked it. Casually, she asked, 'You knew she was going to be here, didn't you? That's why you were so insistent I should come with you. I'm here as a trophy, to let her know you aren't still pining for her, you've already found another woman.'

His face filled with angry dark red, his eyes flashed. 'Don't be ridiculous! I told you, she rarely comes to see Johnny. I didn't expect to see her here!'

She did not believe him. Renata had said she had hinted that she might come, and Randal's pride, his male ego, had needed to convince his ex-wife that he had another woman, she needn't think he wasn't missing her.

Randal had been using her! Pippa felt jealousy and resentment burning deep inside, twisting like a knife in her entrails. All the way here, to the school, she had been wondering what might happen in this hotel, had been trying to work out how to keep Randal at bay, make certain he didn't try to share her bed once his son was asleep. She had been shaking with excitement and passion, too, because even while she was determined he should not make love to her she couldn't help wanting to be in his arms. It might be contradictory, irrational, crazy, but her body ached for his, however hard she tried to convince herself he was forbidden to her.

It hadn't even occurred to her that his ex-wife might turn up, or that Randal might have brought her along as a shield against Renata realising he still wanted her.

Because he must still want his ex-wife, or why would he have been so insistent about Pippa coming with him? She had seen his face at lunch, when he first glimpsed Renata across the room. She had seen his clenched features, the taut jawline, the glitter of his eyes. He still wanted Renata; he was jealous of the tall, tanned Australian golfer who, Pippa angrily decided, was a perfect match for the luscious blonde. They might have been made for each other, in fact, although Randal obviously wouldn't be too pleased if she told him so.

She started unpacking, walking to and fro, sliding clothes into drawers, hanging others up in the tiny wardrobe.

'Do you want me to unpack for Johnny, or will you?' she said without looking at him.

'You're jealous,' he said suddenly. 'You're jealous of Renata, aren't you?' He was at her elbow a second later, grabbing her by the shoulders and swinging her round to face him. 'Ever since we met again you've been trying to convince me you're indifferent, never want to see me again—but you're jealous of Renata, which proves you're nothing of the kind. You can't be jealous if you're indifferent.'

'I am not jealous!' she furiously snapped.

'Oh, yes, you are. I can see it in those big green eyes.' He held her away from him, gazing down into those eyes, his own flickering and gleaming, silvery stars.

'Pure imagination,' she flung back. 'Wishful thinking!'

His voice husky, he whispered, 'Believe me, Pippa, I never expected to see Renata here. I meant what I said—I wanted you and Johnny to get to know each other. And—' He broke off and she watched him suspiciously, trying to probe behind his features, see inside his head, read his mind.

'And what?' she insisted.

He hesitated. 'Nothing. I forget what I was going to say.'

'I don't believe you! Come on, you started to say something—finish it!'

He grimaced. 'Okay, but you won't like it! I was

going to say I wanted to spend the weekend with you!' He pulled her closer, his eyes eating her. 'You kept saying you didn't want to see me again, but I wasn't giving up. I meant to keep in contact with you.' One hand ran down her spine, over the soft silk of her dress, slowly, caressingly. When it reached the hem just above her knees, he pushed her dress upward, slid his hand up inside, between her thighs, fingertips sensuously brushing the inner secret heat, forcing a cry of excitement from her.

'You see? You want me,' he whispered, bending his head. His tongue-tip softly stroked her mouth. 'Close contact, that's what we both need.' He groaned, pulled her hard so that their bodies collided, touched, from shoulder to thigh. 'I need to touch you, make love to you.'

'No, don't! Stop that,' she broke out, trembling violently, her mouth hot from the mere touch of his tongue. She was aware of his body touching hers everywhere, the heat between them intolerable.

'And you need it, too, whether you'll admit it or not,' he muttered, one hand on her back, pressing her hard against him while he cradled her head in his spread fingers with the other, manoeuvring it into position so that he could kiss her.

She would rather die than admit anything of the kind, and she resisted his fierce, invading mouth, struggling so hard he shifted his hand from her spine to her waist and held her possessively, his hand just below her breast.

Her treacherous mouth had parted to admit him, her body clung hotly to his, but she still struggled—so furiously that the two of them swayed and toppled on to the bed, knocking her suitcase off, on to the floor, spilling her clothes in all directions.

'Let go, let go,' she cried, pushing at his wide shoulders.

Randal looked down at her, eyes half-open, smouldering, languorous, and her mouth went dry at the expression in those eyes.

He moved his hand to touch her breast and she drew a shaken breath. He slid an arm under her, lifting her, swiftly pulled her dress over her head, followed by her lacy white chemise and then her bra. She fought him uselessly, tried to stop him stripping her, but his deft fingers were too fast and certain. In seconds she was naked all but her brief white panties.

'You're so lovely,' Randal groaned, letting her slip back on to the bed and lying next to her. His grey eyes wandered freely over her nakedness, sensuously explored her breasts, moved downwards to her hips and thighs. He leaned over to kiss the pale flesh his eyes had just discovered. 'Beautiful,' he whispered.

Her eyes closed helplessly as his mouth heatedly caressed her breast, his hands stroking below, over her hips. Her tiny panties slid down; alarm shot through her as that last barrier went and she recognised that if she didn't stop him now he was going to take her and she would not be able to resist him.

She tried to struggle up, get off the bed, but he pulled her back so that her thighs fell open with him sliding between them. She wished desperately that it did not seem so natural to her to have them there, fitting with her like spoons in a drawer.

'I won't let you!' she gasped.

'Well, I won't force you,' he said thickly, staring down at her smooth bare flesh. 'But I need you,

Pippa, my God, I need you.' He kissed her again, deeply, passionately, and her eyes shut again, her lips moved in hot response, her body quivered. Every time he kissed her, touched her, he got the same reaction; she could not help it, even though she angrily despised herself for being so weak and foolish. Had her mind no control at all over her treacherous body, then?

Through the feverish clouds of her pleasure she suddenly realised Randal was taking off his jacket, then he was shrugging out of his shirt. He was stripping, she thought, appalled! As she realised what was happening she felt his legs kicking his trousers away.

Events were moving far too fast. She must stop it now, before it was too late!

But it was already too late. Randal was between her parted thighs and now he was naked, too, his bare skin brushing hers sensuously, his hands sliding beneath her, lifting her buttocks off the bed so that her knees fell apart.

'Randal, don't!' she groaned. 'I've never...I'm a... It would be my first time and I can't, not like this!'

'Sweet,' he whispered, kissing her. 'That's what I love about you, your innocence, your integrity and sense of self-respect. They are what make you the woman I adore.' His kiss deepened, took fire, until she drowned in it, forgetting everything else but him, her arms round his back, her body clinging to his.

'You're mine. You know you are,' Randal breathed against her parted, hungry lips. 'And I want you to be part of me, for ever.'

She wanted that, too, but she mustn't admit it. Between her thighs he moved in a slow, sensuous rhythm, and she moaned with pleasure, moving, too, opening to the seduction of that brushing contact. The pressure deepened, she felt him pushing into her, then a sharp pain. She gave a cry, 'You're hurting! Don't!' and tried to push him off, her palms flat on his naked chest.

Randal kissed her harder, groaning. 'Don't ask me to stop now, darling, not now, so close...'

Another pang of pain, fiercer, and then he was deep inside her, filling her, and she lay still, breathing wildly, feeling an intolerable ache of pain and satisfaction and desire. What was the point now of denying that she wanted this, had longed to merge with him, be part of him?

His mouth moved down to her breasts, sucked at her nipples, his hands cupping the warm, rounded flesh until she relaxed again, her pain forgotten, and a moment later he began moving again, his hot, hard flesh probing inside her, setting off jangling pulses in places where she had not known they existed, sending waves of ecstatic sensation through her entire body.

Over the next few minutes she almost lost consciousness, mind drowning in physical sensations, holding him, moving with him, mindlessly, sobbing in ecstasy. The next clear awareness she had was of lying still, limp and drained, with Randal collapsed on top of her, while tears ran down her face.

Suddenly he rolled off her. They were separate again and she felt cold and lonely, losing him.

'Don't cry,' he whispered. 'What is it? Did I really hurt you?'

She put her hands over her face, shuddering in sobs, couldn't answer. She didn't even know why she was crying; it certainly wasn't with pain, but in a sort of desolation. After the intense pleasure she had been through she had come down from a wild peak into this darkness and misery.

Randal pulled her hands down, leaning over to stare at her, then began kissing her wet lids shut, kissing her nose, her cheeks, her trembling lips.

'Stop it, Pippa, stop crying. I'm sorry, don't be unhappy. It was selfish of me, but I was afraid you would vanish again after this weekend, and I couldn't bear it. I had to stop you somehow, make you stay. I thought…'

'Thought what?' she muttered, sat up and grabbed her dress, hurriedly put it on, wishing he wouldn't watch her.

He sighed. 'That if you finally let me make love to you, you'd stay. There's an old legend about a mermaid, who fell in love with a human man, but kept going back into the sea until he made love to her and then she became human and they were married and lived happily.'

'Until one day the call of the sea was too strong and she vanished again, this time for ever,' Pippa recalled.

He grimaced. 'Is that how the legend ends? I only remembered…'

'The bit you wanted to come true?' she mocked. 'How convenient! Well, I'm going to have a shower, and I'd like you to go back to your own room, please.'

'We have to talk!'

'We've done enough talking. Randal, I need to take a shower. Please leave.'

He rolled off the bed and collected up his clothes. She knew she shouldn't watch him, but she couldn't take her eyes off that long, lean, supple, naked body which had just taken her to heaven and back. Randal walked to the door without bothering to dress and she padded barefoot after him to bolt the door behind him.

Wryly, she faced the fact that she was locking the stable door after the horse had bolted. All these years she had avoided making love to him, to anyone, and finally it had happened. She was aching physically, body burning, bruised, weary. What did she do now? She asked herself as she went into the bathroom to shower. What in God's name did she do now?

She discarded her green dress and stepped under the shower, washed from head to foot, the warm water sluicing over her, trying to think, trying to understand how everything had changed over what had just happened.

Randal was right. She groaned, closing her eyes. Oh, he was much too shrewd; he understood her far too well. Nothing would ever be the same again. In taking her just now, he had conquered, had shattered all her arguments, her reasons for saying no to him.

He had realised what she had always known, that she had been dying to make love with him for so long, but had resisted him under the lash of her rational mind—and now it had happened, and she was different. As Randal had intended, she felt differently.

Or did she?

She walked out of the shower and put on a white towelling robe, towelled her damp chestnut hair, looking at herself in the cloudy bathroom mirror. Her green eyes held a bleak realisation now.

Had those moments of bliss and intimacy altered anything? He would still put his son first if it came to it. He would never put her first. She would never matter more to him than anyone else in the world.

Nothing important had changed. She still did not want to accept second place in his life. She still couldn't stay with him; she had to go away.

Like the mermaid in the legend she would have to vanish, this time for ever.

CHAPTER NINE

SHE deliberately chose the most demure outfit she had brought with her: a dove-grey straight skirt, a black chiffon shirt which tied at the waist. Contemplating herself in the mirror, she decided it was exactly the look she wanted for the evening ahead. That last thing she wanted was to look sexy, or put ideas in Randal's head. Her chestnut hair she brushed back and clipped at the nape with a black Spanish comb, leaving her face a clear, cool oval. She wore very little make-up: a faint touch of green on her eyelids, palest pink on her lips. As an afterthought she used a flowery perfume, an English fragrance which drifted about with her, leaving a hint of summer on the air.

She tidied her room, now that all her clothes had been put away, and watched TV for a while, although she found it hard to concentrate.

Randal tapped on her outer door an hour later. She checked on her reflection rapidly before she answered. Yes, that was how she wanted to look—remote, untouchable. As far as possible from the wildly responsive woman he had held in his arms on her bed earlier.

She opened the door and caught a flash of surprise in his eyes. He hadn't expected her to look so serene, and noticed at once the demure way she had dressed.

But he made no comment, simply said, 'If you're ready, I thought we might go downstairs and have tea in the reception area. Renata said she'd bring Johnny back before six, and it's five now.'

'Fine, I'd love a cup of tea,' she said, collecting her handbag, sliding the room key into it. The connecting door was still bolted; it would remain that way as long as they were here. She wanted no repetition of what had happened this afternoon; Randal could stay his side of that door.

Despite her desire to stay cool, though, she felt her pulses leap in that dangerously magnetised fashion when Randal put a hand under her elbow to guide her into the lift. Such a light, polite touch, and yet it sent her body into overdrive.

As the doors shut she hastily moved away from him, and felt his quick, probing glance; he was far too observant, and she did not trust him. But she ignored it. It was better not to say anything, give him any opportunity to gain ground.

Downstairs they sat at a table with a good view of the entrance and ordered a pot of China tea. They drank it without milk, a clear, pale straw-coloured liquid with a delicate fragrance, which was very refreshing.

Out of the corner of her eye she noticed Randal's fingers drumming on the arm of his chair as he watched the entrance. He was agitated over whether or not his ex-wife would bring their son back as promised. She felt a pang of sympathy; poor Randal. He would go crazy if Renata had in fact abducted the child. Would she take the boy abroad, if she did? It could be months before Randal saw Johnny again, in that case, and it would turn his life into a nightmare.

To distract his attention, she said casually, 'I was

thinking, just now, that what I need is a holiday, before I start looking for another job.'

'Where are you thinking of going?'

'Somewhere warm—Spain or Italy, probably. I don't know either country. I've had very few holidays abroad; I could never afford it until I started earning more money at the insurance company, and then I bought my cottage, and that ate up any spare cash I had.'

His grey eyes skimmed her face thoughtfully. 'You've had a pretty tough life, haven't you? No family, no real home, and very little money. It was quite an achievement to buy the cottage and do it up yourself, but at least selling it will release a good lump sum. You'll have money now.'

'Yes, I suppose I will,' she agreed, thinking about it. It would be nice to have spare cash with which she could be spontaneous, which she could spend as she wished, when she wished. She had never been in that position before; every penny she earned had been earmarked for something—clothes, food, travelling expenses to and from work, redecoration on the cottage. 'But then I'll have to buy a new home,' she sighed. 'And it will probably cost far more, so I won't have money for long.'

'If you married me you wouldn't need to buy a new home; you would live in mine,' he said casually, taking her breath away.

'Don't make jokes like that!' She knew he didn't mean it, couldn't mean it, was just teasing her. She looked at him with rage and hostility. 'It isn't funny!'

His grey eyes were serious, though. 'I'm proposing, Pippa. I want to marry you.'

She stared fixedly at her cup of pale tea, fighting

with the stab of jealousy in her stomach. 'You're still in love with your ex-wife! I realised that at lunch, when you saw her in the dining room. I saw the look on your face!'

'I was in shock,' he coolly admitted.

'Oh, yes!' she muttered bitterly. 'I know that. The sight of her took your breath away.' Renata was staggeringly beautiful; she couldn't blame Randal for his response to the sight of his ex-wife. After all, Renata had once been his, and now she belonged to another man. That couldn't be easy to take, especially for a very ego-driven male like Randal.

She suddenly remembered his jealousy over Tom—if he felt like that over her, how did he feel over his ex-wife and her new husband?

'The sight of her scared me!' he said harshly, frowning. 'I'd stopped expecting her to turn up to see Johnny. When I saw her I was suddenly worried, afraid she was going to try to take Johnny away from me, take him off to Australia. Mothers tend to get custody in this country, especially if they can afford a good lawyer, and she can, with her new husband's money behind her. I thought Renata would never want custody, she was always an indifferent mother—but who knows? Maybe her golfer has decided he wants a ready-made son to trot around the circuits with him? Good publicity for him, probably.'

She frowned. 'I thought he seemed a decent sort of guy, not the type to think that way at all.' She looked at Randal sharply. 'You're simply jealous of him!'

Dark red rang along his cheekbones; his eyes flashed. 'Don't be absurd! Jealous of him? You're crazy. Why on earth would I be jealous of him! Over Renata? I wouldn't have Renata back at any price.'

His grey eyes focused on her angrily. 'I just proposed to you—doesn't that mean anything to you? All you do in reply is accuse me of being in love with my ex-wife! What do you think that tells me? That you don't know me at all, and, frankly, that I obviously don't know you either, or how could you leap to such an idiotic conclusion?'

He was furious with her; she was very shaken, biting her lip. He was right—how could she have leapt to that conclusion? She didn't know him; she had no idea what made him tick. How could you love someone without knowing them?

'She is very beautiful,' she offered in apology, in feeble placation.

His mouth hardened in cynicism. 'On the outside, maybe, but inside she is far from beautiful. She's selfish, lazy, greedy, materialistic; she was a bad wife and a bad mother. And I wouldn't have her back for a million dollars.'

At that second the swing doors into the foyer revolved to admit Renata, the tall, tanned golfer, and Johnny, who saw them immediately and came running towards them.

'Daddy! I played golf! Alex taught me how to play golf. I hit the ball so hard it went for mile. Alex says I'm a natural. I should play as often as possible, practise every day.'

'Don't chatter on and on, darling,' Renata said in a sort of groan. 'My God, that child babbles. He never stops.' She sank into a spare chair at the table. 'I need a drink. Get a waiter, Alex. Randal, darling, I think Johnny should go to bed; he's tired and so am I—worn out, honestly. I'd forgotten how much energy kids have, and how much of a nuisance they are.'

Randal glowered. 'Not in front of him, please!'

'I'll take him upstairs,' Pippa quickly said, getting up. 'Come on, Johnny. I expect you'll need a bath—is he coming down to dinner, Randal?'

'Oh, please,' Johnny said, 'can't I have Room Service and watch TV instead? I'm tired, and I saw they do a great cheeseburger and fries, and a triple flavour ice cream, and Coke.'

Randal laughed. 'Just as you like, Johnny. Room Service would be more fun, I expect. Say goodnight and thank you to your mother and Alex.'

'Goodnight and thank you,' Johnny gabbled towards them, then took Pippa's hand and began dragging her towards the lift.

In the sitting room he at once grabbed the Room Service menu and sat down with it. 'Can I order now? I'm starving.'

'Why not? I'll stay until the food arrives. Do you want me to order it for you?'

He gave her a scornful look. 'I can do it!' Picking up the phone, he began dialling. 'Hello? Room Service?'

Pippa wandered away to the window, listening as he ordered exactly what he had said he would like. The daylight was fading a little, the spring sky coloured pink and gold. Shadows lay under the trees in the grounds of the hotel. It would be dark soon.

Johnny put down the phone. 'They said it would be fifteen minutes.'

She walked back to sit down near him. 'So you had a good time this afternoon.'

'Yes, Alex is great; I like him. My friends all want to meet him. He's a terrific golfer.' He didn't mention his mother, and went on to ask, 'Am I going to be able to ride tomorrow? Dad said I could.'

'Yes, he said he meant to go with you, but I don't have any gear with me, so I think I'll just stay here and rest.'

'Okay,' Johnny said without interest. 'Alex and Mummy are leaving tomorrow, so I don't suppose I'll see them again.' The thought did not seem to bother him. 'She gets bored easily, Alex says. And she doesn't like the country much; she prefers cities. She talked a lot about Sydney and New York and London, and shopping. She loves shopping. Alex says she has so many clothes they had to buy a new wardrobe. She doesn't play golf, although she always goes with Alex when he's playing in a tournament, but she stays in the bar, he said, and waits for him. And she doesn't like kids much; she says she'd never have another one, not ever. Kids are boring.'

'I'm sure she was joking,' Pippa quickly said. How much had that hurt the boy's feelings? Randal was obviously right when he said Renata was a bad mother; how could any mother say such things to her child?

'She wasn't,' Johnny dispassionately said. 'I could tell. She couldn't be bothered. But Alex is okay; I like him.' He found the TV zapper and flicked through the channels. Pippa's heart sank as he settled on a noisy, blaring cartoon.

It was a relief to her when the Room Service waiter knocked on the door and wheeled in a table on which were spread a silver-covered plate of food, a bowl of ice cream nestling in crushed ice, to keep it cool, and several small bottles of cola.

She signed for the food and tipped the waiter, who

left, while Johnny sat up to the table. Pippa tied his napkin round his neck, suspecting its protection for his clothes would be very necessary.

'I'll just go through to my own room,' Pippa said as he picked up his burger and took a bite. 'If you need me, give me a shout.' She didn't think she could stay to watch him eat; melted cheese and tomato ketchup had already spilled out of the burger bun and on to the napkin.

'Uh-huh,' Johnny said, turning up the TV and feeding chips into his chewing mouth.

Pippa left the connecting door open in case Johnny needed her, then settled down on her bed with a book she had brought with her: a paperback detective story by one of her favourite authors. It wasn't easy to concentrate on the pages, though, with the boom of Johnny's TV in her ears.

After a while she went back to see how he was doing and found him sprawled on the floor on his tummy. Pippa rearranged the table and wheeled it out of the suite, left it in the corridor, then rang Room Service to ask them to collect it.

'Why don't you get into your pyjamas now and watch TV in bed?' she suggested to Johnny, who enthusiastically agreed. 'Better wash and clean your teeth first,' Pippa casually added, an idea to which he was less enthusiastic.

'You don't want your daddy to see you with tomato ketchup all over your face, do you?' she gently said, and he grimaced horribly.

'Oh, okay, then.' He went into the bathroom and was back a minute later. 'Can I have a shower?'

'Of course.'

He was in the bathroom for twenty minutes. Pippa

wondered a little anxiously what he was doing in there, and hoped he wouldn't leave the room looking as if a bomb had gone off, but eventually he emerged looking very clean in his pyjamas and climbed into one of the twin beds, clutching the TV remote control.

Pippa turned off the main light but left his bedside lamp lit. 'I'll be in the next room if you want me,' she said, leaving him. 'Goodnight, Johnny.'

'Goodnight, Pip,' he said, then gave her a grin. 'Do you mind if I call you Pip?'

'All my life people have called me Pip.' She smiled, not adding that she hated the name.

Going through into her own bedroom she changed rapidly into the cocktail dress she had brought with her; a delicate fantasy of different shades of green silk and chiffon, falling to her mid-calf in a flurry, with a scooped neckline and tiny frilled sleeves. She found a silver chain in her bag, from which hung a dark green stone and a silver tassel. Around her throat it gave exactly the right touch to the outfit.

She knew she would never hold a candle to Renata's blonde magnificence, but at least she looked her best, she decided.

A quarter of an hour later, Randal let himself into the suite and found Pippa reading, curled up on the sitting room couch. She lifted her head to survey him expressionlessly, and he in turn contemplated her with what she saw with a gulp of shock to be rage. His grey eyes were molten steel, his mouth taut.

Breathing thickly, he finally erupted, 'What the hell do you think you are doing up here? We were supposed to be having dinner with Renata and Alex; we've been waiting for you for half an hour.'

'Sorry, I was taking care of Johnny and I forgot

the time,' she apologised anxiously. He looked so angry it made her mouth dry and her heart beat harder.

'Where is Johnny?'

'In bed, watching TV.'

He turned on his heel and stalked through into his own bedroom. The burble of the TV stopped, the faint gleam of light was switched off, then he came back.

'He's asleep.'

'Oh, good, I expect he was very tired after all the excitement of today,' she said, getting up and collecting her handbag. 'But we had better leave a low light on in here, and the door open so he can see it, in case he wakes up alone in the dark and gets scared. I explained to him that he could ring Reception and ask for us to be paged, if he needs us.'

'Good idea,' approved Randal. 'Did he eat?'

'Burger, chips and ice cream—yes, quite a lot. And he had a shower. After he was in bed I thought I'd better stay within earshot, in case he needed me.'

'You're very thoughtful.'

'I remember how scared I was of the dark when I was nine.' She shrugged dismissively. But there had been nobody to come to her rescue, then; her foster parents had dismissed her fear of the dark as childish, and told her to pull herself together.

Randal took her arm and hurried her towards the door. 'It was me who needed you, downstairs, helping me to put up with Renata.'

He did not say thank you, she noted—no Thank you for looking after my little boy; no Thank you for going to so much trouble on my behalf! All he was doing was complaining because she hadn't been downstairs with him to protect him from his ex-wife. Men were incredibly selfish creatures.

'I couldn't be in two places at once!'

He urged her into the lift, which started with a jerk which sent her sprawling sideways into him, grabbing at him to stop herself falling on the floor.

His arm came round her, supporting her, holding her close to him, and she felt her treacherous body shudder with awareness.

His head shifted so that he could look down into her wide, disturbed green eyes. She looked away, unable to meet that stare, afraid of what her eyes must be revealing. She must not give away too much; she had already betrayed too much to him. She wanted to clamp a mask on her face from now on, stop him guessing any more about her.

'Pippa, don't look like that,' he murmured huskily, and his mouth came down, skimmed hers for a second before the lift stopped, and he straightened before guiding her out of the lift.

His arm was round her waist, his hand beneath her breast; she was afraid he could feel the fierce beating of her heart, the raggedness of her breathing. Every time he touched her, looked at her, there was this wild reaction; she couldn't stop it. The sooner she could get away from him the sooner she might start to feel safe. At the moment she was living moment to moment, like someone on the very edge of a live volcano.

'You look lovely,' he suddenly told her. 'I love that dress, all those shades of green. And your hair looks wonderful against them, a perfect match, chestnut and green. You look like spring itself.'

She flushed, her throat trembling in pleasure. 'Thank you.'

'Renata and Alex have gone into the dining room;

they'll be waiting at the table,' he told her as they walked through the foyer.

'Has Renata changed for dinner, too?'

'Yes, she put on something black, very formal. I've always been turned off by the sight of women in black; it makes me feel I'm going to a funeral.'

When Pippa saw Renata a moment later she had to be incredulous about Randal's comment. The 'something black' he had said Renata was wearing was body-hugging, sleek, daring black satin with a plunging neckline, revealing a great deal of golden skin and the deep valley between her high breasts, curving down into her small waist and swelling out again, smoothly, over her hips, ending at her knees.

She looked sensational; men at every other table were staring, hardly conscious of what they were eating, while the other women in the room looked daggers at her. There was nothing funereal about her whatever.

'Is that what you call formal?' Pippa whispered to Randal as they walked towards the table.

'Black always is, isn't it?'

'Not when it looks like that!'

A trio was playing light, popular music, seated on a dais in a corner of the room—a pianist, a drummer, a trombone player. Diners talked over them; the room was quite crowded and bustling with waiters coming and going.

As they joined the other two Alex rose, smiling. 'Hello, Pippa, you look very pretty. What an unusual dress.'

'Thank you,' she said, then turned to smile at Renata. 'And you are causing a sensation in that dress, as if you didn't know!'

Renata sipped a champagne cocktail, purring like a cat that had swallowed cream. 'Why, thanks, that's sweet of you. Now, read the menu and choose your meal; I'm ravenous! I ate a small lunch, now I need something more substantial.'

Pippa glanced quickly at the menu, which was rather more extensive than the lunchtime menu, decided on minestrone soup followed by chicken Stroganoff with rice.

The waiter came along to take their order. As he left again, Alex asked her, 'Did Johnny get Room Service?'

'Yes, cheeseburger and fries!'

'I wouldn't mind that, myself. I guess I'm primitive—I prefer junk food to the sort of posh stuff they serve here. Mind you, I have to eat a lot of salads and fruit, to keep my weight down. You can't have a fat golfer, not if you want to win tournaments. Is Johnny okay up there on his own, do you think?'

'He was asleep when we left him, but I told him to ring Reception if he woke up and felt frightened.' She glanced at Renata, who was toying with her champagne flute, looking bored. 'I'm sorry I kept you waiting; I was making sure Johnny settled down in bed.'

Alex gave her a warm, reassuring smile. 'That's okay, it was kind of you to take care of him. He's a good kid. I've got quite fond of him. I promised to take him to one of my tournaments some time. He seemed keen to come along. His friends at school are golf fans, he told me; some of them play at a course near the school. I think he wants to impress them.' He looked at Randal. 'If that's okay with you?'

'In principle, yes, but remember, he's at school a

lot of the time and can't just go off for the day. In the summer holidays he has plenty of free time, but not at other times of the year.'

'Oh, don't worry, Randal, we don't want to drag around with the kid in tow too often, whining and wanting burgers all the time,' Renata said with a snap. 'He's a nuisance, always wanting attention. Unless we hire a nanny to take care of him. I guess we could do that. I can't wait for him to grow up a little. I wouldn't mind a teenager hanging around, someone you can talk to. But little kids are a pain.'

'You're his mother, for God's sake! You're supposed to love him, enjoy taking care of him!' erupted Randal, glaring at her. 'Pippa has ten times more patience with him than you do!'

Renata gave Pippa a derisive glance. 'Yes, well, Pippa's obviously the maternal type, doesn't mind running around after a spoilt, whiny kid.'

Dark red colour splashed Randal's cheeks. 'Johnny is not spoilt, nor is he whiny!'

Alex chimed in, 'No, he isn't. He's fun, a great kid!' He made an apologetic gesture. 'But Renata simply isn't the motherly type, you know.'

'No, I'm certainly not!' she said, tossing her head, the diamond earrings dangling from her ears swinging to and fro.

Alex added, 'Some women are, some aren't.'

'We're not all the same!' Renata drawled, giving Pippa another of those dismissive looks.

Alex said, 'Maybe Pippa has the sort of mother who's a maternal role model, the type who loves kids, cooks, cleans the house—all those old-fashioned things a modern woman doesn't want to waste her life doing.'

'Is it a waste of life?' queried Pippa. 'You think so?' Her tone made it clear she didn't agree.

'Well, no, I guess not, if that's what you enjoy,' Alex placated, smiling at her. 'But Renata's mother was a career woman who left her with a nanny and never bothered about her—you can understand why Renata isn't the motherly type when you know that.'

Brusquely, Randal retorted, 'Pippa is an orphan. She had no mother at all, and grew up in orphanages and foster homes. She had no motherly role model.'

It made her feel odd to hear him defending her, explaining her. She was touched; maybe he understood her better than she had imagined.

Alex looked at her with sympathy. 'That must have been tough; not a fun childhood, I guess. I bet you're dying to have a family now, to finally have all the things you never had as a child.'

'Yes, I suppose so,' Pippa admitted, feeling Randal's eyes on her profile.

Renata drawled. 'Which explains why you're so keen to take care of Johnny! You get a ready-made family right off.'

Their first course arrived in time to save Pippa answering that; she felt resentment burning in her throat and would have liked to slap Renata's face. Instead, she concentrated on the food. When conversation did start again it was Randal, asking Alex about his golf success, and Pippa didn't have to join in; she just sat there, listening. Every so often Renata leaned towards Randal and spoke softly to him, sometimes letting her red-tipped fingernails drift along his sleeve, smiling at him, her long, false lashes flicking up and down.

He watched her with an expression in his eyes that Pippa could not read. At times she felt he disliked his ex-wife; at other times she thought he was still fascinated by her, sexually responsive to her.

Renata was so beautiful. How could any man not be responsive to looks like that? She radiated sex appeal.

'Do you like sport, Pippa?' Alex asked her, and the other two turned to stare at her.

'I like watching it; Wimbledon, for instance. I always enjoy that on TV. But I wouldn't say I was the sporting type. I've never had the time; I've always had to work too hard. I'm afraid I've never even played golf, or watched it. And it's an expensive sport, isn't it? You need clubs and the right shoes, and stuff.'

'Johnny said something about going riding this weekend,' Renata said. 'Are you two going with him?'

'I shall, but Pippa probably won't,' Randal told her.

'I haven't got the right gear,' she said, meeting Renata's contemptuous smile with dislike.

When they were drinking their coffee after the meal people began dancing on a small parquet floor in front of the band's dais. Renata stood up, held out her hand to Randal.

'Shall we?'

He hesitated, but eventually rose and took her hand. They threaded their way through the tables and began to dance the waltz being played. Jealousy stung inside Pippa; she looked down, reluctant to watch them, Randal's arm around his ex-wife's waist, her arm around his neck, their bodies very close, moving in harmony.

'Would you care to dance, Pippa?' Alex asked her

without real enthusiasm, and she shook her head, smiling politely.

'Sorry, I'm too tired.'

'It's not a very good band,' he grimaced.

She laughed. 'No.'

A moment later a waiter came over to them and bent to murmur in her ear, 'Reception has had a message from your suite, madam. Your little boy seems to be upset.'

She was on her feet immediately, relieved to have an excuse for leaving. 'Thank you, I'll go up to him.' She smiled at Alex. 'Please give my excuses to Renata and Randal. It was a pleasure to meet you. Goodnight.'

When she got upstairs and let herself into the suite she heard low sobbing from the double bedroom and hurried through there at once. Johnny was a heap in the bed, lying on his face, crying quietly. Pippa sat down on the bed and lifted him, turning him towards her.

'What's wrong?'

He hiccuped. 'I had a nightmare.'

His face was damp and flushed, his eyes wet. Pippa laid him down again and went to the bathroom, ran water over a flannel, squeezed some of the water out before taking it to bathe Johnny's hot face.

She got him orange juice from the mini fridge in the room, brushed his tangled hair back from his face, made him sit up to drink his juice.

'What was the nightmare about?'

'I was being chased by something. I couldn't see what it was, it was dark, but it made horrid noises.'

'I hate dreams like that,' she said, and his small body fitted itself against her heavily.

'Do you have them?'

'Oh, yes, everyone does, even grown-ups—they're the worst, because you don't know what's after you.'

He finished his juice. She took the glass from him as he yawned.

'Tired?' she murmured, helping him to lie down again. 'You go back to sleep; I'll stay here. You only have to yell and I'll come running.'

His eyes had closed; in the lamplight she saw his lashes flutter down against his flushed cheeks. What had he been dreaming about? she wondered. What monsters haunted his sleep?

When she was sure he was breathing rhythmically, fast asleep, she tiptoed out into the sitting room, leaving one lamp burning beside the bed, in case Johnny woke again.

Going into her own bathroom, she undressed, washed, put on a white silk nightdress and matching robe, brushed her chestnut hair, then returned to the sitting room and lay down on the couch to read her book. She did not want to be out of earshot in case Johnny called her.

At some point she fell asleep; the book slipped to the floor. She did not have nightmares; she was too tired to dream.

She woke with a start, hearing a sound, and looked up to find Randal sitting beside her, his fingers stroking her cheek.

'Oh, hello,' she said, startled, shifting to dislodge his hand. 'Did Alex explain why I left? Johnny had a nightmare, but he's asleep again now.'

'I know. I checked just now. He's deeply asleep. Thanks for coming up to take care of him.'

'That's okay.' Under his possessive stare she was

suddenly conscious of her bare legs, of her semi-transparent nightdress, the silk clinging to her warm body, her breasts visible at the low neckline. 'Well, I'll go to bed myself now and leave you to take care of Johnny.' She tried to slide off the couch but Randal was in the way, his lean body blocking her escape route.

As he bent his head she wailed, 'No, Randal!'

It was a vain protest. His mouth hit hers with a demand that left her too weak to fight the seductive sensuality of that kiss, the caressing hands roaming over her, stroking her bare throat, her shoulders, sliding down inside the nightdress to touch her breasts, wandering up over her bare legs, while all the time she quivered, drawn by the magnetic power of Randal's body against hers.

She knew what would happen if she didn't stop him, yet she was helpless to do a thing about his lovemaking. Every inch of her was shuddering with pleasure under his hands, his mouth; she ached to have him inside her again, to be taken to that wild peak of ecstasy.

Then they both heard a stir in the further room, a whimper from the child sleeping in there, and Randal sat up, his head turned that way, listening.

Pippa took her opportunity and wriggled out from the couch. 'You'd better go and see if he's okay,' she said, and fled, trembling, before Randal could stop her.

CHAPTER TEN

NEXT morning, as they ate a very late breakfast downstairs, Renata and Alex came in to say goodbye. Alex was casual in jeans and a bright yellow sweatshirt. Renata was dressed as for some grand occasion, a film premiére, perhaps, or a fashionable cocktail party, wearing a skintight sky-blue dress with hardly any back and very little above the waist at the front. Other guests, eating egg and bacon or fresh fruit, stopped to goggle in disbelief at this vision.

Her son looked pinkly embarrassed; his mother was not dressed the way he thought mothers should dress at breakfast time.

Randal's brows rose but he was very polite.

'Have a safe trip, and let us know in advance next time you're coming to see Johnny.' He held out a hand. 'Nice to talk to you, Alex; I must bring Johnny along to watch you play some time soon.'

'I'd like that,' Alex said, shaking hands.

'Me, too,' Johnny eagerly chimed in, and everyone smiled indulgently at the boy.

Alex shook hands with Pippa, who was dressed in a pleated brown skirt and dark green sweater, very differently from Renata. 'I enjoyed getting to know you, Pippa. I hope we'll meet again.'

She smiled back. 'Nice to meet you, Alex.'

Renata looked pointedly at her watch. 'We ought to be getting on our way. Do come along, Alex!' She didn't bother with courtesies; she wanted to get away as soon as possible, and made that clear.

Alex obeyed, his expression a little wry. People watched them leave, whispering—no doubt many of them recognised Alex, who was, after all, quite famous.

Renata hadn't spoken to, let alone kissed her son, Pippa realised, wondering if the boy had been hurt. She found Renata's indifference to the pain she might inflict baffling. What sort of woman was she? Across the table her eyes met Randal's; he grimaced silently at her. He had noticed that Renata had ignored their son, too. There wasn't much Randal ever missed.

He returned his attention to the fresh fruit and croissants he was eating. Johnny had decided on a full English breakfast, which he claimed he ate at school most mornings. Pippa couldn't even look at his food; it made her feel sick. She was eating fresh figs and Greek yoghurt, then she might eat a slice of toast.

'This morning, I thought we'd go for a walk around the hotel grounds,' Randal suggested. 'Unless you want to do some shopping, Pippa. There's a large discount shopping centre a few miles away—would you like to go there?'

She shook her head. 'I'd rather go for a walk.'

Johnny beamed at her. 'There's a crazy golf course here; we could have a game.'

'Why not? I've never played any sort of golf, but I don't mind trying my hand.'

'You'll soon learn,' Johnny paternally assured her. 'I'll teach you. I'm quite good, for my age—Alex said so.'

The weather was bright but a little blustery and

slightly cool. The walk was very enjoyable and the game of crazy golf had her and Johnny in fits of laughter. Randal played, too, but seemed abstracted.

Johnny won the game and Pippa bought him an ice cream back at the hotel, as a prize. He took it upstairs to the suite with him and ate it watching the inevitable cartoons on the TV in the bedroom.

Pippa and Randal retreated to the sitting room. She curled up in an armchair; he sat down on the couch close by.

'I talked to the riding stables. They do have some boots and hats for hire,' Randal said. 'But no jodhpurs. They said you could wear jeans, though. You've got some with you, haven't you?'

'Yes, but I'd rather not ride, if you don't mind. I think it would be good for you to be alone with Johnny, for one thing. For another, I'm not wild about riding horses. And I thought I'd take a siesta this afternoon. I've had a very tiring week, one way and another; I need a long rest.'

He nodded soberly. 'Yes, no doubt it's been traumatic, but at least it's all over now, and you know the outcome has been good for you. You'd have been insane to marry Tom; he's a decent enough guy but he's as dull as ditchwater and you didn't love him.'

'Don't talk about him!' she muttered, keeping a wary eye on the door in case Johnny appeared there. 'You don't know what you're talking about!'

'I know you love me,' he coolly informed her, taking her breath away.

She sat upright, face flushing dark red, then turning white. 'You know nothing of the kind! Your vanity is mind-blowing. What on earth makes you think I love you? I've got more sense.'

He sat down on the arm of her chair, caught her face between his palms and kissed her fiercely. She couldn't escape or avoid that devouring mouth, and after a moment of writhing indignation she stopped wanting to, her lips quivering under his, her arms going round his neck.

Without lifting his mouth, he whispered, 'Tell me, Pippa. Tell me you love me. Stop lying to me, and yourself. I love you; you know that. Yesterday I discovered you love me too; you'd never given yourself to me if you didn't. So, tell me! I need to hear you saying it.'

A single tear rolled down from under her closed lids. She gave a small, pathetic sob, pushing at his powerful chest, trying to make him let go of her.

'All you ever think about is what you need. What about what I need?'

'What's that?'

'Time,' she groaned. 'Time to think. I'm so confused. A week ago I was planning my marriage to Tom. Now here I am, with you. I feel as if I've been through an earthquake. The landscape of my life has been torn up; I don't know where I am, or what I want to do. And you keep pushing me, trying to make me do what you want me to do! Leave me alone, Randal. Give me some time and space to work out how I really feel!'

He studied her, frowning, then dropped a light kiss on her nose. 'Okay, we'll talk about it some other time. But you do like Johnny, don't you? I've been watching you with him; I can see you do. I know you said you wanted to be first with anyone you married, not come second after their child—but that was before you got to know Johnny. Do you still feel the same?'

She worried her lower lip, sighing. 'I don't know. No, I suppose not. Seeing him with his mother, I felt so sorry for him. I had a loveless childhood, myself—that's why I badly want to be loved, to come first with the man I marry. I can understand where Johnny's coming from, though; I've been through what he's going through. And I think it's worse for him, because he does have a mother who's alive, but seems quite indifferent to him, whereas I had nobody. I was lonely and neglected but I wasn't getting hurt the way Johnny is.'

Grimly, Randal said, 'Renata's a selfish woman who puts herself first, always has. You see, that's what happens when a woman demands to come first.'

'That's not fair!' she protested angrily. 'I never said I'd put myself first if I ever had a child!'

'No, I believe you wouldn't, but Renata does, always has. There's no room in her life for a child. The less Johnny sees of her, the better. He won't get so badly hurt if he doesn't see her too often. But I don't want him blaming me, telling himself I kept her away. I have to let her visit him if she ever feels like it, although I wish I could stop her seeing him.'

They kept their voices very low, neither of them wanting the boy to hear what they were saying.

'I made a terrible mistake when I married her,' Randal dryly said. 'If I'd known what she was really like I wouldn't have got involved, but I was a lot younger, and she was really lovely.

'Still is.' Pippa shrugged. 'Don't deny you couldn't stop looking at her; I saw you staring.'

His mouth quirked sideways in amusement. 'Well, she is quite a knock-out! In fact, I'd say she's lovelier now than ever. She knows how to dress and use make-up.' He gave her a mocking smile. 'I knew you were jealous, little green eyes!'

'I was not!' she flared immediately, and he laughed.

'Oh, yes, you were. But you didn't need to be! I told you that yesterday. Yes, she's drop-dead gorgeous, but I'm not a romantic boy any more. I want a woman to have a lot of other qualities. Beauty isn't everything. In fact, beauty isn't very much at all. It's just a façade. To be a real woman you need a heart, warmth, caring. And I want a woman with a sense of humour, brains...all Renata offers is what she looks like, and that isn't enough for me now.'

His grey eyes were deadly serious; she had doubted him yesterday but now she was ready to believe him. She had seen the cynicism in his face as he watched his ex-wife. Renata didn't take him in.

Johnny ran into the room a moment later and his father got up to greet him, raking back his slightly dishevelled black hair.

'Hello, enjoyed your cartoons?'

'Yeah. When are we having lunch?' the boy demanded.

Randal looked at his watch, made a surprised face. 'It's half past twelve. Do you want to go down now?'

'Yes, please.'

'You've got ice cream round your mouth,' Pippa gently reminded him. 'Maybe we should all go to the bathroom before we leave?'

'Okay.' Johnny streaked away and his father shuddered.

'I wish I had his energy! Not to mention his stomach. He's hardly digested that ice cream but already he's thinking about more food!'

'He's a growing boy!' Pippa grinned; she found Johnny's unashamed delight in food amusing. But then she liked the boy a lot; in some ways he reminded her of his father, in other ways he was very much himself. She had grown very fond of him.

After lunch Johnny and Randal changed into their riding clothes to go to the stables. Pippa curled up on a couch in the sitting room and watched a TV programme.

While Johnny was putting on his boots, Randal said quietly to her, 'You're sure you won't come?'

She shook her head, keeping her face blank. 'I'd rather stay here and rest.'

He hesitated, eyeing her shrewdly. 'I hope you aren't planning to bolt again? You will be here when we get back?'

She tossed her hair back, making a face. 'Oh, don't be tiresome! Just go, will you?'

Johnny appeared before Randal had the chance to say anything else, and the two of them left.

As soon as they had gone Pippa hurried into her bedroom and packed everything. She could not stay here; she had a sense of impending disaster. It was blindingly obvious that if she didn't get away she would find herself being stampeded into marrying Randal, and every time she thought about that violent alarm bells went off inside her head and heart.

She took her case down to Reception and asked them to get her a taxi to the nearest railway station.

'Will the other members of your party be staying on, or are they leaving too?' the receptionist asked, looking at her suspiciously, obviously wondering if she was bolting without paying the bill.

'Yes, they're staying tonight, but they've gone riding at the local stables. They should be back in a couple of hours. Their luggage is all upstairs.'

The receptionist rang a taxi firm, then told her, 'The cab should be here in ten minutes.'

She sat down and waited, gazing out into the hotel grounds. The trees tossed restlessly in the brisk wind but the sun was shining and wallflowers in a large raised bed sent waves of strong scent into the hotel foyer.

The taxi arrived and drove her to the railway station. She was lucky; there was a train to London only a quarter of an hour later. She got to town in time to catch her connecting train into Essex and was back at her cottage by six.

Her nerves were on edge, wondering if Randal would ring, but the evening passed without hearing from him.

She made herself scrambled egg on toast for supper and went to bed quite early, feeling absolutely exhausted. She woke up in the night crying, tears pouring down her face after a dream she couldn't remember at all except that it had left her with a sense of terrible loss and loneliness.

She got up and went downstairs, made herself hot chocolate and took it back to bed, sat up against banked pillows sipping it, trying to remember what her dream had been about. She couldn't track it down, though, just remember the feelings.

The trouble was, her mind was in confusion: torn, divided, constantly swinging between dread of seeing Randal again, of having to face his insistence that she must marry him, and a yearning to be with him, to be in his arms, in his bed.

He was right, of course; now that she had got to

know Johnny she liked him, was already fond of him. Randal had shrewdly guessed that that would happen. By introducing her to his son he had hoped to disarm her and he had done it. She knew she no longer resented Johnny's place in his father's affections, no longer wanted Randal to put her first at his son's expense. How could she want to supplant that poor, sad little boy, whose mother couldn't be bothered with him, who had been starved of Renata's affection all his short life?

Johnny was a lively, intelligent child who mostly hid his emotional problems, but Pippa had learnt that they existed, had seen the boy's hurt response to his mother's rejection.

No, she no longer wanted to come first with Randal. Johnny needed his father's love as much as she did.

But she still couldn't marry Randal. She had been puzzled at first, hadn't been able to work out why she was so scared, but in the silence of that spring night she faced up to the reasons. She couldn't take the risk. It was that simple. She was scared. Marrying Randal would be like bungee jumping off a cliff, afraid the rope would break, afraid she would hit the ground and be killed or horribly maimed.

She had been emotionally maimed last time. Four years ago she had had the guts to walk away from him, but she had been damaged by doing it. When they'd met again she had rationalised her instinctive need for flight, for getting away from him, had told herself it was because he had chosen his wife and child over her before and she needed a man who would put her first every time, but now she knew it hadn't been that at all.

She was simply afraid of getting hurt again. It was a case of the burnt child fearing the fire. She couldn't take the risk.

Finishing her hot chocolate, she switched off the lamp and lay down in the dark. She must clear her mind of Randal, mustn't let herself think about him, must not keep turning over thoughts of him. She had to get some sleep. She was so tired. And no more dreams!

The answer was to think of something else. A holiday! That would keep her mind busy. Where should she go? Spain? Italy? At this time of year anywhere in the Mediterranean would be wonderful—not too hot, not too crowded. She must go to a travel agent and book herself two weeks in some lovely place.

She would probably go to a seaside resort, but one which could offer fascinating places to visit too. Somehow Italy seemed to her at this moment to offer more. She would get a brochure and choose somewhere. Anywhere, it didn't matter where, because she knew nothing much about Italy. Wherever she went it would be new and exciting.

She must have fallen asleep quite quickly because the next time she woke up it was morning and the room was full of golden light.

It was a lovely morning; spring was slowly turning into summer, the lilacs were out in clusters of white and purple, the roses were budding and the air was rich with the scent of blossom.

Pippa got up, showered, put on jeans and a white T-shirt, blow-dried her chestnut hair, then went downstairs for breakfast.

She had bran cereal with fresh fruit, which she sliced into her bowl: apple, banana, grapes. With it she drank a small glass of orange juice and then a cup of black coffee. After that she did some housework and then went out into the garden to mow the lawn.

While she was doing that Tom arrived, came round the side of the house to find her.

'Where have you been?' he demanded.

Switching off the mower, she smiled at him, pushing back her hair from her sun-flushed face.

'Hello, Tom. I was visiting a friend.'

'What friend?' He had that belligerent look she was coming to recognise. 'I suppose you mean Harding?'

'Tom, don't start on one of those inquisitions. I don't have to tell you who I see, or where I go. So don't bark at me.'

He made a growling noise in his throat like an angry dog and showed his teeth. 'We may not be getting married, but I still worry about you. The man's pure poison. Stay away from him!'

'I'm not discussing him with you, any more than I'd discuss you with him!'

'What does he say about me?' he broke out, very red in the face.

She groaned. 'Oh, for heaven's sake, Tom! Why are you here and what do you want?'

After a seething pause, he said, 'I wanted to work out a timetable for the sale of the house. I can put down a deposit whenever you like, but when, exactly, do you want to exchange contracts?'

She took off her gardening gloves. 'Come in and have a coffee and we'll work something out.'

They sat in the kitchen, drinking coffee and writing out a proposed timetable for the sale.

'I don't want you to feel you're being forced out,'

Tom assured her. 'You suggest a date when it would be convenient for you to move out, then if you need to stay on for a while we can adjust the date later.'

'You're very thoughtful, Tom,' she said, smiling at him. He was a kind man, too; she appreciated the way he tried to make things easier for her. If only he would stop trying to interfere in her life!

'Have you decided where to go on holiday?' he asked.

She shook her head. 'I'll check that out tomorrow. What about you? I thought you would be going away today; that was the plan originally, wasn't it?'

'I had to change the flights. I rang to explain that I'd only need one seat, so they suggested I went tomorrow. It's easier to sell two seats than one, they said. More couples go on these holiday flights. So I'm off early tomorrow. That's why I had to see you today, before I went.'

'Well, I hope you have a lovely time, Tom.'

'I intend to!' He looked at his watch. 'Look, come and have lunch at the pub—you've always liked their roast Sunday lunch.'

It seemed a good idea, it would save her having to cook a meal for herself, so she agreed and they left ten minutes later. The pub was only half full when they arrived, but as time wore on more and more people crowded into the timbered room, with its shining horse brasses and silver tankards hanging on the wall behind the bar counter.

They both chose carrot soup followed by roast beef with light, crispy Yorkshire pudding, roast potatoes, carrots and Brussels sprouts.

'Their gravy's terrific, too,' Tom said, as he finished. 'Not to mention the horseradish sauce.'

They knew a few of the other customers and got into a game of billiards after the meal. It was nearly four o'clock before Tom drove Pippa home.

'Thank you for lunch; it was great,' she said. 'Do you want to come in for tea or coffee?'

'I have to pack, yet,' he said. 'I'd better scoot home now.'

'Have a wonderful holiday!' she said, and stood waving as he drove away.

She was grateful to him for having taken up the whole afternoon. If Randal had pursued her here he would have found her not at home, so she would have avoided a difficult confrontation.

If only she could fix a holiday at once! Then she would be able to put off seeing Randal for weeks. For the rest of the day she was on tenterhooks, and was very relieved when night fell and she could lock up the cottage and go to bed to read and listen to music.

There were no bad dreams that night and she slept well. When she got up it was raining, a light, thin rain which came in sudden showers. She showered, dressed, had breakfast, then did some housework.

Mid-morning, she drove to the nearest travel agent, was given a brochure of Italian holidays and took it across the road to a café, where she read it, drinking another cup of coffee.

Tom would be in the air by now, *en route* for what would have been their honeymoon. Lucky Tom.

She was attracted by the idea of a fortnight on the Adriatic coast; there she could combine a beach holiday with a visit to the Byzantine church at Ravenna and a trip to Venice, which she had always longed to see. So she went back to the travel agent and booked two weeks at a hotel right on the beach road, with full board, starting in a week's time. She would fly there, of course, from Gatwick Airport, and would be taken by coach to her hotel.

A trouble-free holiday, she decided. She couldn't wait.

After doing some shopping she drove home to find Randal's car parked outside the cottage, with him sitting in the driving seat.

While he watched her sardonically, she sat in her own car, paralysed, drumming her fingers restlessly on the wheel, feeling like driving off again and staying out until she could be sure he would have gone. But what was the point? She could put it off, but sooner or later Randal would catch up with her; she knew how persistent he could be.

So she drove on to her forecourt and parked. As she got out of her car, Randal got out of his, but she ignored him, hurrying to open her front door. Before she could shut it in his face he was beside her, pushing his way inside on her heels.

'Where have you been?' he demanded, as Tom had done yesterday.

'Shopping and booking a Mediterranean holiday,' she defiantly told him, walking into the kitchen with her shopping basket and beginning to unpack what she had bought.

'You'll have to cancel that,' he said with calm arrogance. 'We'll go abroad for our honeymoon!'

'There isn't going to be one!' she snapped.

He coolly put the kettle on and got out the instant coffee, just as if he lived here too, set out two mugs, got milk from the fridge, then leaned against the kitchen counter, watching her.

'Make yourself at home,' she said with irritation. Who did he think he was?

'I've just been to Tom's place,' he drawled. 'But there was no sign of him. His next door neighbour told me he was away, on his honeymoon!'

She finished unpacking and put her shopping basket away, not commenting. Randal's grey eyes had a dangerous glitter.

'I thought maybe you'd changed your mind and married him after all!'

'No,' she calmly answered, and his eyes flashed like lightning.

Moving with pantherish grace and speed, he caught hold of her, pushed her up against the wall, holding her there with his own body, forcing her to confront him.

'Don't try to be funny!'

'I wasn't. You asked if I'd married Tom, I said no; that's all!'

'I was out of my mind,' Randal grated. Inches away, his face was white with rage. 'I couldn't be sure you wouldn't do anything so stupid! I just don't understand you. But I was terrified you might have done it just to get away from me.'

Her heart crashed like a burning plane. She couldn't breathe properly, couldn't meet his probing, furious eyes.

'You promised me you'd be at the hotel when Johnny and I got back from the riding stables,' he accused. 'But the minute we'd left you packed and went. They told me at Reception. Why? Why did you run away again? You said you liked Johnny, and I know you want me...'

'No,' she denied. 'That's the point. I don't.'

'Liar.' He caught her face between his hands and kissed her hotly, sensuously, making her legs give way under her. 'Do I have to show you all over again? I'll make love to you in here, on the floor, if I have to. You want me. Admit it.'

'That's just sex,' she huskily conceded.

'Call it what you like. You want me. I can have you any time I feel like it.'

'How dare you?' she angrily broke out. 'I'm not some bimbo you can just…' She stopped, so insulted she couldn't get another word out.

'I didn't say you were! You may call it sex, but we both know it's love. That's what we feel for each other. So why do you keep running away?'

She closed her eyes, a sob forming in her throat, salty tears welling behind her lids.

'I can't take the risk!'

'What risk?' he impatiently insisted.

'Of getting hurt. Last time I nearly died of misery; it was months before I got over losing you. Now I'm afraid of…oh, of everything. How I feel, what might happen if I do marry you, getting hurt again if it doesn't work out between us, the future—everything!'

He put his warm mouth on her wet eyes, kissed them gently, slid his mouth down her cheeks, whispering between kisses, 'I didn't realise you were such a coward. Pippa, darling, I love you and I want to be with you for ever. Do you want to be with me? And don't lie this time. Tell the truth. Do you want to be with me for the rest of our lives?'

She made a wailing noise, keeping her eyes shut. 'Don't ask…'

His mouth touched hers gently. 'I am asking. Tell

me the truth. Do you love me? Do you want to be with me for ever?'

She drew breath, shuddering, then took the final terrifying leap into the truth. 'Yes. Yes.'

He drew her even closer, held her, his mouth against her hair, rocking her as if she was a baby.

'I love you. Say it too.'

'Yes,' she groaned. 'I love you. I love you.'

And felt the fear and tension draining out of her body. She had been afraid of love all this time, afraid of giving herself, of getting hurt, afraid of life itself.

Now she wasn't; she never would be again. She wound her arms around his neck and gave herself up to him, kissing him passionately, with unleashed desire.

THE CORPORATE WIFE

by

Leigh Michaels

Leigh Michaels has always loved happy endings. Even when she was a child, if a book's conclusion didn't please her she'd make up her own. And, though she always wanted to write fiction, she very sensibly planned to earn her living as a newspaper reporter. That career didn't work out, however, and she ended up writing for Mills & Boon® instead – in the kind of happy ending only a romance novelist could dream up!

Leigh likes to hear from readers: you can write to her at PO Box 935, Ottumwa, Iowa 52501-0935, USA.

Don't miss Leigh Michaels' new novel out in the summer.

CHAPTER ONE

ERIN put down the telephone and picked up the yellow memo form which her secretary had just laid on the corner of her desk blotter. "Sarah, would you see if you can get four tickets to Thursday's performance of *Swan Lake* in Forest Park? The Senator's secretary says he has a yen to see a ballet presented on an outdoor stage." Her eyebrows drew together as she read the message. "Wait a minute. 'Jessup called to say the fresh flowers aren't'? They aren't what?"

"Fresh, I presume," the secretary said. "He didn't go into detail. I told him you couldn't talk to him right now about *this* dinner party because you were on the phone organizing the *next* one, and he just sighed."

A smile tugged at Erin's lips. "There have been a lot of them lately, haven't there? I'll call him. I suppose I should have known better than to give that florist a second chance after last time."

"When they sent the centerpiece that would have looked more at home in a mortuary than on a dinner table? Even tired tulips and droopy daisies are an improvement over that," Sarah pointed out. "Also, Mr. Livingstone asked if you'd come into his office when you have a minute, and Cecile Worth wants to talk to you."

Erin had already picked up the telephone. She took it away from her ear. "The worthy Cecile wants to talk to *me?*" she said unbelievingly. "Not Mr. Livingstone?" Only when she saw the secretary's half smile did she realize that she'd picked up not only Sarah's nickname for the woman but her ironic tone of voice.

"He's having all his calls held for the rest of the afternoon. But come to think of it, she didn't even ask to speak to him—she just wanted to be put through to you."

Erin shook her head a little. Slater Livingstone's latest—and it appeared, his most blazing ever—flame, wanting to talk to Erin Reynolds, the mere personal assistant? "Do you have her number?"

"Do I ever," the secretary said with feeling. "She's a gold digger and a—oh, you mean her phone number. You don't need it, she's on hold."

"You left Cecile Worth on hold?"

"It wasn't exactly my doing. I told her it might be some time before you were free, but she insisted on waiting."

"Not a good sign," Erin muttered. She stabbed the eraser end of her pencil against the blinking button on the phone. "Ms. Worth? I'm sorry to keep you waiting."

A low, sultry voice replied, "Oh, don't bother to apologize, Erin dear. I was just sitting here anyway, getting a manicure, while I waited. An *entire* manicure."

Erin winced. Why was it that barbs couched in polite tones dug so much deeper than the ones which were openly catty? Not that Cecile Worth wasn't a master at both kinds.

"But think nothing of it," Cecile went on. "About this party tonight—"

And jolly well time for you to ask, Erin thought, *especially since you're officially the hostess.*

"I do hope the guests aren't going to be the same sort of dull lot that the last batch were."

The last batch of Slater Livingstone's dinner guests, Erin reflected, had included a Nobel-prize-winning physicist and his college-professor wife. Erin had shown them around the office herself before the party and had been charmed by the unassuming pair—but obviously Cecile had a different definition of interesting.

"I assume, from the long silence, that they're exactly the same kind?" Cecile said shrewdly. "No, don't bother to answer. Telling me they're exciting when you know perfectly well they're not isn't going to make things any better. But couldn't you at least make an effort to convince Slater to entertain his clients somewhere besides that stodgy apartment of his? Even a change of scene would help."

Stodgy was hardly the adjective Erin would have chosen for Slater Livingstone's home, but trying to change Cecile Worth's opinion would get her exactly nowhere, so Erin gritted her teeth and kept silent.

"At least if we went to a club there'd be fun and dancing and other people to talk to."

Cecile sounded like a whiny child, Erin thought uncharitably. "That's exactly why Mr. Livingstone's dinner parties need to be private, Ms. Worth. The conversation at these events is apt to be a bit sensitive—not the kind you hold in a public place where just anyone might overhear."

"Then he ought to keep business in his office, and save the evenings for fun," Cecile announced. "If he even knows what fun is."

Though Erin wasn't about to admit it, she wondered sometimes if Slater Livingstone's undeniable preoccupation with his business might explain why he found Cecile, with her air of brittle sophistication, so attractive. The woman provided a contrast, that was for sure.

But it wasn't true that he didn't have any fun. Slater played racquetball on a regular basis and golf often enough to keep his handicap low, though Cecile would probably argue that since he generally played with clients or business associates—or even rivals—the games weren't really pleasure after all.

"The only thing he's interested in besides business is his musty old books," Cecile said with disdain. "What a hobby!"

Erin tried not to smile. Some of the *musty old books* Slater Livingstone bought had been delivered to the office; just last week Erin had gotten a glimpse of a couple of rare first editions and the manuscript copy of a popular modern novel.

Cecile had gone on, but she was obviously talking more to herself than to Erin. "—Just a weekend in New York, that's all I want."

At the moment, maybe, Erin thought. *But that wouldn't be the end of it.*

"Of course, he won't take me. This annoying habit of his, expecting me to fall in with his plans all the time, while he never does what I want—"

Erin had heard enough; the conversation was not only pointless but Cecile's accusations were overblown. "I'm surprised you put up with it, Ms. Worth," she said crisply.

A low giggle startled her. "Are you? Well, take a good look, Erin darling—not only at Slater but the balance in his bank account—and you might dimly see what I'm talking about. Look, I'll send over a guest list of my own tomorrow, so next time you put together one of these ghastly parties, you can include some people who aren't quite ready to be embalmed, all right?"

Erin bit her tongue, but it wasn't necessary; Cecile had slammed the telephone down.

The worst of it, she thought, was that she could walk into Slater's office right now and tell him precisely what the worthy Cecile had said about him, and he'd probably laugh and make a quip about Cecile's fantastic sense of humor. And Cecile obviously knew how he'd react, or she wouldn't have been so careless about what she said.

Erin shook her head and picked up the small thick notebook which held every detail of her life and work. Fortunately, Slater Livingstone's private life was none of her affair. If he chose to make a fool of himself over a woman as shallow and frivolous as Cecile Worth, that was his business.

As Erin came from her office into Sarah's, the secretary glanced up over her half-glasses and said, ''Good, you're finally here. He's acting like a tyrannosaurus rex all of a sudden.''

''And you've scheduled me to be his afternoon snack?''

''Well, he's asked twice now what was holding you up, and I didn't like to tell him you were talking to his lady love.''

''So you made lame excuses instead? Thanks a lot, Sarah.''

''I didn't know if you'd want to admit it,'' the secretary said reasonably. ''If the two of you were simply exchanging girlish confidences—''

''If I ever start thinking of the worthy Cecile as a pal,'' Erin said firmly, ''just take me out and shoot me, all right?''

She tapped once on the walnut door of Slater Livingstone's office and without waiting for an answer pushed it open.

The room was spacious, occupying a corner high in one of St. Louis's newer office towers. Behind the desk a wall of windows provided an incredible view of the Gateway Arch. Late afternoon sunshine glinted off the polished stainless steel, and as Slater Livingstone rose from his ebony and glass desk, the gleaming monument behind him momentarily framed his head.

Almost like a halo, Erin thought whimsically. Or a knight's helmet.

She didn't have to take a good look at her boss to know what Cecile Worth had been talking about—but Erin looked anyway. At thirty-five, Slater Livingstone wasn't handsome in the strictest sense of the word; his face was too craggy for that, and his ears a little too large. But his eyes were gorgeous, dark brown flecked with gold and surrounded by thick curly lashes which would make a fashion model envious.

More important, there wasn't a woman in the world—or a man, for that matter—who could ignore him. He had a presence which commanded any crowd in which he appeared, a presence which was no less effective for being apparently unconscious. Slater didn't seem to realize it, but when he walked in, people noticed. They sat up straighter and prepared to pay attention.

Though she'd seen it happen a hundred times in the year she'd worked as his personal assistant, Erin had no idea precisely what it was about him which caused such a reaction. He was tall, square-shouldered as an army general, always carefully tailored. His gaze was direct, his handshake firm, his smile sincere. But those things were true of many other men, too—men who couldn't bring a room to attention by merely stepping across the threshold.

Perhaps, she thought, it was because he was obviously so much at ease with himself and his surroundings, no matter what they were.

"Hello, Erin." He waved a hand at her customary chair, next to his desk.

Or maybe it was his voice, she thought. Low and warm and smooth as twenty-year-old Scotch, his voice inspired confidence and trust and liking. It was a good thing, she thought, that he'd chosen an honest way to make a living, for Slater Livingstone could have been one of the world's most successful swindlers.

He tipped his head inquiringly, and Erin recalled her wandering thoughts. "Sorry to take so long. I was talking to Ms. Worth." She briefly considered quoting Cecile even though the warning would no doubt be futile, but settled for the safer, more conservative approach. "She had some last-minute questions about the party tonight."

"What to wear, no doubt?" He didn't sound particularly interested. "You sent her flowers, didn't you?"

"Of course." *I just wish I'd had her corsage made from a Venus flytrap,* Erin thought.

He reached for a sheaf of papers lying on the corner of his desk. "Whatever her concerns, I presume you got it sorted out between you."

"Yes, sir," Erin said dutifully. "If you want a report on the plans for the Senator's visit at the end of the week—"

Slater shook his head. "I'm sure you have it entirely under control. Just tell me when and where to show up."

"And what to wear?" The question was out before Erin could stop herself. "Sorry."

Slater leaned back in his chair and rubbed the knuckle of his index finger against the cleft in his chin. A long, slow smile lit up his face and his eyes sparkled. "Does that mean you have something adventurous planned?"

The smile, Erin thought, didn't diminish his con-man potential in the least. "Not exactly. But the Senator likes open-air theater, and Ms. Worth indicated she'd like a change from entertaining at your apartment, so I thought perhaps I'd arrange a casual picnic in Forest Park before the ballet." She didn't know where the words had come from; nothing had been further from her mind. But the image of Cecile sitting cross-legged on a blanket and trying to balance a plate of fried chicken, runny baked beans, and potato salad in her lap was almost too good to turn down.

''Why not?'' Slater said casually. ''When he was President, Franklin Delano Roosevelt once served hot dogs to the King and Queen of England.'' He picked up the sheaf of papers once more. ''I had lunch with a friend today—a friend who asked what was new here at Control Dynamics. I took it as a casual question and said, 'Not much,' and he laughed and told me a good bit about the projects our research and development people have been working on in the last few months.''

Erin doodled a square on the corner of her notebook. ''All of which is supposed to be kept under wraps.''

''Precisely. It can't be sealed up entirely, of course, but I didn't expect to hear hints of it at my club.''

''Maybe it's time for another employee refresher course on confidentiality?''

Slater shook his head. ''I don't think it's necessary to go that far. The information my friend had wasn't entirely accurate and had a good many missing pieces, so I don't see any need to make a federal case of it just now. But—''

''I'll keep my eyes open. No wonder you were in a bad mood.''

''Did Sarah tell you I was acting like a velociraptor?''

Erin said slowly, ''T. rex, actually. You know about Sarah's dinosaur scale?''

''Only the general outlines—I'm not sure I've picked up all the distinguishing points.''

''She doesn't mean any harm,'' Erin said. ''It's just that she hears so much about dinosaurs from her little boy that she's got them on the brain. And now there are only the two of them, since her divorce—''

''You don't have to defend her, Erin. Sarah has to let off steam now and then, too—and there are a whole lot worse things to be compared to. Anyway, the possible leak wasn't the reason for my irritable mood. This was.'' He slid an envelope out from under the leather desk blotter and tapped it on the glass top of his desk.

As soon as she saw the monogram on the envelope, Erin's heart sank. The last time Slater Livingstone's aunt Hermione had written to him, Erin had spent the better part of two weeks in dark and isolated archives all over St. Louis, looking up the vital statistics of obscure, long-dead Livingstones. Still... why would that upset Slater's frame of mind?

''She's not just demanding more family tree research,'' Erin said definitely, ''because that wouldn't put you in a foul mood.''

Slater's eyebrows rose slightly. ''It wouldn't?''

''No. You'd just delegate it to me and dust off your hands and forget it.''

His chuckle was low and rich. ''You're right, as a matter of fact—I'm delegating.''

Erin took the letter he held out. ''That's all it is? Really?''

''When you see her list of questions, you might change your mind.''

Her gaze raced over the close-written Spencerian script, then she rolled her eyes and tossed the page back on the desk. ''Oh, now I see what annoyed you. It's the comment about it being time to add a few buds to your particular branch of the family tree that got you, isn't it?''

Slater reached for the letter. ''What? Where does she say that?''

"She doesn't. You wouldn't expect your aunt Hermione to be quite so inept as to come straight out and demand that you get married and produce a namesake for her—would you?"

"Now that's a thought," Slater mused. "A little girl in pink rompers and pigtails, named Hermione. Though I can't quite picture myself saying *Eat your carrots, Hermione. Stop pulling the cat's tail, Hermione.*"

"You could just call her Herm," Erin suggested. "Anyway, I think she disguised her demand very neatly." She picked up the letter again and in her best imitation of Hermione's Bostonian accent said, "'Slater, have you never considered the value of having a stable hostess? Just one, who knows exactly what you like? It would not only make your life immeasurably easier but Miss Reynolds' as well.' Not that you'd worry much about that."

"What? Making your life easier? I didn't realize I was quite so impossible, Erin."

Erin was still re-reading the letter. "Not *impossible,*" she said before she stopped to think, "but certainly *difficult.*"

Slater laughed. "I must have inherited it from Aunt Hermione. One absolute truth about her letters is that they take one's mind off other troubles."

"She does have a point, you know. Having one person in charge of all the entertaining would be..." Her voice trailed off. *Unless, of course, it ends up being Cecile Worth.* Then Erin's life wouldn't be easier. In fact, it would be darned near unbearable.

"Careful, or you'll start sounding like Aunt Hermione."

"Me, sir? I know better than to suggest anything of the sort." Erin slid the letter back in the envelope and tucked it into her notebook. "Will that be all?"

"For now. There's no hurry about answering Hermione's letter, by the way. She's been pruning the family tree for forty years, so I'm sure it'll last a few weeks. Will you be going by my apartment to check on the last-minute details for the dinner party?"

And to take Jessup some fresh flowers, Erin reminded herself. "Is there something I can do for you?"

"Stick around till the party starts, will you? I'm trying to finish up the Universal Conveyer bid this afternoon, so I'm likely to be running late. It won't do for guests to find nobody at home but the butler."

Erin raised an eyebrow. "I can't see that being greeted by your personal assistant would be much better, particularly when the butler in question is Jessup. But of course I'll stay till you get there."

"Thanks." His tone was abstracted, his attention obviously already on the folder he'd just opened on the desk blotter.

Erin knew she didn't have to try to be quiet; the deep pile of the plush carpet would muffle the heaviest of footsteps, and Slater was concentrating so hard he wouldn't hear her anyway. But she found herself tiptoeing nonetheless. Just as she reached the door, Slater spoke, and the abruptness in his voice spun her around to face him once more.

"One more thing, Erin."

"Yes, sir?"

"About Aunt Hermione's letter. Why were you instantly positive that under no circumstances on earth would I get married?"

There were a hundred ways she could have answered Slater's question, and all of them were equally true. *Because none of the lovelies you've dated in the whole year*

I've known you have lasted more than six weeks. Because sometimes I think you have to write their names under the band of your wristwatch to even remember which one you're with. Because you're more married to your business than you ever could be to a woman.

Instead, Erin had mumbled something almost incoherent about him not being the sort to give in to blackmail. And, uneasily aware that she'd come nowhere close to answering the question, she'd fled the office for the anonymity of the elevator and the lobby.

So much for thinking on her feet—the best qualification of the personal assistant. If she'd had her wits about her, she'd have thrown the question right back at him. *Shall I offer Ms. Worth my best wishes on your engagement tonight?* she could have asked. That would have stopped him in his tracks and made him think better of asking silly questions.

Unless he was actually considering marrying Cecile Worth.

Surely not, Erin thought. He had more sense than that.

And yet, the worthy Cecile had outlasted all the others, and there was no sign as yet that her attraction was waning. In fact, the woman seemed more sure of herself with every passing day. So far she hadn't actually started issuing orders to Slater's staff, but Erin expected that day wasn't far off.

"And it will be closely followed by me starting a job search," she muttered. The idea of answering to Cecile was intolerable, but Erin had no doubt that once she was established as Mrs. Livingstone, Cecile wouldn't hesitate to treat Slater's employees as her personal flunkies.

But not Erin, she decided. Thanks to an excellent salary, she had reserves to carry her through a few months without a job. And there were other companies, other bosses—probably not as good or as interesting as Control Dynamics and Slater Livingstone were, but…

Erin was so preoccupied with sketching out a job search that she walked past the tiny florist's cart in the lobby and out the door. She was retracing her steps when a voice called her name from across the lobby and she turned to see one of Control Dynamics' mid-level advertising executives coming toward her.

It was too late to duck into the gift shop, and if she tried he'd probably follow her anyway. "Hello, Dax." She tried to keep her tone friendly but without enthusiasm; the last thing she needed was to encourage Dax Porter to develop any more interest in her. He was already hanging around the office more than she liked—hand-delivering things which could perfectly well have been sent through interoffice mail, telling Sarah jokes, and asking Erin out. The fact that she hadn't yet accepted an invitation didn't seem to faze him.

He dropped into step beside her as she approached the wicker cart, his highly polished wingtips clicking against the granite floor. "A pretty woman like you shouldn't have to buy flowers for yourself."

"Thanks, Dax," Erin said crisply, and smiled at the young man behind the cart. "Tonio, I need every stem you have left, I don't care what kind as long as it's white. And I also need you to start a delivery service outside the building, so I can stop worrying about flowers every time Mr. Livingstone throws a dinner party."

Tonio grinned and with practiced ease began selecting flowers from the burst of beauty on the cart and laying them carefully on a sheet of waxed paper.

"Another party?" Dax said. "If you can call it a party when it's business—and a pretty dull business at that."

Erin gathered up the bundle. "That dull business is

what pays our salaries,'' she reminded. ''Tonio, if you can take the bill up to Sarah, she'll make sure it's paid right away.''

''Sorry,'' Dax said. ''I didn't mean to insult your precious Mr. Livingstone.'' He snagged a red rose from a water-filled cup and presented it to her with a bow. ''For the woman who's always buying flowers, here's one just for you.''

How could she refuse a gesture of apology, even one which she suspected was half intended to be mocking? Erin took the rose, admiring its deep color, its heavy fragrance. ''It's very thoughtful of you, Dax.''

He was pulling out his wallet as she crossed the lobby. Erin looked down at the rose with true appreciation—for paying for the flower had slowed Dax down just enough that he couldn't manufacture an excuse to join her.

If the worthy Cecile really thought Slater's apartment was stodgy, the woman needed her head examined, Erin thought as she said hello to the doorman in the lobby and took the Art Deco elevator to the top floor. Though the building had started life more than a hundred years ago as a department store, the process of converting it had created luxurious homes which boasted not only every possible convenience but the light and air and space which no builder could afford in modern construction. Where else could one have a living room with an eighteen-foot ceiling—as Slater did?

When she had time, Erin loved to lean over the balcony rail outside Slater's front door and look up at the stained-glass dome, only a few feet overhead, which sent rays of colored light cascading down through the atrium to the department store's old crest, still inlaid in the mosaic-tile floor eight stories below.

But today there was no time. She rang the bell and shifted her burden of flowers to a more comfortable angle.

Jessup opened the door, and a wave of relief crossed his normally impassive face as Erin stepped into the marble-floored foyer. "I knew I could rely on you, Miss."

"What's gone wrong?"

"The flowers, of course. And then the caterer showed up without the extra waiter we asked for. Said the man just didn't come to work today, and they didn't have a substitute. They've always been so reliable before, we've never had a problem—"

"And with ten for dinner, you could use a hand. I'm afraid I'm no good at actually serving—I'd stick my thumb in the duchesse potatoes for sure. But I can keep things organized in the kitchen so you can concentrate on the dining room."

"That would be most helpful, Miss. Of course—" Jessup's voice was dire. "There'll be something else go wrong before the party's over. Things always happen in threes, Miss. But now that you're here—"

Erin feigned horror. "You're relying on *me* to prevent disaster? But I was relying on *you*, Jessup!" She laughed at his stern frown. "Come on, things will be all right. Start making me a list of what needs to be done in the kitchen while I take a stab at the flowers."

He'd been right; the centerpiece which had been delivered looked as if it had been left to sit without water for hours. She was weaving the last of Tonio's carnations and mums into the arrangement when Jessup came quietly into the dining room.

"Miss Reynolds, I'm very much afraid that the guests will be arriving any minute."

Erin turned the centerpiece around so she could inspect it from all sides. "And Mr. Livingstone's not here?"

''He came in a few minutes ago, and he's changing clothes. But Miss Worth hasn't arrived.''

Erin checked her wristwatch. She'd definitely told Cecile when the party would start, and it was well past the time when a careful hostess would have been ready for her guests. ''She's probably been held up. There's disaster number three, Jessup, so now you can relax. Drinks in the living room?''

''The tray is already in place. I'll clear the debris here, Miss.'' Jessup set the centerpiece on the table and began gathering up loose stems and discarded flowers. ''If you'd like to freshen up—''

Erin glanced down at her off-white linen suit, too crumpled from a day at the office for easy restoration. ''Do you honestly think it'll do any good?'' she asked, but she meekly followed his directions toward the bedroom wing.

She'd never before gone beyond the more public portions of Slater's apartment, and she had to admit to being intrigued. The living and dining rooms, with their enormously high ceilings and dark oak moldings, bore the tasteful touch of a master designer, complete with Oriental rugs and elegant furnishings. They were showpieces, but they were also as comfortable as such formal spaces could be. Still, she doubted Slater spent much time there.

She presumed the room opposite the dining room, on the other side of the grand foyer, was an office, but on her other visits the doors had always been closed. When she'd arrived earlier, they'd once more been sealed off, the room silent and mysterious as always. Now she was surprised to see that the rich wood panels had been pushed partway back into the wall pockets, and the temptation to take a look was more than she could bear.

Beyond the half-open doors lay a wonderland, and Erin's eyes widened in astonishment. Though there was a desk in the center of the room, this was far different from the efficient and uncluttered office where Slater spent his days. This room, like the more public ones, was two full stories high, and a spiral stair led halfway up to a balcony which ran around all four sides of the room. The walls on both levels were lined with bookshelves. Many were fitted with glass doors, and behind them gleamed rich gold trim on leather bindings.

Musty old books, Cecile had called them—and for someone who didn't appreciate the beauty not only of old leather bindings but of the words housed inside, this room might well seem dull.

Erin took a deep breath, savoring the scent of supple leather and old ink and fragile paper.

The occasional shipment to the office had given Erin no idea of the true extent of Slater's collection. Even the thousands of old and no doubt rare editions didn't fill the space. Most of the shelves were open, pleasantly stacked with an assortment of books so random and eclectic that it was obvious this was no designer's showcase library but the real thing, well-used and loved.

''One thing's sure,'' she said to herself. ''Cecile doesn't know a good thing when she sees it.''

She wondered if Slater would recognize a bad one.

CHAPTER TWO

ERIN did what she could with limited resources, but she still felt sadly inadequate when she left the guest bedroom with her makeup refreshed and her skirt smoothed as best she could. A lacy camisole to substitute for her tailored blouse would have helped, as would a splashier pair of earrings and a nice gold necklace. As it was, she was going to stand out wildly against the other women in the group. And what would be worse—letting them feel insulted because their hostess hadn't bothered to dress up for the occasion, or telling them that the real hostess hadn't bothered to show up at all?

In something close to desperation, Erin checked every drawer and closet shelf in the entire guest room closet, hoping that somewhere in the miscellaneous clutter which usually built up in guest rooms—left-behind magazines, odd bits of jewelry, an overlooked scarf—she might find something useful.

There was nothing to be found but an empty laundry bag. Either Jessup was extremely conscientious about returning things to their owners, or Slater's overnight guests had been a pathologically neat bunch.

Or else, she thought wryly, *the visitors most likely to leave things behind—the feminine ones—hadn't used the guest room.*

''And just what would you expect?'' she mocked herself. Only a fool would assume that Slater's female friends were platonic ones.

She almost ran headlong into Slater himself at the library door; just as she hurried toward the living room he stepped into the hallway and turned to pull the doors closed behind him. He was immaculately dressed in a perfectly-fitted black tuxedo, and he looked as if he'd had all afternoon to make sure every detail was in place.

Erin thought he was looking at her a bit oddly—but of course, he wouldn't have expected her to be in the private wing.

"Thanks for staying till everything's taken care of, Erin."

"Is Cecile here, then?" Relief surged over her, followed instantly by droll humor. This was the first time she'd felt so much as a twinge of eagerness to see the worthy Cecile.

The living room was mere steps away; rather than answering, Slater strolled down the hall. At the column-flanked archway which separated living room from foyer, he paused, surveyed the empty room, and said, "Apparently not." He turned to Erin and one dark eyebrow quirked upward.

"She knew to the minute when she was expected," Erin said, and then forced herself to stop. She had no reason to feel responsible for Cecile's tardiness, but the surest way to cause herself trouble was to act defensive. If it appeared she had something to feel guilty about, Slater might even think she'd arranged this non-appearance to make Cecile look bad…

That was doubtful, Erin thought dryly. *If I had engineered this, I'd have taken care to provide myself with better clothes!*

The doorbell rang, and a couple of minutes later Jessup appeared in the archway with the first guests. Erin thought he looked a bit frazzled. Perhaps, even though he'd been the one to suggest she should prepare herself to play hostess, he was only now recognizing the situation's implications. If Erin was occupied with the guests, she could hardly be any help in the kitchen.

If he's right that bad news comes in threes, Erin thought, *Jessup's working on his second set of the evening!*

All eight of the guests had arrived and Jessup was serving hot hors d'oeuvres in the living room when the bell rang once more. Erin froze for an instant, forced herself to smile at the guest whose last sentence she had only half heard, and then set her wineglass down so she could take the silver tray from Jessup's hands. "I'll take care of this, Jessup, while you answer the bell."

He gave her a speaking glance and crossed the foyer, leaving the living room doors half open. Cecile Worth fluttered in, shrugged her satin cape to the floor so Jessup had to bend over to retrieve it, and rushed across the foyer. Ignoring the guests, she went straight to Slater. "Darling, I'm so sorry to be late. I do hope I haven't missed anything?" She managed to offer her cheek to be kissed and at the same time give the room a professional survey. "No, I see I haven't," she added very softly, before raising her voice once more. "How elegant that you've acquired a maid—oh, no, it's just little Erin. I'm so sorry, dear, for mistaking you for something you aren't."

I, on the other hand, Erin thought grimly, *have never suffered any illusions about what you really are!* She handed the silver tray back to Jessup, murmured to the guest she'd been talking to, "Perhaps sometime we'll have a chance to finish our conversation, Mrs. Brannagan," and excused herself.

A few minutes later, in the kitchen, Erin gave the soup kettle a last, almost violent stir and sent fragrant broth surging over the side. She swore and grabbed the corner of her apron to mop up the mess.

Jessup handed her a damp cloth. ''The best method,'' he said without looking directly at her, ''would be ground glass in the oysters. If she notices it at all, she'll think it's just sand, and it'll kill her very painfully.''

Erin laughed. ''Thanks for the tip. I'll keep it in mind.'' With her sense of humor back in proportion, she poured consommé into a china tureen, garnished it with herbs, and moved on to the next item on Jessup's list.

By the time dinner was finished, she had a much greater respect for caterers, waiters and butlers. ''And I wasn't even dealing directly with the consumer,'' she said. ''I don't know how you do it, Jessup. I'm going home this minute to put up my feet.''

Jessup set the remainder of the chocolate torte on the counter. ''Mr. Livingstone asked me to give you the message, Miss, that he'd like to talk to you afterward.''

Erin could think of a dozen possible topics, none of which she really wanted to tackle at this hour. ''Has he considered the office, in the morning?'' she asked. ''That's enough *afterward* to suit me.''

''I don't think that was what he had in mind. They've almost finished dessert, and these parties don't generally last long after that. If you'd like to wait in the library, I'll bring you some tea.''

Erin wavered, and surrendered. She didn't much care where she rested her feet; she might have a problem with getting up again once she sat down, but she'd deal with that later. And she might never get another excuse to look more closely at Slater's books.

''Add a slice of that torte,'' she bargained, ''and I won't even notice how late the party lasts.''

Despite the coziness of the book-lined walls and the

overstuffed furniture, the library felt chilly—a combination, Erin thought, of its windowless position toward the center of the building and the dark, cold glass of the skylight overhead, frosted to provide soft daytime illumination while filtering out the harsh rays which might harm the delicate books. Jessup lit the gas log in the fireplace, and Erin settled contentedly in front of it with her torte, her cup of tea, and a biography of Napoleon which happened to be lying on the floor beside her chair with a slip of paper protruding from chapter twelve.

But it wasn't long before she'd abandoned dessert, drink, and chair to survey the treasures which surrounded her.

She was so absorbed by a case filled with miniature books that she didn't notice the whisper-quiet movement of the pocket doors. Not until she heard Cecile's voice did she look around, and then she realized that she was under the balcony, in the farthest and most shadowed corner of the room, where they might not see her. Even Slater, though he'd asked her to stay, might not realize she was in the library; suggesting she wait there might have been entirely Jessup's idea. Unless one of them spotted her abandoned tea tray…

Cecile flung herself invitingly onto an overstuffed couch. ''At least that's finally over,'' she said. ''Call Jessup to get us a drink, darling, and then come here and…relax with me.''

Slater closed the library doors. ''You've already had plenty to drink, and I'm not interested in relaxing. I asked you to be my hostess, Cecile. When you agreed, you took on certain responsibilities—including, if necessary, concealing your boredom from my guests.''

Cecile bristled.

Erin considered knocking a book off the shelf just to

let them know she was present, but she suspected that Slater might see that as a worse sin than mere eavesdropping. She moved out into the light, forgetting the tiny volume she still held in her hands. ''Pardon me, I'll just slip out while you—''

Cecile's eyebrows soared. ''What's *she* still doing here?''

''That's my business,'' Slater said crisply, ''not yours.''

Cecile shook her head, almost sadly. ''Slater, you poor innocent, if you can't see what she's up to—''

Erin looked through her and straight at Slater. ''If you'll excuse me, sir,'' she said, ''surely whatever it was you wanted to tell me will keep till tomorrow?''

Cecile sniffed.

Slater stepped into Erin's path. ''Please wait, Erin. This won't take long.'' He faced Cecile. ''We are not going to sidetrack this conversation by discussing Erin. We're talking about you.''

''No, we're not,'' Cecile said. ''You're giving me a lecture, and I won't stand for it. I told you why I was late. I couldn't help it.''

''Running into friends is not a good enough excuse. At the least, you owe Erin an apology for having to stand in for you.''

Cecile's gaze flicked disdainfully over Erin. ''You actually think she minded the chance to play grown-up? Slater, can you really be as naive as you sometimes appear?''

''On the whole,'' he said, ''it's doubtful.''

Erin heard the warning in his voice; Cecile apparently didn't, for she went straight on. ''You should be glad I agree to put up with these stuffy people for any length of time at all. I've asked you before to invite some of my friends—''

''To provide a contrast?'' Slater sounded perfectly polite.

''Naturally. If you're going to expect me to play hostess to this crowd, the least you could do is let me have some interesting people, too. Next time—''

''But my dear Cecile,'' Slater said, ''I wouldn't dream of subjecting you to this sort of torture again.''

Cecile blinked, and then smiled. ''Well, at least you finally understand how much you've been asking of me. And as long as you're flexible about who we invite, of course I'll do my part in return and put up with your business acquaintances once in a while—''

''*We* are not going to be inviting anyone. And you will not be asked to act as hostess here again. Is that clear enough?''

Cecile's jaw dropped. ''You're just going to dump me? After all I've—''

''—Invested in trying to capture me?'' Slater said. ''Please, Cecile, if you must be tedious, go and do it somewhere else.'' He took two steps toward the fireplace and touched a bell under the mantel. ''Jessup will make sure you have cab fare.''

Jessup arrived so quickly that Erin couldn't help but wonder whether he'd been hovering in the hallway. She stayed in the shadows as the butler ushered a stone-faced Cecile out. The gas log hissed, but there was no other sound in the room.

Slater was standing very still, one elbow braced on the mantel, staring down at the fire as if he'd just completed the hardest job he'd ever faced.

Erin was startled. She'd never thought of Slater as the tender-hearted sort. Certainly he didn't hesitate when business grew cut-throat, and he was not inclined to mince words, no matter whose feelings might be hurt in the process. Besides, so far as Erin could see, Cecile didn't have any feelings to hurt.

She was surprised—given Cecile's bad behavior—that it had apparently taken so much resolve for Slater to givc the woman her comeuppance. But why else would he be staring at the fire as if he was looking at eternity—and not liking what he saw?

No matter what the cause of his preoccupation, he seemed oblivious to Erin. He hadn't spoken or even looked in her direction since Cecile had stalked across the room. Perhaps, she thought, he'd asked her to stay only in order to have a witness, and now he was wishing she'd just slip away?

She started to edge toward the door, but she'd made little progress by the time Jessup spoke from just outside the library. ''Ms. Worth is on her way, sir.''

Slater turned. ''Thank you, Jessup. That'll be all for tonight. I'll lock up after I drive Ms. Reynolds home.''

Erin drew herself up straight. ''There's no need to bother,'' she said. ''I'll take a cab myself. I should have walked down with Cecile and saved Jessup a trip to the lobby—but I can't say I'm sorry not to have her company.'' She smiled at the butler. ''If you wouldn't mind seeing me out—''

''Good night, Jessup.'' Slater's voice was quiet, but there was no mistaking the command in it.

Was it Erin's imagination, or was there a glimmer of sympathy in the butler's fleeting glance at her? ''Yes, sir.'' His retreating footsteps were almost silent on the marble floor.

Slater waved a hand at the pair of armchairs in front of the fire. ''Sit down, Erin.''

She didn't move. ''If I'm being called on the carpet—''

''What on earth for?''

"I have no idea," she said frankly. "But you're barking orders as if you think I set Cecile up to be late."

A half smile tugged at the corner of his mouth. "*And* suggested that the best way to my heart was to be rude to my guests. What a talented manipulator you are to have convinced Cecile to believe that one. Will you sit down, please?"

Erin complied. The tapestry upholstery had grown warm from the gas log, and the heat absorbed by the chair soaked into her back as she sank against it, relaxing muscles she hadn't realized were tense. "How did the party go?"

"Progress, I think. There were no firm commitments made, of course, but Brannagan loosened up as the evening wore on, so I'm sure it'll be all right. I'll need a letter of intent on my desk first thing tomorrow morning—I want it ready the moment he decides to sign it."

"I gave the draft to Sarah this afternoon."

He leaned back in his chair and studied her. "Are you psychic, Erin, or just confident I'd pull this deal off?"

"Neither." The dancing flames were almost hypnotic, she thought. "It's sheer laziness."

One dark eyebrow quirked. "Oh, really?"

"Of course. If I hadn't roughed out that document this afternoon, I'd have to get up at a ghastly hour in the morning, try to think before I'd even absorbed my first cup of coffee, and probably type the thing myself to boot."

"Laziness," he agreed, but there was a twinkle in his eyes. "And of course that's why you stayed around all evening and helped Jessup in the kitchen, too."

"No," Erin said. "That was so I could sample the leftovers."

She expected him to throw back his head and laugh.

Instead, Slater watched her thoughtfully, and there was no amusement in his voice. ''You're always there, Erin. Anticipating what needs doing, pitching in—''

Warily, she said, ''If you're suspicious that Cecile might have some reason for that crazy accusation of hers, let me assure you that I am not trying to snare you, I'm merely doing my job.''

''Of course,'' he agreed. ''And doing it very well.''

Despite the compliment, Erin found herself feeling a little flat—the effect of pure exhaustion, no doubt. If the reason he'd wanted to talk to her was a fairly routine document, why hadn't he dismissed her as soon as she'd told him it was already on his desk? She realized belatedly that she was still holding the small, slim volume she'd picked up just as he and Cecile entered the room, and set it down on the table next to her chair. ''I really can take a cab, you know—''

Slater nodded toward the volume. ''You like my books.''

''It's a remarkable collection. I had no idea you'd acquired so many rare and interesting things. I'd think anybody—''

''Oh, no. When I walked in a few minutes ago, you looked like a debutante who'd been turned loose in Tiffany's after closing time and told to fill her pockets.''

''Did I?'' Erin was cautious. ''They say diamonds are a girl's best friend, but I always thought they wouldn't be much company on a lonely evening. Too cold, too hard, too self-centered.''

He sounded puzzled. ''Self-centered?''

''All the fire is concentrated on the inside.'' Erin felt a little foolish at having to admit the fanciful image.

''I see.'' Almost abruptly, he added, ''Cecile owed you an apology.''

It was fascinating, Erin thought, that her description of something which was totally unrelated had obviously brought Cecile to his mind. Perhaps it hadn't been as difficult for him to send her away as it had appeared—if the words *cold, hard,* and *self-centered* made him think of her. "Yes, she did," Erin agreed. "Is that why you wanted me to listen in to that little spat?"

"May I make an apology for her?"

"I doubt she'd appreciate your stepping in. Besides, *you* don't owe me one."

"I invited her in the first place."

Erin smiled. "All right. I'll accept your regrets for that. And I'm glad you sent her away. She—" She leaned back in her chair, soothed by the warmth of the fire, suddenly too tired to edit her thoughts or to wonder if tomorrow she would regret the personal nature of what she was about to say. "She wasn't right for you."

"I don't suppose you'd like to tell me why you think so."

If you don't already know, what's the point of elaborating? Erin thought. "Not particularly. And I don't suppose you'd really like to sit there and listen to my diagnosis, so—"

"You were much more flattering about me this afternoon, when you said I'm not the sort to give in to blackmail."

"That wasn't flattery," Erin protested.

"I know it wasn't. That's what made it such a compliment. Still, whether or not she was attempting blackmail, Hermione hit on a good point. Several of them, as a matter of fact."

Erin was feeling more lost by the moment.

Slater looked around the room, as slowly and carefully if he was seeing it for the last time and memorizing each detail. Then he leaned slightly forward in his chair, and the firelight cut his face into sharply-shadowed planes as he said, "Erin, will you marry me?"

The words seemed to echo inside her head, and the room suddenly felt like a carnival fun house in which everything looked perfectly normal but was bent at impossible angles. Erin stared at him; her fingers clenched the arms of her chair in an effort to keep herself from sliding onto the floor. *"What?"*

Slater didn't answer. He crossed the room to a shelf she hadn't noticed before and lifted a decanter. "A glass of brandy?"

"No, thanks," Erin said crisply. "And if you need a bracer even to repeat the question, I think that ought to be the end of the entire subject, don't you?"

"Not at all." He poured two snifters and handed her one. "Just in case you change your mind. It's very good brandy. I'm not reluctant to repeat the question, Erin, I just don't think that would get us anywhere. I'd rather tell you why I asked it."

"It's really not—"

"Necessary? What was it you told me just last week, about the need to have all the pertinent information before making a decision, in order to be certain of reaching a wise one?"

"I was talking about a very important contract."

"And the one I'm suggesting would also be."

Once started, Erin realized, he was obviously not going to stop. There seemed to be no option but to listen and then let him down as easily as possible. Or would it be better, perhaps, to treat the whole thing with humor? She let a note of amusement creep into her voice. "Well, please don't tell me that your aunt Hermione's letter inspired you to realize that you've fallen in love with me—because the idea is absolutely ludicrous.''

He smiled, slowly and gently, as if she was being very foolish. ''Give me some credit for knowing that you're not gullible enough to swallow a tale like that. You're quite right, it *is* ludicrous.''

At least he's being sensible about that much, Erin thought.

''You're also not vain—you know perfectly well that a declaration of affection which was based on an old lady's eccentric ideas wouldn't be very complimentary.''

''Any man who couldn't figure out how he felt without Aunt Hermione's interference wouldn't be much of a prize,'' Erin agreed.

''Exactly. And if you were either gullible or vain enough to believe a story like that, you'd hardly be the sort of woman I was looking for, anyway.''

Despite herself, Erin was intrigued. ''What kind of woman *are* you looking for?''

''Maybe it would be easier to list what I don't want. I'm not interested in a trophy wife whose only function is to be decorative—''

''Thank you,'' Erin said crisply. ''I think.''

''I didn't say you weren't decorative, I said beauty alone isn't enough. I'm also not looking for a woman who thinks only of herself and wants me to be constantly entertaining her.''

She couldn't stop herself. ''Like Cecile.''

''And a few others,'' Slater agreed. ''The women I meet in the run of things aren't at all the kind I'm looking for as a partner.''

''Maybe you're looking in the wrong places.''

''Amazingly enough, that idea had occurred to me.'' His voice was dry. ''It's the main reason why we're having this talk—because when I looked around, I saw... you.''

''And what exactly made me eligible for the short list?''

''The qualities which attracted me, you mean? You're solid. Sensible. Practical.'' Slater sipped his brandy.

''Very flattering.''

''As a matter of fact, it's intended to be. Would you rather hear a silly ode to your beautiful eyes?''

''Of course not.''

''I didn't think so. The job of corporate wife isn't really much different from what you're doing right now, you know. That's why I'm so certain you're right for the position.''

''So what you're really proposing,'' Erin said thoughtfully, ''is a sort of business marriage. A personal assistant, if you will, who just happens to have a very long-term employment contract.'' Just when, she asked herself in astonishment, had she stopped thinking this was funny and started taking him seriously?

''And some extra perks, of course.''

Erin's muscles tightened. Precisely what about this incredible proposal did Slater think would be a bonus?

He seemed not to notice her sudden stillness. ''For instance, there will be a certain amount of travel.''

Erin thought wryly that Slater's kind of traveling could hardly be considered a benefit. He'd been around the world, but it seemed to Erin he'd seen little more than airports and offices.

''A lifestyle that's far from shabby.'' He glanced around the library once more as if to emphasize the point. ''A great deal of freedom to do exactly as you liked—I certainly wouldn't expect that every moment of your time be devoted to my projects. A wardrobe, probably far more extensive than you have now. A substantial private income.''

''In effect, you'd be paying me more for doing the same work I am now.''

''Essentially, yes.''

''Why?'' Erin asked baldly. ''So you'll never have to fuss about finding a hostess again?''

''That's a good part of it.''

Erin gave him points for honesty. ''Saving you from the Ceciles of the world...what a mission.''

''And also because I happen to think we fit—you and I. We work together well. This gives us a chance to guarantee a good combination—to make it permanent.''

''That's a benefit from your point of view,'' Erin said. ''Having a personal assistant who can't ever resign.''

''And for you—there's the security of knowing you'll never have to worry about a paycheck again. Or much of anything else, either.''

For a long moment the only sound in the room was the soft hiss of the fire. Erin stared at the flames and wished she could pretend none of this was happening. If only they were simply sitting beside the fire, having a friendly chat about books...

But Slater had asked a question, and he was waiting for an answer. ''Look,'' she said, ''I'm very flattered. And I'm sorry—''

''Don't say things if you don't mean them, Erin.''

''All right,'' she said irritably, ''I'll be blunt. The answer's no. I hope you won't take it personally, because it's not you I'm refusing, exactly. It's just that I want more than a marriage of convenience. I want a family—'' She felt as if she was stumbling over her own tongue. ''Someday, I mean, not right now. But you must see that I can't honestly—''

"So do I." His voice was so soft that for a moment Erin wasn't certain she'd heard him correctly.

She swallowed hard. "You can't mean... You're actually suggesting... But of course you are. It's part of the corporate executive's wife's job to produce the perfect little family, isn't it? Football players and ballet dancers, I suppose, and honor students as well?"

Slater was silent for so long that she began to regret letting the sarcastic note creep into her voice. Had she hit a nerve so deep he wasn't going to answer at all?

"I would very much like to have a family," he said finally. "Like you, I'm in no hurry. And I don't have any particular requirements for my children, either."

Erin felt just a little ashamed of herself.

"I quite understand that you aren't comfortable with the idea just now, and I'm content to leave the final decision for the future."

"And if—assuming I was to accept this incredible offer—the time never came that I was comfortable with the idea?"

"Then we would still have the partnership we started out with."

The gas log hissed. Drops of rain spattered against the skylight far above.

How sad for Slater, Erin thought, that he honestly believed that the deal he was offering was the best that a marriage could be. And how doubly sad it would be if he committed himself to such a makeshift marriage and then found a woman he truly loved—for his sense of honor would hold him to his promise.

"Thank you," Erin said. "And I really mean that. I *am* honored. But—" She couldn't bring herself to say the words again.

"But your answer is still no?"

She took a deep breath. ''Listen to yourself, sir.''

''Do you suppose you could drop the *sir,* Erin?''

''You're settling for something that wouldn't even be second-best, and down deep you know it—I can hear it in your voice.''

From the way his eyes darkened, Erin knew she'd hit the mark precisely. Not that she expected him to admit it openly, of course.

''Someday,'' she said, ''a woman will come along that you can really care for, and when you feel the magic of loving someone, you'll know the difference.''

''That's a magic you've experienced in the past, obviously. Or do you mean you're experiencing it now?''

Erin hesitated. *When exactly would I have time?* she wanted to ask, but she expected he'd just turn that around into another reason for accepting him. ''Believe me, I know what I'm talking about.''

Slater shook his head. ''I think it simply means you're very innocent. It's been my experience that magic is greatly overrated where relationships are concerned. It so frequently turns to melodrama instead.''

He sounded very tired.

Erin put her half-full brandy snifter aside and stood up. ''Not every woman's like Cecile,'' she said. ''And when you meet the right one, and discover that I'm absolutely correct about that magic—just send me a thank-you card, all right?''

CHAPTER THREE

ERIN offered once more to take a cab, but Slater briskly told her not to be ridiculous. "At this time of night there'll be a half-hour wait just to get one dispatched. If you let me drive you, you'll be home before that, and so will I." He walked down the balcony hallway beside her and summoned the elevator.

"I just thought—" she began weakly.

He stepped back to let her precede him, and pushed the button for the garage level. "If you're worried about me annoying you," he said shrewdly, "you needn't. Only an idiot would believe that some fool stunt like kissing you goodnight would change your mind."

Erin felt herself coloring a little. He didn't quite have it right, but he was uncomfortably close to reading her thoughts. It wasn't the question of Slater's behavior that concerned her; he might be merciless in the boardroom, but she couldn't begin to picture him forcing her—or any woman—against her will. She couldn't imagine him wanting to use coercion on an unwilling woman when there were plenty who would happily cooperate.

No, she wasn't afraid of *him.* She was afraid that their conversation tonight would change everything—the easy atmosphere in the office, the smooth working relationship between them, the effortless exchange of ideas. If she had to start watching everything she said for fear of how he might interpret each word…

"Can we just forget this happened?" she said plaintively.

''I think we'd be better off not to try.'' He guided her toward a red convertible in a sheltered corner of the garage. ''But you needn't be concerned that I'll bring the subject up again. I asked my question, and I got my answer. I'm not crazy enough to think that merely asking it again would get me a different one.''

''Good,'' Erin said. ''Because I do like working with you, and I'd hate to have that messed up.'' Relieved, she settled into the deep leather seat. ''This is new, isn't it?''

''The car? Yes.''

''I never suspected you were the convertible type.'' Too late, she realized that she'd practically issued an invitation for him to tell her all sorts of things she'd never known about him. The kind of personal things she'd just as soon not know about a man who was—despite that incredible proposal—never going to be anything more than her boss.

But Slater was as good as his word; he didn't seize the excuse. ''Just consider it part of my mid-life crisis,'' he said dryly.

Erin, grateful for the teasing note in his voice, wrinkled her brow. ''You're not old enough to have one.''

''A sports car?''

''A mid-life crisis. You've got at least ten years to go.''

''I was always precocious. Just ask my aunt Hermione.''

Erin laughed and put her head back against the leather seat. She half wished he'd taken the time to put the top down. Though the night air would be too crisp for true comfort, there was something inviting about the idea of a chilly breeze tugging at her hair and refreshing her brain, clearing away the complicated thoughts of the last hour and leaving only enjoyment.

When the car pulled up in front of her town house, Erin noted that the living room lights were on. At this hour, her mother would normally have doused all but the hall light and gone to bed. She certainly wouldn't be waiting up for Erin; that had been part of their pact two years ago when Angela Reynolds had moved in to share her daughter's home.

She might have company, of course, though Erin's quick glance up and down the street didn't reveal any cars she recognized. Angela hadn't dated much since her divorce, but there had been a couple of men. Men sort of like Dax, Erin thought with a smile—more interested in Angela than she was in them.

"Just drop me off in front," she said.

As if he hadn't heard, Slater parked the convertible in the space nearest the town house and came around to open Erin's door.

"Really," she protested. "You don't need—"

"You might as well save your breath, Erin, because I'm going to walk you to the house no matter what you say." There was no argumentativeness in his voice, only a simple statement of fact.

And though Erin could have pointed out that she got herself home after dark on a regular basis without any escort at all, she knew it would be a waste of time. "Yes, sir," she said and dropped into step beside him.

He glanced down at her, one eyebrow raised in a silent comment on her assumed meekness. After a year of working together, Erin thought, he didn't need to say a word to get the message across.

He didn't touch her, not even to take her arm. Nevertheless Erin found herself almost holding her breath as she put her key in the lock. Despite his reassurances earlier, would he try to take advantage of the situation? *Only an idiot would believe some fool stunt like kissing you goodnight would change your mind,* he'd said. And yet...what would she do if he tried?

Her back was turned to him as she fumbled with the key, but she was aware that he was standing very close; she could feel the warmth of him blocking the chilly breeze. He reached over her shoulder, and his sleeve brushed her hair. Erin jerked away just as he pushed the door open and stepped back.

"See you tomorrow," Slater said, and a moment later he was gone into the shadows of the night.

Look who's talking about idiots, Erin told herself. *Have you ever known Slater Livingstone not to keep his word?*

The living room lights were dimmed, and the television murmured. On the long couch, Angela Reynolds sat up and flicked the remote control. "Did I hear someone with you outside?"

"Mr. Livingstone brought me home."

"Why didn't you invite him in? I'd like the chance to meet him."

"At this hour?"

"How late is it?" Angela peered at the clock. "It must have turned into quite a party."

"That's for sure." Erin considered dropping down beside the couch and telling her mother about Slater's impossible proposal. But she'd already dealt with the question; what else could Angela add? "I thought you'd be in bed."

"I must have dozed off," Angela said. "I had a headache earlier, and an upset stomach. Probably ate something that didn't agree with me." She yawned and pushed herself up off the couch.

Erin said goodnight and retreated to her own room. But the darkness she had longed for didn't bring oblivion, only a swirling kaleidoscope of thoughts and images. Again and again, however, she saw Slater's face as he had so earnestly asked her to marry him.

What an absurd, unforeseen question it had been. She'd tried to handle it sensitively, defusing an awkward incident before it led to an impossible situation—before it threatened the job she had come to love. She'd done her best, and there was nothing more she could have done.

You could have said yes.

The whisper in the back of her mind was like an electrical shock forcing her upright. Then she began to laugh at the foolishness of the whole idea. Marry Slater Livingstone? She was too exhausted to think straight, that was the problem, and her mind was playing tricks on her.

She'd given him the only answer she could. The only sensible answer—for both their sakes.

Hadn't she?

Erin overslept, making her doubly glad that she'd already prepared the documents Slater would need when he met with Bob Brannagan that morning to clinch their deal. "And something tells me," she muttered as she stood under the hottest shower she could bear, "that even if I'd said *yes* last night instead of *no,* if that letter of intent wasn't on his desk by nine this morning he wouldn't be very understanding."

She was already mentally sorting the day's list of things to do when she came into the office, and she almost ran headlong into Dax Porter when he slid off the corner of Sarah's desk into her path.

"Sorry," Erin said automatically, and wondered why he'd been sitting there. Surely Sarah wasn't encouraging him to hang around the office—was she?

One look at Sarah dispersed her suspicions, for the secretary was her imperturbable self, with not a hint of guilt or self-consciousness. ''Dax brought up the latest results from the new direct-mail campaign for you.'' There was a teasing glint in her eyes.

As if they wouldn't have survived interoffice mail. ''Very kind of you,'' Erin murmured.

''I thought maybe you'd like me to go over them with you,'' Dax offered. ''There are some interesting trends in the—''

Erin cut him off. ''I'll look over them when I have time.''

''Oh. You are a little late this morning—Livingstone's party got uproarious, no doubt.''

That, Erin thought, was unworthy of comment. ''Sarah, if the Universal Conveyer bid is ready, would you bring it into my office?''

''I've got it here.'' The secretary closed a folder which was lying on her desk blotter and handed it to Erin. ''But the boss wants you right away.''

Dax said, ''If you have any questions about the campaign—''

''I certainly won't hesitate to call you,'' Erin assured him. ''But I'm sure you have work to do in the meantime.'' She waited, trying not to tap her foot impatiently, till Dax was out of sight. ''Can't that man take a hint? Was he annoying you?''

''He's harmless, Erin. He only flirts with me to make a point with you.''

''The point being that I'd better not wait too long or another woman will grab him? If only someone *would.* Why does Mr. Livingstone need me? Was something wrong with the Brannagan letter of intent?''

''I don't think so. He's being an iguanadon today.''

That was a new one, Erin thought. ''Which means?''

''Ferocious-looking but basically harmless. I keep forgetting that you have no reason to know about the more obscure dinosaurs. Those of us who have eight-year-old boys, on the other hand, learn all of this in self-defense.''

''I'll keep that in mind if I ever have a son,'' Erin said.

Slater's words seemed to echo in her head. *I'd very much like to have a family,* he'd said last night...

And just how long am I going to have flashbacks of that conversation? Erin asked herself. *Knock it off, Reynolds—it's over!*

She tapped on the door and went straight in.

Slater's morning mail was laid out neatly on the blotter; on one corner of the glass-topped desk lay a still-folded newspaper. Slater was standing at the window, looking out over downtown St. Louis toward the Mississippi River, but he turned away from the view when he heard her. ''Good morning, Erin.''

The deep timbre of his voice was the same as always, the greeting just as professional, his smile perfectly normal. All she had to do was return the cheerful words and go to work.

But there was a difference anyway. When she looked at him this morning, Erin saw not only the boss she respected but the lonely man who had asked her to share his life.

She'd suggested last night that they ignore the entire episode. But she realized now that she'd been naive to think it was possible. Slater had already known that, obviously. *We'd be better off not to try,* he'd said. And he'd been right; things *had* changed, and there was no changing them back.

''You wanted to see me, sir?'' she asked.

''You forgot something at my apartment last night.''

She frowned, trying to recall what she might have left

behind. She hadn't missed anything. A hairbrush? A lipstick?

Slater moved across the room to the credenza behind his desk and picked up a slender crystal vase containing one red rose. "Jessup seemed to think this was important to you."

Dax's rose. Too bad she couldn't have made use of it last night, but its deep red would have glared in the midst of the all-white centerpiece, so she'd laid it aside while she arranged the rest of Tonio's flowers. She'd forgotten all about it, the poor thing—but Jessup must have picked it up with the discarded stems and put it safely away for her.

She took the vase and sniffed the rose's heady fragrance. It was a particularly beautiful bloom, and it wasn't the flower's fault that it had been Dax who gave it to her. Regardless of the source, it served as a sort of wake-up call, pulling her back to reality before she could let herself drown in a sea of sympathy. She had her own life, after all, and she couldn't fix whatever was wrong with Slater's…

My goodness, aren't we feeling important? she mocked herself. For all she knew, even though he'd been seemed serious last night, perhaps he'd spoken without truly thinking things through. He'd certainly been frustrated enough with Cecile's conduct to have acted in haste—and he might even be feeling this morning that he'd had a lucky escape when Erin hadn't accepted his offer.

She smiled at him over the rose. "Thank you for bringing it, sir. I'll return the vase, of course."

"No hurry." His voice was level. "Jessup will be pleased to know how happy you are to have the flower back. If I'd realized you were seeing someone, Erin, I wouldn't have bothered you with that nonsense last night."

She opened her mouth to assure him that the rose meant nothing, that there was no one special in her life. Then it occurred to her that he might take it personally if she told him, in effect, that she had refused to consider his proposal because she preferred having no one at all in her life to having him. Confused, she glanced up at him and bit her lip. *And you thought you could just pretend this never happened!*

"There's no need to explain," Slater said. "I certainly understand. Now, shall we get down to work, before Bob Brannagan comes in?"

When Erin came out of Slater's office an hour later, carrying the crystal vase and a to-do list which would take her the better part of three days to finish, Sarah eyed the red rose with undisguised interest. But she didn't comment, just waved a thin sheaf of message slips at Erin.

"Anything important?" Erin asked. Her hands were too full even to reach for the bits of paper.

Sarah riffled the slips as if she were dealing cards. "Depends on your point of view. The Senator's secretary called to cancel his visit for Thursday because of an important vote—something to do with the Pentagon."

Erin groaned.

"Know anybody who wants four non-refundable tickets to the ballet?" Sarah went on imperturbably. "Because I just managed to get my hands on them this morning, about ten minutes before she called."

"I'll ask Mr. Livingstone if there's anyone else he wants to invite. Otherwise we'll just put a notice out to the employees—unless you want to take your son?"

"To a ballet? Unless it's set in prehistoric times—"

''Afraid not.''

Sarah shrugged. ''They're missing a sure bet. Dinosaurs in tutus—I bet a lot of people would pay to see that. Also, Mrs. Brannagan called—said she wanted to thank you for the party last night.'' Her eyes were bright with interest. ''Not Mr. Livingstone. Not the worthy Cecile. *You.*''

''We had half of a very nice conversation,'' Erin said. ''And by the way, before you put any more calls through to Mr. Livingstone from Cecile Worth, be sure to ask him if he wants to take them.''

Sarah looked intrigued. ''Another one bites the dust? That's a comfort. I was beginning to think we were stuck with her permanently. I don't suppose you're going to tell me what happened, either.''

Erin lifted an eyebrow. ''Why do you assume that I know?''

''Because you always do. It's like you have radar where his girlfriends are concerned. There are times, you know,'' Sarah grumbled, ''when your standards regarding office gossip are truly annoying.'' She thumbed through the bits of paper. ''I wonder who'll be next. It's about time for a redhead, don't you think? Have you noticed how he almost never goes for brunettes? Do you suppose it's because he has us?''

''No doubt,'' Erin said. She couldn't help but wonder what Sarah would say if she knew about that conversation last night. And she speculated, as she turned away, what Sarah had meant by radar. Didn't any good personal assistant make it a point to know what was going on with the boss?

At lunchtime, Erin left her list on her desk and a file folder open to the task she'd just begun, and told Sarah she was going down to the cafeteria in the lobby. ''Want to deliver

Tonio's check and save me the trip?'' Sarah asked. ''How many flowers did you get yesterday, anyway?''

Erin glanced at the figures on the check and said, ''More than we're paying for.'' She tucked the slip of paper into the pocket of her pin-striped jacket.

Tonio was helping a customer choose the brightest pink carnations from his supply, and Erin waited patiently till he was finished. ''About this bill,'' she said as she handed over the check. ''I'd like to talk to you about it.''

Tonio looked past her, as if he was uneasy. ''Some other time, Miss?'' he murmured and greeted the next customer.

Puzzled, she went on into the cafeteria, picked up a salad from the display, and looked around the crowded dining room for an empty seat. The lobby cafeteria was very good, but it had its drawbacks—including being almost too handy to the office. That, coupled with the fact that it was one of the busiest places around, meant it was a rare day when customers didn't have to share tables, and so co-workers tended to gather in clumps.

And the only empty seat she could see was at a table for four, where Dax Porter was beckoning to her. Across from him, smiling at Erin, were two women who worked in the advertising department.

Erin tried to smother her irritation. With a salad already in her hand, it was too late to pretend she hadn't come for lunch, so she crossed the room and joined them. To make matters worse, she thought, the empty seat was the one next to Dax. If he'd planned it that way, he couldn't have done a better job.

The two women were soon brainstorming an ad slogan, and Erin wanted to point out to them that doing so in public was probably not the wisest way to keep a campaign under wraps.

Dax leaned toward her and said quietly, ''You look worn out. I always thought Livingstone's parties couldn't be much fun. Everybody sitting around talking about systems controls and the best designs for new switching mechanisms...what was the topic *de jour* last night? Fine-tuning safety measures for nuclear power plants?''

''More likely how to keep communications satellites doing precisely what they're supposed to do.''

''It figures. If you brought up a Broadway play, none of them would know what you were talking about.'' Dax looked over her shoulder into the lobby. ''Who's that with Livingstone? Just getting out of the elevator.''

Erin turned to look. Was it the slightly wavy glass of the wall which made Slater—and Bob Brannagan, for that matter—look a bit somber? Or were they just on their way to lunch somewhere, with the fine points of their deal still undecided?

''That's the satellite king of the western hemisphere.'' She poured a little more dressing on her salad and raised her voice in order to cut through the discussion across the table. ''Does anybody here like ballet? We've got some orphaned tickets for Thursday night—''

''Muscular men in tights?'' Dax made a face. ''It's not my kind of thing. But of course if you're going, Erin—''

That was not the best move you've ever made, Erin told herself. ''Sorry, I'm busy that night.''

He nodded. ''That's when the Senator's due, isn't it? Of course you'll be up to your neck in that affair.''

A cafeteria worker appeared beside the table. ''Ms. Reynolds? Your secretary needs you right away.''

Grateful for the reprieve, Erin pushed her salad away. ''Sorry, everybody.''

''Who's the boss up there, anyway?'' Dax asked. ''Sarah?''

"Sometimes," Erin said lightly. She didn't figure it was worth explaining that if Sarah was panicked enough to interrupt her at lunch, something was definitely wrong.

The instant she walked into the office she got the picture. Sitting near Sarah's desk, a magazine open on her lap and her legs elegantly crossed, was the satellite king's wife.

Mrs. Brannagan looked up with a smile. "I'm so sorry," she said. "I didn't realize you'd gone to lunch. I just came along with Bob on the spur of the moment, you see. I was hoping that we could finish the delightful conversation we were having last night when that young woman arrived and you suddenly disappeared. But I didn't realize I was dragging you away from your break."

"It's nothing, Mrs. Brannagan. Would you like to come into my office?"

"Can't I make it up to you by taking you out for lunch? You can't have enjoyed your food—if you had time for any at all—and it would make me feel so much better."

Erin thought of the list of projects lying on her desk, but she knew that none of them would be as important in Slater's eyes as the good will to be gained from better acquaintance with Mrs. Brannagan. The only thing that surprised her about the situation, in fact, was that he'd actually left the office before being assured the woman was properly entertained.

But of course that was Erin's job, and he obviously had faith that she'd carry through. "I'd be delighted, Mrs. Brannagan. Is there somewhere in particular you'd like to go?"

The woman picked up her handbag. "That's part of my problem," she confided. "I know absolutely nothing about St. Louis. So perhaps I can also pick your brain about where to shop, and what to see? And I'd love to go to the top of the Arch, but Bob doesn't like heights and I don't want to go alone.''

''Then we'll do that after lunch,'' Erin said.

Mrs. Brannagan beamed. ''My dear, does Mr. Livingstone have *any* idea how fortunate he is to have you?''

Will you marry me? he had said. *We fit, you and I.*

Solid, sensible, practical Erin, who had turned down a very long, very secure employment contract…

Erin managed to keep her voice light. ''I doubt it. But he hasn't threatened to fire me, so I suppose it doesn't really matter.''

Erin spent most of the afternoon with Frances Brannagan and arrived back in the office just as Sarah was shutting down her computer for the day. She perched on the corner of Sarah's desk and glanced toward Slater's closed door. ''Is he still here?''

''Oh, yes.'' Sarah rolled her eyes. ''I'm not going home, I'm escaping.''

''T. rex?''

''Megalosaurus,'' Sarah said in dire tones.

''That's worse?''

''Infinitely. They preferred even bigger prey.''

The door of the inner office opened and Slater appeared, buttoning his jacket. ''Sarah, if Erin gets back before—'' He paused. ''Did you have a pleasant afternoon?''

Erin shrugged and smothered the desire to point out that she had not, after all, been playing hooky. ''That must be the thousandth time I've ridden to the top of the Arch, but other than that, it was all right. I'll get through as much of the list as I can this evening, sir.''

''It can wait. You're as tired as the rest of us.''

She could hear the heaviness of disappointment in his voice. Instinct made her say, ''Didn't the Brannagan deal come off after all?'' She could read the answer in his eyes. ''But I thought it was pretty much decided. What happened?''

''Brannagan wouldn't say. Come on, I'll drive you home. It's practically on my way.''

When the parking valet brought the convertible around, the top was down. ''Do you mind, Erin? It'll be chilly.''

''The fresh air will feel good. You must be terribly disappointed—you've worked so hard to put that deal together.''

''Horatio Alger to the contrary, hard work does not always pay off.''

''And the strangest things can kill negotiations.''

''The odd thing about it,'' Slater mused, ''is that I don't think the deal is dead altogether. I'd swear he's still just as interested. But unless I can figure out what threw the wrench in the works and fix it, it isn't going to come back to life, either.'' The convertible drew up at a traffic light and he glanced at Erin. ''I don't suppose Mrs. Brannagan let anything slip?''

Erin shook her head. ''Not a word about business—his or yours. The only things she seemed interested in were shopping, sight-seeing and relationships.''

''Sounds like a very exciting afternoon.'' Slater's voice was dry. ''What kind of relationships?''

''Mine, mostly. And then there was Cecile—Mrs. Brannagan didn't seem to hit it off with the worthy Cecile at all, but she couldn't stop commenting about her.''

''Remind me to give you a raise, all right? I'll consider it in the light of combat pay.''

''Thank you,'' Erin said calmly. ''With a raise, I could almost afford to look at the shops she liked best. I was starting to think the woman's a frustrated matchmaker. Do you know if the Brannagans have a grown-up son?''

''Not offhand. Want me to ask?''

''I have a feeling that won't be necessary. If I passed her daughter-in-law test, I'll find out soon enough.'' Erin glanced at her watch as her town house came into sight. ''Would you like to come in for a cup of coffee?'' She thought she caught a hint of surprise in his face, and added hastily, ''My mother should be home, and she asked last night why I didn't invite you in.'' *Oh, that was a great improvement,* she told herself wryly. *Now what's he supposed to think—that I'm dying to have him meet my mother?*

''Thanks,'' Slater said, ''but I have a couple of things to do.''

''Oh—of course. You said this was almost on your way.'' She reached for the door handle.

''I'll come in long enough to say hello, though,'' Slater said, and parked the car in the only vacant spot in the block.

Erin opened the front door and called her mother's name, but there was no answer. ''Maybe she stayed to work late. I'm sorry.''

''Perhaps another time.'' To her relief, Slater's voice was completely casual. ''See you tomorrow, Erin.''

She stepped inside and began to unbutton her coat, letting her eyes adjust to the dimmer light in the front hallway before she moved around the corner toward the closet. As she reached for a hanger, her gaze fell on the shadowed area at the foot of the stairs, and on Angela Reynolds, sprawled on her side on the carpet like a puppet dropped by a careless child. Her eyes were open and dilated, her face gray and drenched with perspiration.

''Mother?'' Erin's voice shook.

Angela muttered something that sounded like gibberish and raised a hand as if to press it against her temple. But she was too weak; the hand dropped to the floor with a thud.

Erin jerked the front door open. ''Slater!'' There was a note just short of hysteria in her voice.

He was already halfway down the sidewalk, but he needed only three strides to reach her. ''What is it, Erin?''

She couldn't speak. Instead, she seized his arm and pulled him inside the town house, to where her mother lay—just as Angela began to gasp for breath.

CHAPTER FOUR

THE ambulance crew was young, professional, and very efficient; despite the fact that Erin could tell them almost nothing about Angela's collapse, it seemed to Erin to be just minutes before they had her mother stabilized and ready to transport.

She started out the door, without her coat, behind the stretcher, only to discover that the rules forbidding anyone except medical personnel from riding along with the patient were as inflexible as polished granite.

Erin started to protest, her voice shaking, her words almost incoherent, but Slater cut her off. ''I'll take you,'' he said firmly, pulling her back inside the town house, and a moment later the ambulance screamed off down the street.

''That's my *mother,*'' Erin stormed. ''How *dare* they not let me go with her?''

''Because the last thing they need while they're trying to take care of her is for you to have hysterics in the ambulance,'' Slater said calmly.

The comment was like a glass of cold water in the face. ''I wouldn't do anything of the sort.''

''No, because you're not going to have the opportunity. Take a deep breath, and as soon as we've checked the house I'll drive you over.''

Erin seized her coat from the floor where she'd dropped it. ''I'm ready to go right now.''

''You won't be able to be with her right away,'' he pointed out. ''Not till they've at least started to get things figured out. So let's take a couple of minutes to be sure we aren't leaving windows open and bathtubs running, or you'll be sitting at the hospital with nothing to do but worry whether everything's all right here.''

She couldn't summon enough logic to argue, so she trailed after him instead as he walked through every room. When he found the teakettle that Angela must have put on the stove, now boiled dry and red-hot, Erin bit her lip and admitted, if only to herself, that she was far too unnerved to act sensibly.

It was Slater who locked the front door, because Erin's hands were shaking too badly to hold the key. And in the waiting room just outside emergency, he got her a cup of coffee from the vending machine, and then held her hand *and* the lukewarm paper cup till she could keep herself steady once more.

The bitter brew hit her like an ax, dissipating the fog which had surrounded her, and Erin shuddered and sat up straighter. For the first time since she'd dragged him into the town house, she looked directly at Slater. ''I'm sorry,'' she said.

He raised his gaze from the muddy contents of his cup, obviously startled. ''For what?''

''All of it. Acting crazy.''

''You do have some excuse, you know.''

She shook her head. ''Not really. And the way I dragged you into this—you did say you had things to do. So—''

''Nothing as important as this.''

''I just meant that if you need to go, sir, I understand.''

''A little while ago,'' Slater mused, ''you used my name.''

''Did I?'' She could hardly remember anything she'd said; she simply knew that at the moment she'd seen her mother lying limp and helpless, her only thought had been that Slater would know precisely what to do. ''Anyway, thanks for bringing me. But there really isn't any need for you to stay now.''

''Are you kicking me out?'' he said levelly. ''If you want to be alone, Erin—''

''No,'' she admitted. ''No, I don't. But—'' She reached almost automatically under the open collar of her blouse for the delicate chain which hung around her neck, rubbing it between two fingers as if it was a talisman.

''Then I'll stay awhile. Is there anyone you need to notify? I'll make the calls, if you like.''

Erin felt a tinge of humor trickle through her. ''You can actually dial a phone? Sarah will be impressed to hear that.''

''Be a sport, Erin—you aren't really going to tell her, are you?'' His tone grew suddenly serious once more. ''Do you have sisters or brothers?''

''No. Neither.'' The weight which had so unexpectedly—and so briefly—lifted crashed back onto her shoulders again. She was entirely alone; if there were decisions to be made, choices Angela couldn't make for herself, it was Erin who would have to carry the burden.

''Don't assume the worst,'' Slater said sharply, as if he'd read her mind. ''Wait till you've got some hard information. In the meantime, there's nothing to be gained by exhausting yourself fretting about the unknown. Keep your strength up for when we know something.''

''Easier to say than do,'' Erin muttered, and was ashamed of herself for carping at him. ''Sorry. I know you're only trying to help.''

Slater didn't answer directly. ''I assume, since your mother lives with you, that your father is deceased?''

"No," Erin said. "Far from it, in fact. But there's no need to call him."

"They're divorced?"

She sighed. "It's been about two years since it was final. So this is really nothing to do with him."

"Still, perhaps your mother would want him to—"

"No." Erin's voice was firm. "Believe me, if she woke up to find Jack Reynolds standing beside her bed, she'd go straight off into a seizure and then we'd really be in the soup."

He was watching her intently, she realized, his gaze focused on her fingertips as she rubbed the dainty chain. She let it drop back out of sight under her collar. "How could I not have known something was so very wrong?" she said. "She told me last night she'd had a headache and an upset stomach, but nothing on this scale. If I'd had any idea—"

"Of course you didn't know. Besides, Erin, she's an adult, fully capable of looking after herself—and obviously she didn't think it was anything serious."

"It could have happened yesterday, when I was gone so long. I might not have found her till too late—"

"Knock it off." His voice was almost rough. "You're driving yourself crazy with could-haves, Erin, and there's no reason for it."

"But she could have lain there for hours before I got home." She stared at him, wide-eyed. "She might have, anyway—because I don't have any idea when she came home from work today."

"I don't think it had been more than a few minutes. Remember the teakettle? It wouldn't have taken long, once it got good and hot, to boil dry."

"Oh, that's right. I'd forgotten about the kettle." She felt herself start to shiver. "It could have started a fire."

"But it didn't. And if you don't cut it out, Erin, I'm going to shake you."

She was silent. "Slater—"

"Yes?"

She didn't know what—if anything—she'd intended to say. Perhaps she'd only been trying out the name. "Nothing. Just—thanks."

They sat in silence while ambulances came and went, while the groups of patients and families in the waiting room formed an ever-changing pattern as the minutes ticked inexorably by.

"Is there anyone else you'd like to have with you?" Slater asked gently. "The man you're so fond of, for instance?"

She was hardly listening. "Which man?"

"The one who gave you the necklace you're caressing."

She hadn't realized she was fingering the chain again. "Oh, this. Actually—"

"And the rose."

Dax? Almost involuntarily, she smiled at the very thought of Dax being summoned to her side. "No, thanks. Not just now."

Slater's paper coffee cup collapsed in his fist. He looked at it for a long moment as if trying to figure out how such a thing had happened, then unclenched his hand and wiped the last few drops of muddy liquid off his fingers with his handkerchief. "Why? Because you don't want to bother him?"

Erin looked at him in surprise before she realized that since Slater didn't know where the rose had come from, he couldn't possibly recognize the humor in the suggestion he'd made. But she couldn't exactly explain it, either. After this morning, when she'd let him believe that there was a special man in her life… *This,* she thought, *is getting incredibly complicated.*

Only then did she pick up the second meaning in his words. ''And I *am* bothering *you,* aren't I? I'm sorry, Slater, really I am. You don't have to stay, just because I said I don't like the idea of waiting alone.''

He glanced down at the wreckage of his cup and said mildly, ''How about some decent coffee?''

''There isn't anything but the machine, is there?''

''No, but within mere blocks there is a world-famous coffeehouse.''

''I don't want to leave here just now,'' Erin pointed out. ''But we'd have to go over, since they don't deliver.''

Slater gave her a slightly wicked grin. ''Do you care to make a bet?'' He dropped his cup in the nearest garbage can and headed for a pay phone.

Erin was toying with a slab of almond biscotti and drinking perhaps the best coffee she'd ever tasted when an emergency room clerk appeared at the waiting room door and called her name.

She'd waited forever for this summons—it seemed years since she'd sat down in the worn vinyl chair. And yet, now that the moment had come, she was terrified. So long as there had been no word, she realized, she'd known that the doctors were still working, that her mother was still fighting. But had the clerk come to give her a diagnosis, or to tell her that Angela was gone, the battle over?

Her fingers were too numb to keep her cup upright. Slater, sitting next to her, caught it, set it aside, and helped her to her feet.

The clerk said, ''Your mother's being moved to intensive care, Miss Reynolds. I'll show you the way.''

Her relief that the news wasn't worse gave way to a

different, almost deeper fear. "Slater," she said in little more than a breath. "You'll come?"

Across the waiting room, an elderly man badly in need of a shave picked up a biscotti from the enormous box the coffee bar had delivered and held it to his forehead in a parody of a salute. "Thanks, Mister!" he said. "This is almost as good as doughnuts!"

There was a chorus of agreement from the other family members, most of whom were holding cups of gourmet coffee.

The clerk looked bemused. "You ordered in enough coffee and biscotti for the whole crowd?"

Slater said earnestly, "Only because when I called the coffee bar, the manager told me they never delivered orders under five hundred dollars."

"It was pretty foolish of him to think that would discourage you," Erin murmured.

"But that's nonsense," the clerk said. "Of course they deliver—for the hospital, at least. We're always calling down for something."

Slater looked momentarily disturbed—not, Erin thought, because he felt he'd been conned into paying far too much, but because he'd been caught doing a good deed.

"Well, please don't tell the crowd in the waiting room," he told the clerk. "They really enjoyed the story about the minimum order, and they were more than willing to help take care of the excess—just to do me a favor."

Erin tried to swallow her sudden case of the giggles and only managed to give herself hiccups.

The clerk led them down the corridor to a cross hallway and gave detailed instructions for the rest of the trip. As soon as she was out of sight, Erin gave way to a fit of laughter. ''The expression on her face....'' she managed to say. ''She was looking at you as if she was quite sure you could benefit from some serious testing yourself!''

The reminder of their reason for being there tipped her laughter over almost into tears, and in sudden white-faced silence she clutched Slater's arm.

She told him again, sometime in the small hours of the morning as they sat in yet another waiting room, outside the intensive-care area where Angela was still undergoing what sounded like every test known to man, that she'd be fine and there was no need for him to stay longer.

''It's a long time between visits when you can only go in for a few minutes at a time,'' he said simply, and he didn't move.

Erin was too touched by his compassion to argue. ''You know first-hand what this is like, don't you?'' He didn't answer right away, and curiosity flared deep inside her. She knew so much about the obscure long-dead Livingstones, and so little about this one... ''Your parents?''

''My mother was killed in a senseless accident,'' he said finally. ''There wasn't time to say goodbye. My father—well, there was far too much time, at least from his point of view. But that's all ancient history, except for the fact that yes, I do know what it feels like to have a parent in danger. And I don't have brothers and sisters to share the load, either.''

''No wonder Aunt Hermione is trying to marry you off,'' Erin murmured. ''If you're the only twig left on your branch of the family tree...'' It was quite a challenge, she thought hazily, to picture Slater as a twig. An entire trunk, perhaps—but not a mere slender shoot. ''I suppose she'd expect a half dozen little Livingstones.''

''I think I can safely ignore what Aunt Hermione wants.''

''That's what I told you. Remember?'' She yawned and sat up straighter, shaking her head in a feeble effort to clear the fog.

''It's a long time till morning, Erin. Try to rest.''

She wriggled against the vinyl couch, trying to find a more comfortable position. Her voice heavy with exhaustion, she said, ''The heck with Aunt Hermione. How many do you want? Kids, I mean.''

''Eight, at least. That's why I think it's safe to ignore what Hermione wants.''

Erin blinked up at him, doubting her ears.

''I thought that would get your attention,'' Slater said calmly. ''Go to sleep, Erin. That's an order.'' He put an arm around her and drew her close to his side, cradling her against the hard support of his body.

She was too worn out even to tense, much less pull away—but within seconds she realized there was nothing in the least sensual about his gesture. He might have been a big brother offering her a shoulder to lean on.

And yet...

The scent of his aftershave was a familiar one, but she had never before smelled it like this—so faint that it was nothing more than a hint of aroma which was somehow all mixed up with the warm comfort of his body and the strength of his arm around her, creating a soft sensation which wrapped her like a blanket.

Under different circumstances, she thought, it might be quite enjoyable to sit like this, snuggled so tightly against him that she wasn't quite sure where his warmth left off and hers began. If she was to tilt her head back just a trifle, her lips would—accidentally, of course—brush the strong line of his jaw. And if he then turned his head and looked down at her, and leaned even closer for a kiss…

It's your boss you're thinking about, Reynolds, she reminded herself. But Slater could hardly blame her for wondering—when it was he himself who'd introduced the question with that crazy proposal of his—what his kisses would be like.

Competent, of course, just like everything else he did. Maybe even efficient, with no wasted time or effort…

She smiled and turned her face into the curve of his neck while she thought about it, and soothed by the even rhythm of his heartbeat under her cheek, she slept.

Sunlight roused her. Though it was still very early, the day promised to be a brilliant one, and for a moment she exulted in the beauty pouring through the windows. Then she realized how stiff and sore she felt, and that her head was still pillowed on Slater's shoulder, and she remembered.

She pulled away and sat up straight. ''I shouldn't have slept so long.''

''If there had been anything you could do, I'd have awakened you.''

She tipped her head to one side and inspected him. She'd never seen him needing a shave before. She was surprised, for he didn't look unkempt or careless; somehow the shadow of beard just made his eyes look bigger and darker, his jaw stronger. His clothes were another matter; they looked quite simply as if they'd been slept in. Except, she realized, he obviously hadn't slept at all. He had sat there and held her through the night…

Her stomach felt full of butterflies at the idea—which was silly, she told herself. Yes, she'd had a few fancies last night, but she'd been half asleep at the time. There was nothing romantic about the way he'd held her. Nothing at all.

''You're worn out,'' she said. ''I've had—thanks to you—enough sleep to pull myself together, and now that I don't have to face the night demons along with everything else, I'll be fine. Please don't make me feel any guiltier than I already do, Slater.''

He must have been even more exhausted than he looked, she thought, for he didn't argue.

''If you're sure,'' he said, ''there are a couple of things at the office—''

Erin closed her eyes in pain. ''The office. I'd actually forgotten that list you gave me yesterday—''

''Don't think about it. You have more important things to do just now.''

''That reminds me, though. A couple of advertising people were talking down in the restaurant…was it only yesterday? I've lost track of time. Anyway, they were discussing an upcoming ad campaign. Nothing secret, or even particularly sensitive—but are you certain you don't want to put on a reminder course about confidentiality for all the employees? I could—''

''No, you couldn't—not right now, anyway. We'll talk about it later, though, because you've got a good point. Reminding everyone doesn't single anyone out.'' Slater stood up, stretching slowly to relax muscles obviously cramped by holding her so long. ''You'll let me know how things go here, Erin?''

''Of course.'' She walked a little way toward the entrance with him, telling herself that she needed a good stretch herself. But when he left her there and went on, she stood in the corridor feeling very small and insignificant and alone.

* * *

When Erin left the hospital a few hours later, the sunshine was no longer beautiful; it was like the glare of a searchlight instead, hurting her eyes, probing every thought and feeling. The warmth of it against her skin should have been comforting, but in fact it mocked her with the contrast to the cold within her heart.

The nurses had suggested she go home for a while, take a shower, lie down. There were still some tests to do, and the most important thing for Angela right now was calm and quiet—so Erin wouldn't be able to spend much time with her mother anyway. And—what no one had said, but they had all obviously been thinking—she would need her strength even more tomorrow, when Angela went into surgery. Knowing they were right, Erin had complied.

The cab was halfway to the town house when she changed her mind, leaned forward and told the cabbie to take her to the office instead. The driver looked askance at her rumpled appearance, but he did as she asked, and she rewarded his lack of chattiness and curiosity with a larger-than-usual tip.

For the moment, the lobby was almost deserted. The cafeteria had just stirred to life but it was early yet for lunch, while people who had business in the high-rise were mostly already in their appointed places. The street-level boutiques were open, but customers seemed to be few. At the flower cart, Tonio was rearranging carnations, separating them into several cups so they were no longer smashed together. The slightly spicy, bruised fragrance of the flowers made Erin want to sneeze.

She would have hurried by, but the elevator door opened just then and Dax, briefcase in hand, stepped out. Erin turned toward the cart and ducked her head, hoping he wouldn't spot her. But he seemed drawn to her like a magnet; he came straight across the lobby.

''What's up, Erin?'' His gaze drifted over her from head to foot. ''You look even worse than the boss does this morning, you know. Last night must have been the party to end all parties.''

''Hardly.'' Her voice was tight with strain.

Dax looked intrigued. ''You mean it was personal instead?''

She tried to go around him. ''I don't have time for this, Dax.''

He stepped into her path. ''Touchy today, aren't we? Seriously, if you don't want to be the butt of some pretty heavy joking upstairs, you might be better off to change clothes at least. Coming to work in the same suit you wore yesterday—''

Erin cut across the levity in his voice. ''I spent the night in the hospital with my mother.'' It was the first time she had said the words out loud, and she had to steady herself. ''She has a tumor, and she'll have surgery tomorrow.''

He sobered. ''Hey—that's a tough break, kid.''

Erin started to shiver. Had she perhaps been a little too harsh on Dax? Even rough-edged sympathy could be sincere.

''Cancer's a bummer,'' Dax said. ''I hope for your sake it doesn't drag on too long. It's downright depressing for everybody not to be able to make plans. Catch you later, if you're around.''

He strolled on toward the revolving doors, swinging his briefcase.

If Erin had been run over by a steamroller she couldn't have felt flatter. *So much for sympathy,* she thought. But then she shouldn't have expected anything more from Dax.

A few feet away, Tonio cleared his throat. ''I'm sorry

about your mother, Miss Reynolds. But don't pay any attention to that jerk.''

She kept her voice level. ''The only really surprising thing is exactly how little class he has.'' She took two steps toward the elevator.

Tonio shifted a cup of daisies to a different corner of the cart. ''You know, about that red rose he gave you the other day—''

Erin paused, curious in spite of herself. She'd almost forgotten the rose, still in the crystal vase on the corner of her desk. ''What about it, Tonio?''

''He didn't pay me for it.''

Erin was too stunned to speak. ''But I saw him—''

''Oh, he pulled out his wallet.'' Tonio nodded emphatically. ''But as soon as you were out of sight, he put his money away and told me to add it to Mr. Livingstone's bill, that he'd never notice it anyway. I didn't do it, of course. But that's why when you asked about the bill yesterday, I thought maybe you realized what he'd done.''

''And thought you'd cheated?'' Erin shook her head in disbelief. ''Not you, Tonio. Dax is quite the guy, isn't he? Spontaneous, generous, understanding, sympathetic—'' The irony in her voice spilled over. ''Or maybe just *calculating.*''

Tonio was eyeing her in concern. ''I'm sorry, Miss Reynolds. After what he said about your mother, I thought it might make you feel better to know once and for all what he's like, but I guess I shouldn't have—''

Erin smiled. ''Thanks, Tonio. You're a pal.'' She took out her wallet. ''How much was the rose?''

Tonio held up both hands. ''I didn't tell you what he did so you'd pay for it,'' he protested. ''I just thought you should know he's not such a prize as he thinks he is. I didn't want to see you hurt.''

The really frightening thing about that, Erin thought, was that Tonio thought she might have been taken in by Dax's shenanigans…

Slater's door was closed and Sarah was filing documents in the outer office when Erin came in. The secretary dropped a folder and rushed across the room. "Mr. Livingstone told me," she said. "What have they found? How is she? How are *you?* Oh, Erin—"

"Is Slater in?" Erin's lips felt stiff.

"Yes, though he's got Bob Brannagan with him. But I'm sure he wouldn't mind—"

"No, don't interrupt him." Erin thought she saw a tinge of curiosity in Sarah's eyes, and abruptly realized what had caused it. The secretary wasn't used to first names around the office, so Erin's slip alone would account for her inquisitiveness. "The Brannagan deal's far too important. But when he's free—ask if he'll come into my office, will you?" Suddenly she felt she could not stand to say—or hear—another word, as if each one was a nettle rubbed against her skin. Without waiting for an answer, she turned toward the quiet of her own little retreat and closed the door.

The list and the open folder that she'd left on her desk yesterday were still in place. How long ago it seemed—and how much had changed since then. The room looked almost unfamiliar now, as if she hadn't seen it in months.

Her gaze fell on the rose Dax had stolen from Tonio, its color already fading, its petals slightly limp and darkened around the edges, as if it was drooping in shame. *It isn't the rose's fault that Dax is a cretin,* she told herself. But her hands seemed to move of their own volition, one gripping the base of the bloom while with the other she pulled a silky petal loose and dropped it into the wastebasket. Then another, and another…

At least, she realized, letting herself feeling anger was energizing. It was a whole lot better right now to be angry than to think about her mother, for dwelling on a situation she could do nothing about only made her ache all over.

When the stem was bare, she plucked it from the vase and bent it between her hands. Instead of giving a satisfying snap, the stem twisted limply, and an overlooked thorn tore at her thumb. The stem fell into the wastebasket as Erin put the wounded thumb into her mouth.

Only the vase remained. She reached out for it almost automatically, half intending to smash it as well. But the small voice of conscience stopped her. The vase had nothing to do with Dax, it reminded. It was Slater who had provided the vase, equally as exquisite—in its own way—as the rose. But there was a difference. Unlike the flower, given carelessly and doomed to crumble into dust, the crystal vase had been provided with consideration and thoughtfulness, and it would last forever…

Behind her, the office door opened. ''Erin?''

She had known it was Slater, even before he spoke her name. She'd felt his presence there, filling the doorway—and the room—with strength.

Slowly, she turned to face him, and every drop of composure she'd managed to hang on to throughout the morning's onslaught abruptly deserted her. Before she realized what she was doing, she was in his arms, her face pressed into his shoulder, sobbing like a child.

CHAPTER FIVE

SLATER held her till Erin's shuddering sobs died into hiccups and then to silence. "I'm sorry," she said finally, and tried to smile. "I've said that before, haven't I?—and then I just keep on interfering and expecting more and more from you—"

He didn't answer. Instead he held her a little away from him, his hands on her shoulders, so he could see her face. "It's bad, then."

"They found a tumor." Despite her best efforts, Erin's voice shook. "It's called a…oh, I can't remember. Some incredibly long and melodious name."

Slater muttered something she didn't quite hear.

She took a deep breath. "It could be worse, I suppose. The odds are good that the tumor isn't malignant. But it's located on her adrenal gland, and that means it's thrown the hormone balance off in her whole body, and that has sent her blood pressure through the roof. You know that so-called adrenaline rush you get when you're in danger?"

"The fight or flight reaction?"

"Yeah. It's supposed to correct itself after a few minutes, once the immediate danger's past. Only in Mother's case, it can't go back to normal because the tumor just keeps on producing the hormones that cause it in the first place." She stepped away from him and reached into her desk drawer for a tissue. The box was empty. "So it's like she's locked in a pit full of rattlesnakes. She can't fight, she can't flee—and she certainly can't relax.''

Slater reached into his breast pocket and gave her a handkerchief. ''If they take the tumor out, will that solve the problem?''

''They've scheduled her for surgery tomorrow morning. Only it's not that simple, Slater.'' Erin wiped her eyes. ''The doctor explained it all to me, complete with the technical terms. But in plain language, what he told me was that with the hormone levels so high, just putting her under anaesthesia could send her blood pressure up so much it'd blow holes in every artery in her body.''

Slater rubbed the back of his neck.

''If she makes it through that, simply touching the tumor as they try to take it out could set off the same reaction. Or, just to add to the fun, once it's out everything could go the other way—her blood pressure could drop, she could go into shock. People die of shock, Slater.''

''I know.'' There was an odd heaviness in his voice. ''My mother did.''

Erin put a hand out to him. ''I'm so sorry. I'm acting as if I'm the only one who's got problems—''

He shook his head. ''It's a long time ago. I only meant that I know first-hand how serious it can be.''

She refolded his handkerchief, concentrating on each crease as if it was the most important task she'd ever undertaken. ''And since Mother's supposed to stay as calm as possible—for fear she'll have a stroke or a heart attack before they can get her stabilized—they haven't even told her about all the dangers. Only me.'' Her voice was trembling. ''They told me all this, and then they suggested that I go home and calm myself down so I won't frighten her—''

''Erin. It's all right to be scared.''

She wasn't listening. ''It's no wonder she's had headaches. The only surprise is that she didn't have a massive stroke, or heart failure, or sudden blindness, before—''

''Erin, stop it. None of that happened. They'll take care of this.''

''Will they? I signed the papers, Slater, giving permission for the surgery. But if something happens to her—'' She couldn't look at him, so she walked across to the window and stared out at the mirrored wall of the neighboring office building.

''What happens if they don't operate?''

She didn't turn around. ''The stroke, or the heart failure, or the blindness. Or a combination.''

''Then you didn't have a choice.'' His voice was firm, and oddly reassuring—and also very close; he'd moved across the room to stand behind her. ''You did the only thing you could, Erin.'' Gently, he began to massage her shoulders. ''If it isn't too ridiculously mundane to ask, are you going to be all right for money? This isn't going to be inexpensive.''

''I know. And her health insurance isn't all that good anymore, now that she's not working full-time. But it doesn't matter what it costs.'' Erin's voice was low, almost hoarse. ''I'll sell the town house if I have to—it's worth more than I paid for it. There are a few shares of stock that my father bought for me. I'll take a second job—'' Her gaze fell on the lengthy list still lying on her desk blotter. ''Well, maybe not that—I don't know where I'd find time. But we'll manage somehow.''

She put her hands to her temples and tried to rub away the tension. If she could only *think*—

Slater said, ''You know perfectly well you don't have to worry about the money, Erin. No matter how much it is, I'll take care of it.''

The words dropped like stones into the puddle her brain seemed to have become. Erin froze, her fingertips still pressed against her temples, waiting futilely for the ripples to quiet. Surely, she thought, he couldn't have meant…

His voice was quiet, calm. ''All you have to do—''

She couldn't bear to hear him say it, to patiently and reasonably put a price tag on her. ''All I have to do is marry you,'' she said bitterly.

For a moment, utter stillness filled the office. Then Slater caught her arm in a fierce grip and whirled her around to face him. His jaw was set, his eyes ablaze. ''Dammit, Erin, do you really believe I would offer you a bargain where the price is your mother's life?''

She stared at him in utter horror, her throat so dry she couldn't speak. She had never before seen him like this. He'd been angry sometimes, yes—but nothing she'd seen in the course of business had been even a shadow of this fury. She took an involuntary step backward.

He didn't let go of her. ''You said once I'm not the sort to give in to blackmail. Well, I don't use it to get my own way, either.''

She managed to swallow the sawdust that coated her throat. ''Of course not,'' she whispered. ''I'm sorry.''

He stared down at her for what seemed eons before, very slowly, his hand relaxed. His voice was gruff and his strained smile didn't reach his eyes, but the outrage was gone from his voice. ''There you go again with the apologies.''

Erin felt as if she'd caught herself on the very brink of a cliff as the edge crumbled away under her feet. Her heart settled slowly back into place. He was on the way to once more becoming the Slater she knew—calm, reasonable, approachable, controlled.

''If you're willing to loan me the money,'' she said carefully, ''I appreciate it more than you can ever know.''

For a few seconds she thought he wasn't going to respond at all, but finally, he said, ''All you have to do is let me know how much you need. But I'd suggest you not tell your mother it's a loan. She might not like that idea any better than selling your house.''

Erin could see the sense in that. ''Maybe I'll tell her I've earned a big bonus—though goodness knows how, with all the work I've left undone.'' She glanced at the clock on her desk. ''I have to get back to her now.''

''Will you be all right?''

She knew what he was really asking. ''I'm still scared, but I think I can keep her from seeing it now. Slater...'' She hesitated. How could she even begin to thank him? He'd let her cry and rage and tremble in fear—and now, thanks to his patience and warmth and support, she could go back and face her mother with a reassuring smile.

Without giving herself a chance to think twice about it, she put a hand on his arm and raised herself on tiptoe in order to kiss his cheek.

She intended it to be a friendly kiss, a grateful kiss—no more. But something went awry; Slater turned his head at precisely the wrong moment, and her lips brushed his—and clung.

Her hand still rested on his arm, but there was no other touch save for that achingly sweet, almost tender kiss. He didn't even move to put his arms around her, and yet what should have been no more than a casual gesture—gratitude expressed, thanks accepted—was the most sensual caress Erin had ever experienced. Her body almost vibrated with the force of it.

She'd been right—*and* wrong—in her speculations about his kissing techniques. Slater was every bit as efficient as she'd expected; she'd never known any man who could pack such a punch with so little apparent effort. But he was a whole lot more than merely competent.

She was quivering when she pulled away from him, and she didn't look back as she left him standing there beside her desk—for she knew she'd find herself apologizing yet again, this time for miscalculating so badly.

And she had to admit she didn't want to.

Erin tiptoed into the cubicle where her mother lay, half sedated. Beside Angela's bed, an automatic blood-pressure monitor clicked and whirred into life, and Angela sighed and opened her eyes. ''Darling,'' she said softly. ''They told me you'd gone home. But you don't look rested at all.''

Treat it casually, Erin told herself. *Pretend this hospital stay is all routine, that there's nothing to worry about.* What better way to imply that things were perfectly normal than to say she'd gone back to work? Besides, in this case it had the advantage of being the truth—or at least part of it.

She managed a smile. ''Maybe that's because I ended up at the office instead.''

Angela's brow furrowed. ''I thought Mr. Livingstone was a little more compassionate than that.''

''He is,'' Erin said. ''He didn't demand that I come in, I volunteered.'' She leaned against the high bed rail and reached for Angela's hand. ''Is there anything I can bring you? Anything you'd like?''

''A really good cup of coffee.''

''They wouldn't let you drink it. No caffeine.''

''I know. Spoilsports—just because I'm having surgery in the morning.''

Angela sounded tired and sluggish, but that must be the

effects of the sedative, Erin thought, for she could feel the too-quick flutter of Angela's pulse.

"Erin—this is really risky, isn't it? The surgery?"

Erin tried to keep her voice steady. "What makes you ask that, Mom?"

"Because the nurses and doctors are all so cheerful about it. Anymore, when you so much as have a cavity filled they have to tell you all the risk factors—but I haven't even heard the standard lecture about the dangers of anesthesia."

"Maybe they've figured out you already knew it, so they weren't going to bother you again. Anyway, you know your blood pressure's high, so they want you to stay calm."

"Well, I'd be calmer if I knew exactly what was going on."

Angela's gaze drifted past Erin, and pain wrenched her face. It wasn't physical discomfort, Erin thought, but emotional torment, and her heart twisted in compassion.

Angela's voice was a mere thread. "Oh, Erin—there are so many more things I wanted to do."

The nurses had warned her that Angela might experience a roller coaster's worth of emotional outbursts, not only because of the hormone imbalance but also from the drugs she was getting to combat its effects. The best way to counter the moodiness, they'd said, was to be practical and matter-of-fact.

Erin took a deep breath. "Mom, don't be ridiculous. You're going to do them all. The doctors will fix this, and you'll be home in a few days, ordering everyone around and making your list of things to do as soon as you feel up to it."

"With the first item on it being getting a second job to help pay for this siege," Angela said dryly.

"You're not to worry about money, Mother."

"Easy to say. You obviously haven't considered what this is going to cost. I, on the other hand—"

"It doesn't matter," Erin said firmly. "It's taken care of."

Angela's eyes narrowed. "Oh, really?"

Erin's heart sank. The self-pity had abruptly vanished; Angela's shrewd appraisal was the same one Erin had learned to dread as a child, for it meant she was not going to be able to pull off anything the slightest bit shady. Once Angela had her teeth into a question...

"And what makes you so certain?" Angela murmured. "I didn't realize you were in the habit of playing the lottery. How convenient that it would pay off this very week... Or did you end up in the office today instead of going home to rest because you're planning to borrow the money from your boss? Just what kind of interest rate is he giving you? Or is there something else going on that I should know about?"

The bonus, Erin reminded herself. *Tell her about the bonus.*

Before she could decide how to launch her story, however, so that her mother would be most likely to accept it, Angela seemed to relent. "I'll say one thing for the man, he doesn't waste any time. Did you see what he sent me?"

"Who? Slater?" Too late, Erin spotted the interest which flared in her mother's eyes as the name registered. But Angela didn't comment, merely waved a hand at a small stand in the corner, where ivy cascaded from a big earthenware pot.

Erin hadn't noticed it before. She thought it had probably escaped her attention because neither the ivy leaves nor the container were showy enough to stand out amidst the tangle of machinery. The arrangement was plain, simple, homey, looking as if it had grown right there.

A plant, she thought. Not fragile cut flowers which would fade in a few days and be discarded, but a sturdy ivy plant with its roots deep in earth, its tendrils clinging to everything it touched. Something which would fight for life. Something which would last.

A symbol of recovery. How beautifully he had said it, without uttering a word.

Tears stung Erin's eyelids. She rubbed a fingertip across the rough surface of the earthenware pot. She didn't know why the squat, rounded, obviously heavy brown pot should make her think of the graceful, fragile crystal bud vase which was still standing on her office desk because she'd forgotten to give it back to Slater this afternoon. The two things were so different.

And yet, Erin thought, they were alike as well. Both solid, both lasting...and they were both overshadowed by their contents. Trailing ivy dripped over the edges of the pot, almost hiding its wonderful texture. Dax's showy rose had drawn the eye so that the vase had faded into the background, almost unnoticed.

But with the rose gone, the vase shone in its full glory—a thing of beauty which would last forever.

This is not really about flowerpots and vases, she realized. *It's about solidity and security. It's about the contrast between good things and things that merely look good.*

But she would need time to consider all the implications and figure out why her insides felt so strange all of a sudden—time she didn't have just now, for Angela's mood seemed to have shifted again.

"In case I don't make it, Erin..." Angela's voice was little more than a whisper.

"That's enough nonsense, Mother."

Angela shifted restlessly, pushing herself up higher against the pillows which propped her almost upright. "It's not nonsense. After the divorce, I set things up so you wouldn't have to do it all—but I've never told you where all my papers are or what final arrangements I've made."

Erin felt panic rising. The last thing her mother should be doing was to dwell on the worst possible outcome. But how on earth was she to stop her? Distraction, that was the key... She raised her voice. "Well, I think it's awfully selfish of you to waste time telling me about a funeral you're not going to need anytime soon," she said firmly, "when I have some really exciting news to share with you."

She didn't know where the words had come from; to her own ears, her voice sounded almost alien. And how on earth was she going to follow up that announcement?

The door burst open and a nurse appeared. She shot a look from Angela to the machines monitoring her, and then visibly relaxed. "All this moving around disconnected a wire, Mrs. Reynolds," she pointed out, "and judging by the monitors out at the station it looked as if you'd suddenly checked out entirely. What have you been doing in here, anyway? Calisthenics?" She rigged the sensor back in place. "Your anesthesiologist's on the floor doing rounds now," she said. "He'll be in to talk to you in a few minutes."

After the nurse left, Angela lay very still, staring thoughtfully at Erin. "Well? What's the news?"

She needs something positive to think about, Erin told herself. *Something to look forward to. Something to hang on to as she goes into surgery. Something to make her want to come back…*

Erin looked over her mother's head at the monitors, beeping and blinking and racing in their cryptic, hypnotic patterns. She noticed the door opening behind her once more, no doubt as the anesthesiologist came in. She saw her mother's gaze drift past her to the doorway.

And, feeling as if she was watching herself in a dream, she launched herself into an audacious calculated risk. ''Slater's asked me to marry him. And I'm going to tell him yes.''

She braced herself, expecting—even hoping for—surprise and shock. Angela might not exactly disapprove, but she wasn't likely to be pleased. She couldn't possibly be thrilled to hear that her daughter intended to marry a man Angela had never even met.

Erin was betting, however, that Angela's consternation would promptly be outweighed by determination. Not only was an announcement like that bound to take Angela's mind off her own problems, it was positively guaranteed to spark her maternal instincts. Any mother worth her salt wouldn't give up on life till she'd made sure her daughter's crazy notions were properly sorted out…

Which was what made the whole idea absolutely perfect, Erin thought—for as soon as the danger was past, she'd just quietly cancel her pretend engagement. Angela would be pleased, Erin would have accomplished her purpose, and Slater would never know anything about it.

It was Erin, however, who was surprised. Her mother didn't react at all; it seemed as if Angela hadn't even heard her.

This doctor must have horns and a tail, Erin thought, *if he can take my mother's mind off an announcement like that!* She turned to steal a look.

The man in the doorway not only didn't look like the devil, but he was not wearing a white coat or a stethoscope. He was dressed in a dark gray business suit that she had seen very recently...

Erin felt like a days-old party balloon; all the air was slowly seeping out of her lungs, leaving her limp.

''Hello, Mrs. Reynolds,'' Slater said. ''I hoped you wouldn't mind me dropping by.''

He didn't look at Erin, and her heart skipped madly as she considered the question of what he might say or do.

''Of course I don't mind,'' Angela said gently. ''I'm delighted to meet you, Slater—especially since it appears we shouldn't waste any time in getting onto a first-name basis.''

''I'll consider it an honor, Angela,'' he said.

The door opened once more and to Erin's relief the cubicle suddenly overflowed with medical personnel—not only the anesthesiologist they'd expected but an entire troupe of students who trailed after him.

Erin inched through the crowd and finally reached the hallway, where she leaned against the wall and dragged in a much-needed deep breath. But she'd scarcely begun to enjoy the cool influx of air when Slater braced a hand on the doorjamb just above her shoulder and said, ''Do you want to tell me what brought that on?''

Erin parried, ''My little announcement, you mean?''

''That's what I had in mind, yes. Why? Is there anything else I need to be warned of?''

She shook her head. ''I can't think of anything.''

''So I think you'd better tell me how we managed to get engaged.''

Erin shrugged. ''She guessed that I was planning to borrow the money. In a million years, she wouldn't have believed the bonus story.''

"So you spun her a different sort of tale."

An aide hurried by with a stretcher; Slater stepped closer to Erin in order to leave more room in the hallway. Though he wasn't touching her, she could feel his warmth.

She tried not to shrink back against the wall. "And she started talking really crazily about 'final arrangements' and how she didn't expect to live through the surgery. So I thought I'd give her something else to think about."

"I'd say you succeeded. As a change of subject, that one boggles the mind."

She couldn't quite meet his gaze.

"Of course, it leaves me with a question," Slater said. "Pardon me for interrogating you, Erin, but I'd like to know where I stand. Did you really mean what you said? Or was that little announcement simply meant to occupy your mother's mind for the moment?"

Erin closed her eyes. She could hardly tell him the truth—that she hadn't even considered the question he was asking now, because the words had just been there on her tongue and she'd said them before she'd even thought them through.

He was offering her an easy way out. All Erin had to say was *Of course I didn't mean it, really. If we can just pretend for a few days, till she's had the surgery and she's better—*

It was, of course, the sensible thing to do. All the reasons that had prompted her to refuse him a couple of days before were still just as large, just as weighty. If it hadn't been for her mother's gloomy mood, Slater's proposal wouldn't even have come to Erin's mind again. So of course she hadn't meant what she'd told Angela. She had no intention of making this incredible engagement real.

And yet…

Angela's door swung open once more and the students trooped out in a ragged line. The doctor came last and paused to hold the door open. ''You can go back in now. You're Mrs. Reynolds' daughter, is that right? Do you have questions about the procedure?''

Erin was too frazzled to think of anything reasonable to ask. ''You'll take good care of her?'' she murmured, and felt incredibly foolish.

The doctor's steel-sharp gaze softened. ''Of course we will. I don't know how much the surgeon's told you, but—''

In the next five minutes, Erin got an explicit and incisive explanation of everything that would happen in the operating room tomorrow. Only at the end of the lecture did she realize that Slater wasn't beside her any longer; when the doctor said goodbye and once more held the door for her, she saw Slater leaning over her mother's bed, holding Angela's hand as if they'd just shaken on a million-dollar deal. Not that either of them looked precisely happy about it, Erin reflected; in fact, Angela appeared almost somber. Did that mean she'd seen through this story as well? What had Slater been saying to her?

Warily Erin came up to the other side of the bed. Angela gently tugged her hand away from Slater's and turned to Erin with a pensive smile. ''I must say you two know how to take a woman's mind off everything else,'' she said. ''Now run along for a while, will you? You've given me far too much to think about to have you hanging around complicating things. Slater, take Erin out to dinner, and make sure she eats—all right?''

Erin was speechless at the sudden dismissal. Obediently she leaned over to kiss her mother's cheek, and she didn't find her voice till they were almost to the nurses' station. ''What did she mean, *too much to think about?*'' Erin asked. ''What did you tell her? And why didn't you just wait till I could go in, too?''

''Because you were too busy with the doctor to see the summons she gave me.''

''She wanted to talk to you alone?''

''That seems a reasonable conclusion. Where would you like to have dinner?''

''I'm not hungry,'' Erin said automatically. ''Did she seem suspicious at all?''

''I don't know her well enough to judge that. If you don't have a preference on restaurants, I'll choose. There are a couple of places close by, and I'll leave my pager number at the nurses' station in case your mother needs you.''

Erin gave up. After a year of working for him, she knew perfectly well that if Slater didn't want to answer a question, he wouldn't. But she couldn't stop chewing over the problem. Had Angela simply wanted a moment alone to welcome a new family member? Had she taken the announcement at face value, or had she been laying a trap?

Why can't anything be simple? Erin thought irritably.

At the restaurant, she merely glanced at the menu and shook her head. Slater consulted with the waiter, and a few minutes later he pushed a wineglass across to Erin. ''Drink this, at least,'' he ordered.

She picked up the glass, more to have something to do with her hands than because she wanted the wine. ''So here we are,'' she said, ''because my mother told us to go out for dinner. I wouldn't have thought that you would be quite so agreeable to being ordered around.''

Slater shrugged. ''Surely you didn't expect me to argue with her—a woman in her condition. To say nothing of the fact that she was right. You do have to eat, whether you want to or not. You'll need all your strength tomorrow, and there's nothing you can do for her tonight anyway."

"So you decided to humor her."

"And now you're wondering how far I'll carry that? Quite a long way, actually."

The waiter set a basket of bread between them. The rich, yeasty aroma tugged at Erin's senses. Perhaps she was feeling a little hungry after all.

Slater said, without looking at her, "She asked me whether I was in love with you."

Erin's heart gave a strange little flutter. "And you said..."

Slater reached for a bit of bread and began spreading herbs and warm olive oil on it. He looked thoughtfully across the table. "You surely don't think I'd have confided in her that of all the women who filled out applications for the position as my wife, you were the one who had the best references. Do you?"

"Even though it's sort of true." She smiled just a little at the thought of what Angela would have said about that. "So you told her what she wanted to hear?"

"As best I could guess what it was—yes."

"Did she believe you?"

"Just because I had very little success a few days ago in convincing you that I was sane, logical and sensible, it doesn't mean I can't be reasonably persuasive on occasion." He handed the piece of bread across the table. "Try this. And you still haven't answered my question, Erin. Did you mean it? Or were you just pretending for your mother's peace of mind?"

Erin took the bread, but she hardly knew she was holding it. She looked straight into his eyes and thought of fading red roses and crystal vases, of images and reality, of solidity and sensibility and security.

We fit together, he'd said. They were a good combination, and they could make their partnership permanent…

So why not?

She trusted him. She had turned to him for comfort, for reassurance, for help—and he had been there.

It wasn't love, of course. It wasn't magic. But what was it he'd said about love—that magic sometimes turned to melodrama?

What Slater proposed to give her wasn't wild, soaring, breathtaking romance. It was a partnership which could be expected to last forever because it had already proved itself.

The marriage he was offering wasn't a fairy tale built of spun sugar. It wasn't glamorous and showy, like Dax's glorious red rose.

But roses faded, wilted, withered. Spun sugar crumbled.

Not everything was like that. Some things lacked the initial glamour of the velvety flower, the elegance of spun sugar, but they didn't fade or wilt or disintegrate. They were built on a far solider foundation. They lasted.

Things like Slater's crystal vase.

Things like… Slater himself.

Erin took a deep breath. "I meant it," she said. "I'll marry you."

CHAPTER SIX

VERY slowly, Slater set down his wineglass. Erin thought he looked like a man caught in a vat of syrup, having to exert himself in order to move at all. He was reacting as if he wasn't quite sure what he'd heard.

Or, perhaps, as if he'd heard all too well, but the news wasn't precisely welcome...

For the first time, Erin wondered why he'd offered her the alternative of a pretend engagement, instead of a real marriage, at all. Had he actually been hoping she'd take it?

Why had it even occurred to him to wonder if she'd made up her own terms instead of accepting his? There'd been nothing vague about the way she'd announced her decision. Of course, the fact that she'd told her mother before mentioning the matter to her intended husband did have a suspicious aroma—but then, these were unusual circumstances.

There was also the minor detail that just two days ago, she had turned him down—and pretty definitely, at that. Had Slater, in the meantime, moved on to other options? Even started looking at other...how had he put it? Applicants for the position as his wife—something like that.

Erin sat up a little straighter. "Of course, if you've changed your mind—" She couldn't keep her gaze fixed on his face; she found herself staring at the neat knot in his striped silk tie instead. "I wouldn't blame you," she added honestly. "The last couple of days I haven't exactly been that model woman you proposed marriage to. You remember—the solid, sensible and practical person you thought I was.''

''I haven't changed my mind,'' Slater said. ''I just want to be certain that you know what you're doing—and why. And let me point out once more that marrying me isn't a condition for my helping with your mother's medical expenses.''

''Because you're not a blackmailer, I know. We've been over this before.''

''We haven't discussed precisely this variation. I wouldn't put it past you to have gotten some crazy notion in your head that if I'm financing Angela's treatment, the best way to pay me back would be to sell yourself to me.''

The tension had begun to seep out of Erin's body, and she could actually begin to see a little dark humor in the situation. ''Considering what her hospital bill is likely to be...'' She shrugged. ''Frankly, Slater, I doubt I'd be worth that much.''

She raised her gaze to his and wasn't surprised to see the quick flash of appreciative laughter in his eyes. What did amaze her was how every line of his face seemed to soften with his smile. She'd never before seen him look quite so relaxed, and she watched him for a long moment in utter bemusement.

Slater stretched out both hands across the table to her. ''Partners?''

Erin hesitated for only a fraction of a second before laying her hands in his, palm to palm. His fingers were warm, steady, reassuring. ''Partners,'' she whispered.

''Good. Then I just have to break the rest of it to you.''

That sounded positively ominous. Startled, Erin tried to pull away, but his grip had tightened. ''What do you mean?''

''Nothing much, really—only the fact that your mother has already scheduled the wedding for three days after her surgery. She'd no doubt have made it earlier than that, except it does take a certain amount of time to get a marriage license in Missouri.''

Erin's jaw dropped. *''Three days?''*

''I suspect by now she's got the caterer lined up and she's started to look for a dance band.''

''But she can't—''

''It's a good thing you decided to go through with it, I'd say.'' Slater's eyebrow arched slightly. ''What's the matter, Erin? I thought you said you *wanted* to take your mother's mind off her medical condition.''

The surgical waiting room was drab and worn, its chairs uncomfortable. The morning stretched out before Erin; they'd warned her that this delicate kind of surgery might take hours. Erin wriggled deeper into her chair and idly flipped the pages of an old magazine, not even seeing the print. She was thinking about Angela, squeezing Erin's hand as she was wheeled off and murmuring, ''I'm so glad, Erin. About Slater, I mean.''

Erin was just relieved Angela hadn't said anything about caterers or dance bands—or even wedding dates. Slater might have been right about Angela's intentions, she thought, but he must have overestimated her stamina. At any rate, there would be time to sort all that out later. There wasn't any hurry, after all; surely Angela, once her equilibrium was restored, would recognize the sense in putting off any wedding plans till she was fully recovered. She'd need Erin, after all—for a while at least.

She felt Slater come in—or rather, she felt the change in the room as people around her sat up straighter or looked toward the door. She wasn't surprised by their reaction—Slater was known for bringing rooms to high-pitched attentiveness just by showing up—but she was startled by the wave of gratitude that swept over her at the sight of him. She hadn't expected him to come to the hospital this morning; she certainly hadn't asked him to come. What good would it do for both of them to sit there and wait?—and no one knew better than she the amount of work he must have left behind. But she was unreasonably pleased to see him nevertheless.

Slater was more casually dressed than she'd seen him before, in an open-collared shirt and corduroy blazer. He was carrying not the briefcase she'd have half expected to see, but a wicker basket.

She moved a stack of magazines from the chair next to her, and he sat down. "Are you doing all right, Erin?"

"I'm better now," she said honestly. Even the room seemed to have grown brighter, as more sunshine spilled in through the skylight above them. "Mother asked about you this morning. You seem to have taken her by storm."

"I was lucky enough to catch her at a vulnerable moment."

"Right," Erin said dryly. "I'd like to know how you really managed it. You couldn't have had any more than five minutes alone with her yesterday, but the pair of you obviously covered an immense amount of territory."

"Oh, it was an incredible conversation," Slater said genially. "I was quite impressed with her decision-making abilities. There's no doubt where you inherited your talents. Can I interest you in breakfast?"

"No, thanks, I'm not hungry. Besides, I tried the cafeteria here yesterday, and believe me, if hospital cooks can turn oatmeal into rubber, I don't want to see what they can do with eggs."

"I suspected the food here might not be any better than

the coffee, so I asked Jessup to create something you'd like.''

As if on command, the heavenly aroma of hot cheese, tomato, and green pepper drifted toward Erin, and her mouth watered. ''On the other hand,'' she said thoughtfully, ''I wouldn't want to hurt Jessup's feelings by refusing to eat.''

''Now that is an attitude I applaud. We definitely want to look after Jessup's feelings.'' He glanced around the room. ''The trouble is, it smells so good I expect we'll be mobbed the instant I start to unpack it. But there's a little alcove just down the hall that's empty at the moment.''

The deserted alcove even contained a tiny table. Erin took the plate Slater handed her, inhaled deeply and poked a fork into the aromatic square. ''It's sort of like quiche without a crust, isn't it?''

''I believe, if you approve, he's planning to name it Eggs à la Erin.'' Slater laid out sourdough toast, butter and jelly, and got a plate for himself. ''By the way, Jessup asked me to tell you he's very pleased that we're to be married.''

Erin felt a little curl of tension deep inside. She hadn't given much thought to what people would say when they heard about the sudden engagement; she only knew she wasn't ready to face the reaction. But if Slater had already told his butler…

Not that she had any room to complain about whom Slater told or when, Erin reminded herself, for she was the one who'd broken the news to her mother before Slater knew it himself!

She didn't realize how hungry she had been till her plate was empty. ''That was wonderful,'' she said as

Slater packed up the remains once more. "Now I feel as if I can face anything. Thanks, Slater."

He looked up from the wicker basket, eyebrows raised. "Is that a dismissal?"

"Well, I just assumed... I know how busy things are, and with me not there to help—"

"I'll stay as long as I can. But you're right, there's a little matter of a bid that's due this afternoon."

"Universal Conveyer," Erin said unhappily. "It's in my office because I wasn't finished putting the finishing touches on it."

"Don't start feeling guilty. It's good for me to be reminded now and then of how many everyday details you've relieved me of."

"But I should—"

"You should stay with your mother. I'd say the heck with the bid and stick around, too, if it wasn't that the Universal Conveyer job will come in awfully handy to help support Aunt Hermione's six nieces and nephews."

"I thought you said there were going to be eight." She said it carelessly, and only when Slater grinned did Erin really hear herself. She felt a wave of color sweep through her. "I mean..."

"I thought you were too nearly asleep for that conversation to register."

"I must have been," Erin said tartly. "I certainly didn't mean—" She was only getting herself in deeper. Oh, *why* hadn't she just pretended not to remember that silly exchange?

Slater sobered. "You're not having second thoughts, are you?"

She realized he wasn't watching her face but her fingertips, once again caressing the delicate chain at the open throat of her blouse. She hadn't realized what a nervous habit it had gotten to be. ''And third and fourth ones,'' she admitted.

''Forget the nonsense about kids and just think about the partnership.''

''It's a big change, Slater.''

''Not really. Nothing much will be different at all—not until you're ready.''

''And if I'm not *ever* ready?''

''We've covered this ground before, Erin.''

She must have still looked doubtful.

His index finger gently traced the line of her jaw. ''It'll be all right,'' he said softly. ''You'll see.''

But she couldn't help but wonder if he had simply been reassuring her—or himself as well.

The surgery took hours, and the surgeon looked tired when he came out to make his report. Erin found herself clutching Slater's hand and forced her fingers to relax.

''It went very well,'' the doctor said. ''I think it's safe to say that in the long run we've got a cure. Now you go home and get some rest—she'll need you even more tomorrow when she's starting to feel better.'' He patted Erin's shoulder and was off to his next patient.

She sat perfectly still while tension she hadn't realized she was feeling drained slowly from her body.

''Don't pass out on me,'' Slater warned.

He stayed till Erin got her balance back and left her with a quick, almost brotherly kiss on the cheek. She was glad of that, she decided as she wove her way through the hospital corridors toward her mother's room. Things were complicated enough without a public repetition of yesterday's sultry kiss.

Though she wasn't altogether certain it was the *public* part which was making her insides quiver.

* * *

When Erin appeared in the office, still wearing the casual slacks suit she'd worn to the hospital that morning, Sarah looked astonished to see her. ''Mr. Livingstone told me you'd be taking the rest of the week off.''

''Leaving you to the mercies of whichever dinosaur he's been imitating lately? I couldn't be so cruel, Sarah.''

''You know, it's really odd,'' Sarah said meditatively. ''I'd have thought with you gone he'd be worse than usual, but he hasn't roared once, not even when I couldn't find a file he wanted from your office. All he said was thanks for trying. What kind of magic spell have you worked on him, anyway?''

Now that was a strange reaction, Erin thought. If Slater had told her about the engagement, Sarah wouldn't be puzzled at all, so the only logical conclusion was that he hadn't told her. Of course, it was fine with Erin that he hadn't broadcast the news, for she had enough to think of right now without the consequences of a public announcement.

And confiding in Jessup was different than telling a secretary, too. Erin hadn't considered till just now that the butler might well have some serious adjustments to make in the household before a wife actually moved in. For one thing, just because the guest room she'd used on the night of the party had borne no sign it had ever been occupied by someone else, it didn't mean the rest of the apartment was so pristine...

She didn't quite know if she was pleased Slater had been thoughtful enough to make arrangements so she wouldn't get a shock if she stumbled across evidence of other women in his past, or annoyed at the possibility that he'd had to.

''Anyway,'' Sarah was saying as she followed Erin into her office, ''just because he's been behaving like a well-mannered diplodocus so far today doesn't mean he won't revert to allosaurus status any minute—so now that you're here, could you possibly show me where you've hidden the specs we put together for Universal Conveyer *before* he changes his mind and chews me up for not knowing where they are?''

''I forgot to tell him I'd locked them in my desk.'' Erin fumbled for her keys and found the folder in the bottom drawer.

''I owe you one,'' Sarah said as she slapped the folder against her open palm. ''Oh, one more thing—Dax Porter was in earlier about the ad reports he brought up. I didn't know where to find those either.''

Erin pulled the folder from the bottom of a stack on a shelf. ''Maybe I should draw you a map.''

''I could have searched, I suppose, but it didn't seem worthwhile. He just wanted to know if you'd had a chance to review the report and pass it along, because if not he'd just bring up another set for Mr. Livingstone.''

''The last thing we need is more paper piled in this office.''

Sarah grinned. ''Or Dax offering to buy you lunch so he can impress you by explaining it all?''

''There's only one thing wrong with that scenario, Sarah—Dax wouldn't offer to buy. If he bothers you again, tell him I'll try to get to the report today.''

Erin was just settling to the task she'd left half finished two days before when Slater tapped on her door. ''What are you doing here, Erin? The doctor ordered you to rest.''

''This is restful—in comparison.'' She put her pen down and leaned back in her chair. ''Unless, of course, you came in to add a few items to my list.''

He smiled. ''I don't think I'd dare. How's your mother?''

''That's what I'm escaping. She came out of the anesthesia babbling about wedding gowns and champagne punch.''

''You said you intended to get her mind refocused on something positive. I'd say you accomplished what you set out to do.''

''Well, I didn't intend for her to get tunnel vision. Slater, she's making plans for a wedding on Monday, and she's going to be awfully disappointed when you tell her—because *I'm* certainly not going to break the news—that we aren't getting married on Monday because we don't have a license.''

Slater suddenly seemed very interested in the doodles on Erin's desk calendar.

''You didn't get a license, did you?'' She could see the answer in the set of his jaw. ''*You did?* Why? And when did you have time?''

''This morning after I left the hospital. And as for why—surely you don't want me to quarrel with my mother-in-law before the relationship's even official.''

Erin groaned. *Life was a lot less complicated when I was only working for him,* she thought. *Or at least when my main title was personal assistant, not soon-to-be wife…*

''Look,'' he said briskly, ''there really isn't any reason to put this off, and a whole lot of good ones for going ahead. For one thing, the calendar's full for the next several weeks—''

''And you'd like to have an official hostess on board.''

''It would make things easier for you, too—being right on the spot, so to speak, as you're planning all those parties. It would actually leave you more time to spend with your mother than if you're having to run back and forth. And in case you don't find that a compelling reason, let me remind you of the whole wedding scene. If we push ahead right now, your mother's illness makes a wonderful excuse for a small, intimate ceremony. If we wait—''

''—There are hundreds of people who will expect to be invited.''

''And they'll be disappointed if it isn't the event of the century. So what about it, Erin?''

She closed her eyes. ''I just can't wait for Monday,'' she said, irony dripping from her voice.

''That's what I thought you'd say. So—'' He set a small blue velvet box in the precise center of her desk blotter, then pulled a straight chair around and straddled it so he could watch her face.

Erin drew back from the box as if it were a glowing ember. She hadn't had time to think of—much less anticipate—all the details that went along with an engagement, but even if Slater's proposal was a great deal more business arrangement than love affair, he'd never bypass something as obvious as a diamond ring.

Maybe, just because of the irregularity of their agreement, he was even more likely to go overboard than the average man and buy a ring which was splashy and attention-getting—in the belief that it would look more romantic than a simpler one.

She stared at the blue velvet box and reminded herself that in the year she'd worked for him, she'd never seen Slater display a splinter of bad taste. But then, she'd never known him to buy feminine jewelry, either.

And when it came to engagement rings, all bets were off. He wouldn't be the first man to think that where diamonds were concerned bigger must be better regardless of quality, or to believe that the more ostentatious the ring the more his lady would like it. That must be how so many women ended up with engagement rings so gaudy they looked as if they'd come from a prize-vending machine instead of a jewelry store.

"If you're thinking it was a little presumptuous of me not to give you a choice on your engagement ring," Slater said, "let me assure you that I agree. Since it's you who'll be wearing it, you ought to be able to choose what you like."

She looked up at him in puzzlement. "Then why—"

"Because I think that very soon your mother will expect you to turn up wearing one."

The thought was not a reassuring one. If he'd selected a ring more to impress Angela than to please Erin...

Her fingertips trembled against the velvet.

"If you don't like this one," Slater said, "the moment things settle down we'll find a ring you do approve of. But would you at least look at it?"

Erin's stomach settled approximately back into place and she pressed the tiny gold catch. The box flew open and she caught her breath as she saw the ring inside.

The center stone was a pure, deep blue sapphire, breathtakingly beautiful but not so big as to be pretentious. The gold ring itself, perfectly scaled for her hand, was dainty and delicate, and the sapphire was set low, surrounded by tiny diamonds but with no protruding prongs to snag clothes or scratch skin.

Practical, she thought with a twinge of humor. Why had she ever doubted that it would be?

She looked up at him. "It's awfully pretty, Slater." She took the ring from the box and turned it back and forth, watching the stone catch the light. Sometimes the blue looked almost purple, sometimes it carried a tinge of green. "Diamonds can be so chilly. This is...gorgeous. It's just that—"

"What don't you like about it?"

Erin shook her head. ''No, that's not what I mean. It's perfect, really. But would you mind awfully if I didn't wear it right away? Except for Mom, I mean?''

''Because of the nine-days-wonder our wedding's likely to be?''

''That's it, exactly. I know I'm only postponing things, but for right now...''

Slater reached across the desk and took both the ring and her hand. He slid the sapphire into place on her finger and looked at it for a long moment.

He was putting no pressure on her hand as he gently cradled it in his, but Erin could feel the throbbing of her heartbeat in the tips of her fingers. She wondered what he was thinking, as he stared at the ring—the physical symbol of their agreement. Was he feeling hopeful? Confident? Cautious? Apprehensive?

''It looks nice,'' he said. ''I thought it would—but I'm glad you approve of it.'' Casually, he slipped the ring off her finger and put it back in the box, then set the box in her palm. ''Wear it, or not, as you like.''

Erin felt just a little deflated. To Slater, obviously, the ring carried no more sentimental meaning than would a fountain pen he'd used to sign an important contract. As far as he was concerned, it wasn't a symbol of anything—it was only a ring.

She dug into the bottom drawer of her desk to tuck the box into the safest compartment in her handbag, and when she straightened up once more there was another velvet box, a black one this time, on the blotter.

''Oh, now really,'' she began.

''This is different,'' Slater said. ''You said your mother wouldn't believe you've earned a bonus, so I thought you might like something concrete to show her.''

''A bonus? For what?''

He simply looked at the box, and Erin realized he didn't intend to answer till she'd opened it.

Inside the box, gleaming against the white satin lining, was a pair of earrings, each sapphire nearly the size of the one in her engagement ring, and perfectly matched in color. She looked helplessly from the earrings to Slater. ''Now if you'd like to tell me how I possibly earned these...''

''Bob Brannagan signed the deal this afternoon.''

For a split second the news didn't even register. ''I don't see what— He did? That's marvelous! Then you figured out what his hesitation was?''

''Not exactly,'' Slater said. ''You did.''

Erin considered, and shook her head. ''I can't possibly have had anything to do with it.''

''On the contrary. You said, *Mrs. Brannagan didn't seem to hit it off with the worthy Cecile,* and when I asked him if that was true—''

''You can't be serious. He put the entire future of a billion-dollar satellite communications business on hold simply because Frances Brannagan didn't like *Cecile?* Any fool could tell that Cecile wasn't what she—'' Erin stopped dead, uneasily aware that she'd gone a bit farther than tact would have suggested.

Slater sounded perfectly calm. ''Oh, there's no doubt she'd read Cecile like an X-ray machine. What stopped her—and I can't blame her, exactly—was that I didn't seem to know the difference. And because Mrs. Brannagan was so convinced my judgment was flawed, Bob had begun to wonder himself whether he really wanted to do business with me.''

Erin put two fingers to her forehead, right between her eyebrows, and pressed hard. ''Because his wife didn't like your taste in women.''

"Strange things can derail deals, Erin. You said that yourself, too."

"So you told him Cecile was history, and he signed? I wonder what his wife will have to say when she hears you're marrying me."

"She said she'd like an invitation to the wedding," Slater murmured. "I told you this would be a good partnership, Erin. Didn't I?"

When Erin came into Angela's room on Monday evening, she was startled to see how well her mother was looking. She was still pale, she obviously tired easily, and there were a few new lines in her face, but for a woman who just days ago had been on the edge of death, Angela looked wonderful.

Her hair had already been styled and a hospital volunteer was bending over her wheelchair, makeup tray in hand, putting the finishing touches on her eye shadow.

"If I didn't know better, Mother," Erin said dryly, "I'd say you were the visitor instead of the patient."

Angela waved the volunteer away. "If you make me look too healthy, they'll kick me out of my room, and I'm not ready to go home till tomorrow."

The volunteer laughed. "And you wouldn't want to outshine the bride."

Angela tipped her head to one side and studied Erin. "*That* wouldn't be hard to do. Please tell me you're wearing that ratty old trench coat of mine as a cover-up, not a fashion statement."

"I'm wearing it because it's raining," Erin said, "and because I seem to have misplaced mine." Feeling incredibly self-conscious, she laid the trench coat across the foot of Angela's bed and turned slowly, making the spangles on the bodice of her white cocktail dress sparkle for her mother's inspection.

Angela sighed. "Much better. That's a lovely dress, dear. I've always thought so. Of course, I had no idea when you bought it for that convention last spring that it would end up being your wedding gown."

"It's my *something old,* that's all."

"I've always envisioned you in embroidered white satin, with a train and a long lacy veil—"

"The train would just get in the way of the wheelchairs and stretchers."

Angela smiled reluctantly. "I expect down deep you think I'm selfish, insisting on this hurry. Don't you?"

"Not selfish at all—I think you're just being silly. It would make a lot more sense to put off the wedding till you're back on your feet. Did you say you're going home tomorrow? You can't be by yourself, Mother—"

"I won't be. You know all that volunteering I've done for the last ten years? Well, people are standing in line to help me, so you can feel free to concentrate on your husband."

Erin didn't trust herself to answer that.

An aide came into the room. "Your mother looks better than she feels, Miss Reynolds," she said, "and we don't want to tire her out too much. I hate to hurry you along, but perhaps you'd better go on down to the solarium. Sorry about protocol, but this guest will be the last to arrive and the first to leave."

Erin leaned over to kiss her mother's cheek.

The hallway was—incredibly—deserted, and the walk to the solarium seemed to stretch out forever.

Exactly like the consequences of this decision, Erin thought. Was she doing the right thing?

"Fine time to ask yourself that," she muttered.

What she was feeling was only last-minute nerves anyway, she told herself. Every bride had butterflies, no matter what the circumstances of her wedding day.

She took a deep breath and walked the length of the hallway to the solarium, a small lounge where patients normally could relax in the sunshine. Today, late in the afternoon and in a pouring rain, the room was probably not going to provide the most cheerful atmosphere. But then, the surroundings didn't matter any more than did white satin and lace, or cascades of flowers, or the gleam of candlelight—none of which were to be part of her wedding day, either.

There would be just Erin and Slater, a judge, a ring, Angela and her hospital aide as witnesses...and that was all. Erin wouldn't have bothered with anything more than regular business clothes if she hadn't known that her mother would be disappointed if she showed up in an ordinary suit. In fact, having the ceremony at her mother's bedside would have been just fine with her, but Angela had insisted; the solarium wasn't much, she'd said, but it was the best she could manage. And Erin, knowing how much effort it had taken for Angela to be wheeled down to look at the room in advance, could do nothing but agree.

Erin turned the corner to walk toward the solarium, and her step slowed as she saw Slater standing in the hallway just outside the little lounge. Her hand raised to her throat, her fingertips caressing the fine gold chain she always wore around her neck.

''Still having doubts, Erin?''

''Does it show so clearly?''

''You're playing with your necklace again.''

''Oh. I guess I've gotten in the habit of rubbing it between my fingers when I'm stressed. Slater, will you promise me something?''

''That depends entirely on what you're asking.'' His voice was grave.

She tried to continue to meet his eyes, and couldn't. ''I know you think now that you'll never fall in love, but if you do find that magic someday—''

''This is a solemn and unbreakable contract, Erin.''

She raised her voice just a little. ''I want you to promise me if it happens, you'll tell me.'' He didn't answer, and after a long moment she opened her eyes very wide, as if she was astonished. ''Why should you hesitate to give me a promise that you're so sure you'll never have to keep?''

Slater smiled slowly. ''Remind me to object if you decide to go to law school. You're dangerous enough just as you are.''

Before Erin could point out that he hadn't answered the question, she heard the click of rapid footsteps, and Sarah practically skidded around the corner, cradling a foot-square white box in her arms. ''There you are, Mr. Livingstone. I just grabbed the box from Tonio and ran, and I still thought I was never going to make it over here on time, with the traffic.'' She handed him the box and blinked in obvious surprise as she saw the shimmering spangles on Erin's cocktail dress.

Slater opened the box and lifted out a double handful of dainty flowers tied with trailing white ribbons.

Sarah's eyes went wide. ''That's a bridal bouquet,'' she said.

Slater handed the bouquet to Erin and the empty box back to Sarah. ''Erin, on Sarah's next employee review, be sure to note that she's quite observant.''

Erin was holding up the bouquet, studying each perfect flower. ''It's beautiful, Slater.''

He smiled down at her. "I can't turn the solarium into a cathedral, but I saw no reason you shouldn't have flowers for your wedding."

"You're getting *married?*" Sarah's voice was almost a squeak. "Oh, I'm observant, all right—I have *observed* that the two of you seemed faintly interested in each other." She hit the heel of her hand against her temple. "Here I thought I was bringing flowers for Erin's mother because Tonio doesn't deliver, and I couldn't understand why it was so critical to get them here at five o'clock on the dot."

"Now you know," Slater said. "Come on in, Sarah. You can be a witness." He pushed open the solarium door.

Erin's first glimpse of the room made her think it was tiny—much smaller than she remembered from inspecting it with her mother a couple of days ago. But her second glance told her that the room was still pleasantly large, it was simply filled to overflowing with people, with flowers, with helium balloons tied with satin ribbons. Despite the gloom outside, the room was brightly lit and cheery and warm. She saw Jessup, in his usual plain black, and Frances Brannagan, smiling and holding a lacy handkerchief as if she expected to need it. All of Angela's nurses were there, and even the surgeon, wearing scrubs and a smile. On a table in the corner was a punch bowl and a large, pillared cake.

Erin felt almost dizzy. *I can't turn the solarium into a cathedral,* he'd said. But he'd obviously done his best to provide all the other trappings…

The crowd shifted, and a man she hadn't spotted before took three steps toward her and stopped, just arm's length away. "Hello, Erin," he said softly.

She stared at him for one endless moment.

Oh, yes, she told herself bitterly. Her so-thoughtful future husband had managed to provide *all* the other trappings…

She turned on Slater, fury warming every cell of her body. Her voice was low and hard-edged. ''I don't suppose you'd like to explain,'' she said, ''exactly how my father happened to hear I was getting married—and what on earth made him think I'd want him to come?''

CHAPTER SEVEN

SLATER said calmly, ''He heard about it because I called and told him.''

Erin's throat tightened. ''You just took it upon yourself to invite him—without even asking me what I wanted?''

Jack Reynolds took two steps forward. ''Erin, there's really no need—''

She didn't even look at him. ''Stay out of this, Dad.''

Slater's voice was low and level. ''I thought he had a right to know about his daughter's wedding.''

''And what would you know about it?'' Erin said. ''Did you even consider how my mother's going to feel about this? Or did you think she hasn't been through enough in the last week, so with things looking up, it was time for a really nasty surprise?''

Slater's gaze remained steadfast on her face, but Erin thought she saw a flicker—of doubt perhaps? of guilt?—in his eyes. But her feeling of grim satisfaction at making him realize how badly he'd blundered didn't last long, for only a moment later the door opened and the aide guided Angela's wheelchair into the solarium.

Since the three of them—Slater and Erin and Jack Reynolds—had been practically huddled by the door, there wasn't even an instant for Erin to try to warn her mother, to soften the blow. Angela's wheelchair actually grazed Jack Reynolds' shin as it halted, and he turned to look down at his ex-wife.

Erin wanted to cover her eyes, but she was too mesmerized to move. She saw shock in her father's face and watched as it was quickly masked. Reluctantly, fearing the worst, she glanced at her mother.

Angela, she thought, must feel as if she were seeing a ghost.

Gently, Jack Reynolds laid his hand on his ex-wife's shoulder, and Angela reached up to touch his fingertips.

Erin's gaze focused on the shiny narrow gold band on her father's left hand. That was odd. She supposed she shouldn't really be surprised that he had married again; the divorce was two years past now. What stung was that he hadn't bothered to tell her.

"Jack," Angela said softly. "Thank you for coming."

Her mother's calmness stunned Erin. Angela couldn't possibly have carried off a surprise like that without showing so much as a flicker of agitation. Which meant...she'd known it was coming. She'd been warned.

The accusation Erin had leveled against Slater, that he'd acted without even considering Angela's feelings, had been hasty and presumptuous—and wrong.

She looked up at him. "I was too surprised to think, Slater. I should have known you wouldn't do something like that without asking her. But why didn't you warn me?"

Slater's tone was full of irony. "She didn't want you to get your hopes up in case he couldn't come."

Erin frowned. "You can't mean it was her idea." But crazy as it sounded at first, it was the only conclusion that really made sense. "She asked you to call him," she said slowly. "And you were going to take the blame if I didn't like it, rather than let me be angry with my mother."

He didn't speak, but she could see the answer in his eyes.

Beside her, Jack Reynolds cleared his throat. "Erin," he said very quietly, "This is your special day, and I know you don't particularly want me here or you'd have asked me yourself. Your mother thought you'd regret it someday if I didn't come, but it's up to you. I'll leave right now if you want me to—but I'd like very much to have the pleasure of attending my only daughter's wedding.''

The world seemed to hang in the balance. Slater stood very still. Angela seemed to have stopped breathing.

Erin laid her hand on her father's arm and said, ''If we can find an aisle here somewhere, Dad, perhaps you'll walk me up it?''

The crowd parted as neatly as if the maneuver had been rehearsed, and Erin saw the black-robed judge waiting for them, silhouetted against the windows at the far side of the room.

The wedding ceremony itself was little more than a blur in Erin's mind, each sentence punctuated by the spattering of raindrops against the glass. She couldn't stop thinking of how readily she had concluded that it was Slater's idea for her father to be present, that he'd made the decision carelessly and without thought of how it might affect others. It would have been an action completely unlike him; how had she so easily persuaded herself he could do such a thing?

She sneaked a glance up at him through her lashes. He looked very serious, almost somber.

She wouldn't much blame him if he was feeling some doubt right now about this whole idea, Erin admitted. He might well be debating whether he really wanted to marry a woman who could jump to such dramatic and faulty conclusions. It was no surprise that he'd been sarcastic a few minutes ago—the wonder was that he'd stopped at that.

And if he was having second thoughts, what on earth was the man supposed to do about it? Announce before the whole crowd that he was inclined not to go through with this wedding?

Slater would never do that. He would never go back on his word in public without so much as a warning. But even if he'd wanted to draw her aside to hash out his doubts, there hadn't been an opportunity for that quiet moment; by turning to her father, Erin had quashed the possibility—unintentionally, but no less efficiently.

So here they were. She looked up at him once more, trying to read his thoughts. Slater took her hand; his fingers were warm and strong and steady as he slipped her wedding ring into place, and she relaxed a little.

Then it was finished. "You may kiss your bride," the judge said, and Erin, quivering inside, obediently raised her face as Slater slipped an arm around her.

She didn't expect that this kiss would be anything like that first sudden, accidental, exploratory caress had been; how could it be, with an audience? She was almost right, too, for there were many differences. This kiss was slow, deliberate, and knowledgeable, not focused entirely on her mouth but drawing her whole body into the caress as he pulled her closer. Instead of instant flame crackling over her skin like summer lightning, this kiss created heat which rumbled through her bones like a volcano. The only things that hadn't changed, she found herself thinking, were the way he left her dizzy and reeling and the fact that he'd managed to knock her so completely off balance without any obvious effort at all. The man wasn't only efficient and way beyond competent, Erin told herself, he was versatile as well.

She wondered where he'd learned it all.

Slater kept an arm around her, turning her to face their guests. For a long moment everything looked static, as if she was staring at a still photograph, and then the crowd mobbed them.

It seemed much later when the aide in charge of Angela's wheelchair tapped Erin on the shoulder. "It's past time for your mother to be back in bed," she said, "but she doesn't want to go."

Erin set down her punch cup, excused herself from the nurse she was talking to, and hurried across the room to Angela's side. She could see the strain of fatigue in her mother's face. "You've overdone it," she ordered, "so stop giving everybody a hard time and go rest."

Angela forced a smile. "It's been worth every instant," she said. "Even if I ache till next Tuesday for staying up this long. You'll stop by my room before you leave?"

It was Slater who answered. "Of course."

Angela looked past them both. "I'm glad you came, Jack," she said and held out her hand. "I know how busy you are these days. Have a safe trip home."

Jack Reynolds clasped her hand for a moment and stepped back to let the wheelchair pass. Almost as soon as it was out of sight, he turned to Erin. "I'll be going, too, Erin. I've just got time to get to the airport for my flight back to San Diego."

Erin told herself it was completely irrational to be disappointed that he was leaving when she hadn't even considered inviting him to come in the first place. "You're going back so soon?"

His smile was slightly twisted. "It was a rather sudden trip," he pointed out.

"Of course. And I'm sure you have other obligations." At least some of them, she thought, were represented by that shiny gold ring he was wearing. She stood on her toes to brush his cheek with a kiss. "I'm glad you came, Daddy. Really."

''I'm glad I did, too, Shamrock.'' His voice cracked. ''If... Well, Slater's got my number—if you ever want it.'' He thrust a hand out to Slater and was gone before Erin could answer.

''Shamrock?'' Slater said under his breath.

She didn't look at him. ''He used to say I was his lucky charm, like a four-leaf clover. So—'' She had to stop to clear her throat, and then with determination she smiled and returned to her guests.

The party lasted for another hour and broke up only as the hospital itself began to settle down for the evening. There were still a few people relaxing in corners, drinking punch and talking, when Slater asked if Erin was ready to leave.

Panic sizzled through her. But it wasn't leaving the party that made her hesitate, it was all the other questions he was asking. Was she ready to go with him? Ready to make his home her own? Ready to be his wife?

''What about the wreckage?'' she asked, looking around the solarium. ''We can't leave it this way.''

''It's taken care of. The balloons go to the pediatrics wing, the flowers to the long-term nursing unit.''

''That's sweet.'' She straightened a ribbon on her bouquet. ''You said we'd stop to see Mother.''

''I'm betting she'll be asleep. If so, we'll leave a note instead of waking her.''

Angela was not asleep. Her door was standing half open, and though Erin couldn't see her visitor she could hear the murmur of voices. Her eyes widened. ''My father's in there!''

''So much for his flight back to San Diego,'' Slater said.

''You don't sound surprised.''

He shrugged. ''Seems to me they'd have plenty to talk about.''

''*That* would make a nice change,'' Erin muttered.

''I gather you don't want to interrupt?''

She shook her head. ''It'd be a bit awkward, I think.'' She wrote a note for her mother instead and left it at the nurses' station.

At the hospital door she hesitated, feeling suddenly shivery. The rain had stopped, but night had settled in earlier than normal because of the heavy clouds, and the damp air was chilly against Erin's face after the hours she'd spent in the crowded and over-warm solarium. ''My raincoat is in Mother's room.''

''And you'd rather not go back after it.'' Slater took off his trench coat and draped it around her shoulders. The soft, light wool was warm from his body and scented with his aftershave, and though the coat was far too large to fit her it settled down around her like a blanket. Or a hug, she thought. She couldn't quite decide if it was comforting or possessive.

Slater's apartment was dim and quiet. Erin was surprised to see only a few small lights, just enough to indicate the outlines of the rooms. She slipped out of his trench coat, and the spangles on her dress caught and magnified the faint light.

''I like that dress,'' Slater said. He took the coat to hang it up. ''I've seen you wear it before, haven't I? Or is that one of those questions husbands shouldn't ask?''

Husband, she thought. There'd been a little twist in the way he'd said it, as if it felt as strange to his tongue as it did to her ears. *Husband...*

Erin's smile felt forced. ''No, you haven't seen the dress before. I bought it for the opening party at the convention we threw last spring for all our customers, but I wasn't moving in your circles then, I was still in the public relations department.''

Slater nodded. ''That was the convention where I wandered by the PR booth on the last day just as you were launching a promotional pitch, and I heard the best presentation ever for Control Dynamics.''

''The speech that got me promoted to be your personal assistant? That's the one.''

''Tell the truth, Erin. Did you really not know I was there when you started talking?''

''Of course I didn't—and it's a good thing, too. If I had, I'd have been completely tongue-tied.''

Slater half smiled. ''You? I doubt that.''

''Cross my heart.'' She looked around the foyer; she'd never seen it in such deep shadow before. ''I thought sure Jessup would have the place ablaze in celebration. He left the party a couple of hours ago, didn't he?''

''He's taking a day or two off.''

I wonder, Erin thought, *whose idea that was.* She suspected that Jessup could fade into the wallpaper at the drop of a hat, but Slater might have felt her adjustment would be easier if it was just the two of them. And perhaps he was right. ''Very thoughtful of him.''

''He said he'd leave a casual supper for us.'' Slater crossed the foyer and snapped on the living room lights, adjusting the momentary glare down to a soft glow. In front of the fireplace was a small table, draped in white linen and set for two, with gleaming crystal, silver flatware, and covered appetizer plates already in place. Nearby, on a glass cart, was a warming tray which emitted heavenly smells.

''A two-course meal is his definition of a casual supper?'' Erin said.

''Oh, I'm sure he's left dessert somewhere.''

''That makes three.''

''Unless he assumed we'd be bringing the rest of the wedding cake home instead of leaving it for the hospital staff. Perhaps I should have warned you that Jessup is quite the romantic.'' Slater lit the gas fire and held Erin's chair.

''If this is casual, I wonder what he called the breakfast you brought to the hospital.'' She was uneasily aware that she was talking almost at random. She'd never had so much trouble finding things to say to him, at least not since the day shortly after that convention, when she'd been summoned to his office without a hint of the reason and been offered a new job.

Slater uncorked a champagne bottle, removed the silver covers from the appetizer plates, and seated himself across from her. Erin looked down at her soup, pale green creamy cucumber swirled together with rich tomato bisque, served on a plate which had been packed in chipped ice. ''If this wasn't cold, the red and green combination would make it perfect for a Christmas party,'' she said.

''We'll keep it in mind.''

His noncommittal tone made Erin think of the upcoming events and schedule of customer visits, and that reminded her of the fat leather notebook where she kept the details not only of her schedule but Slater's. At the moment, she couldn't remember where she'd left it. On her desk, perhaps? She'd never lost track of it before—but today with its wedding nerves had been far from ordinary. ''I don't even remember what's coming up next,'' she admitted. ''The Senator, maybe? I forgot to ask Sarah if that's been rescheduled.''

''No, it's still hanging at the moment. I sent the ballet

tickets to a dance studio Sarah had heard about that gives free lessons to underprivileged kids.''

''Wonderful idea. I'd forgotten all about the tickets—I'm glad they didn't go to waste.'' She tried to smile. ''If I don't get my scattered brain under control pretty soon, you'll no doubt be looking to hire a different personal assistant.''

''It's good for me to be reminded now and then of all the things you normally take care of. How efficient you are, how levelheaded—''

Erin managed, with effort, to keep her voice steady. ''Am I hearing a little sarcasm there?''

''Not at all. Why?''

''Just that it wasn't very levelheaded of me to conclude that you'd decided, entirely on your own, to patch up the rifts in the Reynolds family, without even bothering to get a clue what they might be.''

''What else would you think?''

''Now that I stop to consider, you didn't precisely say it was your idea to invite my father. But you didn't tell me it wasn't, either.''

''Let's just say I wasn't as hopeful as your mother was that if you found yourself face-to-face with your father, you'd be pleased to see him.''

Erin was silent for a long moment. ''Slater...if I'd thrown a tantrum about it—''

His eyebrows arched. ''Are you telling me that *wasn't* a tantrum? You could have fooled me.''

She ignored the interruption. ''Would you really have let me keep on believing you'd been such a bungling meddler?''

She thought for a moment he wasn't going to answer. ''Probably,'' he said finally. ''Your mother was worried about how you'd take it, and if you'd blame her.''

"Then why did she do it?"

"Because she was even more worried that when things slowed down and you had a chance to think, you'd regret not inviting him."

Erin spooned up the last bite of her soup. "Maybe she's right."

"I'm sure she'll be pleased to hear it."

"And at least she'll know for certain that it was worth putting herself through the strain," Erin agreed. "Even though it wasn't as bad as it might have been. I still can't believe he was in her room, just shooting the breeze. I wonder..."

Slater removed the soup plates to the side cart and served the main course, a spicy chicken-and-rice casserole with steamed vegetables on the side. "What?"

"Whether he was telling her about his new wife."

"I noticed he was wearing a wedding ring. You didn't know he'd remarried?"

Erin shook her head. "No. Though why shouldn't he? Mother's dated, off and on—she just hasn't found anyone she wanted to marry. I wish he'd told me, though." She took a deep breath. "I didn't even have a chance to talk to him today."

"He said you could call him anytime," Slater reminded.

"And chat with his new wife? The one whose name I don't even know? I suppose I should keep in touch, though—I might have little brothers and sisters someday."

"Who knows? They might even like to come and play with Aunt Hermione's nieces and nephews."

Erin was paying no attention. She'd put a hand to her throat, reaching for the slender gold chain around her neck, and she panicked when she didn't feel it.

''What's wrong, Erin?''

''My necklace—'' Her fingertips fumbled past the silky collar of the cocktail dress. ''I must have broken the—oh, no, here it is. It was caught on one of the spangles.''

Slater was looking at her oddly, but Erin was so relieved that it took her a second even to register his expression.

She pulled the chain free. ''How incredibly lucky that it didn't break. It would be just too ironic to lose my mother's wedding ring today, of all days.''

''That's what you cherish so much? Your mother's wedding ring?'' Slater's tone was almost flat.

Erin tipped her head to one side in puzzlement. ''Of course. She gave it to me when the divorce was final, and I've worn it ever since.''

He neatly dissected a broccoli stalk. ''I thought perhaps it had something to do with the man you're so fond of.''

For a moment Erin was honestly puzzled. ''What man? Oh, the one you thought I'd want with me at the hospital? There's nobody, Slater.'' She saw his eyebrows lift and suddenly it was horribly important to convince him, to reassure him that he had no competition. ''If there had been someone special in my life, I would never have...''

She stopped herself, but it wasn't in time; the unspoken words echoed through the room nonetheless. *I would never have married you—because you're not special...*

''I mean...'' she said faintly. ''I didn't mean that the way it sounded.''

''Of course you didn't. You were just reminding me of our partnership.'' He glanced at her plate. ''Don't you like the casserole?''

I would choke if I tried to eat another bite. On the other hand, maybe it would be better to choke on food than on words... ''It's wonderful. I'm just not very hungry.''

"Then I won't go searching for dessert."

She looked down at Angela's ring, still clenched in her hand. There was something odd about it, she thought, and dismissed the notion as fanciful. In any case, she had more important things to think about. She couldn't let that tactless comment fester. "I'm sorry, Slater."

He began to gather up the dishes. "Sorry for what? Keeping to the rules we set? Don't be silly." His voice was perfectly calm.

Oh, he'd really needed reassuring, all right, Erin told herself. He'd married her thinking there was another man in her life, a man she cherished—so why should she expect that the idea that there wasn't one would bother him? It hadn't, of course, because it simply didn't matter to him whether there was or not. So long as they lived by the rules...

You're a fool, Erin Reynolds... Erin Livingstone...

"You look exhausted, Erin."

She stood up. "I'm not too tired to help clear the mess. At least I presume you're not planning to leave it for Jessup whenever he gets back?"

"No—but all I'm going to do is load the dishwasher, and then I'm going to settle down with Bob Brannagan's technical drawings for a while so I'll be ready for our conference tomorrow. So why don't you get some sleep? Jessup's put your things in the guest room next to the library."

Erin's hands stilled on the plates she was stacking.

It was absurd to be surprised at the arrangements he'd made, she told herself. The first time they'd discussed the possibility of making their marriage more than businesslike had been on that crazy evening when he'd brought up the idea in the first place, when he'd said the decision would be hers to make—and it had ended up a moot point because she'd turned him down.

Since then—yes, they'd joked about Aunt Hermione's nieces and nephews, but in a kind of unfocused, *maybe someday* kind of way. They'd never approached the question seriously again. Erin had actually let it slip from her mind—which was pretty astonishing in itself, come to think of it.

She knew she ought to be feeling grateful that Slater was keeping his word, that he was too much of a gentleman to force the issue. He'd said he'd wait till she was comfortable with the idea, and he…

And precisely when, she asked herself in astonishment, had that happened? Exactly when had she gone from uneasiness with the entire idea of a physical relationship to expecting that their marriage would include lovemaking? Because there was no denying that she had changed her mind.

Erin didn't remember a decisive moment. She only knew that her thinking had altered sometime in the last few days. Perhaps it was just part of the reality she'd accepted when she'd decided to marry him without love on either side. Perhaps she'd simply realized he was right; even though they wouldn't ever feel the blinding passion of love for each other, they could still have the comfort of family. Raising children would be just another facet of their partnership.

But this, of course, was a difficulty neither of them had foreseen. *I'm content to leave that decision for the future,* Slater had said, and that was exactly what he was doing. But they'd left *the future* undefined.

How was Erin supposed to let him know that she'd changed her mind? Drop hints? Wait for him to read her thoughts? Send him a telegram?

She supposed the most direct way would be to throw herself into his arms and say, *By the way, I'm absolutely panting to go to bed with you.* She could feel her face growing hot at the very idea.

His fingertips brushed her cheek. "It's all right, Erin. Don't torment yourself." His lips pressed briefly against a feathery lock of hair at her temple, and then he pulled back and smiled down at her. "Goodnight, dear."

And what else could she do but walk away?

The bedroom to which he'd directed her was the one she'd used on the night of the dinner party. The addition of a few of her own things had softened the edges, but the room was still just as impersonally beautiful as when Erin had first seen it. Her hairbrush lying on the polished dresser, her suitcases lined up precisely in the closet, her sweaters neatly folded in the drawers, were not enough to make it hers. Only time could do that—and she was quite sure she didn't want it to. She didn't want to be comfortable here—for as long as she used this room, she was nothing more than a guest in his house.

At home, in her bedroom at the town house, she would have dropped her spangled cocktail dress in a heap on the bench at the foot of her bed as a self-contained reminder to take it to the dry cleaner's. Here, she thought, she would feel guilty about doing anything of the sort, so she hung the dress neatly in the closet even before she put on her nightgown.

The sheets were cream-colored satin—gorgeous, luxurious, and completely impractical. No matter how carefully she folded them back, they slipped and slid, and her silky gown didn't help matters at all. She constantly felt that she was sliding out of bed, and every time she tried to pile up the pillows into a nice stack to prop herself up, at least two of them squirted out of the heap and shot across the room.

This is ridiculous, the little voice at the back of her brain whispered. *There's no reason for you to be here. What you need to do is march down that hall and into the library and interrupt Slater at his blueprints and tell him you've decided you don't want separate bedrooms after all....*

She quailed at the thought. But maybe she could just tell him she wasn't comfortable in this room. Or she could ask if there were some ordinary sheets to use instead.

Before she'd quite decided what she was going to say, she found herself at the library door, already easing it open.

She was trying to brace herself for the questions he would inevitably ask when she realized that apart from a moonbeam flickering through the skylight, the room was dark. So was the living room, the dining room, and the hallway which led to the kitchen wing.

Either Slater had changed his mind about reviewing Bob Brannagan's technical drawings, or he'd taken them to his bedroom. Wherever that was.

Erin had never felt so alone in her life.

The moon ducked behind a cloud, and the dim, ghostly light which had shown her the outlines of the library vanished. Erin felt her way to the nearest chair. Perhaps if she just sat here quietly for a while, soaking up the sense of his presence which seemed to remain in the room, she'd feel better. Maybe then she'd choose the dullest book she could find and take it back to bed with her.

But despite her resolution not to feel sorry for herself, tears brimmed and overflowed, and very quietly she began to sob.

A door opened on the balcony almost directly above

her, a door she hadn't noticed before because it appeared to be part of the bookshelves, and a shaft of light cut through the library. ''Erin?'' Slater stepped onto the balcony. His shirt was unbuttoned, his tie loose.

She turned her face into the cushioned wing of the chair and tried to smother her sobs. It would have been difficult enough simply to have told him why she'd come looking for him, but to be discovered crying about it…

He came down the spiral stairs from the balcony, his step light, and perched on the arm of her chair. ''Poor darling. You've had about all you can take, haven't you?''

The gentle touch of his fingertips against her hair, soothing her as he might comfort a child, was the last straw. She sniffed and said, illogically, ''You didn't even kiss me goodnight!'' She remembered the brush of his lips against her temple. ''Not a real kiss.''

As if in shock, his hand stilled on her hair, but though she couldn't see his face, she knew from his tone that he was smiling. ''And you wanted me to?''

''Of course not!'' she flared, sensitive to the hint of laughter. ''Only…'' Her voice quavered. ''Only if you felt like it.''

''Oh, I felt like it.'' The last trace of humor had vanished. ''Shall I show you how much?''

He didn't wait for an answer. Slowly his hand tightened on the back of her neck, and he leaned closer.

The moon peeked forth once more, showing Erin the shadowed angles of his face for a moment before she closed her eyes and gave herself up to his kiss.

Slowly he explored her, his lips tender as he caressed and nibbled her temple, her cheekbone, her ear—then growing urgent as he returned to her mouth, becoming demanding as she answered with an urgency of her own.

When ultimately he raised his head, his breathing was

as unsteady as Erin's own. "I don't want to stop, Erin." His arms were still around her; slowly his hold loosened.

She leaned against him, her voice shaky and almost hoarse, her face pressed against his bare chest. "You don't have to. Stop, I mean."

He was very still. She could feel the thud of his heartbeat against her cheek. "I want you to feel right about it."

"I do." The simple words were every bit as much a vow as when she had said them that afternoon, before the judge.

He said something under his breath, and he kissed her again. Only then did she begin to realize how firmly he'd restrained himself before, for this embrace left her gasping for oxygen—and for him.

He guided her up the spiral stairs, kissing her on each step, and across the narrow balcony to the door he'd left open. Beyond it lay a bedroom so huge the corners lay in shadows despite the golden glow of the bedside lamps. But Erin had no time or energy to notice more, for she was in his arms again in a world where nothing existed except the two of them and the need to satisfy his hunger—and her own.

CHAPTER EIGHT

MUCH later, Erin lay beside him, so relaxed that she could barely blink, and watched him sleep.

The last of the rain clouds had floated by, and the moon was unimpeded. But though its silvery light poured in the tall windows at the far side of the enormous bedroom, glistening against a tabletop where a half-rolled set of engineering drawings lay, it cast only a faint glow over the big bed.

Erin didn't need more. She lay very still and looked at Slater, studying the arch of his eyebrows, the way his long lashes curled, the fine lines at the corners of his eyes.

My husband. She tried the words out in her head and savored the unfamiliar feel of them, and wondered at the serenity she felt. He'd been more right than she had believed possible, she thought, in his conviction that they could be content with the partnership they were building. Except it was even more than that—they could be happy.

She curled up next to him, thinking that she'd made the best choice of her life in marrying this man she loved—

With an almost audible pop, all her sleepy contentment vanished.

This man she loved.

''What a fool I am,'' she whispered. Impossible as it seemed, she hadn't recognized love until it had hit her between the eyes. Instead, she'd rationalized and justified and defended her decision to marry him. She'd told herself she was being—what was that list of qualifications

Slater had cited?—solid and sensible and practical, when the truth was that she'd wanted nothing more than to be his wife. *Because she loved him.*

No wonder she'd been so anxiously breathless in that moment, right after she'd told him that she'd marry him, when she thought that he might have changed his mind. No wonder, when he'd offered the option of a temporary engagement purely for her mother's peace of mind, she'd found a way around it. No wonder, instead of continuing to be concerned about whether he found the woman who could show him the magic of love, she'd ended up grabbing him for herself.

Even this afternoon, though she'd tried to make him promise that if he ever found love he'd tell her, she had to admit that she'd been relieved when he hadn't given her what she'd asked for.

She'd honestly believed, the night Slater had proposed and she'd turned him down, that she had no romantic interest in him at all. Had his proposal actually sparked her fascination, or only fed oxygen to an ember that had already been smoldering deep inside her?

It didn't really matter, she supposed. The results were the same—his offer had focused her attention on him, made her notice things she would have missed before. Things like his kindness and generosity, of course—but also his sheer physical strength and the way he moved, the splendor of his smile, and how good it felt just to be close to him.

Little things—but together they had added up to a knockout punch.

The finishing touch, of course, had been his restraint. Erin hadn't seen it at the time, but she could admit it now; there hadn't been a day, since his proposal, that she hadn't wondered what it would be like to make love with him.

And the fact that he hadn't even kissed her—that he hadn't used physical attraction, much less force—in order to make his point had intrigued her. How ironic that without even touching her Slater had been infinitely seductive.

This is one dangerous man, Erin thought. *And there are a lot of women out there who aren't morons like the worthy Cecile. Women who won't just see a wallet but an intriguing, exciting, very sexy man…*

Could one of them make Slater feel the magic Erin had once promised he would someday find? And if there was such a woman…what about the magic Erin felt for him?

Magic so often turns to melodrama, he'd said. He wouldn't seek out love because of its uncomfortable side-effects; that was, after all, why he'd proposed to Erin in the first place, and she knew he'd stand by his plans. But what if, despite his lack of interest, love found him anyway? What if that special woman were to discover him?

And the difficulty cut the other direction, too. What if his sensible, practical, solid wife fell in love with him and Slater ended up with all the uncomfortable side effects he'd been trying to avoid?

Unfortunately for Erin, however, there was no longer a *what if* in that equation, and it was far too late to put it back.

She couldn't change what had happened. So she'd just have to be sensible, practical, and solid enough not to show it. Not to descend to melodrama. Not to watch every woman he encountered and wonder if this was the one he could love. Not to display jealousy even if it was turning her toenails green.

The answer was obvious. The problem was going to be that figuring out a solution was a great deal easier than making it work.

* * *

Erin knew even before she opened her eyes that she had slept far past her normal time, but she was horrified when she sat up and looked at the clock on Slater's bedside table to see that it was well past nine.

The apartment was oddly quiet—but then of course it would be; Slater had said he was meeting with Bob Brannagan again this morning, so he must have been gone for an hour at least.

Under different circumstances, she would have enjoyed the opportunity to putter around the apartment, exploring and familiarizing herself with her new home. But she was running so far behind schedule that would have to wait.

In any case, she reflected, there wasn't much to explore at this end of the apartment. The upper level of the entire wing was devoted to the master suite—the huge bedroom, an equally luxurious bath, and a couple of walk-in closets. Windows on two sides looked out over the skyline of St. Louis, and there were two entrances—a discreet stairway in one corner which led down to the hall near the guest bedrooms, and the door they'd come through last night from the library.

She should have expected, she supposed, that Slater would have arranged these rooms for maximum convenience. Why should he have to go all the way downstairs and around if he wanted bedtime reading, when cutting an extra doorway was so easy?

Efficient, she thought. *Practical. Solid.*

The reminder of last night's blinding moment of insight and the resolution which had followed made her stomach flutter. How could she look at him this morning and not let the love she felt show in her eyes, in her smile, in the way she touched him?

It would help a little, she hoped, seeing him the first

time in the office instead of waking up next to him. Nevertheless…

In the green marble bathroom, Erin cast a longing look at the whirlpool tub and hurried through a shower instead. She sat down at the built-in vanity to dry her hair, and couldn't help wondering why such a deliberately feminine nook had been so carefully fitted into what was otherwise a very masculine bathroom.

This is exactly what you can't let yourself do, she thought. Of course there had been other women in his life—she could hardly pretend otherwise when she'd seen them for herself. But speculating about them would get her nowhere. Instead, she must concentrate on the fact that she would be the one who lasted, the one who spent her life beside him…

Propped up against the mirror was an envelope bearing her name. It contained a key, the codes to the apartment's security system, and a note. Eagerly, she unfolded the sheet of embossed notepaper.

I'm going on to the office, Slater had written in the strong and spiky hand she knew so well. *Take as long as you like, and give your mother my best.* And he'd signed his name. That was all.

Her heart was as flat as the paper.

For Angela, he'd sent his best. For Erin, there was nothing…except permission to be late to work.

What he was really offering her, she remembered saying the night he'd proposed, was a new job, not a marriage. *A personal assistant with a very long-term employment contract,* that was all she really was. Despite the stunning passion they had shared last night—

At least, Erin had felt passion. She had been stunned. And she had believed they were sharing equally. But what had Slater felt?

She tried to blot out the trickle of doubt. "Get over it," she told herself. "You accepted the terms. Now you're going to have to live with them."

Sarah greeted Erin with undisguised relief. "Thank heaven you're finally here. I've been calling everywhere I could think of."

Erin frowned. "I stopped by the hospital to pick up my mother, but she'd already checked out and gone home. What's wrong?"

Sarah rolled her eyes. "The boss has created a whole new king of the tyrant reptiles. Every one he's ever imitated before would turn tail and run if they met him this morning."

That was odd, Erin thought. His note might not have been the love sonnet she'd have liked, but it had been perfectly civil—precisely what she'd have expected of Slater. But if he was so unhappy he was threatening to bite anyone who crossed his path—

Sarah said, "It's the Universal Conveyer bid that went in just last week—for the control systems on that new assembly line."

How foolish, Erin thought, *to think he might have been irritable because of me.*

"What about it? Was something wrong?" *Did I overlook something? Put it together wrong? Mess up the numbers?*

Sarah shook her head. "He just got the word that MacDonald Associates underbid us."

"That's impossible. They couldn't be doing it for less—not unless they pared the bid to the bone. And why would they want the job if they can't make money on it?"

"Well, feel free to go tell Mr. Livingstone that he must

have heard the news wrong, all right? I hope you don't mind if I don't follow you—I'd prefer to stay out here and crawl under my desk to wait for the explosion.''

''Sorry, Sarah—I didn't mean... I don't understand how they could do it, though.''

''Well, just to make matters worse, it's something like fifty cents less.''

''As if they knew precisely what our bid was,'' Erin mused. Her stomach twisted into a knot. Slater had been concerned last week about an information leak, but in that case the details had been wrong and the effects minimal. This case was obviously quite different.

''And just to top things off,'' Sarah went on, ''the Senator's secretary called.''

Erin looked at her with foreboding. ''Please tell me he's not coming this week.''

''Thursday. I've already checked on the ballet, but the series finishes up tonight, so that's out. I don't know how you're going to entertain him, but you've got just about forty-eight hours to figure it out. Oh, and the secretary said he's bringing his daughter.''

''So what does that mean? I'm supposed to arrange child care, too?''

''Hardly. She's twenty-five.''

''Then it's good news—I don't need an extra woman to keep the numbers straight at dinner. Of course that small blessing is balanced out by the fact that Jessup's taking a few days off...'' Erin rubbed the back of her neck. ''I'll think of something.''

''Well, while you think, can you watch the office for a while? I've got to take the Brannagan drawings down to the copy center.''

''What's the matter with the machine behind your desk?''

"It'll feed one sheet of paper, quit, and need resetting. If I'm lucky the repairman will be along before the end of the year. In the meantime, since the boss wants seventy-two thousand copies, more or less—"

Erin raised an eyebrow.

Sarah grinned sheepishly. "Okay, he only needs fifteen sets. But since he's being particularly touchy this morning about confidential information—"

"For good reason, I'd say."

"—It means I'll have to stand over the whole mess to be sure there isn't an extra copy slipped through."

Erin held up both hands in surrender. "Go. I'll cover."

She considered moving out to Sarah's desk, but unless the copy center two floors down was unexpectedly busy, the work shouldn't take more than half an hour. Instead, she settled down in her own office, leaving her door open. From this angle, she couldn't see Sarah's desk, but she would hear anyone who came in. According to Sarah's calendar, the only person Slater was expecting this morning was a supplier's representative.

Bad timing for that poor guy, Erin thought, *when he walks in and meets a T. rex in need of an attitude adjustment.*

A few minutes later, a rustling from the outer office drew her attention, and she put her work aside and went out to greet the rep. The person in the outer office, however, was Cecile Worth, and the rustling Erin had heard hadn't been a sales representative organizing his presentation but the papers scattered on Sarah's desk as Cecile stirred them up.

"Can I help you find what you're looking for?" Erin said crisply.

Cecile didn't even blink in surprise. "I stopped by to see Slater."

''I doubt you'll find him lurking under a manila folder on Sarah's desk.''

''But maybe she has a nail file,'' Cecile said sweetly, and fluttered a hand to show off her scarlet polish. ''Which I am desperately in need of. By the way, Erin, I understand congratulations are in order. So you listened to my advice and took a good long look at his wallet, hmm? Of course, even then who would have thought you'd actually get the job done?''

''Slater's very busy today, Cecile. I doubt—''

''—That you'll try very hard to pencil me in. Well, I suppose if I can't talk to him, I may as well settle for you. I'll make it worth your while if I can meet the Senator this week, Erin. Being his dinner partner would be nice, but I'll settle for sitting across the table.''

Erin was furious at the woman's gall, but even more, she was startled that Cecile so plainly knew that the Senator's visit had been rescheduled. Last night, even Slater hadn't known, yet here the worthy Cecile was...

''I'll keep your wishes in mind when I plan the guest list,'' Erin said. ''But satisfy my curiosity, won't you? What's so attractive about the Senator?''

''Oh, just that he's very interesting,'' Cecile purred. ''And as for what I said about making it worth your while, Erin, maybe I should put it this way—if I don't get an invitation, I'll make your life hell.'' She smiled coolly. ''You know, now that I think about you and Slater, it should have been obvious. His idea of exciting pillow talk is no doubt discussing the profit and loss statement—and who better to do that than little Erin?''

Despite her best efforts, Erin felt soft color wash over her cheeks. Balance sheets had been just about the last thing on her mind last night.

Cecile smirked. ''Was it *that* exciting? Or does it just

take so little to thrill you? I'm pleased for you, darling. Those who don't expect much shall not be disappointed." She flipped her hair back over her shoulder and swept out.

Erin muttered under her breath and started to straighten up the papers the woman had disarranged. She would have expected the worthy Cecile to carry a nail file everywhere she went...

And even if she didn't, why had she been podging around the trays on top of Sarah's desk instead of in the shallow center drawer where such things would most likely be kept?

What had she really been looking for?

Surely her actual reason for coming couldn't have been the Senator's party. The woman wasn't an idiot; she must realize that the likelihood of Slater inviting her to be his guest wasn't much greater than the chances that he'd ask her to act as his hostess again—in other words, nonexistent. And Erin had even less reason to want the woman around. As for both Cecile's threat and her promise, they'd been global and indefinite—hardly something to take seriously.

So what had she really wanted?

Erin picked up a stray memo, a copy on Universal Conveyer's letterhead, and slid it back into the proper folder. Careless of Sarah to leave it out—or had Cecile moved it?

Her eyes narrowed as she wondered whether Universal Conveyer's control systems had been mentioned at the dinner party where Cecile had played hostess. It was quite possible, she thought. One of the engineers working on the proposal had been among the guests, she remembered. And one of the accountants, too, because those same people were also involved with Bob Brannagan's project.

And if Cecile had been listening...

Erin shook her head in disbelief. Frankly, she couldn't imagine Cecile paying much attention to something she'd so clearly find boring, or realizing the importance of what she'd heard.

Though, Erin remembered uncomfortably, she herself had reminded Cecile that the reason Slater's parties weren't held in public places was because the conversations had to be kept private. She might just as well have announced that information gleaned at those parties could be worth money.

But even if Cecile had wanted to capitalize on her position, how would she have known what was important, or who would want to buy it?

Unless, Erin reflected, someone at MacDonald Associates had discovered Cecile had been at that party. It wouldn't have been hard to pick her brain of anything she did recall. And a shrewd operator, putting together bits and pieces, might be able to figure out just about what the bid would be…

She had just finished straightening all the papers and gone back into her office when she heard footsteps leave the tiled corridor and stop just inside the door. Annoyed that she hadn't been able to so much as pick up a pen, she went back out to greet the newcomer.

Dax was standing near Sarah's desk, and when he looked up she saw surprise flicker in his eyes.

That was no wonder, Erin thought. Finding out the woman he'd been trying to date had abruptly married the boss must have come as a stunning surprise. She suspected that Dax didn't shock easily—though of course that was mostly because he seemed impervious to hints and insensitive to anything which didn't fit into his egocentric view of the world. So the impact of the announcement must have been staggering.

"Erin," he said. "I didn't expect you to be here, with your mother ill."

"She's doing fine." Erin's voice was crisp. "What can do I do for you, Dax? If it's the advertising reports, I haven't gotten to them yet."

"It is, actually. Sarah said she'd find them for me and leave them on her desk."

That didn't sound like Sarah's version of the conversation, Erin thought. "I'll get to them today, but I don't know when Mr. Livingstone will have time to look at them. It's been a little busy around here this morning."

"That was my copy," Dax said. "And I could really use it, so if she could make another, I'll pick it up this afternoon."

"I'll tell her to have it delivered." Erin waited beside the desk till he was gone.

Only a couple of minutes later, Sarah reappeared, slightly breathless and carrying a stack of copy paper more than two feet high.

"That's just fifteen sets?" Erin asked.

"Big project." Sarah set the stack on the corner of her desk. "It'll take me the rest of the morning just to get them sorted out and distributed."

Suspicion trickled through Erin's veins. Was this what Cecile had been hoping to find? Surely not. This set of plans had nothing to do with the Universal Conveyer deal. And yet—if she *had* been paying attention at that party, and figured out how important the Brannagan plans would be… "Sarah, has the worthy Cecile been hanging around here lately?"

"Haven't seen a single scarlet fingernail since last week. Before the party for the Brannagans, I think. Do you want to take your set right now?"

Erin lifted the top bundle and stood idly flipping the

pages. Before she'd moved from the public relations department into Slater's office, these drawings would have been absolute Greek. Even now, she knew just enough to interpret the basics. Without any experience, someone like Cecile wouldn't have a clue what these specifications meant—or even how to tell which papers were important and which were not. It wasn't as if they were labelled *Important—Steal Me First.*

The door of Slater's office opened. ''Sarah, would you...''

Erin turned toward him. She was startled at the strength of her reaction, for how many times had she seen him like this—coat off, sleeves rolled up, apparently preoccupied...

But those other times, she'd been looking at her boss. Not her husband. Not her lover. Not the man she loved.

Today, she saw the strength in his body and felt once more the security and comfort she'd experienced last night as he'd held her. She saw the way he moved and relived, just a little, the ecstasy of making love with him. She saw his preoccupation and hit reality with a thud, remembering that business would always come first with him. He had, after all, married her because of his business...

''Erin,'' he said. ''Come in, please.''

''Let me grab my notebook.''

''No need.'' He ushered her into his office and waved her to a chair. ''Sarah's told you about Universal Conveyer.'' It wasn't a question.

''Yes. I can hardly believe it, but... There's no doubt?''

''Do you mean am I sure we've lost the bid? Yes. And I know exactly how much the difference was, too. It wouldn't buy a bag of peanuts at the circus.''

She nodded. ''I suppose the first thing you'll want to do is run down the leak.''

Slater shook his head. "I'll deal with that when I get back."

"Back?" Erin's voice felt raspy. "Where—"

"I'm catching the next commuter flight to Chicago, to talk to the Universal Conveyer people."

"Then you don't think the deal's dead?"

"Let's just say I want to be sure they know the kind of people they're doing business with. But in the meantime, we'll have to assume that Universal Conveyer is out of the picture, so the Brannagan project just got even more important. While I'm gone—"

Erin didn't quite understand. How could Slater know that the Brannagan project was safe until he found out why Universal Conveyer hadn't been? If it was painfully clear to her that the information had been deliberately leaked, Slater had to realize that the underbidding couldn't be an accident. And that meant it could happen again.

Why was he willing to take any chance at all of a repetition?

But it wasn't up to her to second-guess his decisions. Erin pulled her attention back to his crisp list of instructions, committing them to memory and wishing she'd insisted on getting her notebook after all. "Of course, sir."

Slater frowned. "I thought we were past that."

Too late, Erin heard the title echoing through the almost-silent office. "Sorry," she said. "It just slipped out—but you were being particularly bossish, you know."

He leaned back in his chair and smiled, the first hint of relaxation she'd seen since she'd walked in. "I was, wasn't I? How's your mother doing?"

"I'm not sure. I understand my father took her home this morning."

Slater's eyebrows climbed. "I wonder what his new wife will think of that."

''The question occurred to me. Then I realized what was bothering me last night...'' She paused. ''I mean, when I thought I'd lost Mother's ring. I guess I've been wearing it so long I'd stopped seeing it—if that makes sense.''

Slater sounded a little doubtful. ''So you looked at it last night—'' he prompted, ''and you saw—''

''It wasn't till this morning that I realized what I'd seen. The wedding ring Dad was wearing yesterday wasn't shiny because it was new, it gleamed because it had been polished. It matched the one I've got, you see.''

''He's still wearing his wedding ring....'' Slater gave a low, long whistle. ''I wonder how long it'll be before she asks for hers back.''

''If you're starting a betting pool, put me down for *within a week.*'' She said, tentatively, ''That reminds me, though. I never even asked if you wanted a wedding ring.''

''You had a few other things on your mind. And it doesn't matter, Erin. Really.''

Of course not, she thought with a trace of cynicism. Now if he'd married her to hold off other women, instead of just to be his hostess, he might have wanted to wear her ring... *Pretend it isn't important to you that love has nothing to do with it—and maybe eventually it won't matter at all.*

Maybe, Erin thought, she was actually starting to get the hang of this corporate wife business.

Slater glanced at his wristwatch. ''I have to leave.'' He started to unroll his shirtsleeves. ''Where did my damned cuff links go?''

''You'll be back for the Senator's visit, won't you?'' Erin stood up.

''With time to spare, I hope.'' He found the cuff links

in a tray on his desk, settled his tie into place, and put on his suit jacket. Hands on hips, he paused to give Erin a speculative look. "What will you do if I don't give you a goodbye kiss?"

Kick you, she thought. *Scream. Break my heart…* No—the proper answer to a playful question was a playful answer. "Sure you want to find out?"

Slater smiled. "Nope." Casually, he pulled her close. But there was nothing nonchalant about the way he kissed her, and by the time he let her go Erin felt as if her insides had turned to lava. "I'm sorry I won't be home tonight," he whispered, and was gone before she could answer.

Which, she thought, was probably just as well. If her brain really had melted, which was certainly how it felt, the would-be perfect corporate wife might have blown her cover sky-high by telling him she loved him, or something stupid like that.

She didn't feel like facing Sarah, at least until her heart stopped skipping beats, so Erin settled down at Slater's desk to list all the instructions he'd given about the Brannagan deal. She was deep in thought, trying to remember the last of them, when she heard voices from the outer office and realized Slater had left the door partway open. *That's going to get annoying real fast,* she thought, and considered walking over to shut it. But the next thing she heard stopped her in her tracks.

"I can't show you something like that," Sarah said. "Go through channels."

A man's voice, lower and tightly controlled, answered. "They'll say advertising doesn't have a need."

Advertising, Erin thought. No wonder the voice sounded familiar; Dax Porter had returned. Now she was really glad she was in Slater's office and not her own; he wouldn't think to look for her there. She turned her attention back to her list.

''And they're right, of course.'' The secretary sounded thoughtful. ''So why are you interested, anyway? It's not like we have to sell the idea to the public.''

''Would you at least stop playing dumb? You know what's been going on as well as I do. Look, Sarah, you've had as much fun romancing me as I have flirting with you, but I don't have time for the runaround right now.''

Erin's eyes widened in shock.

''I can't afford to spend weeks prying bits and pieces out of you so I can put them together like a jigsaw puzzle,'' Dax said irritably. ''I want the drawings for the switches that are going to control Bob Brannagan's new satellites, and I want them now.''

''So you can sell them to Fritz MacDonald.'' Sarah's voice was taut.

''Or whoever will pay the most. So far, it appears to be Fritz. And you're going to get them for me, or I'll tell your boss precisely what happened to the Universal Conveyer job.''

Erin closed her eyes in pain. The shocking thing, she thought, was the fact that she was not surprised to learn Dax Porter was the culprit, the source of Control Dynamics' leaking information. She must have had her doubts, at some level, ever since Tonio had told her about the stolen flower—because a man who would steal a simple rose rather than pay for it would probably do things which were a great deal more unethical as well.

What was wrenching her to bits was the fact that his source was Sarah.

It wasn't Cecile who had unwittingly provided information to some corporate spy. It was *Sarah.*

Sarah, who had been Slater's confidential secretary for

years, long before Erin had come into the office. Sarah, who looked after him, fixed his coffee just so, teased him with her dinosaur code…and betrayed him by giving out confidential information. It sounded as if she wasn't even selling it, but giving it away for the fun of flirting with Dax—and that hurt Erin even more.

"Look," Sarah said crisply, "there's nothing I can do to get you the drawings."

"You've had your hands on them already."

"And I've passed them on."

"Well, you'd better figure out a way to get a set back."

"Or you'll tell Mr. Livingstone? If you tried to throw me to the wolves, you'd be admitting your own theft." There was a thread of relief in Sarah's voice.

"You can bet I'd be careful not to say it in front of witnesses. Or hasn't it occurred to you that the accusation doesn't need to stand up in court in order to ruin you? Just raising the question would be enough."

That was perfectly true, Erin knew. Once suspected, a confidential secretary was doomed. Of course, from the sound of things, Sarah deserved it, but…

"Besides, I've got other plans for my life than advertising." Dax gave the word a twist as if it was obscene. "My resignation letter's already written. Maybe I'll take it straight to Livingstone—and tell him I'm quitting because I can't square it with my conscience any more to be the conduit for you to sell information. Or maybe," he went on thoughtfully, "we'll leave me out of it entirely. If Fritz MacDonald were to let it slip that you were the source of his information… He and Livingstone play racquetball together now and then, you know."

Erin had never understood, considering the rivalry between the firms, why the two men at the top would find sharing a sport an engaging pastime—but that was one of the masculine mysteries she would probably never comprehend. The point was that Dax was right. If Fritz MacDonald was to point a finger, seemingly by accident…

Not that it would come to that, of course, because Slater would know long before Fritz MacDonald had a chance to play his role. Erin was going to have to tell him.

"So what's it going to be, Sarah?" Dax was obviously losing patience. "Stop stalling. I need the details of that switch—especially the drawings. Do you get them for me, or do I talk to Livingstone?"

Erin held her breath.

"I'll get them." She heard Sarah's voice as if it was coming from a great distance. "But it'll take a while."

There was a long pause, as if Dax was weighing his options. "I'll give you forty-eight hours, but that's all. And don't think just because I'm not hanging around that I've changed my mind. You know where to find me when you've got the plans."

Erin heard the rapid tap of his heels as he left. The silence which fell over the office suite weighed so heavily on her that she thought she would never be able to move again. But eventually she pushed herself to her feet and crossed the thick carpet to the half-open door.

Sarah was sitting at her desk, elbows on the blotter, her face buried in her hands.

Erin pushed the door wider. The hinges creaked, and Sarah jerked upright. Her face went gray with shock.

"I think," Erin said, "that you'd better come in, Sarah. We have some things to talk about."

CHAPTER NINE

SLOWLY, Sarah stood up. She moved like a mechanical doll, Erin thought, or a rusty tin soldier. She followed Erin into Slater's office and stood in front of the desk, not even responding to the offer of a chair. She licked her lips and blinked her eyes very slowly, like someone who had just roused from a bad dream and wasn't yet sure if she was awake—or whether she even wanted to be.

Erin sat down behind Slater's desk and waited.

Finally Sarah's gaze focused once more. "I didn't know you were here."

"That much was fairly obvious."

"I had to run down to the copy center again for just a minute, and when I came back your office was empty, and Mr. Livingstone was just leaving. I thought you'd gone to lunch." Her voice trailed off. "But none of that matters, does it? Oh, Erin, what am I going to do?"

The desperation in her voice startled Erin. She'd never before thought of Sarah as a world-class actress, completely wasted in a secretarial position. But how could the woman possibly be sincere? Erin's voice was dry. "I'd say that depends on what you've already done. You've been pretty busy, haven't you?"

Sarah's eyes widened. "You don't think I did this on purpose!"

"What else am I supposed to think? You admitted giving Dax the Universal Conveyer information, you promised to get the Brannagan drawings for him—"

"I had to buy some time. A chance to think." Horror

dawned in her eyes, and Sarah sank down onto the edge of the chair. "You don't believe me, do you? Erin, I need this job. I have a child to support. You don't think I'm stupid enough to risk it—do you?"

Erin didn't answer, but doubt bubbled up in her mind. She'd noticed, even in the midst of her shock, that it didn't sound as if Sarah had profited financially from the information Dax was selling. So why *would* she have done it? Merely for the dubious pleasure of having Dax Porter hanging around? Balanced against the risk she was taking, that made no sense at all. And she couldn't possibly be carrying such a grudge against Slater that she'd put herself at such risk in order to get even...

"Well, I am stupid." Sarah's voice was full of self-loathing. "I was too dumb even to see what was happening. Remember how many times Dax dropped into the office while we were working on that bid? And you know yourself the kind of careless, naive questions he asks. I can hardly even remember what I said to him—but it wasn't any more than crumbs, I'd have sworn it wasn't. And maybe he got a glimpse of the paperwork—heaven knows there was plenty of it, all over the office. I never gave it a thought, Erin. He's supposed to be on our side!"

I can't afford to spend weeks prying bits and pieces out of you so I can put them together like a jigsaw puzzle, Dax had said. Erin had assumed that meant Sarah had tantalized him with information, feeding it to him slowly to maximize his attentions. But it could equally well be that Sarah was telling the truth—that Dax had picked her brain without her even being aware of what he was up to.

In this case, of course, innocence was no defense. A personal secretary was supposed to be as confidential as an attorney—or maybe even a confessor. They were never to speak without thinking, no matter what. They were never to tell secrets. So if Sarah had talked—even if she was acting gullibly and foolishly rather than with malicious intent—she was still responsible. She had, however ingenuously, treated her boss with disrespect and his business with abandon. And she would have to face the consequences.

Erin took a deep breath. "I'll have to tell Slater, of course."

"Tell him what? I didn't steal information, Erin. I didn't leak it. I swear I didn't." Her voice faded. "Not on purpose. It could have happened to anyone. I mean, are you absolutely certain *you* didn't let anything slip? Dax spent as much time talking to you as to me. He must have thought it was worth his while—and now that it's painfully obvious he's more than just a skirt-chaser—"

Erin felt the accusation explode in her head. Was it possible she, too, had been caught in Dax's trap? Sarah was right that he was a master of the casual question. Only now did Erin remember that he'd asked her, over lunch in the lobby cafeteria, about Bob Brannagan, his dealings with Slater, and the conversation at the dinner party the night before. Of course, he hadn't phrased things quite that directly; she hadn't even noticed at the time that he was doing anything more than carrying on a casual conversation.

But what about Erin's answers? *Had* she let information slip? In her annoyance with Dax, her haste to get away from all those unwelcome encounters, had she said the wrong thing?

Had she betrayed her husband? Violated Slater's trust?

If so, her actions had been even worse than Sarah's. If a secretary had to be secretive, a personal assistant was supposed to resemble a tomb. And as for a wife...

There would be nothing she could do which would be

worse, in Slater's eyes, than let confidential information slip. Having an affair, she thought, would be nowhere on the same plane; after all, theirs was hardly a love match, and so long as she wasn't late for an important dinner party...

Gallows humor isn't going to fix this, she told herself.

She gritted her teeth and replayed as best she could every conversation she'd ever had with Dax Porter. So far as she could remember, she hadn't let a piece of information slip. But could she be absolutely certain? Dax was not only slick, he was diabolical; he'd not only snared Sarah but he'd managed to keep her in the dark even while he was teasing out everything she knew...

Was it only luck that had kept Erin herself from falling into the trap?

She looked at Sarah with considerably more sympathy, realizing how close she herself had come to disaster.

But it was still no excuse. The damage done by Sarah's careless tongue had been immense. Could Erin ever trust the woman again? More to the point, could Slater?

A bit of that overheard conversation nagged at her once more. "You told Dax you'd get him the plans," she reminded.

"I didn't mean it, Erin. I just had to delay him, somehow."

"Why? To buy yourself time to figure out what to do?"

The secretary was nervously folding the hem of her skirt into pleats. She nodded and said, almost to herself, "My job. I need my job."

"I don't know if it can be saved." Erin felt brutal, but she knew that honesty was the only way to handle this now. It would do Sarah no good to give her false hope. "I'll still have to tell Slater about this."

Sarah looked directly at Erin, took a deep breath, and

squared her shoulders. ''At least let me be the one to tell him what happened.''

''Confession being good for the soul?''

''It'll be better to tell him myself.''

''He's likely to think that you know the truth's going to come out, so you're just trying to limit the damage by putting the best possible face on your actions.''

''Well, isn't that exactly what I'm doing?'' Sarah said bitterly. ''It's the only chance I've got, Erin. If I can explain what happened, make him believe that I didn't mean to do it—''

Erin didn't think it would make a great deal of difference, but Sarah was right about one thing—her only chance with Slater would be a full, open, honest explanation. Then at least he might let her stay at Control Dynamics, though doubtless it would be in a much less sensitive job. Otherwise, Sarah would not only be unemployed, she'd be without a reference to help her get another position anywhere.

And no matter what the results had been, in Erin's mind carelessness didn't deserve the same harsh punishment as deliberate action would.

''The sooner the better,'' Sarah said. The words were firm, but her voice trembled. ''As soon as Mr. Livingstone gets back from lunch—''

''He hasn't gone to lunch. He went to Chicago, to try to salvage something from the Universal Conveyer deal. Didn't he tell you?''

Sarah's face fell. ''I just caught a glimpse of him going down the hall as I came back from the copy center. When will he be back?''

''I don't know. He said he'd try to be here for the Senator's visit.''

''But that's Thursday night. After—'' Sarah gulped.

"That's hours after Dax's deadline. Dax could be waiting for Mr. Livingstone at the airport to tell him. And he will, just to get even with me."

"A phone call..." But Erin knew better. A face-to-face discussion was Sarah's best—her only—hope. *Besides,* she thought, *I don't even know where Slater's staying.* For that matter, he might not know yet himself; it was Sarah who normally made arrangements for hotels and plane tickets.

And there was a horrible irony in the idea of calling him at Universal Conveyer to let him know what had caused the very problem he was trying to solve...

"I have to stop Dax in the meantime," Sarah said. "It's not just for my sake either, Erin. I don't know where else he's getting stuff—but it occurred to me, along in the middle of that lecture of his, that I may not be the only source he's using. If I tell him I won't give him the drawings, or even that I can't get hold of them—"

"You believe he may be able to get them somewhere else?"

"Why not? If he thinks I'm not going to come through, why wouldn't he try another route? Erin, there are fifteen sets of those drawings floating around this building. I handed them all out myself."

Erin felt sick.

"Dax didn't offer to cut me on in the finances," Sarah said dryly, "because his source of supply depended on keeping me acting dumb. And I'm sure he'd still prefer to get information from me because he's got such a hold on me he knows he won't have to pay for it. But what about the others? If he offered enough money—"

"Those plans have to be worth a million dollars to Fritz MacDonald."

Silence settled over the office.

''If I'm the cause of another deal going bad,'' Sarah said drearily, ''I'll kill myself.''

''No, you won't.''

''I'm glad you're so sure of it.''

''I mean we'll stop him.''

''How, exactly, do you propose to do that? Call in all fifteen sets of drawings? For all we know they've been recopied already. Besides, the engineers *need* them. They don't have all the time in the world to do this project—''

Erin was shaking her head. ''We'll give Dax exactly what he asked for.'' She smiled. ''We'll give him the Brannagan drawings.''

Not the real ones, of course, just a fairly close facsimile. But her brainstorm was more difficult to carry out than Erin had expected.

The alterations themselves were simple enough. The Brannagan plans were not only complex, they were also far from neat. Obviously several draftsmen had worked on them in stages, some using computer technology, others making additions and corrections by hand—and no one had bothered to take the necessary time to smooth out the final version and make it pretty. So it was easy to add a line here and take one out somewhere else without leaving obvious signs of precisely when the drawings had been changed, or by whom.

But knowing what to move, what to draw in, what to delete, was another question; she was no engineer, and neither was Sarah. It seemed self-evident that with such sensitive equipment, a minimum of change would throw off the whole. After all, if this one infinitesimal switching mechanism were easy to build, Bob Brannagan wouldn't be so agreeable to the idea of paying multimillions to get the work done. But how would Erin know whether she'd changed enough? Exactly which alterations would be most disruptive?

Just as important, what would be least obvious?

On the other hand, Erin reflected, her experience, limited though it was, had to be more extensive than Dax's. She'd been working with things like this for a year; in his job, he'd probably never seen an actual set of plans. So long as the changes didn't leap out at him as obviously wrong, Erin's plan would work. Dax would pass the drawings along as the real thing—and he wouldn't have any reason to keep looking for another set.

They could buy at least a few hours...enough, Erin hoped, for Slater to get home and for Sarah to make her confession. Then he could decide what to do about Sarah, and Dax, and Fritz MacDonald.

So, with Sarah hovering nervously over her, Erin rubbed out a few lines, altered an equation here and there, turned a chip the opposite direction, and smudged the connections for a fuse. Rather than risk using the copy center in the building, Sarah smuggled the resulting plans down the street to a commercial printer and made a set for Dax.

Erin was quite pleased with the results. It seemed to her that even someone with experience in reading plans and specifications would have trouble making sense of these drawings. Or—perhaps even more importantly—realizing that they made no sense at all.

With any luck, Erin thought, Fritz MacDonald's people wouldn't realize they'd been conned until after the Brannagan project was so far along it couldn't be harmed. Then, most likely, they'd fume in silence rather than admit they'd been bested at corporate espionage.

With any luck, Sarah could confess and maybe even keep her job—for she had, after all, saved the Brannagan project.

And with any luck, Slater would never have to know that Erin had taken a hand in the situation at all.

Erin was just finishing arranging the centerpiece for the Senator's dinner party when Jessup came in to remind her of the time. "Mr. Livingstone hasn't arrived yet?" she asked, already knowing the answer. Surely she'd have heard him. Surely he'd have come in to say hello.

"He's probably caught in rush-hour traffic," Jessup said gravely. "It's only a few minutes till the guests will be here, Mrs. Livingstone."

"I know. I just hoped..." She put the last pink anthurium into place and stood back to admire the result. The silver bowl with its matching tray had been a good choice; the flowers' reflection in the shiny surface made the arrangement even more impressive.

As she climbed the stairs to the master bedroom, Erin couldn't help remembering the last dinner party, when Jessup had sent her off to the guest room to ready herself because she might have to fill in for Cecile. How different things were now—and yet how much the same.

She was just pulling her white-spangled cocktail dress—her wedding dress—over her head when Slater came into the bedroom.

Her heart began to pound. He looked tired, she thought, as if his trip hadn't been much of a success. But despite the weariness in his face, he was still the most gorgeous sight she'd ever seen.

He didn't even say hello, just came to stand behind her at the mirror. "I know I told you I like that dress," he said, and kissed the nape of her neck. "But that doesn't mean it's the only thing you can ever wear."

"I haven't had time to shop." Erin settled the neckline into place.

Slater zipped the dress. ''Besides, why take a chance of spilling red wine or something and ruining it? Shouldn't you put it away to keep?''

''For posterity? Do you really think any of Aunt Hermione's nieces would want to be married in it?''

''Why not? If it was good enough for their mother...'' He slowly turned her to face him.

Erin was reluctant to meet his gaze, for fear he'd see in her eyes that there was something she didn't want to tell him. *Tomorrow,* she thought. *As soon as he gets to the office, Sarah will confess... and then I won't have secrets anymore.* At least, she wouldn't have quite so many of them.

The intercom buzzed, and she stepped away from Slater. ''That's Jessup,'' she said quickly. ''That's the signal that the doorman just called to tell him the first guests are on their way up.''

''Then you'd better go.'' He pulled his tie loose. ''I'll be down just as soon as I can.''

''At least have a hot shower to relax you. In just a few minutes we'll be going downstairs for the cocktail party and the Senator will be swamped for the next two hours, so it really doesn't matter if you're a little—''

''Cocktail party?''

''In the lobby. Didn't I tell you about that? The Senator wanted to meet as many of Control Dynamics' employees as he could, so—''

''Is it election year?''

''Isn't it always? Since he's only going to be here overnight, it seemed the best way to fit everything in. We'll appear at the party, then come back up here for dinner.''

There was a twinkle in Slater's eyes. ''That's much easier than having the party here and actually getting everyone to leave on time.''

"It certainly is. Anyway, you may as well take your time. I'll look after things."

"I know you will."

Of course he knew, Erin thought. He had faith in her abilities, or he'd never have married her. The perfect corporate wife...

He vanished into the bathroom, and she turned toward the stairway. Apart from zipping her dress, she thought unhappily, he had hardly touched her.

The Senator was bluff and hearty, white-haired and red-faced, the stereotypical politician. He greeted Erin like a long-lost pal, except that the kiss he pressed on her was slightly more than friendly, and introduced his daughter. "It turned out to be a good thing, really, that I had to postpone my trip until this week," he said, "because it meant Katrina could come with me. She works with disadvantaged children, and they need her so badly that she seldom takes time off."

"Dad," Katrina said. "Stop trying to make me look like a saint, all right? Nobody believes you, anyway." Her voice was the audible equivalent of hot fudge sauce—slow-moving and rich and very, very appealing.

Furthermore, she was not only the most gorgeous woman Erin had ever encountered—an obviously natural blonde with porcelain skin and huge, improbably brown eyes—but there was an instant warmth about her which made her very hard to resist. If her father had taught her the politician's trick of seeming to be everybody's chum, Erin thought, he'd done a good job.

The Senator made noises of disagreement, but he didn't actually argue the point. Erin was amused enough at his attitude to forget the overzealous way he'd kissed her, until she saw Katrina glance over Erin's shoulder toward the doorway with unmistakable interest in her eyes.

There was no doubt in Erin's mind what Katrina was looking at, for she'd heard Slater's step in the hallway. He came to stand beside Erin's chair, one hand on her shoulder. She glanced up at him, feeling proud that he was hers, ready to make the necessary introduction.

And saw bemusement in his eyes as he took his first good look at the Senator's daughter. Bemusement—and fascination, which was even more frightening because she'd never seen it there before. He'd certainly never looked at Erin that way...

Her heart dropped like a stone.

Someday you'll find a woman you can love, she'd told Slater blithely on the night he'd first proposed to her. But she hadn't really believed it would happen—or rather, even without realizing how she felt, she had hoped to be that woman. She'd let herself be convinced at some unconscious level that someday he would come to see her as more than a useful adjunct. And so she had put her perfectly sensible prediction out of her mind and married him, and trusted that someday it would be all right.

And when, on her wedding night, she'd realized that she'd been fooling herself all along, she'd made up her mind to play the game. She'd been logical and reasonable and cool in her decision to be the wife he wanted—the perfect corporate wife.

But all that logic and reason wasn't doing Erin any good right now. It was one thing to prepare herself for jealousy in the abstract sense, but quite another to stand toe-to-toe with it. It was one thing to think of a hypothetical woman—faceless and without personality—and tell herself that she wouldn't watch Slater, she wouldn't question his feelings, she wouldn't wonder if this woman was the one.

But Katrina was neither faceless nor without personality. And Erin could try all she wanted not to wonder about Slater's feelings, but the truth was she didn't need to speculate; he looked as if he'd been hit over the head with a telephone pole.

Erin wished she could say the same about herself. It would have hurt a great deal less than the knife blade she was feeling in her heart.

She concentrated on her breathing, and she managed to smile as she introduced them. And then, because it was too painful to watch as her husband took Katrina's hand as carefully as if it were glass, she turned back to the Senator and asked about the Pentagon matter which had delayed his trip last week.

A few minutes later she set her wineglass down and said, "I believe it's time to go down to the lobby for the cocktail party."

The Senator set down his glass. Katrina didn't seem to hear at all; she sat very straight, glass in hand and still as full as when Erin had poured it for her, looking over the rim at Slater. Slater looked as if he'd never heard of a cocktail party before, much less been told about this one.

The Senator laughed. "Don't feel bad," he rumbled to Erin. "Happens all the time—people get so wrapped up in Katrina they forget everything else."

The people in question, Erin thought grimly, no doubt being of the male persuasion...

"I don't mean to brag," he went on. "But my little girl—"

Is seducing my husband, Erin wanted to say. *And she deserves to be spanked for it.* She bit her tongue hard and told herself that this was no way to deal with jealousy.

The chatter of the cocktail party, already in progress, carried up through the atrium all the way to the top floor. She linked her arm through the Senator's and guided him into the confusion, stopping here and there to introduce the senior staff. But it wasn't long before the Senator had both hands outstretched as he worked the crowd with supreme efficiency, and so Erin turned away, running a practiced eye over the guests in search of problems in the making. The person who was too shy to leave the corner, the one who was drinking too much, the one who wanted to monopolize the guest of honor…

Her eye fell on Katrina just as the young woman stretched out her lovely slim hand to take the glass Slater had fetched for her. Erin saw the brush of the woman's fingers against the back of Slater's hand, saw her lashes sweep up and then tantalizingly down again. And she saw Slater smile down at Katrina, with a warmth and ease that made her heart ache.

Beside her, Dax Porter was watching, too. Erin wasn't surprised to see him; though it took incredible gall to appear at a company party when one was stealing from the host, his absence would be noticed—and she supposed, despite what he'd said to Sarah about his long-term career plans, Dax wasn't planning to give up his position at Control Dynamics as long as he could get his hands on saleable secrets.

"Interesting," he murmured. "You made such a determined play to get the man, and now before you've even had a chance to relax and enjoy the triumph he's found other interests. Poor Erin. Maybe you shouldn't have set your sights quite so high."

And grabbed for you instead, Dax? Erin clenched her teeth to keep from saying that she'd sooner immolate herself than settle for a traitor, liar and cheat. The last thing she could do right now was let Dax suspect that his secret was out. Tomorrow, it would all be over, but tonight she had to smile and treat him just as she always had—pleasant, no-nonsense, with no more than a hint of irony. "Thanks for sharing your insight, Dax," she said sweetly and turned toward the portable bar.

Sarah was standing off to the side, watching the crowd. It was the first time Erin had seen her since she'd handed over the altered plans, and she casually worked her way across the room. "How'd it go?" she asked.

Sarah wrinkled her nose. "He was awful," she said. "Arrogant and pompous and condescending. He actually had the nerve to thank me—in a sneer, of course."

"Of course, the good news is that means he swallowed the bait."

"Yes." Sarah's gaze drifted across the room. "Do you think I could talk to Mr. Livingstone tonight?"

Drag him from Katrina's side? Erin thought. *Good luck!* "I think it would be better to wait. There'll be fewer distractions in the office tomorrow."

"I know. I just want to get it over with."

"That makes two of us." Erin drifted away, headed toward a guest who was standing alone near the punch bowl.

A little later, she noticed that Slater and Katrina, still deep in conversation, had edged off toward a corner. A few minutes after that she ran almost headlong into her husband near the bar. No doubt, she thought, Katrina had wanted fresh ice.

"I hope you and the Senator are finding time to talk," Erin said, her tone as sweet as she could manage.

"Oh, we'll take care of the details after the party breaks up. Katrina's a darling, isn't she?"

The worst of it was, Erin thought, that she couldn't even honestly disagree.

Before she could say anything at all, however, Slater had gone on. "It's a nice party, Erin."

To Erin's ears, the words sounded almost careless, a throwaway compliment that meant little. His voice had been level, with none of the enthusiasm he'd shown just a few moments ago. So Katrina was a darling, was she? And what about Erin? She was solid, practical, sensible...and dreary.

She said flatly, "Of course it's a nice party. That's my job, isn't it?" And without even looking for a reaction, she spun away from him and headed, almost blindly, toward the nearest group of guests.

The evening was finally over—but even then Slater didn't seem willing to see it end, for he insisted on going downstairs with the Senator and Katrina while they waited for their taxi.

Through the evening, Erin's nerves had slowly frayed till now even the soft, rhythmic click of the spangles and beads on her dress as she moved was enough to push her over the edge into a screaming frenzy. She told Jessup that the cleanup could wait, turned her back on the mess and retreated to the master bedroom.

She dropped her dress on the floor and sat down to brush her hair, trying to get control of herself. In a few minutes, Slater would walk through the door, and she had to react like a good corporate wife. She must smile and greet him cheerfully, ask whether the Universal Conveyer people had seen reason after all, offer to rub his back...

She must not let slip even a hint of the depressing news which would greet him tomorrow at the office. She must not be sarcastic about Katrina. And if Slater turned to her tonight and wanted to make love, she must not wonder if he was thinking of the Senator's gorgeous daughter...

And that, she knew, would be impossible.

She turned the light off, and when he came in through

the library she was lying on her side, curled up and breathing as evenly and softly as she could.

Slater paused for a moment, then closed the door softly behind him. He undressed in the dark and slid into bed. He leaned over her for a moment, then sighed and gently ruffled her hair and settled back against his pillow.

Erin's hands clenched. He'd patted her on the head like he would a pet, she thought. One who had performed as expected.

Good Erin, you did that trick just perfectly. Now sit and stay till I want you again…

And she would. She'd stay, and she'd do her best on every trick he asked of her, because she loved him.

And if someday—maybe someday soon—he didn't want her anymore…

A silent tear slid down her cheek and hid itself in her pillow.

For a change, Erin was the first one to reach the office in the morning. She'd expected Sarah to be there waiting—haggard from a sleepless night, perhaps, but early nonetheless—and the too-neat desk and the still-covered computer made her nervous. Had Sarah chickened out? Had she reassessed her chances of persuading Slater and, deciding that there was no hope of anything but rejection, decided not to humiliate herself by begging for her job?

But just as Erin was filling the coffeepot on the cart in the corner of Sarah's office, the secretary appeared. Her jaw was set, her face was pale, and her eyes were full of dread. "Is Mr. Livingstone here already?"

Erin shook her head. "He was already gone when I woke up. But he left me a note—he went to the gym and will be a little late this morning."

Sarah's face twitched.

Erin knew exactly what Sarah was feeling—half relief and half disappointment. It was precisely the same mix she'd experienced on waking to find herself alone. She'd been disappointed that there was only a note on the dressing table—a note just as cool as the one she'd found the morning after her wedding—to remind her she had a husband. And yet she'd been relieved as well because she hadn't had to face him with a bright smile in celebration of a successful party.

''A half hour one way or the other isn't going to make any big difference,'' Erin pointed out.

''I know. It's just that I had myself braced for it.''

''How about some coffee? That might make you feel better.''

''It might. Though even arsenic couldn't make me feel worse,'' Sarah said. ''Having to face him with what I've done...''

Erin, knowing that nothing she said could make things easier, poured her own coffee and retreated toward her office.

At the same instant, both of them heard the footsteps in the hallway—firm, decisive, definitely male.

And angry, Erin thought. But what—

She met Sarah's eyes, and sudden, horrible understanding flared between them.

He'd gone to the gym, Slater's note had said, and Erin had thought no more about it. But the gym was where he and Fritz MacDonald played racquetball from time to time. Slater might well have gone in search of Fritz this morning, looking not for a game but a chance to challenge him about Universal Conveyer.

And if he'd found him, Slater might have gotten a great deal more than he bargained for.

Erin braced herself in the door of her office, where

she'd be just out of Slater's line of sight but only a step from Sarah's defense. If he came in shouting—or worse yet, deadly cold and controlled—the least she could do was help to explain, to tell him that all they'd done, really, was to try to make a horrible situation just a little easier to bear.

But it wasn't Slater's voice she heard, it was Dax's, and at the first words Erin's muscles froze.

"Dammit, Sarah," he said, "it doesn't work!"

Erin forced herself out of the doorway. Dax didn't see her standing there; all his attention was focused on Sarah. He shook a thick sheaf of paper—the set of Brannagan drawings she'd given him just yesterday—in her face.

"You shouldn't have come here, Dax." Sarah's voice shook.

"How stupid can one woman be? Don't you get it?" Dax's voice was shrill. "The damn thing doesn't work!"

Erin stepped forward. "Keep your voice down, Dax. The whole nineteenth floor's going to hear you, and you'll have security people breathing down your neck inside of two minutes."

He twisted round to glare at her. "You keep out of this, Miss Virgin Pure. Nobody asked you." Then his eyes narrowed, grew cunning. "You're in this up to your neck, aren't you? You know perfectly well what your precious little Sarah's been up to. I ought to have known she wouldn't be so cooperative without your approval. What's in it for you, Erin? Power?"

Erin's brain seemed to be stuck in low gear.

"I suppose you're going to want a cut of the money, too," Dax growled. "Well, you won't get it, because for the last time, I'm telling you the damned thing doesn't work!"

None of them had heard Slater come in. Erin didn't

even know he was there until he spoke, quite calmly, from directly behind Dax. ''Of course it doesn't, Dax,'' he said. ''You didn't really think we'd give you the genuine drawings—did you?''

CHAPTER TEN

ERIN'S heart hit her toes. Slater obviously didn't need an explanation of what was going on in his office; even though Dax hadn't been specific, Slater had gone straight to the heart of the matter. There had been no surprise in his voice, only a kind of sadness. Obviously he not only knew the Brannagan plans were in the wrong hands—but he also knew exactly who had put them there…

And he's going to think I'm in it up to my neck, Erin thought. Which, of course, she was. Her attempt to mitigate the damages had backfired; instead of a loose cannon they were suddenly faced with a nuclear warhead gone berserk.

She shot a look at Sarah, who merely looked confused. Then the secretary's face grew even whiter, and Erin turned her head just as two uniformed security officers appeared in the hallway.

Sarah's hands clenched the back of her desk chair as if it was the only thing keeping her from sliding off a cliff.

We're in for it now, Erin thought.

Slater's upraised hand halted the two men in their tracks, and he took another step toward Dax. "Well?" he prompted. "Surely you're not fool enough to think Erin and Sarah would give you the real drawings."

Erin's heart soared high again. It was going to be all right, she told herself. Because of course that was exactly what had happened. Slater must have realized in a flash that Dax's set had been sabotaged.

Except… Slater couldn't know.

He might—just possibly—suspect what Erin had done, but he couldn't be certain. There was no evidence; she'd made sure of that.

Even if he'd turned her office inside out—something he'd had no opportunity to do since he'd returned from Chicago, even if he'd wanted to—he would have found nothing except her own set of plans. The real ones.

The copies on which they'd actually made the changes had gone into the shredder, and the set Dax was brandishing hadn't been out of Erin's sight, or Sarah's, from the moment they'd been created in the print shop till Sarah had handed them over to Dax yesterday.

So, if Slater wasn't certain of what they'd done, was he simply bluffing when he said the plans weren't the real ones?

Erin didn't think so; the note of authority in his voice would have been very hard to deliberately assume, even for someone as experienced in the game of business poker as Slater was.

Besides, she realized, there was another and far more sensible interpretation of what he'd said—that he was simply telling the truth.

Dax's plans didn't work—there was no question about that. But maybe the failure hadn't come from the changes Erin had made…but from something else altogether.

She was still contemplating all the ramifications of that possibility when Slater confirmed it. "What you have there, Dax, are preliminary drawings, ones that don't incorporate the final, most important innovations that make the switches unique. And of course before I released those copies I made sure there were a few small—shall we say—*corrections* made to them as well."

So that's why the drawings had looked rough and unfinished, Erin thought—because they were only preliminaries. Not that their precise history mattered, of course. The important thing was that the plans had been altered—Slater had changed them himself, or had them changed—before Erin had ever laid hands on a set. The drawings she and Sarah had started with had been false ones.

No wonder Fritz MacDonald's engineers hadn't been able to make sense of the drawings; they'd been sabotaged long before Erin had started moving lines and changing numbers. And they had been changed by someone who didn't have to guess—as Erin had guessed—how to create a failure. Slater of all people could ensure that the drawings would be both intriguing and completely worthless.

But he hadn't told Erin what he was planning to do. Even though she was his personal assistant, his right hand, his executive officer, he hadn't trusted her enough to confide in her.

No wonder Slater hadn't seemed anxious to pursue the source of the leak, even after the Universal Conveyer disaster. He simply hadn't wanted to tell Erin that he was already doing so—in his own way—by planting false information throughout Control Dynamics and waiting to see where it turned up.

He hadn't trusted her. *Not even her.*

Slater waved the security men into the office. His voice was crisp and level. "Porter, these gentlemen will escort you out of the building. Your final paycheck and your personal possessions will be forwarded to you. Don't set foot on Control Dynamics' property again."

Dax's reply shocked her; Erin had heard the words before, of course, but never expressed with such venom.

Slater stepped back, turning slightly to give the security people room, and Dax's fist shot out in a short, vicious jab. Erin tried to call out a warning, but her throat was so tight she could barely squeak. Slater had obviously expected something of the sort, however; his hand came up, knocking Dax's blow aside and breaking his hold on the bundle of loose papers. The Brannagan drawings hit the office floor with a thud and sprayed out to cover half the carpet.

Dax stared at the mess for an instant, and then as if all the energy had gone out of him, he turned away. Each of the security guards took an arm; he tried to shrug them off, but they maintained their grip as they marched him toward the elevator.

Slater closed the door between office and hallway. To Erin, the click of the latch sounded as loud as a shotgun blast. "I think we've aired enough of this affair in public," he said grimly. "Erin, into my office. Now."

She was startled. "But I—"

Sarah stepped forward bravely. "Sir, I have to talk to you."

"You'll be next. In the meantime, pick up this mess so it doesn't get into another wrong set of hands. Erin, I'm waiting."

He sounded like a stranger. There was a rough edge to his voice, one she'd never heard before.

Erin stumbled as she crossed the threshold to his office. Slater caught her arm, but there was no gentleness in his grip.

He pointed at a chair. Erin thought hollowly that now she knew firsthand why Sarah had preferred not to sit during their confrontation, and she stayed on her feet.

Slater walked around behind his desk, as if to put a safe distance between them. "So you were in on it, too."

She couldn't deny it, precisely, for she *had* been involved. And she knew quite well that he wouldn't listen to the whole explanation—not now, when his anger was so raw, and perhaps not ever. So she only shook her head a fraction and said nothing at all.

"No wonder you spent so much time huddled in corners at the cocktail party last night—with Dax, with Sarah, with who knows who else." His eyes were dark with fury. "Dammit, Erin! I knew the source of that leak had to be close to the top. There were too many bits of information that simply weren't known anywhere else. But to think that *you*—"

"Don't expect me to believe that you're shocked." The words felt like jagged glass cutting her throat. "You suspected me, Slater, or you wouldn't have gone behind my back when you changed those plans in the first place."

"I suspected that somebody—maybe you, maybe Sarah—was being careless. That's why I decided not to let anyone know about the faked plans. But I never in my worst nightmares thought it was intentional. The idea that *you*—"

She opened her mouth to explain, to defend both Sarah and herself—and knew from the black anger in his face that it would do no good. Why on earth would he believe her protests, when he had the evidence of his own eyes to prove differently? Not only had Dax showed up this morning with the fake set of plans in hand, he'd clearly implicated Sarah—made it plain she'd known exactly what she was doing. And it would have been obvious to anyone with the intelligence of a doorknob that Erin had known, before the man had ever started slinging accusations, exactly why he was there. So why on earth wouldn't Slater think that she'd been involved from the beginning, and in the most sordid way possible?

And even if someday he would listen to the truth, would he ever trust her again? If he hadn't had faith in her even before this last calamity, how could she even hope that this wound could be healed?

She had done it to herself. She'd acted with the best intentions in the world, of course—to save him pain by keeping Dax from getting the real plans somewhere else, to buy time for Slater to seal the leak once and for all, to give Sarah the one-in-a-million chance of saving her job.

But by trying to help, Erin had not only sacrificed her own professional standing, she'd inflicted a mortal wound on an already problematic marriage.

''Why the hell did you do it, Erin? Was it money, to start with? Or the sheer fun of it? Maybe Fritz MacDonald's supposed charm?''

She shook her head, more in pain than in denial.

''Not for Dax, surely. You can't possibly have imagined yourself in love with that—''

''No!'' She almost screamed the word, and it hurt her throat.

I made a mistake, she wanted to say. *But I did it because I love you...*

And wouldn't that feeble explanation just fix things up nicely? she thought bitterly. If it didn't make him even angrier, it would probably send him off into spasms of sarcastic laughter.

She folded her arms across her chest in a feeble attempt to keep herself from shivering. Her pride told her to leave under her own conditions, rather than waiting for him to tell her to go. Holding on to that last remaining bit of dignity wouldn't be much comfort, but it was something. She would hold her head high and look him in the eye—

But she couldn't. Instead, she focused her gaze beyond him, on the stainless steel Gateway Arch which gleamed in the sun in contrast to the muddy brown of the river which lay just behind it. ''Do you mind if I pack up my personal items myself, Slater? Or would you prefer to let security do it and forward them to me?''

He dropped into his desk chair, his fingertips pressed to the furrow between his eyebrows, and Erin knew it was all the answer he was going to give her.

She tugged her rings—the sapphire she had thought so beautiful, the matching wedding band—from her left hand, and placed them carefully on his desk blotter. ''As it turns out, it's a good thing I didn't bother to get you a wedding ring,'' she mused. ''It would just be one more for you to take back to the jewelry store.''

She was almost to the door when he spoke. ''Erin—'' He sounded tired. ''Where are you going?''

Erin didn't look at him. ''I don't see why you need to know, sir. Unless, of course, you're trying to avoid me, and in that case you don't have to bother. I'll do all the avoiding for both of us.''

She quietly closed the door behind her.

Sarah's eyes were wide, almost wild. ''What—''

Erin shook her head. ''I don't know what to tell you, Sarah—except that I'd rather face your whole lineup of real dinosaurs than Slater in the rage he's in now.''

Sarah squared her shoulders. ''I'm going in there and tell him everything,'' she said. ''Every last detail.''

''Good luck,'' Erin said. ''But don't expect it will make a difference.''

She glanced into her office, but she didn't have the heart to take her pictures off the walls. She didn't have the patience to sort out what was hers.

She picked up Slater's crystal vase, the one which had once held Dax's stolen red rose. She had thought of it as a symbol of solidity, something which would last forever. Now she saw only its fragility. How little it would take to shatter it, to turn its beauty into shards which would cut and tear whatever they touched.

Just as her marriage had shattered, leaving behind only pain.

In the end, Erin took nothing at all. The things she left behind, she knew, didn't matter in the slightest. She had no need of physical reminders to cause her grief; her memories would be painful souvenirs.

She walked, without watching where she was going, and she tried not to think. It was midafternoon when Erin found herself wandering down a row of antique stores and specialty shops—only a few blocks from Control Dynamics in actual distance, but a million miles away in mood—and realized with a jolt that she'd better start making some decisions. She had no clothes except what she was wearing, no money except for a couple of dollars she found stashed in her skirt pocket, no identification or credit cards, and no place to go for the night.

She could go home…not to Slater's apartment, of course, but to the town house. She was still the official owner, and in any case she knew she'd always be welcome in Angela's home. But that was part of the problem—her mother was there, and Angela would have a whole lot of questions when her daughter turned up shaken, stone-broke, and alone.

And as if this mess wouldn't be hurtful enough to a woman who was still recovering from a life-threatening illness, Erin would have her father to face, too. Jack Reynolds had answered the phone every time Erin had called to check on her mother; it was painfully apparent that he'd simply moved in to look after her. Until this moment, Erin had been minding her own business about her parents' decisions, glad just to know that Angela was being well-cared for. But she also knew that whatever uncomfortable questions Angela didn't think of, her father was sure to.

Furthermore, once she'd told them even the bare bones of her story—the minimum she could get by with—there was no predicting what either of them might do. Erin didn't think her father would issue some sort of macho challenge to the man who'd hurt his daughter—he might, she thought, be more likely to give Erin herself a good lecture—but it would be a whole lot easier not to take the chance.

Which left her right back where she'd started. Why hadn't she had the brain to pick up her handbag, at least? With a credit card she could at least have checked into a hotel and bought a few necessities....

But thinking of the things she should have done was only putting off the inevitable. She didn't have a choice; she was going to have to go back to Slater's apartment and get some clothes and the couple of hundred dollars she'd stashed in her lingerie drawer. And she'd better do it soon, before the end of the business day, or she'd run the risk that Slater would be there.

Only when she pushed through the revolving door into the lobby did she realize that the doorman might well forbid her from going further. If Slater had told the security people that she was no more welcome here than Dax was at Control Dynamics' office building...

But the doorman touched his cap and smiled. ''Nice afternoon, Mrs. Livingstone,'' he said.

Erin agreed, without being quite sure if the man was being straightforward or sarcastic. *Was* it a nice afternoon? She hadn't been in any condition to notice.

Her key was still at the office, of course. She rang the doorbell and hoped that Jessup hadn't gone out for the afternoon. Despite the heavy door and the thick walls, she could hear the chimes, though they sounded faint and far off. The last notes had not yet died away when the door swung silently open.

It was the first time in the year she'd worked with Jessup, organizing party after party, that she'd ever truly seen him lose his composure. "Mrs. Livingstone—" His voice cracked.

Erin bit her lip. How much things had changed in a few hours, since she'd drunk her morning coffee in the kitchen while Jessup finished the party cleanup, and felt guilty because she wasn't helping.

Obviously, she thought, *he's had his orders.*

But did it really matter what Slater had told the butler? The only things she'd come for were the belongings she'd brought with her. Surely Slater couldn't object to her taking what belonged to her. "I've come after my clothes, Jessup," she said coolly. "That's all. I don't care whether you pack them or watch me while I do it, to make sure I don't get anything that isn't mine. I'll wait out here while you gather them up, if that's the way it has to be. I just want my things."

"Of course," Jessup said. He stepped back. "But there's no need for me to supervise."

"I'd rather you would," Erin said. "Just so it's clear what I'm taking." She stepped into the foyer.

There was no lingering evidence of last night's party, not so much as a hint of Katrina's perfume…

Just last night, she thought, *my biggest concern was Katrina and the way Slater was looking at her.* What a fool she had been, those few hours ago—intuitively knowing that her marriage was in danger, but completely ingenuous about the source of the threat.

Erin avoided the library—it would always be, for her,

a memory that made her ache—and started down the hall toward the back stairs which also led up to the master bedroom.

Jessup didn't follow her. "Would you like me to bring you a cup of tea, Mrs. Livingstone? Perhaps a snack?"

She'd forgotten that she hadn't eaten since breakfast, but then she had no interest in food. She gave him a half smile. "The tea would be wonderful."

She found her stash of money first and tucked it safely into a pocket, then pulled her biggest suitcase from the closet and opened a drawer. There was no need to be neat, she thought, just fast.

The door opened and she heard the click of china. "Thanks, Jessup. Put it on the table, please. Do you know if my ivory silk blouse has come back from the cleaner's?"

"I haven't a clue," Slater said.

Erin's hands clenched on a frilly bit of underwear and she heard the lace tear under her nails.

"I must say, Erin, as avoidance techniques go, this one isn't terribly successful."

If he'd attacked once more, Erin would have walked out rather than pursue a futile argument. If he hadn't said a word, she'd have gone away rather than cause him more pain. But that careless, don't-give-a-damn comment made her angry. She had a right to her own possessions. And what was the matter with the man, anyway?—did he honestly think she'd *expected* to find him at home in the middle of the afternoon? That she'd *wanted* to renew the morning's bitter quarrel? "Go to hell, Slater. I didn't ask you to come up here, so why don't you send Jessup to act as your watchdog and just go away?"

"We need to talk, Erin." His tone was so mild it frightened her more than any amount of bluster could have done.

She dumped a few more things into her suitcase. ''About what?''

''Details.'' His tone was crisp and completely unhelpful.

''All the trivial technicalities of a divorce, you mean? If you insist. You don't mind if I keep packing while you talk, do you? I wouldn't want you to think I was trying to stretch out my time here.''

After a moment, wondering why he was so quiet, she turned to face him. The leisurely way he was surveying her, his gaze moving with slow precision from head to foot and back, made her nervous. Had the man never really seen her before?

She tried to ignore him. ''You did bring up the tea, didn't you?''

''Of course.'' But he finished his inspection of her, still taking his time, before he poured a cup for her.

She sipped it and watched him warily over the cup's gold rim. ''If you're worried about what I might ask for in a divorce...''

''No, I wasn't.'' His gaze was steady. ''What in the hell were you thinking of, Erin?''

Not this again, Erin thought. But it wasn't the same, she realized; what had been an angry accusation this morning sounded more like an honest question now. Would he actually listen to an honest answer? It was worth a try, she supposed.

''Dax took advantage of Sarah—and then he threatened to tell you she'd been the brains of the operation all along.'' As explanations went, it sounded pretty feeble, Erin knew, but she didn't quite know how to go on. ''And I—''

''Because you felt so bad about Sarah letting secrets slip, you gave away more.''

Why had she even let herself hope? ''I suppose that's the bottom line, yes. If you don't mind, Slater, I'd really just like to pack up my things and go.''

She set her cup on the bureau and glanced into her suitcase. The contents were as jumbled as if they'd been through an airplane crash, and they were just about as useful. She'd thrown in all her lacy lingerie, but not a sensible blouse or a pair of jeans or a shoe without heels....

''Why didn't you tell me you changed the drawings, Erin?''

She tried to swallow the sudden tightness in her throat. If he knew what she'd tried to do... Was there the slightest hint of hope after all? ''Sarah told you that?'' she whispered. *And you believed her? You listened to her? Why not to me, Slater?*

''She told me. So I compared them myself, line by line.'' He sat down on the foot of the bed, next to her suitcase. ''Well, Erin?''

She couldn't get a full breath, and her voice was little more than a thread. She tried not to think about how important this might be, if he believed her...or if he didn't. ''I'm sure Sarah told you all her reasons—not knowing if Dax had other sources, trying to buy some time so she could tell you herself what had happened.''

He nodded. ''And yours?''

''I wanted Sarah to have a chance. She's not criminal, Slater. She's—I don't think she's even all that careless. Dax used her, and she's breaking her heart over what she did. I'll guarantee nobody will ever have the opportunity to do that again.'' She sighed. ''And I hoped that when Fritz MacDonald realized that they'd gotten a bogus set of plans, Dax would lose credibility with the people he was selling to—they wouldn't trust him anymore.''

''Were you even going to tell me?''

''Of course I'd have told you—as soon as you got home. But I thought it was better if Sarah did. And in the meantime, somebody had to do something to stop Dax.''

His face showed no hint of what he might be thinking.

''I thought that preventing him from getting his hands on the real Brannagan drawings might be a way for Sarah to make up for her mistake. Because it *was* a mistake, Slater. Only a mistake.''

She could hear the tick of the gold clock on the mantel; in the quiet room it sounded like a bomb timer counting down.

''You know,'' Slater said finally, ''you really haven't answered the original question. Why didn't you tell me this morning about the changes you'd made in the drawings?''

''Would you have listened?''

He didn't admit it, but he didn't argue the point either. She thought, from the long harsh breath he released, that he knew exactly what she meant. He said, ''You think I should give Sarah another chance.''

''I don't have anything to say about it, sir.''

''Dammit, Erin, will you stop that?''

''Why should it matter what I call you?'' she flared. ''And if it helps…''

''If it helps what?''

''Never mind. As I was saying, before you interrupted me, my judgment's hardly been a model to look up to lately.''

''On that matter,'' he said dryly, ''I can wholeheartedly agree.''

Erin's last faint hope had faded into ash; yet she found

herself thinking that Slater looked just as unhappy as she felt. *But of course he does,* she told herself. His perfect, effortless little marriage of convenience had blown up in his face. Erin hadn't been the perfect corporate wife after all—she'd turned out to be the perfect nuisance.

"You didn't even take your purse this morning," Slater said softly.

"So what?" She knew she sounded cross, and she didn't care.

"You stood in my office while I yelled at you, and you looked at the river. And then you turned your back on everything as if you had no use for it anymore, and you walked away."

"I don't—"

His voice was harsh. "Don't you know what I thought, Erin?"

"That I was going to throw myself into the Mississippi?" She shook her head. "I wasn't thinking clearly enough to make a decision quite that final."

"That's usually not what stops a suicide," he said wryly.

"Though it would have served you right."

"Yes, it would." He sounded as if the words hurt his throat. "I yelled at you, Erin. I accused you. I wouldn't listen to you. I drove you away." His voice dropped almost to a whisper. "And I'd never even told you that I love you."

Erin's heart slammed into her ribs so hard she thought it was going to break through. "No," she said uncertainly. "You absolutely cannot expect me to believe that in the midst of this mess, you suddenly realized you'd fallen in love. So what the—"

"Nothing of the sort." His voice was perfectly matter-of-fact. "In the midst of this mess, I was furious with you. I fell in love long before that—which might help explain why I was too angry to consider that you might have had perfectly good reasons for what you'd done.''

Erin's ears were ringing.

''I was so sure, you see, that you wouldn't betray me. A slip of the tongue, maybe—but to give away confidential information on purpose, no. Then I walked into the office this morning to find Dax screaming at both you and Sarah, and suddenly it was right there in front of me—or at least it seemed to be—and I lost my head.'' His eyes were dark, pleading. ''Afterwards, when I saw in black and white what you'd really done—and realized that our marriage was so meaningless to you that you walked out instead of bothering to defend yourself...''

''No.'' She could hardly get her breath. ''No, Slater. That wasn't why I left. You and your solid, practical, sensible ideas about marriage, and how magic always turns to melodrama... Well, maybe you didn't plan to lead me on till I fell in love with you, but—''

''Erin,'' he said, and held out his arms.

She shook her head and took a step back. ''But you did a remarkably good job of it, and if there was any justice in the world you'd feel so guilty you wouldn't be able to sleep at night!''

She didn't know how she ended up in his arms, but within thirty seconds, as he kissed her, she didn't care anymore.

When he finally stopped kissing her, he nestled her even closer against his chest and said contentedly, ''I don't know about guilt keeping me awake. It sounds pretty uncomfortable. But if you don't want me to sleep at night, I know a way you can—''

Erin looked up at him through her lashes. ''You

know,'' she said pleasantly, ''you *deserve* to fall for Katrina and have her break your heart.''

''But I don't have one. I gave it to you.''

Erin rolled her eyes. ''First thing tomorrow I'm buying you a wedding ring. You're too dangerous to be let loose without displaying a warning sign.''

''That's what I was forgetting.'' He reached into his pocket and slid her rings back onto her finger, kissing them into place. ''All the symbols in the world can't make me feel more married, Erin. That's why, when you asked if I wanted a ring, I said it didn't matter.''

He kissed her till her toenails threatened to dissolve, and then, instead of releasing her, he led her to the wing chair beside the fireplace and pulled her down onto his lap.

Erin snuggled closer, savoring his warmth and strength, the scent of coffee and aftershave, and the slightly unsteady rhythm of his breathing—which by itself said quite a little about the way he felt. *I fell in love long before that,* he'd said, and suddenly suspicion began to nag at her. ''Slater—exactly how long have you known you love me?''

He didn't even hesitate. ''Six months, give or take a couple of weeks. That's when I realized what was happening, you understand. How long I've loved you is a little different question—more like a year.''

''I've only worked for you a year.''

''Then that's how long it's been.''

Erin shook her head in confusion. ''So when you proposed that sensible, practical, solid marriage, you knew you were in love? And you didn't tell me?''

''Guilty. I thought for a while you'd caught me, you know. When you said I was not only settling for second best, but I knew it… Of course I knew it, love. I was just hoping it wouldn't stay that way."

"You told me it was ludicrous to think you'd fallen in love with me."

"Oh, no. I said it was ludicrous to think that Aunt Hermione's letter would have prompted me to realize it."

He'd been very careful what he'd told her, Erin thought.

As if he'd read her mind, Slater said, "If I'd laid out the truth, you'd have been gone before I'd finished the sentence. What was I supposed to do, Erin? You were totally oblivious—I don't think you ever saw the man, just the boss."

"Oh, I saw. I just didn't want to admit it." She looked up at him through her lashes. "And you were an awfully good boss…sir."

"Knock it off, Erin."

"Yes, dear," she said meekly.

"I didn't expect marriage to be quite such a tightrope, though," Slater mused. "One instant you were smiling and generous, the next you were skittish. You'd be warm and loving and incredibly sexy, and a minute later you'd start muttering that you were a fool—"

"You heard that?"

He sounded astonished. "You don't really think that on my wedding night, with you in my arms, I'd have gone to sleep—do you?"

"Well, whatever I said, you have to admit that it wasn't any picnic from my point of view, either—realizing after I signed on that I'd really like to change the rules."

"Consider them changed," he said comfortably.

"It may take me a while to forgive you, though, for letting me think you didn't understand what love was. I actually felt sorry for you when you told Cecile to get lost.''

''Why?''

''Because you looked so miserable—as if the world had fallen on you.''

''I was bracing myself to play the most important hand of poker I'd ever held.''

''Nice of you to deal me in.''

''But darling, you always held all the cards.''

''Oh, really? I suppose you're going to insist you gave me all the pertinent information so I could make a good decision about marrying you?''

''Don't you think it was a wise choice?''

''That's beside the point.''

''No, it isn't. What else did you need? It isn't that I couldn't have given you an ode to your beautiful blue eyes—and they are beautiful—I just didn't think you'd sit still for it.''

''Probably not,'' she admitted. ''What about Aunt Hermione's suggestion that you get yourself a hostess? You used that deliberately in order to make me start thinking about you, didn't you?''

''Oh, it's worse than that,'' he said cheerfully. ''I needled her into writing that letter.''

''I ought to have seen through you,'' Erin muttered. ''I have *always* known that you could be the most successful swindler on the whole continent if you made up your mind to it.''

''Thank you.''

''But I didn't think anybody could influence Aunt Hermione.''

''You just have to know how. I plan to teach all of her nieces and nephews exactly which buttons to push so—''

''All eight of them?''

"Or six. Or one. Or none. Whatever we end up with is fine with me, Erin. It's you I want—so badly I'd have tried anything I thought might jolt you out of your complacent view of me as part of the furniture. Including Cecile and all the others—not that you seemed to care."

"I cared. I was so jealous of Cecile I couldn't stand it—I just didn't know that's what it was. I thought I was furious with her for not appreciating you. I needed a jolt, all right, but not so I'd notice you, Slater. Just to realize how much you meant to me." Her throat was tight. "I can still hardly believe—"

"That I love you? You can always ask your mother. I told her I loved you that afternoon when you announced our engagement."

"You said," Erin reminded, "that she asked, and you told her what she wanted to hear."

"I did. It simply had the added advantage of being the truth."

"So that's why she was so anxious to marry me off that she wouldn't even wait to get out of the hospital."

"She wasn't, actually," Slater admitted. "I was the one who was anxious—but it made an awfully good excuse. And she seemed to think I could make you happy."

"I wouldn't be surprised if she knew what I was thinking better than I did." She snuggled closer to him. "About that announcement I made…telling Mom I was going to marry you. It took a while for me to understand that I did it because I already knew I loved you, I just didn't want to confess even to myself that I wanted you so badly. That cool little proposal of yours—the whole idea of giving your wife a job description—scared me."

"Speaking of jobs and scares—I think you're right about Sarah having had the fright of her life."

"You're going to give her a second chance?"

Slater nodded. ''And I'm really glad you didn't clean out your office, because you have more important things to do tomorrow than put all the pictures back on the walls. We've got not only Bob Brannagan's switches to build, but Universal Conveyer's controls—''

Erin hugged him tighter. ''You did it!''

''The CEO's no fool—and he doesn't like dealing with crooks. Anyway, we're going to be busy. Unless,'' he added thoughtfully, ''you'd like to try your hand at engineering for a while.''

She was astonished. ''Why?''

''Because those little innovations you put on Dax's copies of the Brannagan drawings are really quite interesting.''

''You're joking. Aren't you?''

Slater shook his head. ''It'll probably come to nothing, of course. But it started me thinking in an entirely new direction—and if you really have stumbled across improvements, the bonus will make your sapphire earrings look like penny candy.''

Erin whispered, ''The only bonus I'll ever want is you.'' She tipped her head back, inviting his kiss.

After a while, he said unsteadily, ''That can be arranged. By the way, if you ever call me *sir* again—''

Erin raised her head from his shoulder. ''Oh? What will you do to me?''

''For starters, this.''

Erin thought she'd been held firmly before, but she'd been wrong. And the way he kissed her was neither tender nor tentative; it was the kiss of a hungry lover, and it promised delights almost beyond bearing.

Several minutes later, he let her come up for air. ''Well?''

''I see what you mean,'' Erin managed to say. ''And of course I'll always do *whatever* you ask...'' She flashed a saucy smile. ''...sir.''

THE BOSS'S SECRET MISTRESS

by

Alison Fraser

Alison Fraser was born and brought up in the far north of Scotland. She studied English literature at university and taught maths for a while, then became a computer programmer. She took up writing as a hobby and it is still very much so, in that she doesn't take it too seriously! She currently lives with her husband, children and dogs in Birmingham, and is in her early forties – she doesn't know what she wants to be when she grows up!

CHAPTER ONE

'LUCAS RYECART?' Tory repeated the name, but it meant nothing to her.

'You must have heard of him,' Simon Dixon insisted. 'American entrepreneur, bought up Howard Productions and Chelton TV last year.'

'I think I'd remember a name like that,' Tory told her fellow production assistant. 'Anyway, I'm not interested in the wheeling and dealing of money men. If Eastwich needs an injection of cash, does it matter where it comes from?'

'If it means one of us ending up at the local job centre,' Simon warned dramatically, 'then, yes, I'd say it matters.'

'That's only rumour.' Tory knew from personal experience that rumours bore little relationship to the truth.

'Don't be so sure. Do you know what they called him at Howard Productions?' It was a rhetoric question as Simon took lugubrious pleasure in announcing, 'The Grim Reaper.'

This time Tory laughed in disbelief. After a year in Documentary Affairs at Eastwich Productions, she knew Simon well enough. If there wasn't drama already in a situation, he would do his best to inject it. He was such a stirrer people called him The Chef.

'Simon, are you aware of your nickname?' she couldn't resist asking now.

'Of course.' He smiled as he countered, 'Are you?'

Tory shrugged. She wasn't, but supposed she had one.

'The Ice Maiden.' It was scarcely original. 'Because of your cool personality, do you think?'

'Undoubtedly,' agreed Tory, well aware of the real reason.

'Still, it's unlikely that you'll fall victim to staff cuts,' Simon continued to muse. 'I mean, what man can resist Shirley

Temple hair, eyes like Bambi and more than a passing resemblance to what's-her-name in *Pretty Woman*?'

Tory pulled a face at Simon's tongue-in-cheek assessment of her looks. 'Anyone who prefers blonde supermodel types... Not to mention those of an entirely different persuasion.'

'I should be so lucky,' he acknowledged in camp fashion, before disclaiming, 'No, this one's definitely straight. In fact, he has been described as God's gift to women.'

'Really.' Tory remained unimpressed. 'I thought that was some rock singer.'

'I'm sure God is capable of bestowing more than one gift to womankind,' Simon declared, 'if only to make up for the many disadvantages he's given you.'

Tory laughed, unaffected by Simon's anti-women remarks. Simon was *anti* most things.

'Anyway, I think we can safely assume, with a little judicious eyelash-batting, you'll achieve job security,' he ran on glibly, 'so that leaves myself or our beloved leader, Alexander the Not-so-Great. Who would you put your money on, Tory dearest?'

'I have no idea.' Tory began to grow impatient with Simon and his speculations. 'But if you're that worried, perhaps you should apply yourself to some work on the remote chance this Ryecart character comes to survey his latest acquisition.'

This was said in the hope that Simon would allow her to get on with her own work. Oblivious, Simon remained seated on the edge of her desk, dangling an elegantly shod foot over one side.

'Not so remote,' he warned. 'The grapevine has him due at eleven hundred hours to inspect the troops.'

'Oh.' Tory began to wonder how reliable the rest of his information was. Would Eastwich Productions be subject to some downsizing?

'Bound to be Alex,' Simon resumed smugly. 'He's been over the hill and far away for some months now.'

Tory was really annoyed this time. 'That's not true. He's just had a few problems to sort out.'

'A *few*!' Simon scoffed at this understatement. 'His wife

runs off to Scotland. His house is repossessed. And his breath smells like an advert for Polo mints… We do know what that means, Goldilocks?'

At times Tory found Simon amusing. This wasn't one of them. She was quite aware Alex, their boss, had a drink problem. She just didn't believe in kicking people when they were down.

'You're not going to do the dirty on Alex, are you, Simon?'

'*Moi?* Would I do something like that?'

'Yes.' She was certain of it.

'You've cut me to the quick.' He clasped his heart in theatrical fashion. 'Why should I do down Alex…especially when he can do it so much better himself, don't you think?'

True enough, Tory supposed. Alex was sliding downhill so fast he could have won a place on an Olympic bobsleigh team.

'Anyway, I'll toddle off back to my desk—' Simon suited actions to his words '—and sharpen wits and pencil before our American friend arrives.'

Tory frowned. 'Has Alex come in yet?'

'Is the Pope a Muslim?' he answered flippantly, then shook his head as Tory picked up the phone. 'I shouldn't bother if I were you.'

But Tory felt some loyalty to Alex. He had given her her job at Eastwich.

She rang his mistress's flat, then every other number she could possibly think of, in the vain hope of finding Alex before Eastwich's new boss descended on them.

'Too late, *ma petite*,' Simon announced with satisfaction as Colin Mathieson, the senior production executive, appeared at the glass door of their office. He gave a brief courtesy knock before entering. A stranger who had to be the American followed him.

He wasn't at all what Tory had expected. She'd been prepared for a sharp-suited, forty something year old with a sunbed tan and a roving eye.

That was why she stared. Well, that was what she told herself later. At the time she just stared.

Tall. Very tall. Six feet two or three. Almost casual in khaki trousers and an open-necked shirt. Dark hair, straight and slicked back, and a long angular face. Blue eyes, a quite startling hue. A mouth slanted with either humour or cynicism. In short, the best-looking man Tory had ever seen in her life.

Tory had never felt it before, an instant overwhelming attraction. She wasn't ready for it. She was transfixed. She was reduced to gaping stupidity.

The newcomer met her gaze and smiled as if he knew. No doubt it happened all the time. No doubt, being God's gift, he was used to it.

Colin Mathieson introduced her, 'Tory Lloyd, Production Assistant,' and she recovered sufficiently to raise a hand to the one stretched out to her. 'Lucas Ryecart, the new chief executive of Eastwich.'

Her hand disappeared in the warm dry clasp of his. He towered above her. She fought a feeling of insignificance. She couldn't think of a sane, sensible thing to say.

'Tory's worked for us for about a year,' Colin continued. 'Shows great promise. Had quite an input to the documentary on single mothers you mentioned seeing.'

Lucas Ryecart nodded and, finally dropping Tory's hand, commented succinctly, 'Well-made programme, Miss Lloyd…or is it Mrs?'

'Miss,' Colin supplied at her silence.

The American smiled in acknowledgement. 'Though perhaps a shade too controversial in intention.'

It took Tory a moment to realise he was still talking about the documentary and another to understand the criticism, before she at last emerged from brainless-guppy mode to point out, 'It's a controversial subject.'

Lucas Ryecart looked surprised by the retaliation but not unduly put out. 'True, and the slant was certainly a departure from the usual socialist dogma. Scarcely sympathetic.'

'We had no bias.' Tory remained on the defensive.

'Of course not,' he appeared to placate her, then added, 'You just gave the mothers free speech and let them condemn themselves.'

'We let them preview it,' she claimed. 'None of them complained.'

'Too busy enjoying their five minutes' fame, I expect,' he drawled back.

His tone was more dry than accusing, and he smiled again.

Tory didn't smile back. She was struggling with a mixture of temper and guilt, because, of course, he was right.

The single mothers in question had been all too ready to talk and it hadn't taken much editing to make them sound at best ignorant, at worst uncaring. Away from the camera and the lights, they had merely seemed lonely and vulnerable.

Tory had realised the interviews had been neither fair nor particularly representative and had suggested Alex tone them down. But Alex had been in no mood to listen. His wife had just left him, taking their two young children, and single mothers hadn't been flavour of the month.

Lucas Ryecart caught her brooding expression and ran on, 'Never mind...Tory, is it?'

Tory nodded silently, wishing he'd stuck to Miss Lloyd. Or did he feel he had to be on first-name terms with someone before he put the boot in?

'Tory,' he repeated, 'in documentary television it's always difficult to judge where to draw the line. Interview the mass murderer and are you explaining or glorifying his crimes? Interview the victims' families and do you redress the balance or simply make television out of people's grief?'

'I would refuse to do either,' Tory stated unequivocally at this mini-lecture.

'Really?' He raised a dark, straight brow and looked at her as if he were now assessing her as trouble.

It was Simon who came to her rescue, though not intentionally. '*I* wouldn't. I'd do anything for a good story.'

Having been virtually ignored, Simon thought it time to draw attention to himself.

Ryecart's eyes switched from Tory to Simon and Colin Mathieson performed the introductions. 'This is Simon Dixon. Alex's number two.'

'Simon.' The American nodded.

'Mr Ryecart.' Simon smiled confidently. 'Or do you wish us to call you Lucas? Being American, you must find English formality so outmoded.'

Tory had to give credit where credit was due: Simon had nerve.

Lucas Ryecart, however, scarcely blinked as he replied smoothly, 'Mr Ryecart will do for now.'

Simon was left a little red-faced, muttering, 'Well, you're the boss.'

'Quite,' Ryecart agreed succinctly, but didn't labour the point as he offered a conciliatory smile and hand to Simon.

Simon—the creep—accepted both.

It was Colin Mathieson who directed at them, 'Do you know where we might find Alex? He isn't in his office.'

'He never is,' muttered Simon in an undertone designed to be just audible.

Tory shot him a silencing look before saying, 'I think he's checking out locations for a programme.'

'Which programme?' Colin enquired. 'The one on ward closures? I thought we'd abandoned it.'

'Um…no.' Tory decided to keep the lies general. 'It's something at the conception stage, about…' She paused for inspiration and flushed as she felt the American's eyes on her once more.

'Alcoholism and the effects on work performance,' Simon volunteered for her.

She could have been grateful. She wasn't. She understood it for what it was—a snide reference to Alex's drinking.

Colin didn't seem to pick up on it, but Tory wasn't so sure about Lucas Ryecart. His glance switched to the mocking smile on Simon's face, then back to hers. He read the suppressed anger that made her mouth a tight line, but refrained from comment.

'Well, get Alex to give me a bell when he gets in.' Colin turned towards the door, ready to continue the guided tour.

Ryecart lingered, his eyes resting on Tory. 'Have we met before?'

Tory frowned. Where could they have met? They were unlikely to move in the same social circles.

'No, I don't think so,' she replied at length.

He seemed unconvinced but then shrugged. 'It doesn't matter. We probably haven't. I'm sure I would have remembered you.'

He smiled a hundred-watt smile, just for her, and the word handsome didn't cover it.

Tory's heart did an odd sort of somersault thing.

'I—I…' Normally so articulate, she couldn't think of a thing to say.

It was at least better than saying anything foolish.

He smiled again, a flash of white in his tanned face, then he was gone.

Tory took a deep, steadying breath and sat back down on her chair. Men like that should carry around a Government Health Warning.

"'I'm sure I would have remembered you.'" Simon mimicked the American's words. 'My God, where does he get his lines? B movies from the thirties? Still, good news for you, ducks.'

'What?' Tory looked blank.

'Come on, darling—' Simon thought she was being purposely obtuse '—you and the big chief. Has he got the hots for you or what?'

'You're being ridiculous!' she snapped in reply.

'Am I?' Simon gave her a mocking smile. 'Talk about long, lingering looks. And not just from our transatlantic cousin. Me think the Ice Maiden melteth.'

Tory clenched her teeth at this attempt at humour and confined herself to a glare. It seemed wiser than protesting, especially when she *could* recall staring overlong at the American.

Of course it hadn't lasted, the impact of his looks. The moment he had talked—or patronised might be closer to the mark—she had recovered rapidly.

'Well, who's to blame you?' Simon ran on. 'He has at least

one irresistible quality: he's rich. As in hugely, obscenely, embarrassingly—'

'Shut up, Simon,' she cut in, exasperated. 'Even if I was interested in his money, which I'm not, he definitely isn't my type.'

'If you say so.' He was clearly unconvinced. 'Probably as well. Rumour has it that he's still carrying a torch for his wife.'

'Wife?' she echoed. 'He's married?'

'Was,' he corrected. 'Wife died in a car accident a few years ago. Collided with a tanker lorry. Seemingly, she was pregnant at the time.'

The details struck a chord with Tory, and her stomach hit the floor. She shook her head in denial. No, it couldn't be.

Or could it?

Lucas could shorten to Luc. He was American. He did work in the media, albeit a quite different area.

'Was he ever a foreign correspondent?'

She willed Simon to ridicule the idea.

Instead he looked at her in surprise. 'As a matter of fact, yes, my sources tell me he worked for Reuters in the Middle East for several years before marrying into money. I can't remember the name of the family but they've Fleet Street connections.'

The Wainwrights. Tory knew it, though she could scarcely believe it. He'd been married to Jessica Wainwright. Tory knew this because she'd almost married into the same family.

How had she not recognised him immediately? She'd seen a photograph. It had pride of place on the grand piano—Jessica radiant in white marrying her handsome war reporter. Of course, it had been taken more than a decade earlier.

'Do you know him from some place, then?' Simon didn't hide his curiosity.

Tory shook her head. Telling Simon would be like telling the world.

'I remember reading about him in a magazine.' She hoped to kill the subject dead.

* * *

'Where are you going?' he asked, watching her pick up her handbag and jacket.

'Lunch,' she snapped back.

'It's not noon yet,' he pointed out, suddenly the model employee.

'It's either that or stay and murder you,' Tory retorted darkly.

'In that case,' Simon did his best to look contrite, '*bon appetit*!'

It deflated some of Tory's anger, but she still departed, needing fresh air and her own company. She made for the back staircase, expecting to meet no one on it. Most people used the lift.

Taking the stairs two at a time, she cannoned right into a motionless figure on the landing, bounced back off and, with a quick, 'Sorry,' would have kept on moving if a hand hadn't detained her. She looked up to find Lucas Ryecart staring down at her. Two meetings in half an hour was too much!

The American, however, didn't seem to think so. His face creased into a smile, transforming hard lines into undeniable charm. 'We meet again...*Tory*, isn't it?'

'I—I...yes.' Tory was reduced to monosyllables once more.

'Is everything all right?' He noted her agitation. He could hardly miss it. She must resemble a nervous rabbit caught in headlights.

She gathered her wits together, fast. 'Yes. Fine. I'm just going to the...dentist,' she lied unnecessarily. She could have easily said she was going to do some research.

'Well, at least it's not me,' he drawled in response.

Tory blinked. 'What's not?'

'Giving you that mildly terrified look,' he explained and slanted her a slow, amused smile.

Tory's brain went to mush again. 'I...no.'

'Check-up, filling or extraction?'

'Extraction.'

Tory decided an extraction might account for her flaky behaviour.

'I'll be back later,' she added, feeling like a naughty schoolgirl.

'Don't bother,' Lucas Ryecart dismissed. 'I'm sure Colin won't mind if you take the rest of the day off.'

He said this as Colin Mathieson appeared on the stairwell, holding up a file. 'Sorry I was so long, but it took some finding.'

'Good…Colin, Tory has to go to the dentist.' The American made a show of consulting him. 'Do you think we could manage without her this afternoon?'

Colin recognised the question for what it was—a token gesture. Lucas Ryecart called the shots now.

'Certainly, if she's under the weather,' Colin conceded, but he wasn't happy about it.

There were deadlines to be met and Alex was seldom around these days to meet them. Colin was well aware Tory and Simon were taking up the slack.

'I'll come in tomorrow,' she assured him quietly.

He gave her a grateful smile.

'Tory is a real workaholic,' he claimed, catching the frown settling between Lucas Ryecart's dark brows.

'Well, better than the other variety, I guess.' The American's eyes rested on Tory. He had a very direct, intense way of looking at a person.

Tory felt herself blush again. Could he possibly know why they were covering for Alex?

'I have to go.' She didn't wait for permission but took to her heels, flying down the stairs to exit Eastwich's impressive glass façade.

Having no dental appointment, she went straight back to her flat to hide out. It was on the ground floor of a large Victorian house on the outskirts of Norwich. She'd decided to rent rather than buy, as any career move would dictate a physical move. Maybe it would be sooner rather than later now Lucas Ryecart had descended on Eastwich.

Tory took out an album of old photographs and found one from five years ago. She felt relief, sure she'd changed almost out of recognition, her face thinner, her hair shorter, and her make-up considerably more sophisticated. She was no longer that dreamy-eyed girl who'd thought herself in love with Charlie Wainwright.

Coupled with a different name—Charlie had always preferred Victoria or Vicki to the Tory friends had called her—it was not surprising Lucas Ryecart had failed to make the connection. Chances were that all he'd seen of her was a snapshot, leaving the vaguest of memories, and all he'd heard was about a girl called Vicki who was at college with Charlie. Nobody special. A nice ordinary girl.

She could imagine Charlie's elegant mother using those exact words. Then, afterwards, Vicki had probably undergone a personality change from ordinary to common, and from nice to not very nice at all. What else, when the girl had broken her son's heart?

It was what Charlie had claimed at the time. Forget the fact that it had been his decision to end the engagement.

She took out another photograph, this one of Charlie's handsome, boyish face. She didn't know why she kept it. If she'd ever loved him, she certainly didn't now. It had all gone. Not even pain left.

Life had moved on. Charlie had the family he'd wanted and she had her career. She still had the occasional relationship but strictly on her terms with her in control.

She pulled a slight face. Well, normally. But where had been that control when she'd met Lucas Ryecart that morning? Lagging way behind the rest of her, that was where.

It had been like a scent, bypassing the brain and going straight for the senses. For a few moments it had been almost overpowering, as if she were drowning and had forgotten how to swim.

It hadn't lasted, of course. She'd surfaced pretty damn quickly when he'd begun to talk. She still bristled at his criticism on the single mothers documentary, regardless of whether it might be fair, and regardless of the fact that he'd bought Eastwich and along with it the right to express such opinions. She just had to recall what he'd said in that deep American drawl and she should be safe enough.

The question floated into her head. 'Safe from what?'

Tory, however, resolutely ignored it. Some things were better left well alone.

CHAPTER TWO

BY MORNING Tory had rationalised away any threat presented by Lucas Ryecart.

It could have been a simple chat-up line when he'd asked if they'd met before. Even if he'd seen a photograph of her, it would have left only the vaguest of impressions. And why should he make the connection between a girl student named Vicki and the Tory Lloyd who worked for him? She hadn't between Luc and Lucas until Simon had talked about his past and no one in Eastwich really knew about hers.

No, chances were he'd already forgotten her. He'd be like all the other chief executives before him—remote and faceless to someone in her junior position.

Reassured, Tory did as promised and went in to work, dressed casually in white T-shirt and cotton chinos. As it was Saturday, there were no calls to answer and, within an hour, she had dealt with most outstanding correspondence on her desk. The rest she took down the corridor for her boss's personal attention.

She didn't expect to find Alex Simpson there, not on a Saturday, and was initially pleased when she did. She imagined he'd come in to catch up on his own work.

That was before she noticed his appearance. There was several days' growth of beard on his chin and his eyes were bleary with sleep. His clothes were equally dishevelled and a quilt was draped along what he called his 'thinking' sofa, transforming it into a bed.

At thirty Alex Simpson had been hailed as a dynamic young programme-maker, destined for the highest awards. He had gone on to win several. Now he was pushing forty and, somewhere along the way, he had lost it.

'It's not how it looks.' He grimaced but was obviously relieved it was Tory and no one else. 'It's just that Sue's husband is home on leave and I've had no time to make other arrangements.'

Tory held in a sigh but she couldn't do anything about the disapproving look on her face. Officially Alex was lodging with Sue Baxter, a secretary at Eastwich, while he fixed himself up with more permanent accommodation. Unofficially he was sleeping with her while her Naval Engineer husband was on tour of duty. Tory knew this because *in*discretion was Sue Baxter's middle name.

She was a shallow, slightly vacuous woman, and what attraction Sue held for Alex was hard to fathom, but Tory kept her opinion to herself. Alex seemed intent on pushing his own self-destruct button and Tory felt ill-qualified to prevent him.

'You won't say anything, will you?' He smiled a little boyishly at Tory, already knowing the answer.

She shook her head, her loyalty guaranteed. She didn't fancy Alex, though many women did. Nor was she sure if she liked him at times. But he had a vulnerable quality that brought out a protective streak in her.

'You'd better not hang round here, looking like that,' she said with some frankness.

'I suppose not.' Alex made another face. 'I hear the new chief exec appeared in person yesterday.'

Tory nodded. 'I said you were out researching a programme.'

'I was, sort of,' he claimed. It was as unconvincing as his rider of, 'Pity I missed him.'

Tory looked at him sceptically, but refrained from pointing out that, had Lucas Ryecart met Alex while he was in this condition, Alex might not still be on the Eastwich payroll.

'Tory, I was wondering—' he gave her an appealing look '—if I could go to your place. Just to clean up. And maybe get my head down for an hour or two.'

Tory's heart sank. She told herself to refuse point-blank, but it came out as a less definite, 'I'm not sure, Alex. You know how tongues wag round here and if anyone saw you—'

'They won't,' he promised. ' I'll be the soul of discretion.'

'Yes, but—' Tory didn't get the chance to finish before Alex smiled in gratitude at her.

'You're a great girl.' He jumped up from his desk with some of his old enthusiasm. 'A wash and brush-up, that's all I need, and I'll be a new man.'

'All right.' Tory was already regretting it as she relayed, 'I have a spare key in my desk.'

Alex picked up the quilt from the couch and stuffed it into a cupboard, before following her back down the corridor to her office.

'You'll need the address.' She wrote it down on her telephone pad. 'You can use the phone to find a hotel or something.'

'Kind of you, Tory darling—' he looked rueful '—but I'm afraid hotels are out till pay day. My credit rating is zero and the bank is refusing to increase my overdraft.'

'What will you do? You can't keep dossing down in the office,' Tory warned.

'No, you're right. I don't suppose you could...' he began hopefully, then answered for himself, 'No, forget it. I'll find somewhere.'

Tory realised what he'd been about to ask. She also understood he was still asking, by not asking. His eyes were focused on her like a homeless stray.

She tried to harden her heart. She reminded herself that Alex earned a great deal more than her for doing a great deal less. Was it her problem that he couldn't manage his money?

'Never mind.' He forced a brave smile. 'I'll be back on my feet soon. I'm due my annual bonus from Eastwich next month—that's assuming this American chappie doesn't cancel it.'

Or cancel him, Tory thought as she looked at Alex through Lucas Ryecart's eyes. He was a shambolic figure whose past awards would be just history.

'Look, you can use my couch,' Tory found herself offering, 'until pay-day.'

'Darling Tory, you're a life-saver.' A delighted Alex made to give her a hug but she fended him off.

'And strictly on a keep-your-hands-to-yourself basis,' she added bluntly.

'Of course.' Alex took a step from her and held up his hands in compliance. 'No problem. I know you're not interested.'

He should do. Tory had made it clear enough in the beginning and Alex, philanderer though he undoubtedly was, respected the fact. He was also lazy; mostly he ended up with women who chased him. Being handsome in a slightly effete way, he drew a certain type of woman. Tory wasn't included in their category.

'Five days.' Tory calculated when their next salary should appear in the bank.

'Fine.' Alex gave her another grateful smile before turning to go.

'Alex,' Tory called him back at the door, 'try and stay sober, please.'

For a moment Alex looked resentful, ready to protest his innocence. Tory's expression stopped him. It wasn't critical or superior or contemptuous. It was simply appealing.

He nodded, then, acknowledging his growing problem, said, 'If I don't, I'll crash somewhere else. Okay?'

'Okay.' Tory hoped his promise was sincere. He wasn't a violent drunk but she still didn't want him round her place in that state.

After Alex had gone, she wondered just how big a mistake she'd made. She knew it was one. She trusted it would turn out to be of the minor variety.

Rather than dwell on it, she returned to her work, but was interrupted minutes later. Her door opened and she looked up, expecting to see Alex again. She stared wordlessly at the man in the doorway.

Overnight she'd decided it was a passing attraction she'd felt towards Lucas Ryecart. Only it hadn't yet. Passed, that was. Dressed in black jeans, white shirt and dark glasses, he was just as devastating.

'How's the tooth?' he asked.

'The tooth?' she repeated stupidly.

'Gone but not forgotten?' he suggested.

The tooth. Tory clicked. She'd have to acquire a better memory if she were going to take up lying to this man.

'It's fine,' she assured. 'Actually, I had forgotten all about it.'

'Good.' His eyes ran over her, making her feel her T-shirt outlined her body too clearly. 'You didn't have to come in. How do you usually spend your Saturdays?'

The same way, Tory could have admitted, but somehow she didn't think he'd be impressed, even if he now owned most of Eastwich. More like he'd think she had nothing better to do with her time.

'It varies.' She shrugged noncommittally, then glanced down at her work, as if anxious to get on with it.

He noted the gesture, and switched to asking, 'Has Simpson gone?'

'Simpson?' Tory stalled.

'Alex Simpson.' He leaned on the doorframe, eyes inscrutable behind the dark glasses. 'At least I assume it was Simpson and not some passing bum, making himself at home in his office.'

'Alex was here, yes,' she confirmed and went on inventively, 'He came in to catch up on his paperwork.'

'He was catching up on some sleep when I saw him,' countered Ryecart.

'Really?' Tory faked surprise quite well. 'He did say he'd been in very early. Perhaps he nodded off without realising.'

'Slept it off, is my guess,' the American drawled back, and, pushing away from the door, crossed to sit on the edge of her desk. He removed the glasses and appraised her for a moment or two before adding, 'Are you two an item? Is that it?'

'An item?' Tory was slow on the uptake.

'You and Simpson, are you romantically involved?' He spelt out his meaning.

'No, of course not!' Tory denied most vehemently.

It had little impact, as the American smiled at her flash of temper. 'No need to go nuclear. I was only asking. I hear Simpson has something of a reputation with women,' he remarked, getting Tory's back up further.

'And from that you concluded that he and I…that we are…' She was unwilling to put it into words.

He did it for her. 'Lovers?'

Tory found herself blushing. He had that effect.

He studied her, as if she were an interesting species, and her blush deepened. 'I didn't think women did that any more.'

'Possibly not the women you know,' Tory shot back before she could stop herself.

He understood the insult. He could easily have sacked her for it. Instead he laughed.

'True,' he conceded. 'I tend to prefer the more experienced kind. Less hassle. Lower expectations. And fewer recriminations at the end… Still, who knows? I could be reformed.'

And pigs might fly, Tory thought as she wondered if he was flirting with her or just making fun.

'What about you?' he said with the same lazy smile.

'Me?' she asked. 'Oh, I prefer the invisible kind. Much less hassle. Zero expectations. And absolutely no recriminations.'

It took the American an instant to interpret. 'You don't date?'

'I don't date,' Tory repeated but without his tone of disbelief, 'and I don't need reforming, either.'

He looked puzzled rather than annoyed, his eyes doubting her seriousness.

'Is that a targeted response,' he finally asked, 'or a general declaration of intent?'

'Come again?' Tory squinted at him.

'Are you just telling *me* to take a hike,' he translated, 'or are all men off the agenda?'

Tory debated how much she wanted to keep her job. Just enough to show some restraint, she decided, so she said nothing. Her eyes, however, said much more.

'Me, I guess,' he concluded with a confidence barely dented. 'Well, never mind, I can live in hope.'

He was laughing at her. He had to be. He wasn't really interested in her. It was all a joke to him.

He straightened from the edge of her desk, saying, 'Would you have some idea how I might contact Simpson? '

'I...I'm not sure.' Having denied any relationship with Alex, Tory could hardly reveal the fact he was holed up at her place. 'I might be able to get a message to him.'

'Fine. I've asked all senior department heads to meet me, nine a.m. Monday, for a briefing,' he explained. 'It would be advisable for Simpson to attend.'

Tory nodded. 'I'll tell him...I mean, if I get hold of him,' she qualified, anxious to dispel the notion she and Alex had anything other than a business relationship.

'Well, if you can't, don't worry about it,' he ran on. 'It's Simpson's problem if he can't give Personnel a current telephone number.'

Tory frowned. 'But you saw him this morning.'

'So why didn't I wake him up?' he asked the question that was clearly in her mind. 'Let's just say I thought the morning after wouldn't be the best time to meet a new boss. What do you think?'

Tory thought that remarkably fair of the American—to give Alex the chance to redeem himself. Of course, he might simply prefer to sack him when he was stone-cold sober.

'Alex is a very good programme-maker,' she declared staunchly. 'He won a BAFTA three years ago.'

'Simpson *was* a very good programme-maker,' Lucas Ryecart corrected her, 'and, in this business, you're only as good as your last show. Simpson should know that.'

Tory said nothing. Speaking up for Alex had cut no ice with this man.

He also suspected her motives. 'Why so concerned about Simpson? If he goes, it might do your own career some good.'

'I doubt it.' Tory wondered who he was trying to fool. 'Simon is more experienced than me.'

He frowned, making the connection only when she glanced towards the second desk in the room. 'More willing to promote his cause, too, as I recall. Is he the reason you're loyal to Simpson?'

'Sorry?'

'You don't want to work for this Simon guy?'

No, Tory certainly didn't, but she didn't want to do Simon down either.

'You're not homophobic, are you?' he surmised at her uneasy silence.

'What?' Tory was startled by his directness.

'Homophobic,' he repeated, 'Anti-gay, against homo—'

'I know what it means!' Tory cut in angrily, and, forgetting—or, at least, no longer caring—who he was, informed him, 'It might be hard for an American to understand, but reticence isn't always an indication of stupidity.'

'Being brash, loud-mouth colonials, you mean.' He had no problem deciphering the insult. He just wasn't bothered by it.

Tory wondered what you had to do to dent this man's confidence. Use a sledgehammer, perhaps.

'Simon's sexual preference is a matter of complete disinterest to me,' she declared in heavy tones.

'If you say so,' he responded, as if he didn't quite believe her.

'I am *not* homophobic!' she insisted angrily. 'Whether I'd want to work for Simon doesn't hinge on that.'

'Okay.' He conceded the point, then immediately lost interest in it as he looked at his watch, saying, 'I have to go. I have a meeting in London. I'll give you my number.'

He picked up her Biro and, tearing out a slip of paper from her notepad, leaned on her desk to write his name and two telephone numbers.

'The top one is my mobile,' he informed her. 'The other's Abbey Lodge. I'm staying there in the short term.'

Abbey Lodge was the most exclusive hotel locally, favoured by high-powered businessmen and visiting celebrities.

He held out the piece of paper and for a moment Tory just stared at it as if it were contaminated. Why was he giving her his telephone number? Did he imagine she'd want to call him?

'In case you have a problem tracking down Alex Simpson,' he explained, patently amused at her wary expression.

'Of course.' Now she almost snatched the paper from him.

'Still, if you want to call me, regardless—' his mouth

slanted '—feel free. I'm sure we can find *something* to talk about...'

'I...' On the contrary Tory couldn't think of a sensible thing to say. She'd been so presumptuous it was embarrassing.

'Meanwhile—' his smile became less mocking '—it's a beautiful day. Why not play hooky for once?'

The suggestion sounded genuine but Tory felt even more uncomfortable, recalling the fact she'd played hooky yesterday.

'I have some stuff to finish,' she claimed, sober-faced.

'Well, you know what they say: all work and no play,' he misquoted dryly, 'makes for a dull television producer.'

Tory realised he was joking but wondered, nonetheless, if that was how she seemed to him. Dull. What an indictment.

It put her on the defensive. 'I'm not the one travelling down to London for a business meeting on a Saturday.'

'Did I say business?' He raised a dark brow.

Tory frowned up at him. He had, hadn't he?

He shook his head, adding, 'No, this one's strictly personal.'

'I'm sorry.' Tory denied any intention to pry.

But he continued, 'In a way, it involves you. I'm having dinner with the woman I was dating until recently...a *farewell* dinner,' he stressed.

Tory met his eyes briefly, then looked away once more. There was nothing subtle about his interest in her.

'This really is none of my business, Mr Ryecart,' she replied on an officious note.

'Not now, maybe—' he got to his feet '—but who knows what the future might hold?'

He afforded her another smile. Perfect white teeth in a tanned face. Too handsome for anyone else's good.

Tory tried again. 'I shouldn't think we'll meet very often, Mr Ryecart,' she said repressively, 'in view of your considerably senior position, but I'm sure I'll endeavour to be polite when we do.'

This time her message couldn't be missed. 'In short, you'd like me to take a hike.'

Tory's nails curled into her palms. The man had no idea of the conventions that governed normal conversation.

'I didn't say that,' she replied, through gritted teeth. 'I was just pointing out—'

'That you'd touch your forelock but nothing else,' he summed up with breath-taking accuracy.

Tory felt a curious desire to hit him. It took a huge effort to stop herself, to remind herself he *was* her boss.

He held up a pacifying hand, having clearly read her thoughts. He might be brash, but he wasn't stupid.

'Tell you what, let's agree to dispense with the forelock-tugging, too,' he suggested and finally walked towards the door.

Tory's heart sank. What did that mean?

'Mr Ryecart—' she called after him.

He turned, his expression now remote. Had he already dispensed with her, altogether?

She didn't intend waiting to find out. She asked point-blank, 'Should I be looking for another job?'

'What?' Such an idea had obviously been far from his mind. He considered it briefly before answering, 'If you're asking me will Eastwich survive, then I don't know that yet. It's no secret that it's operating at a loss, but I wouldn't have bought it if I didn't feel turn-around was viable.'

It was a straight, businesslike response that left Tory feeling decidedly silly. She had imagined rejecting Lucas Ryecart might be a sackable offence but obviously he didn't work that way.

'That isn't what you meant, is it?' He read her changing expression.

'No,' Tory admitted reluctantly. 'I thought…'

'That I'd fire you for not responding to my advances,' he concluded for himself, and now displeasure thinned his sensual mouth. 'God, you have a low opinion of me…or is it all men?'

Tory bit on her lip before muttering, 'I—I…if I misjudged you—'

'In spades,' he confirmed. 'I may be the loud, overbearing American you've already written me off as—'

'That's not—' Tory tried to deny it.

He overrode her. 'And I may let what's in my pants overrule good sense occasionally,' he continued crudely, 'but desperate I'm not, or vindictive. If you leave Eastwich, it won't be on my account.'

Tory wanted the ground to swallow her up. She started to say, 'I'm sorry, I shouldn't have—' and was left talking to thin air.

Lucas Ryecart might not be vindictive but he had a temper. She experienced its full force as the door slammed hard behind him.

And that's me told, she thought, feeling wrung out and foolish, and wishing she'd kept her mouth shut.

He'd been flirting with her. Nothing more. Perhaps he flirted with all personable women under the assumption that most would enjoy it. He'd be right, too. Most would.

They'd know how to take Lucas Ryecart, realise that anyone that handsome, and rich, and successful, would scarcely be interested in ordinary mortals. They'd be slightly flattered by his appreciative gaze, a little charmed by his slow, easy smile, but they certainly wouldn't be crazy enough to take him seriously.

She glanced out of the window in time to see him striding across the car park. She didn't worry that he'd look up. She was already forgotten.

She watched him get into a dark green four-by-four. It was a surprisingly *un*flash vehicle. She'd have expected him to drive something fast and conspicuous—a low-slung sports car, perhaps. But what did she really know about Lucas Ryecart? Next to nothing.

She tried to remember what Charlie, her ex-fiancé, had said. He hadn't talked much of his dead sister but he'd mentioned her husband a few times. He'd obviously admired the older man who'd spent his early career reporting from the trouble spots of the world. Charlie's mother had also alluded to her American son-in-law with some fondness and Tory had formed various images: faithful husband, dedicated journalist, fine human being.

None fitted the Lucas Ryecart she'd met, but then it had been years since Jessica Wainwright's death and time changed everybody. It had certainly changed his circumstances if Eastwich was only one of the television companies he owned. He was also no longer the marrying kind, a fact he'd made clear. Arguably, his directness was a virtue, but if he had any other noble character traits Tory had missed them.

Time had changed Tory, too. Or was it her current lifestyle? All work and no play, as he'd said. Making her dull, stupid even, unable to laugh off a man's interest without sounding like prude of the year.

Tory felt like kicking herself. And Alex. And Lucas Ryecart. She settled for kicking her waste bin and didn't hang around to tidy up the mess she made.

She took the American's advice and spent the afternoon at the Anglian Country Club, a favourite haunt for young professionals. For two hours she windsurfed across the man-made lake, a skill she'd acquired on her first foreign holiday. It was her main form of relaxation, strenuous though it could be, and she was now more than competent.

Sometimes she took a lesson with Steve, the resident coach. About her age, he had a law degree but had never practised, preferring to spend his life windsurfing. They had chatted occasionally and once gone for a drink in the club but nothing more. Today he helped her put away her equipment and asked casually if she had plans for the evening. She shook her head and he proposed going for something to eat in town.

Normally Tory would have politely turned him down, but Lucas Ryecart's image loomed, and she said, 'Why not?'

Tory drove them in her car and they went to an Italian restaurant. They talked about windsurfing, then music and the colleges they'd attended. Steve was easy enough company.

They went on to a pub and met some of his friends, a mixed crowd of men and women. Tory stuck to orange juice, and, although declining a party invitation, agreed to drive them there.

When the rest had piled out of her car, Steve surprised her with a kiss on the lips. It was quite pleasurable, but hardly earth-moving and another man's image intruded when she closed her eyes. She broke off the kiss before it turned intimate.

Steve got the message. 'I don't suppose you'd like to go home to my place?' he asked, more in hope than expectation.

'No, thanks all the same.' She gave him an amiable smile and her refusal was accepted in the same spirit.

Steve bowed out with a casual, 'Perhaps we can go out again some time,' and followed his friends into the house where the party was.

Tory drove home without regrets. She'd enjoyed the evening up to a point, but she had no desire to have competent, athletic sex with a man whose *raison d'être* was windsurfing. She'd sooner go to bed with a mug of Horlicks and a Jane Austen.

She returned to find her flat empty and felt a measure of relief, assuming Alex had chosen somewhere else to doss down.

No such luck, however, as she was rudely awakened at two in the morning by a constant ringing on her doorbell. Pulling on a dressing gown, she went to the bay window first and wasn't entirely surprised to see Alex leaning against the wall.

'Lost my key, sorry,' he slurred as she opened the outer door and took in his swaying figure.

'Oh, Alex, you promised.' She sighed wearily and for a moment contemplated shutting the door on him.

'Couldn't help it,' he mumbled pathetically. 'Love her, really love her… Know that, Tory?'

'Yes, Alex. Now, shh!' Tory hastily propelled him through the hallway before he woke her neighbours.

'I'm not drunk.' He breathed whisky fumes on her as he lurched inside her flat. 'Just had a drink or two. Her fault. The bitch. Phoned her up but she wouldn't talk to me.'

Tory sighed again as he sprawled his length on her sofa. There would be no moving him now. She should have turned him away.

'Why won't she talk to me?' he appealed with an injured air. 'She knows she's the only one I've ever loved.'

'Her husband was probably there,' Tory pointed out in cynical tones.

'Husband?' He turned bleary eyes towards her, then rallied to claim belligerently, 'I'm her husband. Eyes of God and all that. Better or worse. Richer or poorer. Till death or the mortgage company do us part,' he finished on a self-pitying sob.

'Who are we talking about, Alex?' Tory finally asked.

'Rita, of course.' A frown questioned her intelligence, then he began to sing, 'Lovely Rita, no one can beat her—'

'Shh!' Tory hushed him once more. 'You're going to wake the woman upstairs.'

'Don't care,' Alex announced, this time like a sulky boy. 'All women are vile… 'Cept you, darling Tory.' He smiled winningly at her.

Tory rolled her eyes heavenward. She might have taken Lucas Ryecart too seriously that morning, but she was in no danger of it with Alex. Drunk, Alex would flirt with a lamppost.

'I thought you were talking about Sue,' she stated in repressive tones.

'Sue?' He looked blank for a moment.

'Sue Baxter,' she reminded him heavily. 'Works at Eastwich. Husband in Navy. Woman you've been living with for the last month or two.'

Drunk though he was, Alex understood the implication. 'You think I don't love Rita because I've been shacking up with Sue? But I do. Sue's just…'

'A fill-in?' Tory suggested dryly.

'Yes. No. You don't understand,' he answered in quick succession. 'Men aren't the same as women, Tory, you have to realise that.'

'Oh, I do,' Tory assured him, and before he could justify his infidelity on biological grounds she stood and picked up the blanket and pillow she'd dug out earlier. 'You're an education in yourself, Alex,' she added, draping the blanket over him without ceremony. 'Lift.'

He raised his head and she thrust the pillow under him.

'You're not a woman, Tory,' he told her solemnly, 'you're a friend.'

'Thanks,' she muttered at this backhanded compliment. Not that she minded much. She didn't want Alex's roving eye fixing on her. 'Goodnight, Alex.'

''Night, Tory,' he echoed, already settling down for the night. Soon he would be out for the count.

It was Tory who was left sleepless.

After an afternoon spent windsurfing and an evening in company, she should be tired enough to sleep through a hurricane, yet she couldn't sleep through Lucas Ryecart.

Alex had provided a temporary distraction but now he was just another concern. How could she keep Alex sober tomorrow so he would be presentable on Monday for his meeting with Ryecart?

She tried telling herself it wasn't her problem. And it wasn't, really. After all, what did she owe Alex? He had given her a chance, taking her on as a production assistant when she'd had little experience, but she'd surely repaid him, covering up for him as she had over that last three months. It would be much the wisest thing to let Alex fend for himself.

Perhaps Alex might even hold his own with the American. After all, he was an intelligent, articulate man with a first-class degree from Cambridge and twenty years' experience in the television industry.

Whereas Lucas Ryecart, who was he?

The man who was going to wipe the floor with Alex, that was who, she answered the question for herself, and for the second night in a row fell asleep with Lucas Ryecart's image running round her brain.

CHAPTER THREE

TORY woke in an extremely bad mood, and felt not much better after taking a shower. Dressed in jeans and T-shirt, she went through to the living room to tackle Alex. She had decided: she wanted him gone, a.s.a.p.

Only he wasn't awake yet. With his arms tight round a cushion and his legs bent up on the sofa, he lay there muttering in his sleep. He looked a wreck and he smelled awful, of too much booze and nicotine. She'd never found Alex attractive; this morning he was positively repellent. No way was he going to get his act together by Monday.

But she realised that she wouldn't need to give him a hard time. When Alex woke up, he would feel sorry enough for himself.

She was right. When she woke him with strong black coffee, he was full of remorse.

He'd forgotten his promise not to return to her flat drunk. Apparently he'd had a whisky for Dutch courage before phoning his wife in Edinburgh. When she'd slammed the phone down on him, he'd had several more.

'So, basically it was all Rita's fault,' Tory concluded on a sceptical note, deciding a sympathetic approach wasn't going to help him.

He looked a little sheepish. 'I didn't say that, exactly.'

'Just as well,' Tory muttered back, 'because I haven't met many candidates for living sainthood, but your wife has to be one.'

He looked taken aback by her frankness, but didn't argue. 'You're right. I didn't treat her very well, did I?'

Tory's brows went heavenward.

'Okay, I admit it,' he groaned back. 'I was unfaithful to her a couple of times, but it didn't mean anything. It's Rita I love. After twenty years together she should know that.'

'Twenty years?' Tory hadn't viewed Alex as long-term married.

'We met at college,' Alex went on. 'She was so bright and funny and together. She still is… If only I'd realised. I can't function without Rita,' he claimed in despair.

'Then you'd better try and get her back,' Tory advised quite severely. 'Either that, or get your own act together, Alex, before you lose it all.'

'I already have,' he said miserably.

Tory resisted the urge to shake him. 'Hardly. You have an exceedingly well-paid job doing something you used to love. Give it another week or so, however, and you'll probably be kissing goodbye to that, too.'

Alex looked a little shocked at her plain-speaking, then resentful. 'It's not that bad. Sure, I've missed a few deadlines and been absent for a meeting or two. But Colin understands. He knows I'll be back on track soon.'

'You've forgotten the American.' Tory hadn't.

'Ryecart.' Alex shrugged at the name. 'So, there's a new chief exec. He'll only be interested in the business side.'

'I don't think so.' Tory decided not to pass on Ryecart's comments about their last documentary but decided Alex still required a reality check. 'There's something you should know. He saw you yesterday morning, crashed on your office couch.'

'Damn,' Alex cursed aloud, before saying with some hope, 'Maybe he thought I'd been working all night.'

Tory shook her head again. 'This man's not stupid, Alex. He knew you were sleeping it off… He wants to see you first thing Monday morning.'

'Well, isn't that civilised of him,' Alex sneered, 'not waking a sleeping man? Making me sweat till Monday morning before sacking me.'

That scenario had already occurred to Tory, but she said nothing.

'He was probably too much a coward to do it on Saturday,' Alex ran on speculatively. 'Probably thought I'd turn round and punch his lights out for him.'

Tory sighed heavily. 'Men are ridiculous.'

That deflated Alex somewhat. They both knew he was as likely to punch someone as become celibate.

'All right, so I'm no fighter, but he wouldn't know that.'

'I doubt he'd care. He looks well able to take care of himself.'

'Big?' Alex deduced from her tone.

'Huge.' Tory reckoned the American was at least six inches taller than Alex.

'Upwards or outwards?'

'Both... Well, sort of. He's not fat. He's just...muscly, you might say,' Tory described him with some reluctance.

Alex slanted her a curious look. 'You don't fancy him, do you, Tory?'

'No, of course not!' she protested immediately. 'Whatever makes you say that?'

He shrugged, then smiled a fraction. 'The blush on your face, I suppose. I've never seen you blush before.'

'Rubbish. I'm always blushing. I'm like a Belisha beacon in hot weather,' she declared extravagantly and turned the conversation back on him. 'Anyway, we're not talking about me. It's you that has the problem. You're going to have to make an effort on Monday, Alex, to impress him.'

'Is there any point?' he asked rhetorically. 'Why go in and give him the satisfaction of firing me?'

'Oh, for God's sake, Alex!' She lost her patience. 'Stop being such a wimp!'

For a moment Alex looked seriously indignant. He was her boss, after all. Then he remembered he'd just spent the night sleeping on her sofa, and had pretty much surrendered his right to deference by offloading his problems on her.

'I'm sorry. I shouldn't have said that,' Tory added as his face caved in, exposing his vulnerability.

'No, it's all right. It's what Rita would have said to me. She couldn't stand people wallowing in self-pity.' He looked in admiration at Tory, and her heart sank. She didn't need Alex transferring his emotional dependence onto her.

'Well, it's up to you, Alex. I'm not going to tell you what

to do.' She rose abruptly to collect their coffee-cups and take them through to the small kitchen adjoining.

He followed her and watched as she rinsed them out in the sink. 'I could prepare a schedule of documentaries we propose to make in the coming months.'

Tory frowned. 'What documentaries?'

He shrugged. 'I'm sure we could come up with something.'

'*We?*' she echoed.

'I thought, well, that you might—'

'Give up my *one* day off?'

'Well, if you've plans...' He clearly believed she hadn't.

'You think my life is dull, too, don't you?' she accused, almost wiping the pattern off the saucer she was drying. 'Good old Tory, with nothing better to do at the weekend.'

'No, of course not,' Alex disclaimed quickly, realising he'd touched a sore spot.

Tory scowled, but not at him. It was Lucas Ryecart's comments that still rankled. She couldn't seem to get the man out of her head.

'I just know I'll work better with you as a sounding-board,' Alex added appeasingly.

Tory knew he wouldn't work *at all* if she didn't help him.

She gave in. 'You go wash, I'll make the coffee, then we'll get started.'

'Tory, you're a brick.'

Tory pulled a face as he went from the kitchen to the hall and the bathroom off it. She heard the shower running shortly afterwards and, above it, the sound of him singing. She pulled another face. What did he have to sing about?

Men were unbelievable. One moment Alex was confessing his undying love for his wife and his devastation at her loss, the next he was singing a selection of top-twenty hits from the seventies.

Compartmentalisation. That was the key to the male psyche. Everything kept in separate little cubicles. Love of wife and children. Work and ambition. Fun and sex. Duty and religion. Nip into one cubicle, pull the curtain and forget the rest. Then nip out and onto the next. Never mind tidying up what you've left behind on the floor.

Not all men, of course, but the majority. She thought of Lucas Ryecart. Another compartmentaliser. One moment she was a woman and he was making it damn plain he fancied her. The next she was one of his employees and he clearly had no problems treating her as such. Then he was gone, and no doubt she'd been forgotten the second he'd climbed into his car.

So very different from women. Women stood at windows, watching cars pull away while they sorted out what they felt and why. Women carried their emotional baggage between cubicles until they were bowed with the weight.

There were exceptions, of course. Her own mother was one. Maura Lloyd had a simple approach to life. Create what havoc you liked, then shut the door on it and move on. It had worked for her—if not for the people round her.

Tory had been Maura's only child. She'd had her at eighteen. Tory's father had been a married lecturer at art college. At least that was one of the stories Maura had told her, but at times he'd also been a famous painter, a cartoonist in a popular daily paper, and an illustrator for children's story-books. Tory was never sure whether these were total fantasy or a selection of different men who might have sired her or the same multi-talented many-careered individual. Whichever, Maura had consistently avoided naming the man throughout Tory's twenty-six years, and, having met some of Maura's later partners, Tory had decided to leave well alone.

At any rate, Maura had decided to keep her. After a fashion, anyway, as Tory had spent her childhood shuttling back and forth between gentle, unassuming grandparents who lived in a semi in the suburbs to various flats her mother had occupied with various men.

The contrast couldn't have been sharper, order versus chaos, routine versus excitement, respectability versus an extravagantly Bohemian lifestyle. Tory had never felt neglected, just torn and divided.

She loved her mother because she was warm and funny and

affectionate, but, in truth, she preferred living with her grandparents. When she'd become sick as a child, her mother hadn't pretended to cope. Grandmother Jean had been the one to take her to chemotherapy and hold her hand and promise her her beautiful curls would grow back.

It wasn't that Maura hadn't cared. Tory didn't believe that. But it had been a selfish sort of caring. When Tory had needed calm, Maura would be playing the tragic figure, weeping so extravagantly a ten-year-old Tory had become hysterical, imagining she must be dying.

She hadn't died, of course, and the childhood leukaemia was now a distant memory, although, in some respects, it still shaped her life. She supposed everything in childhood did.

She looked round her kitchen—everything in its place and a place for everything. Grandmother Jean's influence, although she'd been dead ten years and her grandfather for longer.

There was no visible sign of her mother but Tory knew she carried some of her inside. She just kept it locked up tight.

'Tory?' A voice broke into her thoughts. 'Are you all right?'

'Sure. I've made coffee.' She loaded a tray with the cafetère and cups and a plate of croissants.

Alex followed her through and, after a slow start, they began to trawl up some ideas for future programmes.

They worked all day, with only the briefest break for a sandwich lunch, and as Alex got into his stride the man who had won awards re-emerged. Tory remembered why she had wanted to work for him in the first place. When he wasn't bed-hopping or pub-crawling, Alex Simpson was a fairly talented programme-maker.

In the end they came up with four firm proposals for future programmes and a promising outline of another. Alex sat back, looking pleased with himself, as well he might, while Tory had some satisfaction in imagining Lucas Ryecart's reaction.

'Where's your nearest take-away?' Alex asked, consulting his watch to find it after six.

'There's a Chinese a couple of streets away,' she replied. 'I have a menu list somewhere. We can phone in an order, then I'll collect it.'

She went to a notice-board in the kitchen and found the menu list for the Lucky Dragon. They made their selection and she did the calling.

Alex followed her through to the hall, saying, 'I should go,' as he watched her sling on a lightweight jacket.

'You don't know where it is.' Tory slipped out the door before he could argue.

The Lucky Dragon was, in fact, easy to find. The problem was one had to pass The Brown Cow pub on the way, and Tory wasn't sure whether Alex would manage to *pass* it.

She went on foot and the food was ready by the time she arrived. She walked back quickly so it wouldn't go cold. She didn't notice the Range Rover parked on the other side of the street or its owner, crossing to trail her up the steps to her front door.

'I'll do that,' he offered just as she put the take-away on the doorstep so she could use her key.

Tory recognised the voice immediately and wheeled round.

Lucas Ryecart took a step back at her alarmed look. 'Sorry if I startled you.'

Tory felt a confusion of things. As usual, there was the physical impact of him, tall, muscular and utterly male. That caused a first rush of excitement, hastily suppressed, closely followed by the set-your-teeth-on-edge factor as she realised a series of things. He had her address. Her address was on a file. He had her file. He owned her file. He owned Eastwich.

He just didn't own her, Tory reminded both of them as a frown made it plain he wasn't welcome.

'I wanted to speak to you,' he pursued. 'I decided it might be better outside work hours… Can I come in?'

'I…no!' Tory was horrified by the idea. She wanted no one, especially not this particular one, to find out Alex was using her flat as a base.

'You have company?' he surmised.

'What makes you say that?' Her tone denied it.

He glanced down at the plastic bags from which the smell of food was emanating. 'Well, either that, or you have a very healthy appetite.'

Sherlock Holmes lives, Tory thought in irritation and lied quite happily. 'I have a friend round for tea.'

'And I'm intruding,' he concluded for himself. 'No problem, this won't take long. I just wanted to say sorry.'

'Sorry? For what?'

'Yesterday morning. I was way out of line. Wrong time, wrong place, and I was moving too fast.'

Tory was unsure how to react to what seemed a genuine apology.

'I—I…this really isn't necessary,' she finally replied. 'We both said things. I'd prefer just to forget the whole incident.'

'Fine. Let's shake on that.' He offered her his hand.

'Right.' Tory took it with some reservations.

His grip was firm and strong and it jolted her, as if his touch were electric. Warmth spread through her like a slow fire.

Quite alarming. To be turned on by a handshake. Even the thought brought a flush to her pale cheeks.

He noticed it and smiled. Did he know?

'You're very young,' he said, out of nowhere.

She shook her head. 'I'm twenty-six.'

'That's young.' He smiled without mockery. 'I'm forty-one.'

Tory's eyes widened, betraying her surprise. He didn't look it.

'Too old, I reckon,' he added, shaking his head.

'For what?' Tory asked rather naively.

'For girls young enough to be my daughter,' he concluded, laughing at himself now.

No, you're not. Tory almost said the words aloud. But why, when she wanted rid of him? Didn't she?

She looked down. They were still holding hands. She slipped from his grip. The warmth between them remained.

'Colin Mathieson told me you were in your thirties,' he recalled next.

Tory's heart sank a little. Colin *believed* she was in her thirties. It was a wrong impression fostered by Alex when he'd employed her for the job.

'Perhaps he was thinking of someone else,' Tory suggested weakly.

'Perhaps,' he echoed. 'Anyway, if I'd known your real age, I wouldn't have asked you out.'

It was Tory's turn to frown. Did he have some religious objection to women under thirty? Or did he imagine her too immature to interest him?

'You didn't,' she pointed out.

'Didn't I?' He arched a brow before admitting, 'Well, it had been my game plan. I guess I didn't get round to it.'

Now she was too young or inexperienced or whatever for him to bother, Tory surmised with some anger, surely irrational.

'It was Colin who gave me your address,' he went on. 'I told him I wanted to talk to you about Simpson.'

Alex? For a moment or two Tory had forgotten about Alex.

She could tell the American, of course. She could invite him in so he could meet a sober, industrious Alex. Did it matter if he jumped to the wrong conclusions about him being there?

Tory found it did matter, so she said nothing.

'Did you manage to locate him, by the way?' Lucas enquired directly.

She nodded.

'He's looking forward to meeting you,' she fabricated. 'I believe he has some future projects he wishes to discuss.'

Lucas Ryecart looked mildly surprised but didn't challenge it.

'Good.' He then began to say, 'I guess I'd better leave you to your meal—' when the door opened behind Tory.

She turned to see Alex and this time her heart plummeted. He was holding his jacket, obviously on his way out. On seeing her, his face clouded with guilt.

Tory was quick to realise where he'd been going. Tired of waiting for the meal, he'd been off in search of liquid refreshment.

'There you are.' Alex recovered quickly. 'I was worried you'd got lost and was coming to look for you.'

'No, I...' She glanced between the two men but made no effort to introduce them.

Lucas Ryecart, of course, knew exactly who Alex was. His eyes briefly registered the other man, then slid back to Tory and didn't leave her. Dark blue eyes, cold with anger.

'Sorry—' Alex picked up on the sudden drop in temperature '—I can see I'm in the way. Would you like me to disappear for an hour or two? Let you have the flat to yourself?'

Tory could have groaned aloud. Alex made it sound as if they were sharing the place.

'I...no, don't do that, Alex.' She'd spent all day getting his mind back on work. She wasn't giving him a chance to go AWOL on her.

It was the wrong answer as far as Lucas Ryecart was concerned.

'No, don't do that, *Alex*,' he mimicked her anxious tone, reading too much—far too much—into it. 'Miss Lloyd and I have finished any business between us for now.'

Having said his piece, he turned and walked away.

'Damn!' Tory swore in frustration.

Alex, having registered an American accent, began, 'Was that—?'

'Yes!' Tory confirmed and, half tripping over the Chinese take-away, picked the bags up and shoved them at Alex. 'Carry these in!'

Then she raced down the steps and across the street in time to catch Lucas Ryecart opening the door of the Range Rover.

'Wait, please,' she appealed before he could climb behind the steering wheel.

He stopped and turned. His expression was now remote, as if he'd already dismissed her from his mind, but, after a moment's deliberation, he closed the car door and leaned against it.

'Okay, I'm waiting.' He folded muscular sinewy arms across a broad chest.

Tory saw tension and anger beneath the apparently casual gesture. 'I...um...just wanted to clear up any possible misunderstanding. About Alex being there, I mean. You see…well, it's not—'

'How it seems?' he cut across her ramblings with a mocking lift of one dark brow.

'Yes, ' she confirmed, 'I mean, no, it isn't.'

'So that wasn't Alex Simpson,' he drawled on, 'and you aren't about to share an evening meal with him and he isn't currently staying at your flat and you haven't lied to me about your involvement with him.'

Tory saw from his face that she would be wasting her time, telling the truth. Any inclination on his part to kiss and make up had departed with Alex's appearance at the door.

'There's no point in this,' she muttered to herself and would have walked away if a hand hadn't shot out to keep her there.

She tried to pull her arm free. When she couldn't, she lifted her other hand, intending to push him away. He was too quick for her. He grabbed both her wrists and dragged her round until he had her backed against his car.

He did it with the minimum of force. Only her pride was really hurt.

She snapped at him, 'Let me go!'

'Okay.' He released her but stood so close she was still trapped and asked, 'Is Simpson's wife filing for divorce?'

She frowned at the unexpected question. 'Yes, possibly. Why?'

'Well, that explains the need to keep quiet,' he concluded, 'if not the attraction.'

His eyes narrowed in contempt and Tory found herself flaring back, 'You know nothing!'

'You're right. I don't,' he agreed in the same vein. 'I don't know why a bright, beautiful young woman would waste herself on a washed-up has-been with a wife, two kids and a drink habit to support… Perhaps you could enlighten me?'

'Alex isn't a has-been!' Tory protested angrily, recalling the programme outlines they'd prepared to impress this man. Some of their ideas were good, damn good. All futile, now, it would seem. 'And he doesn't have a drink problem.'

He threw her a look of pity.

'Who says love doesn't walk around with a white cane and guide dog?'

She threw him back a look of fury.

'I'm not in love with Alex Simpson! I never have been in love with Alex Simpson. I never shall be. I don't even believe in love!'

She spoke in no uncertain terms and speculation replaced pity in his gaze, but he still didn't release her.

'So you don't love Simpson,' he mused aloud. 'You don't love anybody. I wonder what gets you through the day, Tory Lloyd?'

'My work,' she answered, both literally and figuratively. 'That's what's important to me. That's *all* that's important to me.'

He shook his head, then leaned towards her to say in a low voice, 'If that's true, Simpson must be goddamn lousy in bed.'

Tory reacted with shocked disbelief. 'Do you have to be so…so…?'

'Accurate?'

'Crude!'

'I can't help it,' he claimed. 'I am American, after all.'

His tone was serious, but inside he was laughing. At her.

'Is that what you like about Simpson? Is he suitably refined?'

'More so than you, at any rate.'

Tory had, by this time, given up worrying about job security.

Lucas Ryecart had also abandoned any effort to be a fair, reasonable employer.

'I won't argue with that.' He shrugged off any insult, before drawling, 'But at least I have a certain homespun notion of morality.'

'Really?' Tory sniffed.

'Yes, really,' he echoed. 'If I were married, I wouldn't dump my wife and kids just because a newer, prettier model came along—'

'That's not the way it was,' Tory almost spat at him, 'and who knows what *you'd* do. You're *not* married, are you?'

'Not currently, but I was.' His face clouded briefly.

Tory could have kicked herself. She'd forgotten momentarily his connection with Jessica Wainwright.

'And when I was married, I was faithful,' he added quietly.

Tory believed him. He hadn't cheated on Jessica. He hadn't cheated because he'd adored her.

Her anger faded as she wondered if he still grieved but she didn't want to probe further. She was uncomfortable with the whole subject.

'Mr Ryecart,' she replied at length, 'I don't feel this is any of my business.'

'It will be, *Miss* Lloyd,' he mocked her formality, 'come the day I take you away from Simpson.'

'What?'

'I said—'

'I heard!' She just didn't believe him. Was it a joke?

Blue eyes caught and held hers. They told her it was no joke.

'I've decided I *am* interested, after all,' he stated dispassionately.

They could have been discussing a business deal. She was to be his latest acquisition. Take over, asset strip, move on.

'I thought you were too old for me,' Tory reminded him pointedly.

'I'd have said so, yes,' he agreed in dry tones, 'but as you're already living with someone of my advanced years, you obviously don't share my reservations.'

'I am *not* living with Alex,' she seethed in denial.

'You're simply good friends, right?' He slanted her a sceptical look.

Tory wanted to slap him. She longed to. She'd never had such a violent urge before.

'Oh, think what you like!' She finally snapped. 'Only don't take it out on Alex.'

'Meaning?' Dark brows lifted.

'Meaning: you may fancy me—' she continued angrily.

A deep, mocking laugh interrupted her. 'English understatement, I love it. I don't just *fancy* you, Miss Lloyd. I want you. I desire you. I'd like to—'

'Okay, I've got the picture,' she cut across him before he became any more explicit. 'But that's not my fault or Alex's. I haven't encouraged you. If this affects our positions at Eastwich—'

'You'll scream sexual harassment?' His eyes hardened.

Tory scowled in return. He was putting words in her mouth that weren't there. 'I wasn't saying that.'

'Good, because I've told you before,' he growled back, 'I am quite capable of separating my private life and my position as Chief Executive of Eastwich… If I decide to fire Simpson, you can be sure it'll be for a better reason than the fact he's currently sharing your bed.'

'He isn't!' Tory protested once more, only to draw a cynical glance that made her finally lose it. 'To hell with this! You're right, of course. Alex and I *are* lovers. In fact, we're at it like rabbits. Night and day. Every spare moment,' she ran on wildly. 'We can't keep our hands off each other.'

It silenced him, but only briefly before he drawled back, 'Now who's being crude?'

'It's called irony,' she countered.

'All right, so if you and Simpson aren't lovers…' he surmised aloud.

'Give the man a coconut,' she muttered under her breath.

He ignored her, finishing, 'Prove it!'

'Prove it?' she echoed in exasperation. 'And how am I meant to do that—set up a surveillance camera in my bedroom?'

'That would hardly cover it,' he responded coolly. 'Some couples rarely make it to the bedroom. I prefer outdoor sex myself. How about you?'

Tory didn't have to feign shock at an involuntary vision of a couple entwined in long grass under a blue sky. Not just any couple, either.

She shut her eyes to censor the image and heard his deep drawl continue, 'Not that I was suggesting it as an immediate option. A date will do, initially.'

Tory's eyes snapped open again. 'A date?'

'You know—' he smiled as if he could see inside her head '—boy asks girl out. Girl says yes. They go to a restaurant or the movies. Boy takes girl home. If he's lucky, he gets to kiss her. If he's very lucky, he gets to—'

'Yes, all right,' she snapped before he could warm any more to the theme. '*You're* asking *me* on a date?'

'That was the general idea,' he confirmed.

'To prove I'm not slee—having an affair with Alex?' Her tone told him how absurd she thought it.

'It isn't conclusive,' he admitted. 'But if you were my woman, I wouldn't let another man get too close. I reckon Alex Simpson will feel the same way.'

Tory doubted it. Even if she had been Alex's *woman*—how primitive it sounded—she didn't see Alex fighting anyone over her.

'Alex doesn't work like that,' she said disdainfully. 'He's much too civilised.'

'Really.' He glanced across the street towards her house and the bay window on the ground floor.

Tory followed his eyes in time to see Alex drawing back behind a net curtain. Evidently he'd been watching them. It was hardly surprising.

'He's curious, that's all,' she explained. 'He's realised who you are. It's nothing personal.'

'Yeah, I bet,' he scoffed in reply.

'It's true!' she insisted.

'Okay, so it's true,' he repeated, humouring her, 'in which case he won't mind if I do this.'

'Do wh—?' The question went unfinished.

The American leaned forward and kissed her before she could stop him. His lips touched hers with fleeting intimacy. It was over in a matter of seconds, but she was left feeling the imprint of his mouth on hers.

'I—I…' she stammered, wide-eyed '…you sh-shouldn't…'

'No, I shouldn't,' he agreed, gazing hard at her. 'But now I have…'

Now he had, he would have to kiss her again. His eyes told her that.

Tory had time to protest, turn her head, do anything but stand there looking up at him. Time to move away before his head blocked out the sun and his mouth covered hers, hard and possessive. Time to pull back as he began to kiss as if they were already lovers.

Only Tory had never felt like this before. Totally powerless, her eyes shutting, her lips parting, letting him in. Unable to resist as he stole the breath and the will from her. Boneless and fluid in strong arms wrapped round her waist, drawing her closer.

Passion flared so quickly, it caught them both unawares. Somewhere in the back of her head, Tory knew this was crazy, but she didn't seem to care. Her arms lifted to his shoulders and he dragged her body to his. They fell back against the side of his car, oblivious. He went on kissing her. He started touching her. They forgot where they were.

Her jacket was big for her. Just as well. It hid the movements of his hands, pulling out the T-shirt from her jeans, running up over her back, then round to her small, firm breasts. She wore a crop top rather than bra. He touched her above it, stroking a nipple erect through the material. She moaned in his mouth. He groaned back and tried to push aside the top. She didn't stop him. She wanted this.

Sanity returned only as the front door of the nearest house slammed and a voice exclaimed loudly, 'Look, Mummy, they're still kissing. Don't they know they'll get each other's germs?'

'Shh, Jack,' another instructed, 'and stop staring. Just get into the car!'

The first, childish voice penetrated the mush that Tory's brain had turned into, and the mother's had a sudden, sobering effect.

She pushed at Lucas Ryecart's shoulders. He'd already taken his hand from her breast but was slow to release her entirely. He lifted his head away and they both glanced in the direction of the woman hustling her child into a car parked some yards down the road.

Embarrassed colour filled Tory's cheeks but Lucas Ryecart was unflustered. He didn't hide his pleasure in the kiss but gave her a slow, sensuous smile.

'You'll come back with me.' It was a statement, not a question.

Tory looked blank.

'To my hotel.' He made his meaning clear.

And the blue eyes holding hers made it clearer still.

'I...of course not!' Tory finally mustered up some indignation.

He ignored it. 'Why not? We both want it.'

Tory shook her head, denying it.

He smiled, and the smile called her a liar. He thought her a pushover. Something to do with the fact she'd just acted like one.

Pride reasserted itself and she tried to pull free. He held her easily, large hands spanning her waist.

'You won't have to go back to Simpson,' he assured her. 'I'll help you move out on him tomorrow.'

Tory stared back at him. What was he suggesting?

'We've only just met.' Her tone told him he was absurd.

'So?' He laughed. 'How often does it feel like this?'

She could have said, *Like what?* but he might have reminded her. And she didn't need it. Her body was trembling from the simple touch of his hand on her waist.

'You don't have to move in with me,' he went on. 'Not yet, at any rate. But you can't keep living with Simpson.'

'I'm not living with Alex,' she repeated for what seemed like the twentieth time. 'It's my flat.'

'Even easier,' he reasoned. '*You* can kick *him* out.'

Tory discounted the kiss and finally asked herself why she was having this conversation with a perfect stranger.

'You're crazy,' she concluded with more than a vein of seriousness.

'No, *I'm* honest,' he countered, 'and I don't see much point in fighting the inevitable.'

Him and her in bed together. That was what he meant. Tory didn't need a translation. His eyes told her. His certainty was disturbing. He imagined she was so easy.

It was time to fight back.

'Mr Ryecart—' she gave him a look that would havc soured cream '—you either think an awful lot of yourself or very little of me. Whichever, I would sooner walk over red-hot coals with a plastic petrol can in my hand than go to bed with you. Is that honest enough for you?'

Was it insulting enough? Tory asked herself.

Seemingly not as he made some sound of disbelief and she, losing her temper, pushed him hard on the chest.

Taken by surprise, he stumbled backwards but recovered in time to grab her as she tried to escape.

The smile was gone. His eyes glittered dangerously. 'You can't sleep with Simpson again. Do you understand?'

A shiver went down Tory's back at the unspoken threat. She pulled at her arm but he wouldn't release her.

'Do you understand?' he repeated.

'Yes,' she choked the word out.

He caught and held her eyes, insisting, 'You *won't* sleep with him,' even as he finally let her go.

For a moment Tory returned his stare, and saw something in it, dark and disturbing, that told her she didn't really know who this man was.

Then she was running, running as she should have done earlier, blindly across the road and up the steps, through the door Alex had left on the latch.

She didn't look back. If she had, she would have seen him.

Lucas Ryecart watched her until the moment she disappeared.

CHAPTER FOUR

TORY'S office looked out onto the main corridor. Monday morning she watched Alex and the other senior producers walk towards the conference room at the far end. They were in subdued mood for their first official meeting with the new big chief.

Two hours later she watched them return with a considerably more relaxed air.

Only Alex didn't. He didn't return for another half an hour.

Simon spotted him first. 'Here he is.'

Alex popped his head round the door. 'Tory, can I see you for a moment?'

His manner gave little away as he proceeded to his office.

'Maybe he wants help in clearing his desk,' suggested Simon on a hopeful note.

Tory muttered, 'Shut up, Simon,' in passing as she walked past him on her way to Alex's office, closing the door behind her.

'Everything all right?' she asked tentatively, then listened in bemusement as Alex began to enthuse over the American and his plans for Eastwich.

It was as if he had suffered a blinding conversion on the road to Damascus with Lucas Ryecart in the role of God.

'When he asked me to wait back,' Alex ran on, 'I thought, This is it. The axe is about to fall. But nothing. He just wanted to discuss the direction I envisaged our department taking.'

Tory's gaze was incredulous. Did Alex really believe Ryecart was interested in his opinions?

'Naturally I handed over the presentation package I'd prepared,' he declared smugly. 'He seemed impressed.'

'Really.' Tory tried to convey some of her scepticism.

Alex misunderstood. 'Don't worry, he knows you had a part

in it. He asked me how long we'd worked in such close liaison.'

Tory recognised sarcasm even if Alex didn't and could have groaned aloud. She wondered how she could bring Alex up to speed. The trouble was she'd worked hard to kill Alex's curiosity about Ryecart the evening before. She'd put their evident quarrel down to the American's belief that she'd been less than honest about Alex's whereabouts and fortunately Alex hadn't witnessed the kiss that had followed.

'I wouldn't take what he says at face value, Alex,' she warned at length.

But Alex refused to let her dampen his spirits. 'He seems straight enough to me… Anyway, I feel like celebrating. Come to lunch. Antoine's. My treat.'

Tory wondered how Alex could suddenly afford to pay for such extravagant dining.

'Thanks,' Tory replied, 'but I have an appointment in less than an hour. We could go to the canteen, if you like.'

Alex pulled a face, as Tory had guessed he would, and said, 'I'll pass, if you don't mind.'

'Not at all.' Tory trailed back to her office, still puzzling over Ryecart's game plan.

'Well?' Simon enquired as she returned.

'Everything's fine,' Tory said succinctly and went to pick up her bag from under her chair. 'I'm going to the canteen for lunch.'

'I'll come with you.' Simon wanted to hear more.

They walked along the corridor together and she relayed some of the phrases Alex had used about the American while Simon raised a sceptical brow.

'Miss Lloyd!' Someone called from behind them.

Tory kept walking for a step or two, pretending she hadn't heard. She had no need to glance round to identify the voice.

'Wait up.' Simon grabbed her arm. 'It's the man himself.'

'You don't say!' Her teeth were already clenched as she turned to find Lucas Ryecart bearing down on them.

It was a purely physical reaction. She knew she didn't like him. She'd told herself that a hundred times.

But it had changed nothing. Her heart still stopped for a beat or two, then raced like a runaway train. She heard its engine roar and tried to focus on her dislike, not his looks. Did all women feel the same? Was that why he'd been called God's gift?

Their absorption in each other was mutual and obvious, so much so that Simon said, 'Shall I make myself scarce?'

'Yes!'

'No!'

The answers were simultaneous, but Simon knew which side his bread was buttered. He smiled at Eastwich's new boss before strolling off down the corridor.

Deserted, Tory went on the offensive. 'What do you want?'

'We need to talk,' he responded in a low undertone, 'but not here. It's too public. Come to lunch.'

Tory shook her head. 'I can't.'

'Or won't?' he challenged in reply.

Tory had forgotten he had no time for social niceties. She abandoned them, too.

'All right, I won't,' she confirmed.

He nodded, then looked at her long and hard. 'If it's any comfort, you scare the hell out of me, too.'

Was he serious? Tory wasn't sure, but the conversation was already in dangerous territory.

She deliberately misunderstood him, answering, 'I don't know why you'd be scared of me, Mr Ryecart. It's not as if *I* could sack *you*.'

He made an exasperated sound. 'That's not what I meant and you know it! Can't you forget our respective positions for a single moment?'

'Shh!' she urged before they attracted an audience. 'But, no, since you ask, I can't forget. Neither would you, I imagine, if you were in my position.'

'Underneath me?' he suggested.

'Yes!' She'd walked right into it.

He smiled, giving it a whole new meaning, while Tory blushed furiously.

'If only you were.' His eyes made a leisurely trip down her body and back again.

'You—' Tory could think of several names to call him but none seemed rude enough.

'It's all right, I can guess.' He was more amused than anything.

Tory seethed with frustration and anger. If she didn't walk away, she would surely hit him.

She did walk away, but he followed her to the lift.

It took an age to arrive. She stood there, ignoring him. Which was hard, when she could feel him staring at her.

The lift arrived and a couple of women from Drama stepped out. They nodded at Tory, then glanced at her companion. Their gaze was one of admiration rather than recognition.

Lucas Ryecart was oblivious, stepping into the lift with her.

Tory wanted to step out again, but it seemed an act of cowardice. What could he do in the five seconds it took for the lift to reach the ground floor?

He could stop it, that was what. He could run a quick eye over the array of buttons and hit the emergency one.

Tory didn't quite realise what he'd done until the lift lurched to a halt.

'You can't do that!' She was genuinely outraged at his action.

'Why not?'

'I…you… Because…well, you just can't!'

He grinned, mocking her regard for authority, and she flashed him a look of dislike.

'Don't worry,' he assured her, 'I'll give myself a severe reprimand later… For now, let's talk.'

'I don't want to talk.' Tory eyed the control panel, wondering if she should make a lunge at it.

She rejected the move as overly dramatic until he drawled, 'Fair enough. Let's not talk,' and, with one step, closed the distance between them.

Sensual blue eyes warned her of his intention.

Tory's heart leapt. In alarm, she decided, and raised her arms to fend him off.

'If you touch me—'

'You'll scream?'

So she wasn't original. She was still serious.

'Yes!'

'Well, of course, what else would you do, the lift being stuck and all?'

Tory glowered at him. He had an answer for everything.

He stretched out a hand and lightly brushed a strand of hair from her cheek. Then, before she could protest, he stepped back to his corner of the lift.

'Don't panic. I won't touch you till you ask me to.'

He appeared confident she would.

'We'll both be dead before then,' she shot back.

The insult went wide. His smile remained.

He leaned back against the wall as if he had all the time in the world. 'You never told Simpson about our…our *conversation* yesterday, did you?'

'There was nothing to tell,' she retorted, the ultimate put-down.

He arched a brow in disbelief. 'It's fairly usual for you, I suppose, being propositioned by other men?'

'Happens all the time,' she claimed, deadpan.

He laughed, briefly amused, then regarded her intently before murmuring, 'I can believe it.'

He had a way of looking at a woman that made Tory finally understand the expression 'bedroom eyes'. She tried hard to conjure up some indignation.

He helped her along by adding, 'So why settle for a wimp like Simpson?'

'When I could have someone like you?' she replied with obvious scorn.

'I wasn't thinking specifics. Pretty much any young, free and single guy would be an improvement on Simpson,' he said in considered tones. 'But, yes, since you're asking, I reckon there's every chance you could have me.'

The sheer nerve of him took Tory's breath away. 'You…I…wasn't—'

'After you show Simpson the door, of course,' he stated as a condition.

Tory still didn't believe she was having this conversation. 'And if I don't?'

His eyes narrowed, even as he admitted, 'I haven't thought that far.'

But when he did? Would their jobs be in jeopardy?

Tory found it impossible to gauge. Lucas Ryecart was still a stranger to her.

She glanced across at him. Today he was dressed formally. In dark double-breasted suit, relieved by a white shirt and silk tie, he would have looked every inch the businessman if it hadn't been for his casual stance, hands in pockets, length resting against a wall of the lift.

He caught and held her eye and homed in on her thoughts as he continued, 'If I wanted to fire Alex Simpson, I could have done so this morning with no great effort. I believe he has already had the requisite number of warnings.'

Tory hadn't known that. She'd imagined the executive board of Eastwich ignorant of Alex's recent conduct.

'Had you and he *not* been cohabiting—' his mouth twisted on the word '—chances are I would have. Instead I felt obliged to keep carrying him, at least for the time being.'

Tory frowned, failing to follow his logic. 'I don't understand.'

'It's like this. I *wanted* to fire him and normally would have.' A shrug said it would have given him little grief. 'However, I wasn't a hundred per cent certain why. Most likely it was because he's a sorry excuse for a production manager, but it just could be because he happens to be living with the woman I want,' he pondered aloud.

'I—I...y-you...' His bluntness reduced Tory to incoherence.

'So I decided I'd leave it for now,' he concluded, 'and if he continues to mess up, I won't have the dilemma.'

'You'll fire him, anyway?' Tory finally found her voice.

'Correct,' he confirmed without apology.

'And what if he gets back on form?' she challenged.

'Then he has nothing to worry about it.' He met her eye and his gaze did not waver.

He was either a man of honour or a very convincing liar. The jury was still out on which, but Tory could see the situation was going to be impossible.

'Maybe I should be the one to leave.'

'Eastwich?'

'Yes.'

His face darkened momentarily. 'You'd do that for Simpson?'

The suggestion had Tory sighing loudly. 'You mean hand in my notice while quoting "It is a far, far better thing that I do," etc. etc.?'

His lips quirked slightly, recognising the irony in her voice. 'Something like that.'

'Well, I'm sorry to disappoint you, but self-sacrifice is not part of my nature,' she told him. 'Try self-preservation.'

'From me?' He arched a brow.

'Who else?' she flipped back.

Arms folded, he thought about it some, before querying, 'Do I bother you that much?'

'Yes. No… What do you expect?' she retorted in quick succession and masked any confusion with a glare.

It had little effect. 'I must say, you bother me, too, Miss Lloyd. Here I am, supposed to be rescuing Eastwich from economic collapse, and I can't get my mind off one of its production assistants… What's a man meant to do?' he appealed with a smile that was slow and lazy and probably intended to devastate.

But Tory was wise to him now. 'This is all a joke to you, isn't it?'

'A joke?' he reflected. 'I wouldn't say so. Well, no more than life is generally.'

So that was his philosophy: life was a joke. It was hardly reassuring. For her or Eastwich.

'It comes with age,' he added at her silence.

'What does?'

'The realisation that nothing should be taken too seriously, least of all life.'

'Thank you,' Tory replied dryly, 'but I'd prefer to make up my own mind—when I grow up, of course.'

'Was I being patronising?'

'Just a shade.'

'Sorry.'

He pulled an apologetic face and Tory found herself smiling in response.

'Rare but definitely beautiful,' he murmured at this momentary lapse.

Tory tried hard not to feel flattered and counteracted with a scowl.

'Too late.' He read her mind all too well.

'Could you restart the lift...please?' she said in a tight voice. 'I'd like to go to lunch.'

'Sure,' he agreed to her surprise and reset the emergency stop.

The lift geared into action rather suddenly and Tory lurched forward at the same time. She was in no danger of falling but Lucas Ryecart caught her all the same.

He held her while she regained her balance. Then he went on holding her, even as the lift descended smoothly.

She wore a sleeveless shift dress. His hands were warm on her skin. She still shivered at the lightness of his touch.

She could have protested. She tried. She raised her head but the words didn't come. It was the way he was looking at her—or looking at his own hands, smoothing over her soft skin, imagining.

When he finally lifted his eyes to hers, he didn't hide his feelings. He desired her. Now.

He drew her to him, and she went, as if she had no volition. Only she did: she wanted him to kiss her, willed him to. Needed it. Turned into his arms. Gazed up at him, eyes wary, but expectant.

The lift came to a halt even as he cupped her face in his hands and lowered his mouth to hers. By the time the door slid open, he was kissing her thoroughly and she was helplessly responding.

'Well!' The exclamation came from one of the two men standing on the other side.

Too late Tory sprang apart from Lucas to face Colin Mathieson and a tall, grey-haired man of indeterminate age.

Colin's surprise became shock when Lucas turned to face them also.

The stranger, however, appeared greatly amused.

'We've been looking for you, Lucas, boy,' he drawled, 'but obviously not in the right places.'

He chuckled and his eyes slid to Tory, openly admiring Lucas's taste.

'Chuck,' Lucas responded, quite unfazed, 'this is—'

But Tory, horrified and humiliated, wasn't going to hang around while he introduced her to his American buddy.

'Don't bother!' she snapped at him, and took off.

She heard Colin call after her, half reprimand, half concern. She heard the stranger laugh loudly, as if enjoying the situation. She heard nothing from Lucas Ryecart but she could well imagine that slow, slanting smile of satisfaction.

Yet again, he had proved his point. Good sense might tell her he was like a disease—seriously bad for her health—but she seemed to have little immunity. The only sane thing was to keep out of infection range.

She went to the staff canteen, certain he wouldn't follow her there.

'Where have you been?' Simon demanded when she sat down with a spartan meal of salad and orange juice. 'I was about to give you up for dead—or alternatively *bed*. I wonder if he looks at all women that way.'

'Shut up, Simon,' she muttered repressively.

But Simon was unstoppable. 'Talk about smouldering. I used to think that was just an expression. Like in women's novels: "He gave her a dark, smouldering look." But not since I saw Ryecart—'

'Simon!' Tory glanced round and was relieved to see no one within listening distance. 'You might think this sort of thing

is funny but I doubt Lucas Ryecart would. You have heard of libel, I assume.'

'Slander,' Simon corrected. 'I haven't written it down… Well, not yet.'

'What do you mean, not yet?' Tory told herself he was joking.

Simon grinned. 'I could scribble it on the washroom wall, I suppose. L loves T. Or is it T loves L?' he said with a speculative air.

'It's neither,' she replied, teeth gritted.

Simon arched a surprised brow at her tone, but he took the hint and changed the subject.

Tory didn't linger over the meal but returned on her own to the office and threw herself into work so she wouldn't have to think too hard about anything else.

Alex didn't return from lunch—it seemed he was bent on pushing his luck—but she told herself firmly it wasn't her problem. She worked late as usual and was emerging from the front door just as Colin Mathieson was stowing his briefcase in the back of his car.

As he was a senior executive his bay was right at the entrance and, short of going back inside, she couldn't avoid him.

'Tory.' He greeted her with a friendly enough smile. 'I'm glad I've run into you. I wanted a word.'

Tory waited. She didn't prompt him. She just hoped the word wasn't about what she suspected.

She hoped in vain and stood there, wanting the ground to swallow her up, as Colin Mathieson gave her an avuncular talk which, while skirting round the point, could basically be summed up as: You are lowly, young production assistant. He is rich, charming man of the world. Are you sure you know what you're doing?

It was well meant, which was why Tory managed to mutter 'yes' and 'no' in the right places and somehow contain her feelings until she could scream aloud in the privacy of her own car.

Because it was galling. To be thought such a fool. Colin actually believed she was so naive that she took Lucas Ryecart seriously.

The day she did that, she really was in trouble.

CHAPTER FIVE

AFTER the lift incident, Tory was determined to avoid Lucas Ryecart. It proved easy. The American spent the next day closeted in meetings with various departments before disappearing to the States for the rest of the week.

His absence put things into perspective for Tory. While she'd been fretting over their next meeting, he'd been on a plane somewhere, with his mind on deals and dollars. Perhaps he did want her, but in the same way he'd want any grown-up toy, like a fast car or a yacht. He'd spare a little time for it, enjoy it a while, then move onto something—or someone—new.

She'd almost managed to get him out of her head when the postcard arrived with a bundle of other mail on the Saturday morning.

There was no name on it, just a picture of the Statue of Liberty on one side and the words, 'Has he gone?' on the other.

'Are you all right?' Alex noticed her strained expression across the breakfast table.

'Yes, fine.' She quickly shoved it in among her other letters. 'It...it's just a card from my mother.'

'I thought she'd moved to Australia,' Alex commented.

Realising he'd seen the picture side, she was committed to another lie. 'She's on holiday in New York.'

Alex nodded and quickly lost interest.

Tory reflected on the words in the postcard. *Has he gone?* How she wished!

She slid a glance at Alex, currently unsetting all the stations on her radio. He was driving her crazy.

Fanatically *un*tidy, he left clothes on chairs, take-away cartons on tables and used towels on floors.

Tory had tried a few subtle hints, then more direct comments and he was suitably contrite—but not enough to reform.

Tory wondered if it were her. Maybe she wasn't suited to cohabitation, even on platonic grounds.

At any rate, she longed for Alex to depart. Or had until the postcard had arrived. Now she was torn. She didn't want to seem to be giving into Lucas Ryecart's demands.

In the end she let fate decide it and when Alex returned later that day from an unsuccessful flat-finding mission she surprised him with her concession to stay a little longer.

'You're a star. I'll try to look for a place mid-week,' Alex promised, 'although it might be difficult, with Ryecart returning on Monday.'

Tory pulled a face. 'He's definitely back?'

'Didn't I say?' Alex ran on. 'He sent a fax yesterday, setting up a meeting with our department. Monday morning at the Abbey Lodge.'

'No, you didn't say.' Tory struggled to hide her irritation.

'Don't worry about it,' he dismissed. 'He just wants to discuss the department's future direction.'

'Well, I'll keep a low profile,' she rejoined, 'if it's all the same to you.'

Alex didn't argue. Having been bullied into sobriety by Tory, he had regained some of his old ambition. He would be too busy promoting his own career to spare much thought for Tory's.

In fact, come Monday morning, it was a two-man contest between Simon and Alex.

Simon gained an early lead by simply turning up on time. Caught by roadworks, Alex and Tory were already fifteen minutes late when they reached the Abbey Lodge Hotel and entered the lion's den.

Tory refused to look at the lion even when he drawled a polite, 'Good morning,' in her direction.

It was a small conference room, mostly taken up with an oval table and eight leather chairs. She put Simon between her and the great man, and left Alex to sit opposite and run through a quick explanation for their tardiness.

It did have some semblance to the truth. Alex's car *was* in the garage. She *had* given him a lift. And they hadn't anticipated the council digging up a major section of the ring road.

But, of course, Lucas Ryecart knew the reality: that Alex and she had arrived together because they were living together.

He even gave Alex the chance to confess. 'Do you and Tory live in the same neighbourhood?'

'I...no, not really.' Alex slid a conspiratorial glance in Tory's direction.

He was doing as he'd promised by keeping quiet about their current arrangement.

Tory's heart sank as Lucas drawled, 'That was *generous* of you, Tory, to go out of your way,' and forced her to look at him.

It had been a week since they'd met and in the interim she'd put herself through aversion therapy. She *could* not like this man, brash egotist that he was. She *would* not like this man, even if her job depended on it. She *had* to look at him with dispassion and see the ruthlessness that underlay the handsome features.

This time she was ready—just not ready enough. She saw his age, written in his sun-lined face and the grey round his temples. She saw the imperfection, a scar tracing white down one cheek. She saw the mouth set in an irritatingly mocking curve. But then she met his eyes and forgot the rest.

A deep blue, bluer than a tropical sky, they drew her to him, those eyes, and made her realise that attraction defied any logic. The sight of him still left her senses in turmoil.

But this time she fought it, this involuntary attraction. She got angry with herself for such weakness. She got even angrier with him for causing it.

'Actually, it wasn't out of my way at all.' Her voice held a defiant note.

His mouth straightened to a hard line. He understood immediately. She was answering his postcard. No, Alex hasn't gone.

He went on staring at her until she was forced to look away, then he switched back to business.

He talked frankly of the direction he envisaged the department taking. He wished to concentrate on documentaries with a longer shelf-life. Previous programmes had suffered from delays and hence loss of topicality or duplication from other companies.

Alex clearly felt he was being told what he already knew. 'We are conscious of duplication,' he put in. 'We abandoned a project not so long ago because Tyne Tees was further along on it.'

'How much did that cost Eastwich?' Lucas Ryecart enquired.

'I can't remember,' Alex admitted.

'I can.' Lucas Ryecart stated a figure.

'Sounds right,' Alex said rather too casually. 'Budgets aren't normally my concern.'

Tory, assiduously contemplating the wood grain in front of her, flinched inwardly. Did Alex have to jump into the hole the American was digging for him?

There was a moment's silence before Ryecart returned briefly, 'So I gathered.'

Alex caught on then, and backtracked to make the right sounds, 'Not that I don't try to work within a budget framework. In fact, some programmes have been done on a shoestring.'

'Really.' Lucas Ryecart's disbelief was dry but obvious. 'Okay, surprise me!'

'Sorry?' Alex blinked.

'Which programme was done on a shoestring?'

'I...well...' Alex was left to bluster. 'That's an expression. Obviously I didn't mean it literally, but I believe we're no more profligate than any other department. Look at drama.' He tried to shift focus. 'It's common knowledge that their last period piece cost half a million.'

'And made double that by the time Eastwich had sold it abroad.' Lucas Ryecart pointed out what Alex would have known if he'd thought about it. 'Moving on, Alex has drafted some proposals for future programmes with which I assume you're all familiar.'

Tory assumed the same but, from his tight-lipped expression, Simon was still in the dark.

'I left a copy on top of your desk,' Alex claimed at his blank expression.

'Really.' Simon was clearly unimpressed with Alex's efforts, and Tory didn't blame him.

'Have mine.' She pushed the document towards him. 'I have a spare.'

'Simon, you can get up to speed while we discuss it,' Lucas Ryecart pressed on. 'Okay, folks, at the risk of riding roughshod over anyone's pet project, I propose we can items one and four from the outset.'

'Can?' Alex echoed in supercilious tones although Tory was sure he understood.

'Rule out, bin, expunge.' Lucas Ryecart gave him a selection of alternatives that somehow made Alex look the fool.

Certainly Simon allowed himself a smirk.

Alex came back with, 'Why…if I may ask?'

His tone implied the American was being dictatorial.

'You can ask, yes.' Lucas Ryecart clearly considered Alex pompous rather than challenging. 'Proposal one is too close to a programme about to be broadcast by BBC2 and the costs on four will be sky high.'

Tory watched Alex's face as he woke up to the fact that the American was going to be no pushover like Colin Mathieson.

'Costs are the only criterion?' he said in the tone of the artist thwarted by commercialism.

Lucas Ryecart was unmoved. 'With Eastwich's current losses, yes. But if you want to spend your own money on it, Alex, feel free.'

He said it with a smile but the message was plain enough. Put up or shut up.

Alex looked thunderous while Simon gloated.

'Proposal two…' Lucas Ryecart barely paused '…is also likely to attract mega-buck litigation unless we can substantiate every claim we make against the drug companies.'

'You know that's damn near impossible,' Alex countered. 'We'd have to rely on inside sources, any of whom could be less than truthful.'

'Exactly,' Lucas Ryecart agreed, 'so I'd sooner pass... However, should you wish to take the story elsewhere, I won't stand in your way.'

Alex went from indignant to disconcerted as the American threw him off balance again. He had yet to fully appreciate that behind the pleasant drawling voice there was a man of steel.

'So that leaves us two ideas still on the table,' he resumed. 'Racial discrimination in the Armed Forces and drug-taking in the playground. Either might be worth exploring... In addition, Simon and I both have an idea we'd like to pitch.'

Alex was instantly suspicious. 'The same one?'

'Actually, no.' It was Simon who answered. 'We don't all go in for the conspiratorial approach.'

His disparaging glance included Tory. He'd obviously lined her up on Alex's side. She might have protested, had Lucas Ryecart not been there and likely to scorn any claim of impartiality.

'Tory—' the American turned those brilliant blue eyes on her '—perhaps you have some idea you'd like to put forward as well.'

She already had: at least two of Alex's proposals had originated with her, but, in giving them to Alex, she had effectively lost copyright.

She shook her head, and wondered if he considered her gormless. She had certainly contributed little to the meeting so far.

'As you know, Tory and I worked quite closely on this document.' Alex imagined he was rescuing her from obscurity.

Instead he confirmed what Simon suspected: that they'd worked as a team, excluding him.

It also made Ryecart drawl, 'Very closely, I understand.'

'I...well...yes...'Alex couldn't quite gauge the other man's attitude.

Tory could, only too well. For *very closely* read *intimately*.

She was finally stirred into retaliation. 'Have you a problem with that, Mr Ryecart?'

He fronted her in return. 'Not at all. I look forward to working in close liaison with you myself, Miss Lloyd.'

And let that be a lesson to me, Tory thought, clenching her teeth at the barely hidden double meaning.

She looked to the other two men, but if she expected any support she was in for a disappointment. Alex had put the American's comment down to sexist humour and was chuckling at it, and Simon was enjoying her discomfort.

It was every man for himself.

'Returning to the matter in hand,' Lucas Ryecart continued, 'I suggest each of us pitch our idea for a limited period, say forty minutes.'

He took his watch off and laid it on the table. It was a plain leather-strapped, gold-rimmed affair, nothing ostentatious. If Lucas Ryecart was wealthy, he didn't advertise the fact.

He glanced round the table, waiting for someone to volunteer. No one did. In adversity, they were suddenly a team.

'We're not used to working with time restraints,' Alex objected for all of them.

'I appreciate that, but I find deadlines cut down on bull,' Ryecart said bluntly, 'and forty minutes is the air-time for most documentaries produced at Eastwich... I'll go first, unless anyone objects.'

No one did. Tory felt a little ashamed for them all. They were such rabbits.

'Okay,' he proceeded. 'My idea more or less dropped in my lap. One of our backers, Chuck Wiseman, is a major publisher in the US and is looking to spread his empire to the UK. Specifically, he's bought out two quality women's magazines—*Toi* and *Vitalis*. Anyone read them?'

Tory was the only one to say, 'Yes.'

'Your opinion?' he asked seriously.

She answered in the same vein. '*Toi* is a pale imitation of *Marie Claire*. *Vitalis* is mainly hair, nails and make-up, with the occasional social conscience article.'

'Cynical but accurate.' He nodded in agreement. 'Chuck intends amalgamating the two, keeping the best of both and hoping to create something more original. But it is something of a marriage of convenience, with neither in any hurry to get to the altar.'

'It'll never work,' Alex commented.

'Possibly not,' Ryecart echoed, 'but Chuck's determined and he's a man to be reckoned with.'

'So where do we come in?' Tory was intrigued despite herself. 'Fly-on-the-wall stuff, recording the honeymoon.'

'Sort of,' Ryecart confirmed. 'Chuck's sending both staff on a residential weekend in the hope that familiarity will breed contentment.'

'He's obviously not very hot on old sayings,' Alex commented dryly.

'Still, it might make for a good story.' Simon smiled as he considered the in-fighting that would ensue. 'Where's he sending them? If it's somewhere hot and sunny, you can put me down for that one.'

Ryecart smiled briefly. ''Fraid not, Simon, but I'll note your enthusiasm. It's an outdoor-activity course in the Derbyshire Dales.'

'He has to be kidding!' Tory exclaimed before she could stop herself.

'Yeah, that's what I thought,' Ryecart echoed, 'but Chuck reckons he'll end up with a solid team as a result.'

'If they don't kill each other first,' murmured Simon.

'Or kill themselves, falling off a mountain,' Tory added. 'These courses are fairly rigorous, physically and psychologically.'

'Which is where we come in,' Ryecart rejoined.

'An exposé?' Tory enquired.

He nodded. 'Assuming there's anything to expose. Who knows? The course might be as character and team building as it claims.'

'I would think it would be more divisive,' Tory judged, but saw what he saw, too—the makings of a good human-interest story. 'I mean, if the staff know it's a test, there's going to be tension from the outset.'

He nodded. 'Two groups of individuals spending a weekend in each other's company under difficult circumstances. As fly-on-the-wall TV, it could prove dynamite.'

Alex and Simon nodded too, warming to the idea, even though it wasn't theirs.

'What are we talking here?' Alex asked. 'One of us plus camera crew interviewing these women while they abseil down mountains?'

'No crew,' Ryecart dismissed. 'The centre has continuous camera surveillance and uses camcorders for outdoor events. This footage will be handed over to Chuck's organisation and then to us.'

'Is that legal?' Simon said doubtfully.

'The centre has already signed a waiver, handing over copyright to Chuck,' Ryecart explained. 'The plan is for an Eastwich reporter to go undercover as a new member of staff for *Toi*. They'll have to join the magazine pretty much straight away as the course is this weekend. Whoever goes—' he glanced between the three of them '—I'll drive him or her down to London today for the interview.'

Both Simon and Alex looked at Tory.

'Why me?' She dreaded the idea of a car journey spent with Lucas Ryecart.

'At the risk of stating the obvious,' Simon drawled, 'they're both *women's* magazines. You're a woman. Alex and I aren't.'

'Quite.' Alex supported Simon for once.

Heart sinking, Tory looked towards the American.

He just said, 'It can be decided later,' and switched subjects with, 'Right, who wants to pitch their idea now?'

'I will.' Alex got in before Simon and began to flesh out his idea revolving drugs in the playground.

Alex had a somewhat novel idea, centring his investigation around public schools and the suggestion that a new breed of parents, themselves party-going and pill-popping in their youth, were tacitly condoning their children's drug-taking.

He'd obviously done some research on the subject and claimed to have already made contact with a headmaster willing to co-operate.

Simon cast doubt on the likelihood of that, pointing out that no public school head was likely to help him if it put fees at jeopardy.

'And you would know this, having gone to somewhere like Eton yourself?' Alex threw back.

'I did go to a public school, yes,' Simon said in his usual superior manner.

'A minor, I bet,' Alex guessed, accurately.

'Whereas you, no doubt, were a state grammar school boy,' Simon sneered back.

Tory suspected Simon already knew that, too. Alex was very proud of the fact.

'So?' Alex eyed Simon in an openly hostile manner.

'It shows, that's all,' Simon smirked in reply.

Exasperated, Tory intervened with a dry, 'Well, if anyone's interested, I went to a London comprehensive. Unofficial motto: Do it to them before they do it to you… But I was hoping I'd left my schooldays behind.'

Both Alex and Simon looked taken aback, as if a pet lapdog had suddenly produced fangs.

But it drew a slanting smile from Lucas Ryecart as he realised she was ridiculing their one-upmanship.

She didn't smile back. Simon and Alex might be behaving like prats but the American was still the common enemy.

'Quite,' Alex agreed at length and resumed speaking on his pet project while Simon continued to snipe the occasional remark and Lucas Ryecart refereed.

Tory wondered what the American made of the antipathy between the two men. Perhaps he was harbouring some idea of sending *their* fragmented team on an outdoor-activity course. The idea of Alex and Simon orienteering their way round some desolate Scottish moor, with only one compass between them, made her smile for the first time that day.

'You don't share that view?' a voice broke into her thoughts.

Tory looked up to find Lucas Ryecart's eyes on her again. Having only the vaguest idea of what had gone before, she hedged, 'I wouldn't say that exactly.'

'No, but your smile was a shade sceptical.' It seemed he'd been watching her.

'Possibly,' she admitted, rather than confess she'd been day-dreaming.

'So you don't agree with Alex that most adults under forty will have tried some kind of recreational drug?' he pursued.

Now she knew what they'd been discussing, Tory wasn't any more inclined to express an opinion.

'Tory won't have,' Simon chimed in. 'Far too strait-laced, aren't you, Tory? Doesn't smoke. Doesn't drink. Doesn't pretty much anything.'

'Shut up, Simon,' she responded without much hope he would.

'See... She doesn't even swear.' He grinned like a mischievous schoolboy. 'I somehow doubt her parents were pot-smoking flower children.'

'Well, that's where you're wrong!' Tory snapped without considering the wisdom of it.

She regretted her outburst almost immediately as all eyes in the room became trained on her.

'Would you care to expand on that?' invited Simon.

'No,' she ground back, 'I wouldn't.'

'But if it gives some insight into the subject—' he baited, amused rather than malignant.

'Simon.' A low warning, it came from Lucas Ryecart. 'Leave it.'

Tory should have been grateful. He'd seen her vulnerability. But didn't that make her even more vulnerable—to him rather than Simon?

'Sure.' Simon was wise enough not to want to make an enemy of the American. 'I didn't mean to tread on anyone's toes.'

'That makes a change,' Alex muttered in not so low a voice, then gave Tory a supportive smile.

Ryecart took control once more, 'Simon, would you like to pitch your idea now?'

'My pleasure.' Simon was obviously confident.

Tory listened to him outlining his idea for a docu-soap on

a day in the life of a Member of Parliament. It sounded pretty tame stuff until Simon named the backbencher he proposed using. A controversial figure, with intolerant views, he was likely to produce some interesting television.

'He's almost bound to be de-selected next time around,' Simon concluded, 'so he has nothing to lose.'

'Has he agreed to it?' Ryecart asked.

'Pretty much,' Simon confirmed.

'Know him personally?' Alex suggested.

'As a matter of fact, yes,' Simon responded. 'I was at school with his younger brother.'

Alex contented himself with a snort in comment.

Simon expanded on the approach he'd take and Lucas Ryecart gave him approval to progress it further. He had done the same for Alex.

He wrapped up the meeting by saying, 'All right, we'll meet again in three weeks and see where matters stand. Thank you for coming.'

They were dismissed. At least Tory thought they were, and was breathing a sigh of relief as she picked up her briefcase and led the way from the room. They were out in the hotel lobby when the American said, 'Tory, I'd like to talk to you.'

He didn't stipulate why but he didn't need to. He was her boss.

Alex looked ready to ask but Lucas Ryecart ran on, 'Simon, perhaps you could give Alex a ride back to Eastwich as his car is in the shop?'

'Sure, no problem.' Simon knew better than to object.

Alex, too, accepted the arrangement and Tory was abandoned altogether. That was how it felt, at any rate, as they walked out of the main entrance.

She guessed Lucas either wanted to talk to her about the magazine assignment or her current living arrangements, *vis-à-vis* Alex. Neither prospect was appealing.

'We can talk over lunch.' He began steering her by the elbow.

'In the dining room?' Tory wasn't dressed for five-star lunching.

'We could have a bar meal,' he continued, 'or call room service if you prefer.'

'Room service?' Tory echoed rather stupidly.

'I'm staying here,' he reminded her.

She stopped in her tracks. 'You expect me to go upstairs with you?'

'Expect, no,' he replied, 'hope, absolutely.'

His smile was more amused than lascivious. He just loved yanking her chain.

'So what's it to be?' he added.

'I'm not hungry!' she countered.

'Bar meal it is, then,' he decided for them and switched direction.

'I said—' She was about to repeat it.

He cut across her. 'I heard. You may not be hungry but I am, so you can sit and watch me eat while we talk business.'

Business. The word reminded her once more of their prospective positions. She wondered why she kept forgetting.

'Couldn't we just return to the conference room?' She wanted to keep things on a formal basis.

'And risk being alone together?' He raised a brow. 'Well, if that's okay with you—'

'No.' She hastily changed her mind. 'Let's go to the bar.'

'Sure, if that's what you want.' He inclined his head, making it seem he was accommodating her.

He really was the most aggravating man, Tory thought as they entered the hotel bar.

Large and well lit, it lacked intimacy but was almost empty. He installed her into a corner booth and was about to go and order at the counter when a waiter appeared. Lucas ordered a steak and salad, and insisted she have at least a sandwich.

From the bowing and scraping that went on, Tory assumed Lucas Ryecart was a familiar face.

'Big tipper, are we?' She couldn't resist remarking as the young waiter disappeared.

'Not especially,' he said with a grin, 'but Chuck is, so I guess I get the obsequious treatment through association.'

'Your magazine-buying friend,' she recalled out loud. 'He's staying here, too.'

'Was,' he confirmed. 'A bit too rural for him so he's moved back into the Ritz.'

In London, Tory assumed he meant. 'You make it sound as if he's living there.'

'He is for the moment,' he relayed, 'there and the New York Plaza. He commutes between the two.'

It seemed an odd way of life, even for a successful businessman. 'Has he a family?'

'He's between wives,' Lucas said, 'and has no children apart from a grown-up stepson… You're looking at him, by the way.'

Had she understood correctly?

'Chuck is your stepfather?'

'Is or was—I'm not sure which. He's remarried a couple of times since then.'

'Was, I think,' Tory volunteered, 'otherwise I'd have a multiplicity. Or two officials, anyway.'

Tory was normally reticent about her background but it seemed she'd met a fellow traveller, parent-wise.

'How old were you when your parents divorced?' His enquiry was matter-of-fact rather than sympathetic.

She answered in the same vein, 'They didn't. They were never married.'

He studied her face. 'You find that embarrassing?'

'No!' she claimed a little too sharply. 'Why should I?'

'No reason,' he mollified. 'It's hardly unusual these days… So were they the original pot-smoking hippies?'

Tory resented that question, too. 'Is that relevant to my work at Eastwich?'

'It might be,' he responded evenly, 'if you were to work with Alex on his drug story. It's best to go into these things with an open mind.'

Tory was tempted to argue with him, to say she was as objective as any good documentary-maker should be, but she wasn't sure if she were in this case. The truth was her mother had done drugs in the past. So-called soft drugs, but they had made Maura more feckless than ever. Tory had been old enough to know and disapprove, but too young to do much about it. It was one of the times she'd voluntarily decamped and returned to her grandparents in Purley.

'I would prefer to work on another story,' she declared at length.

'Fine by me,' he acknowledged with a brief smile. 'How convincing do you think you'd be as a features editor for a woman's magazine?'

For a split second Tory thought he was recommending she seek alternative employment, then she realised he was referring to the programme he'd proposed.

'You want me to do the *Toi/Vitalis* job?'

'Well—'

'Because I'm a woman?' That had been Simon's rationale.

'No, not especially,' Lucas Ryecart denied. 'I just can't envisage Alex trekking over moorland unless there's a pub at the end of the road and I don't see Simon in the role of observer, blending quietly into the background.'

Tory couldn't argue with either statement but was left feeling the job was hers through default.

'Right,' she murmured, her expression saying more.

'You're not happy?'

'Do I have to be?'

'Well, yes,' he countered. 'I don't want a good programme sabotaged by a lack of commitment on your part. So, if you're not up to this assignment, I'd sooner you say so now.'

And that's me told, Tory thought as she once more glimpsed a hard businessman behind the easygoing charmer.

The food arrived, giving her a moment or two to consider her response.

'I am up to it,' she claimed in a more positive manner. 'When do I start?'

She'd intended to sound keen but she wasn't prepared for his answer.

'This afternoon. You have an appointment with Personnel at the offices of *Toi*.'

'In London?'

He nodded.

'What if I don't get the job?'

He smiled at her naïvety.

'You already have. The interviews were last month. You've been a feature writer on a regional newspaper and this is your first magazine post.'

While he ran through her proposed cover, Tory suddenly realised what she was really taking on. She was going to have to lie about herself and her background and keep those lies consistent.

'Will anyone know I'm not a bona fide employee?'

'Only the personnel director of the group, and he's aware of your role.'

Tory wasn't altogether sure if she was.

'You don't expect me to provoke trouble?' she asked uncertainly.

'Absolutely not,' he said with emphasis. 'We want no charges of *manufacturing* material otherwise Eastwich's credibility will be blown. Sit back and observe like you did today.'

Tory couldn't help asking, 'Is that a criticism?'

'A comment,' he amended. 'After Alex and Simon's self-promotion, your reticence was almost refreshing although potentially limiting, careerwise... That's advice, by the way, not a threat.'

Tory nodded, accepting what he was saying. She had to push herself forward more.

She did so now, telling him, 'I do have ideas, you know.'

'I'm sure you do,' he responded. 'The trouble is, you let them be appropriated by other people.'

'We work as a team,' she stated a little testily.

'Yeah?' He raised a brow in disbelief. 'Perhaps someone should tell that to Alex and Simon. They seem to be playing on opposite sides. And your loyalty...well, we both know where that currently lies.'

With Alex, he meant, and Tory found herself colouring as if it were true. But it wasn't. Not in the sense he was implying.

'Alex is my boss. That's all!'

'So you keep saying.'

'Because it's true.'

'Okay, I'm your boss, too,' he reminded her unnecessarily. 'Can *I* come and share your flat?'

He gave her a mocking smile.

Tired of defending herself, Tory replied in the same vein. 'Sure. Why not? You could pull rank and pinch the sofa from Alex.'

Their eyes met and his smile faded. 'You're trying to say you're not sleeping with Alex?'

'No, I *am* saying that,' she corrected. 'Ask him, if you like.'

'Then why the pretence that Alex is living elsewhere?' he challenged.

'Because sometimes *other people* take two and two and make five,' she countered pointedly.

His eyes narrowed. '*Other people* have heard of Alex's reputation with women. I understand he's tested out more than one sofa since his wife left.'

Tory knew that was true enough so didn't comment. She said instead, 'Look, I like to keep home and work separate. And as far as work goes, Alex is my boss, plain and simple.'

It begged the question, 'And home?'

Tory felt she'd already answered it, and said flippantly, 'An extremely annoying flatmate who leaves the top off the toothpaste.'

He smiled briefly but disbelief lurked behind his eyes. Why could he not accept the truth?

Tory shook her head and, to her relief, he finally moved the conversation back to the magazine project, briefing her in what he saw as her role—passive but observant.

'When do I actually start work there?' Tory asked with some anticipation.

'Tomorrow,' he replied succinctly.

'Tomorrow?' She hadn't been expecting such short notice.

He nodded. 'That'll give you four days at the magazine before the team-bonding weekend.'

'But the magazine's in London,' she protested faintly.

'Which is where we're going now,' he added, 'or as soon as we've finished lunch and you've gone home to pack.'

Pack?

'You want me to stay over?' Tory was wide-eyed with suspicion.

'Is that a problem?'

He looked back at her, all innocence.

'In London?'

She wanted to make sure she'd understood.

'That's the general idea, yes.'

He nodded.

'With you?' She stared back stonily.

'If you like, although I hadn't planned on it,' he revealed. 'It's certainly an interesting proposition.'

'I w-wasn't…I didn't…I—I…' Tory stammered on until she saw the grin spreading on his face.

'No, I know.' He let her off the hook.

But he still laughed.

Damn the man.

CHAPTER SIX

LUCAS RYECART went on to explain. Tory had her appointment with the magazine at four p.m. and the plan was for her then to stay at a London hotel while she worked the rest of the week at *Toi*. At the same time he had a meeting with an investment banker and would be staying overnight at an entirely different hotel. Both venues were in central London so common sense dictated they travel down together. End of story.

Chastened, Tory accepted his offer of a lift and he trailed her back to her flat so she could pack a case. He waited outside for her.

They then travelled at speed towards the capital and Tory stared out at the motorway embankment rather than engage in further conversation. Having virtually accused him of luring her to the big city for immoral purposes, she felt silence was now her best option.

They'd reached the outskirts of London when her mobile rang.

Taking it out of her bag, she recognised the number calling as her office one. She pressed the receive button and wasn't too surprised to find it was Alex, wondering where she was. She didn't really get a chance to answer before he launched into a diatribe against the American, based on that morning's meeting.

Tory quickly switched the phone to her other ear, hoping Lucas hadn't caught the words 'arrogant ass' as Alex warmed to his theme. It seemed his enthusiasm for the American had dimmed somewhat.

She repeated Alex's name a couple of times in warning tones before actually cutting across him to say, 'Actually, Mr Ryecart's here beside me if you want to speak to him.'

It stopped Alex in his tracks momentarily, then he dropped volume as he proceeded to play twenty questions. Most she managed to field with 'yes's or 'no's and kept her voice carefully neutral.

To say Alex wasn't best pleased at her sudden secondment was an understatement and, in typical self-centred Alex fashion, he began to wonder how he was meant to get to work in the mornings, before he realised her car would still be in Norwich and was, therefore, available. She should have refused, of course. She didn't altogether trust Alex to drive it in a sane, sensible, sober fashion, but he pleaded and cajoled and called her Tory darling until she finally surrendered, more to shut him up than anything else.

When he finally hung up, she waited expectantly for comment from the American. She didn't have to wait long.

'So do you agree with him?' Lucas Ryecart drawled. 'Am I an arrogant ass?'

'You heard.'

'I'm not deaf.'

Tory supposed he would have to have been not to have caught Alex's initial remarks.

She tried bluffing. She was almost certain Alex hadn't used Lucas's name once.

'You're assuming that Alex was talking about you,' she muttered back.

He glanced from the road, fixing her with a sceptical look. 'Unless he happens to have a beef with another *swaggering Yank*. That's always possible, I suppose.'

Tory coloured as she realised he'd heard even more than she'd realised.

'Well, you know what they say about eavesdroppers,' she replied with some idea of putting him on the defensive.

'What?' He gave a short, mocking laugh. 'That they should immediately pull over onto the hard shoulder and climb out of the car while their passengers take abusive calls about them?'

This time Tory didn't argue back. He was right, of course. It was absurd to accuse him of eavesdropping when he could hardly have avoided listening to Alex's rant and rave.

She switched tacks. 'I'm sorry if you've taken offence but it's par for the course to bitch about your boss and you have put Alex's nose a little out of joint.'

She felt she'd laid on the right degree of humility but he made a dismissive sound.

'You think I care about Simpson's opinion? Believe me, I've been insulted by better men than him. The question was: do you agree with him?'

Tory was tempted to say, Yes, she did, but it seemed an act of extreme recklessness in their present situation.

She plumped for a circumspect, 'I have no thoughts on the subject.'

To which he muttered, 'Coward,' but in an amused rather than unpleasant tone. 'By the way, I wouldn't inform Simpson I'd overheard him.'

'Why not?' She would have imagined he'd want the opposite.

'A man in his position has only two ways to go,' he continued. 'He'll either feel the need to climb down and so embarrass us both with an apology I don't want and he won't mean. Or he'll be compelled to back up his remarks with a show of machismo for your benefit which, at the very least, will support my gut instinct that Simpson isn't worth the trouble he causes.'

'Right.' Tory saw the point he was making and the wisdom of it. 'I'll keep quiet.'

'Smart move,' he applauded her decision, then ran on, 'You know what really sticks in my craw about Simpson?'

Tory assumed it was a rhetoric question so didn't volunteer an answer.

Lucas continued, 'Forget the anti-American insults or his pompous posturing, the worst thing is the fact that he's just not good enough for a girl like you.'

Tory sighed loudly, wondering what she could say back to that. She was weary of denying involvement with Alex.

She said instead, 'And who do you imagine is?'

'Pretty much any personable, intelligent man without a drink problem would be an improvement,' he drawled back.

Not himself, then. Did that mean he'd lost interest? Tory supposed she should have been pleased but perhaps she was female enough to feel piqued as well.

She was considering her reply when he switched to saying, 'I'll leave that thought with you. Meanwhile, let's test your navigation skills. There's an A to Z in the glove compartment. We're looking for a Hermitage Road, NW something.'

'Okay.' Tory was glad of a change of subject and did as he suggested.

She didn't have to make much reference to the A to Z because she knew this part of London, and she guided him to the offices of the magazine without too much trouble.

'You're pretty good at giving directions,' he commented as they drew up outside the offices of *Toi*.

'For a woman, you mean?' Tory read the unspoken words in the compliment.

'I didn't say that,' he claimed even as a half-smile admitted it.

'I come from London,' Tory confessed, and, seeing she had five minutes to her appointment, began to collect her things together. 'Is the boot open?'

'Boot?' he repeated, then translated, 'The trunk?'

'Possibly,' she replied dryly. 'I need my case.'

'Won't it keep till I pick you up?'

'You're coming back for me?'

He nodded. 'Sure. I'll take you on to your hotel.'

'There's no need,' Tory dismissed quickly. 'I can get a taxi.'

'To where?'

'My hotel.'

'Which is?'

Tory frowned. What game were they playing now?

'You tell me,' she countered.

'I will when I find out,' he agreed. 'I've left Colin Mathieson's secretary to arrange it.'

'Right.' She should have known he wouldn't bother with any matter so trivial. 'I'll wait here for you, then.'

'I'll give you a call when I'm on my way,' he suggested. 'What's your cell-phone number?'

'I'll write it down.' She started to look in her bag for paper.

'That's okay,' he dismissed. 'Just tell me it.'

She did as he asked, and he repeated it as if it was already committed to memory.

Tory had her doubts. She certainly couldn't memorise an eleven-digit number after one hearing. But who knew what this man could do?

'I'd better go.' She glanced at her watch again. 'I don't want to be late for my interview.'

'Good luck, then.'

'I thought the job was mine.'

'It is,' he assured. 'That's the easy part.'

Tory supposed he was right. Convincing the rest of the magazine staff that she was a bona fide features editor might prove more difficult.

She finally climbed out of the car and walked up the steps of the magazine office, conscious that Lucas had yet to drive away. She turned round and he saluted her briefly. She didn't wave back but went ahead through the revolving doors that opened out into a reception.

'Yes.' An elegant blonde looked her up and down from behind a desk.

Tory said her name and she noticed the blonde's eyes flicker with recognition but no warmth before she was asked to take a seat in Reception.

She'd barely sat and picked up this month's edition of *Toi* when another identikit blonde arrived to escort her upstairs to the personnel director's office.

The interview was, as Lucas had said, just a formality, but she sensed the director wasn't altogether enthusiastic about her reason for being there. He used the expression 'the powers that be' when he referred to the magazine's new owner, Chuck Wiseman, and just stopped short of calling the team-bonding weekend psychological claptrap. He also warned her that, due to the unusual circumstances surrounding her hiring, she might possibly encounter some hostility from the editorial staff.

'I'm not sure I understand,' she queried this statement. 'Do you mean some know why I'm here?'

'Not that, no,' the personnel director assured her. 'If they did, we might have a walk-out on our hands. In fact, I have warned the *powers that be* of just such a consequence if you are discovered.'

'Then why should they be hostile?' she pursued.

'I'm only speculating on the possibility,' he backtracked a little. 'After all, there were at least two junior editors who felt they were in line for your post plus the fact it was never advertised. To all intents and purposes, you appear to have been given the job purely on personal recommendation from, let's say, above.'

'I see.' Tory did, too. She was joining a woman's magazine—a notoriously bitchy work environment, anyway—already viewed as someone's protégé. 'Who do they imagine has imposed me?'

'There are various theories,' he hedged, 'which I won't go into. I just feel you should be warned that you may get a somewhat frosty reaction.'

'Thanks.' Tory pulled a face.

She sensed he wasn't in the least bit sympathetic. Someone had obviously ridden roughshod over him, too.

'I'm afraid there isn't much I can do to improve the situation,' he added in the same cool tones.

'Don't worry, I'll survive.' Tory was sure she would.

The mishmash of types found on a woman's magazine was hardly as scary as some of the loud-mouthed, disaffected girls with whom she'd gone to school. At least no one here was likely to threaten to beat her up for her lunch money.

'I'm glad you're so confident.' He clearly didn't share the feeling. 'Anyway, I'll show you round the editorial department.'

She followed him to the lifts and they went back down to the editorial floor which was largely open plan. Tory trailed in his wake, conscious of curious eyes on her.

They stopped at a closed office at the end and Tory was introduced to Amanda Villiers, the editor-in-chief, who was currently conducting a meeting with several staff.

If she hadn't been pre-warned, Tory would not have understood Amanda Villiers's attitude. While on the surface her new boss was all polite handshake and smiles, there was an edge to every remark she made.

'I read your résumé with interest,' she drawled. '*The Cornpickers Times*, that was your first job, wasn't it? Features editor of the women's page.'

'*Cornwall Times*,' Tory corrected, while knowing the mistake had been deliberate.

Amanda was playing to an audience and several of her staff had dutifully tittered at her remark.

'Whatever.' Amanda Villiers smiled tightly. 'I didn't come up the provincial route. What does one write about for farmers' wives? How to get sheep dye from under their fingernails? Or how to prepare the perfect *Boeuf en Croute*—after one's killed it first, of course.'

Tory laughed, having some idea she wasn't meant to, and Amanda looked a little surprised.

'You've forgotten knit yourself a designer sweater, using your own flock,' suggested Tory on the same theme and took the wind out of Amanda's sails.

'Yes, well, all very fascinating, I'm sure,' Amanda said with a dismissive air, 'but a national women's magazine is, of course, a whole different world. Not that I need to tell you that. You did two years on that French magazine...what's it called again?'

Good question. Tory had spent an hour of the car journey that afternoon memorising her CV but it evidently hadn't been long enough.

'I don't imagine anyone's heard of it,' she murmured evasively.

'No, I certainly hadn't—' Amanda sniffed '—but, do tell, darling, how does one go from the *Cornish Times* to some sub-porno in Paris?'

Tory considered declaring herself not the type of person to work on a sub-porno, but she was already having enough trouble building any credibility without discussing ethics.

'It's a long story,' she told the room at large, 'with which

I may bore everyone when we're lying in our sleeping bags listening to the wind whistling round our tents.'

'Oh, God, the adventure weekend.' Amanda groaned aloud. 'You know about it and you still want to work here? You must be desperate.'

'I'm sure the job will make up for it.' Tory forced some enthusiasm into her voice.

Amanda looked sceptical and turned to a younger woman on her right. 'What do you think, Sam? You've been doing the job for the last six months. Is it worth a weekend in some godforsaken spot in the dales?'

Sam, a woman of about thirty, glanced between her boss, Amanda, and Tory, before making some inaudible comment, then staring rigidly at the notepad in front of her.

The set of her shoulders betrayed anger barely held in check. The only question was, where was this anger directed: at Tory who'd prevented her from being promoted, or the taunting Amanda whom Tory herself already felt like pushing off a cliff, given half a chance?

'Anyway, I'd better introduce you round.' Amanda finally remembered her manners and rattled off names and job titles too quickly for Tory to assimilate. 'When do you start?'

'As soon as possible,' Tory replied briefly.

'In that case, grab a pew,' Amanda suggested and left Tory with little choice.

She couldn't count on rescue from the personnel director because he was on his way out, problem disposed of.

Still, what happened next was familiar territory after that morning. While Amanda conducted a brainstorming session on cosmetic surgery, Tory was once again made to feel part of the furniture. Ideas were thrown up for discussion, opinions sought, criticisms levied but no one sought to include Tory in any of it.

This was not altogether surprising as the rest took their lead from Amanda and, having humiliated Tory sufficiently for the moment, the editor now ignored her totally.

Just as well, Tory realised, because she had little positive to say on the subject of breast implants or liposuction. She accepted some women felt the need for self-improvement but it seemed a growing obsession, the quest for the body beautiful. Magazines were full of such articles and the only question was whether they were documenting or feeding the phenomenon.

'What about you, Victoria?' Amanda finally addressed her. 'Have you had any fine tuning? Boob job, perhaps?' She glanced towards Tory's moderately sized chest, before deciding, 'No, maybe not... That nose, however. Very retroussé. What do you think, girls?'

Two of the women laughed as if she'd said something witty but a young woman at the end of the table seemed to suppress a sigh.

It made Tory wonder just what hidden tensions would be exposed after so many unrelieved hours in each other's company over the weekend.

For herself, she was already glad she worked for Eastwich and Alex for all his faults rather than the autocratic Amanda.

When Tory's cell-phone interrupted the meeting, Amanda gave her a look of pity before drawling, 'A golden rule, darling, mobiles off during meetings. I thought you'd have known that.'

Tory grimaced—as far as she was going to get to apology—and read the number calling. It was another mobile. She guessed it was Lucas.

'Who is it?' Amanda asked impatiently.

'A friend, he's giving me a lift,' Tory explained.

'Man friend?'

'Yes.'

'Lucky you.'

Amanda actually sounded more sincere than usual but Tory waited for the punchline. When it didn't come, she offered, 'I'll ask him to call back later.'

'No, don't bother. Time to wrap up, don't you think, *mes enfants*?'

The others nodded and Tory wondered if any ever disagreed with Amanda. Perhaps any who had were long gone.

'Well, answer him,' Amanda instructed, 'before he gives you up for dead.'

'All right… Hi,' she said into the mouthpiece.

Lucas replied simply, 'I'm outside.'

'Okay, be there in a moment,' she promised and rang off.

'Masterful type, is he?' Amanda concluded from this brief exchange.

'You could say that.' Tory nodded back.

'Love those, myself,' Amanda commented, 'in bed, at any rate. Not so keen when they're strutting about, demanding their socks washed and their breakfast cooked.'

Tory forced a laugh and wondered briefly if it was in the job description—to laugh at Amanda's jokes.

'Well, run along, mustn't keep him waiting, Vicki, darling,' the older woman urged in mocking tones that had Tory gritting her teeth.

But she did as she was told, anxious to get away from Amanda and her coven.

Fortunately she remembered her way back to the lift because no one volunteered to escort her, although she did find herself waiting with one of the other sub-editors. She recognised the girl who went in for sighing rather than sniggering.

'So what's your opinion?' the girl asked as they descended in the lift together. 'Think you'll like it here?'

Tory shrugged. 'Early days.'

'She doesn't get any better,' the girl drawled back, 'and she seems to have developed a pretty instant dislike of you, if you don't mind me saying so.'

Tory actually did mind, especially as it reinforced her own suspicions that working for Amanda was going to be a nightmare. Thank God, it was only temporary.

'I'll live with it,' Tory said at length.

Her lift companion regarded her with a look that seemed to waiver between pitying and admiring before the doors slid open and they parted in the reception area.

Tory didn't hang around. In fact, she almost ran down the steps to Lucas's awaiting car.

'How was it?' he said as she climbed into the passenger seat.

She released a breath of pent-up anger, before responding, 'Don't ask!'

'That bad?' he concluded.

'Worse.' Tory shuddered even before she spotted Amanda emerging from the building.

He followed her gaze. 'Who's that?'

'The editor from hell.' She grimaced. 'Can we go?'

'Yeah, sure,' he agreed easily and, putting the car in gear, drove towards the exit. 'I take it you were introduced.'

'More than introduced,' she relayed. 'After the briefest of inductions, the personnel director abandoned me to the pack.'

'The pack?'

'Editorial staff,' she qualified, 'but, believe me, the lions of the Serengeti would definitely seem friendlier.'

He laughed, then saw from her face she wasn't really joking. 'You don't think your cover was already blown.'

She shook her head. 'More a case of noses out of joint. Apparently one of them has been Acting Features Editor for months so she's hardly overjoyed by my appearance and, as for the editor-in-chief, Amanda Villiers, she resents having some nobody from nowhere imposed on them through suspect channels.'

'Well, never mind,' he tried to console, 'you only have to put up with it for a few days.'

'It's going to seem like weeks,' she complained. 'Forget their open hostility, have you ever tried pretending to be someone you're not?'

'Actually, yes,' he replied. 'I once passed myself off as the deaf and dumb son of a goat-herder in Northern Afghanistan.'

'Is that a joke?' The amused note in his voice certainly suggested it was.

'Not particularly, although it had its humorous moments,' he confided, before explaining, 'I was covering the Russian/Afghani conflict when I ended up in a situation where being an American journalist wasn't good for the health… Mind you, neither's going without food for a couple of days, but I survived,' he finished with a dry laugh.

Tory realised it was a true story. She had forgotten his former life as a foreign correspondent. This was the first he'd alluded to it.

'All right, you win.' She picked up the not-so-hidden message. 'I admit working undercover at *Toi* hardly rates in the danger stakes, but I'm still nervous about blowing it. I mean, I only know in the vaguest of terms what a features editor does. I'm going to be as hopeless as they think I am.'

Lucas pondered the last remark before pointing out, 'But if they're expecting you to mess up, it won't matter if you do, will it?'

'I suppose not,' Tory agreed. 'I just don't want to give Amanda Villiers the satisfaction.'

'Yeah, I've heard she's pretty monstrous.'

'You've heard? From whom?'

'Chuck. At least, I'm guessing it's the same woman. He calls her Mandy.'

'To her face?' Tory didn't think that would go down well.

'I guess so.' Lucas nodded. 'He took her out for lunch once and I don't see Chuck calling her Miss Villiers.'

'A business lunch, you mean?' pursued Tory.

He shrugged. 'Could have been… Is she pretty?'

Tory blinked at the question, before saying, 'Possibly. That was her on the steps.'

'Maybe not business, then,' he judged. 'Chuck certainly has an eye for a pretty lady.'

Tory glanced in his direction and saw the smile slanting his lips. It seemed he admired his stepfather for this.

'Isn't he…well, isn't he…?' She found no tactful way to express her doubts.

He did it for her, saying, 'Too old? Yeah, probably. But women don't seem to mind that. Chuck has a lot of charm. A lot of money, too,' he added dryly.

'And it doesn't bother you?' Tory couldn't resist asking.

He thought about it for a moment, then shrugged. 'Chuck's smart enough to look out for himself.'

It didn't really answer her question. 'But what about your mother? Does she still care?'

He shook his head. 'Mom's been dead twenty years.'

'I'm sorry,' she said automatically.

He gave her a quizzical look. 'What for?'

'Being nosy, I suppose.'

'Don't worry about it. I took it as a good sign.'

'Sign?' She was wary once more.

'That you're at least interested enough in me to ask such personal questions,' he stated, a smile in his voice.

Tory just stopped herself from saying, Don't flatter yourself, and responded instead, 'I was making conversation. That's all.'

'Yeah, okay.' He made a pacifying gesture with his hand. 'But for the record I am a forty-one-year-old widower. Both parents dead. No dependants. Sane. Healthy. Solvent. No unusual vices.'

His autobiography sounded so like a personal ad, Tory pointed out, 'You missed out with G.S.O.H. and W.L.T.M. young, attractive female for fun relationship.'

It drew a laugh before he drawled back, 'I find people who claim to have a good sense of humour often don't, and I've already met the young attractive female, thanks very much, although I'm not sure she goes in for "fun relationships".'

He meant her, of course. At least, Tory assumed he did. But she could hardly know for certain unless she asked him and that seemed a very unwise thing to do.

Her glance found him wearing the amused expression that was pretty much a fixture on his face.

'No comment?' he prompted.

Tory gritted her teeth, 'I doubt she's *your* type, then.'

'We'll have to see,' he replied, smile still in place. 'Meanwhile, let's get you settled in your hotel. It's called The Balmoral, Kingscote Avenue and is somewhere in W10.'

Tory picked up the A to Z once more and located their current position. Finding the hotel was something else. For all its grand name it was tucked away in a back street of a rather down-at-heel part of Earl's Court.

Not that she was about to raise any objections. She'd lived in worse areas with her mother and, although the hotel looked down-market, too, Eastwich's budget didn't usually stretch to much better.

It was Lucas Ryecart who said, 'Don't bother getting out,' when she made a move to do so. 'You're not staying in this dump.'

'It's probably nicer inside.'

'It would have to be.' He pulled a face. 'See that guy who's just walked into the joint? Russian Mafia, I'd say, if I didn't think they could afford better.'

Tory had seen the gentleman. Leather-coated with an upturned collar, he'd had a lean, mean unshaven face and suspicious air, but was probably an innocent foreign tourist.

'Well, if he is,' she suggested, 'think of the story I could write for *Toi*: Russian Mafia plan gold bullion robbery from royally named hotel. That would give the magazine much-needed edge, at any rate.'

'May I remind you, you work for Eastwich, not *Toi*?' he threw back. 'And that if you write bad things about the Mafia, they don't settle for complaining to the Press Complaints Commission. Let's go.'

'Where?' she asked as he pulled away.

'You can have my room tonight,' he replied and, anticipating any objection, added, '*Have*, I said, not *share*.'

'What will you do?' Tory was still not convinced by the assurance.

'Don't worry about me,' he dismissed. 'I'm having dinner with a friend who can probably put me up for the night.'

Friend? Male or female? The question crept into Tory's head, and, when she opted for the answer female, she felt a pang of jealousy, pure and simple. But why? She didn't want to get involved with him, did she?

Every shred of sense said no, but that didn't diminish her attraction to him. It wasn't merely his looks. The sound of his voice stirred something in her, too, and the way he moved, and his directness, though it was often disconcerting.

'In fact,' he resumed, 'when I come to think of it, this friend could probably help you—or, at least, his wife might.'

His wife. A moment's relief was quickly followed by denial. She hadn't really been concerned, had she?

'In what way?' she queried.

'She used to work for a woman's glossy before the kids came along,' he explained. 'She could give you the low-down on what a features editor does on a day-to-day basis.'

'That would certainly be useful.' Tory seriously doubted her ability to bluff through four working days before the adventure weekend.

'Okay, come to dinner, and you can pick her brains.' It was a fairly casual invitation.

Tory still hesitated. 'Won't they mind—you turning up with a total stranger?'

'Why should they?' He shrugged. 'Unless you become a major embarrassment after a glass or two of wine.'

'Not as far as I know,' she stated heavily.

'That's all right, then,' he replied, and, turning into the parking space in front of one of the biggest hotels in London, announced, 'We're here.'

A doorman appeared to open the passenger door while Lucas climbed out and opened the boot. He indicated her case and his overnight bag to the hovering porter before handing over his car keys so the vehicle could be parked somewhere.

'I'm going to leave the car here,' he explained as they went through the revolving door into the lobby, 'and retrieve it in the morning rather than search South Kensington for a parking space.'

She nodded at this information but wondered why he'd let the porter take his bag. Did he imagine she could be persuaded to let him share the room? If so, he was in for a disappointment.

'Reservation in the name of Ryecart,' he announced as they approached the desk, and, when it was located, informed them, 'A Miss Lloyd will actually be using the room. Is it possible to extend the booking from one night to four?'

Four nights? Did he mean for her? It seemed so.

When he'd finished business with the desk clerk, he said, 'You might as well stay here for the duration. Save the bother of finding somewhere else.'

'But surely it's too...' She pulled a face rather than say the word expensive in front of the porter.

'It's on Eastwich,' he said as if that made the money irrelevant.

She supposed it was his decision. After all, he *was* Eastwich in a sense. But hadn't he been griping about budgets to Alex just that morning?

Lucas checked his luggage into the porter's office to be picked up later. 'Why don't you freshen up before we go to my friends for dinner?' he suggested to Tory. 'Take your time. I have some calls to make, then I'll wait in the cocktail bar.'

Tory didn't actually remember agreeing to this dinner date, but wasn't given much chance to object as he turned on his heel and walked off towards the hotel lounges. She was left in the care of the porter who guided her to her room on the fifth floor.

The room was every bit as luxurious as she'd expected and, after the porter had departed, tip in hand, she spent a little while looking across the London skyline. Then, still debating the wisdom of going with Lucas on any date, however innocuous it seemed, she showered, changed into a pale lilac shift dress and spent at least twenty minutes trying to sweep her unruly hair into a sophisticated style before giving up and letting it fall back into a mass of curls.

It wasn't a proper date, of course. It was more in the nature of work. That was what she told herself, even as she checked once more how she looked in the mirror, before draping a cream pashmina round her arms and venturing out to find him.

As it was early evening, the cocktail lounge wasn't crowded. From the doorway Tory noticed him at the bar, talking to a stunning brunette of supermodel proportions. She was considering retreat when he spotted her in turn. He made some final remark to the brunette before crossing to greet Tory.

He noted her change of outfit with a smiling, 'You look lovely.'

Tory replied with a less gracious, 'Humph,' and followed it up by muttering, 'We can pass on dinner, if you prefer.'

'And do what?' He arched an interested brow.

He'd misunderstood so Tory glanced pointedly towards the brunette. 'You could pursue new interests.'

He followed her gaze, then laughed dryly as he curled a hand round Tory's elbow to guide her to the front lobby.

'You're not jealous, are you?' he added in amused tones.

She gave him a repressive glance, claiming, 'Not even remotely.'

'Shame.' He pulled a doleful face. 'No need, anyway. Pros like her don't do it for me.'

Tory assumed he meant professional women and threw back, 'Too challenging, are they? Women in executive positions?'

He looked puzzled for a moment, then gave another laugh. 'I think we may have lost something in the translation. When I say "pro", I mean, well, to put it politely, a lady of the night.'

'Lady of the...' The penny finally dropped with Tory and left her round-eyed with disbelief. 'That girl...she was...no, she couldn't be.'

He nodded before switching subjects to say, 'I'll need your room key.'

'What for?' she queried.

'My overnight bag,' he reminded her slowly and indicated the porter's lodge tucked into a corner of the lobby. 'They'll have it stored under room number.'

'Oh.' She just had to stop reacting with suspicion to everything he said. 'Here.'

She produced it out of her clutch purse and waited while he retrieved his case.

They emerged from the hotel to find it still light and sunny on this summer's evening.

The liveried doorman assumed they'd want a taxi and was already signalling for one from the rank alongside the entrance.

Once they were installed in the back, curiosity had Tory resuming their earlier conversation. 'Did she ask you for money, then? The woman in the bar.'

'Not up front,' he told her. 'She'd be thrown out of the hotel if she went around doing that.'

'Then how did you know?' she pursued.

He smiled a little as he asked, 'Do you think I'm irresistible?'

'No!'

'Well, neither do I. So, when some stunning-looking dame comes up to me in a bar, sits down, uninvited, and asks me if I'm in need of company, I can guess everything's not quite on the level.'

'She *might* just have fancied you,' Tory argued. 'You're not that bad-looking.'

'Gee, thanks,' he said at this grudging admission, 'but, no, I don't think it was love at first sight.'

'What else did she say?'

'She asked me if I was in London on business. She then said she was *doing business*, should I be interested. I told her I was waiting for a friend and she was just offering to find a friend for my friend when you came to my rescue,' he finished in wry tones.

Tory made a slight face. This man didn't need her help to get out of such a situation. He was obviously a man of the world.

'You weren't tempted,' she challenged, 'stunning as she was?'

'Not even remotely,' he echoed her earlier words. 'Paying to have a woman tell me how great I am in bed has never held appeal.'

Tory felt herself actually blushing.

And that was before he leaned closer to murmur, 'Eliciting such information for real, now, that's a different matter.'

For once there was no amusement in his low deep drawl. It was Tory who forced a laugh.

'You don't believe I can?' he added. 'Or was that an invitation to prove it?'

It hadn't been, of course, but he still lifted a hand to her cheek and, when she didn't immediately pull away, turned her face towards his.

He stared at her so long Tory assumed that was all he was going to do. Then he kissed her. Not deeply or intimately. His lips barely touched against the corner of her mouth while a hand lightly pushed back the curls framing her face.

It was over almost before it was begun. He drew away and leaned back against the taxi leather.

Tory was left confused and somewhat irrationally annoyed. If he was going to kiss her, he should do it properly or not at all.

'An ominous silence followed,' he commented as if writing a novel, 'but still he counted himself lucky—at least she hadn't slapped him.'

'Yet,' Tory warned darkly.

But too late. A quick glance confirmed that the amused smile was back in place.

'I'm not sure I want to go to dinner with you,' she added in haughty tones.

'Well, it's too late for a rain check,' he countered. 'We're here.'

Here being a splendid row of Georgian terraced houses. Rich friends, obviously.

'Do they know I'm coming too?' she asked as he selected cash from his wallet to pay the taxi.

He nodded and, paying the driver, helped her out of the taxi before answering, 'Caro does, anyway. In fact, she's looking forward to giving you the low-down on being a features editor. A trip down memory lane, she called it.'

'What does she do now?'

'Stays at home with the children.'

'How old?'

'The twins are about three, the baby is just a few months old… You like children?' he added as they walked up the steps.

'Boiled or fried?' she quipped.

He smiled at the small joke before pursuing, 'Seriously?'

'I like them well enough,' she finally replied. 'Just as long as I can hand them back.'

'I used to feel like that, too,' he agreed. 'Then one day you find yourself thinking it wouldn't be so bad, having your own.'

The admission was unexpected, so much so that Tory stared at him, testing if he was quite serious.

'With the right person, of course.' Blue eyes met hers, half intent, half amused.

Flirting, that was what he was doing. Tory knew that. Yet it seemed important to make a statement.

'I'll never have children.' She was unequivocal about it.

He smiled a little. 'How can you be so certain?'

Tory did not smile back. He obviously thought she was making a lifestyle choice.

'I just am.' She didn't feel like going into reasons.

She had told him. That was enough.

He shook his head, as if he still didn't believe her.

His problem, she decided.

It was only later she wished she'd told him it all.

CHAPTER SEVEN

LUCAS studied Tory for a moment longer, then said, 'You'll see, one day,' before turning to press on the doorbell.

It was answered by a woman wearing a frog apron on top of a smart summer dress. She was slightly older than Tory with a pretty freckled face and red hair escaping from a band at the neck. She looked a little flustered but her face was transformed at the sight of Lucas.

'Luc, lovely to see you.' She gave him a hug and a kiss on the cheek before turning to Tory. 'And you must be the features editor to be. Pleased to meet you. Come through, but mind the toys.'

She led the way down a wide hall, which was strewn with the pieces of a wooden train set, calling out, 'Boys, Uncle Luc is here.'

The effect was immediate as two identical pyjama-clad figures came hurtling out of a room to throw themselves at Lucas Ryecart's legs. Without hesitation, he stooped down and heaved one up in each arm, much to the boys' delight.

'Play trains,' demanded one.

'Build a tent,' demanded the other.

'Pillow fight!' added the first.

'Do the swingy thing,' chimed the second.

And so it went on as the twins began to list endless possibilities now opened up to them at the appearance of 'Uncle Luc'.

'Boys!' their mother eventually called over the excited gabbling. 'Uncle Luc is having dinner. *You* are going to bed.'

This elicited a joint protest of 'Aw' and crestfallen little faces.

'You heard your mother.' Lucas put them both back on the ground. 'But if you're up those stairs by the time I count five,

I may just tell you the really scary thing that happened to my friends, Al and Bill, the time they got lost in a jungle in South America.'

'A real jungle?'

'Honestly?'

The boys' eyes were round with anticipation before Lucas began, 'One…two…'

Then there was a mad scramble as the two made for the stairs and rushed up as quickly as their legs would allow.

'You don't have to,' Caro said as he reached five.

'I'd like to.' He raised a brow in Tory's direction. 'You don't mind?'

Tory shook her head. Caro seemed friendly enough.

'It'll give us a chance to have a girl talk.' Caro grinned wickedly.

'About magazine work, I hope,' Lucas added.

'Of course. What else?' Caro feigned innocence, even as the gleam in her eye suggested he would also be a topic under discussion.

Then one of the twins appeared at the top of the stairs to shout, 'Is it five yet?'

'Shh, the baby's asleep!' his mother called back.

While Lucas promised, 'I'm coming, Jack,' and took the stairs two at a time.

'I don't know how he does it—' Caro gazed after him in puzzled admiration '—but he always gets their names right. Not even their grandmothers can do that.'

Tory wouldn't have managed it either. The boys had looked like clones of each other. 'Does he see them often?'

'He tries to—' Caro pulled a forgiving face '—but he has such a busy schedule. Still, the boys always love it when Uncle Luc comes. He's their godfather.'

'Really?' Tory assumed that was why he was called 'Uncle Luc'.

'Well, one of them,' Caro continued before glancing towards the back of the house. 'Look, do you mind if we chat in the kitchen while I get on with dinner?'

Tory shook her head, offering, 'I'd be happy to help. I'm

not much of a cook but I can peel vegetables with the best of them.'

'It's all right.' Carol smiled, leading the way through. 'Most of it's done. I just have to keep watch over various pots and pans. Poached salmon—I hope you like it.'

'Sounds delicious.' Tory meant it. 'A welcome change from chicken salad or tuna pasta, the heights of my own culinary achievements.'

Caro laughed. 'Oh, you're definitely one up on me. I used to live on a diet of sandwiches and yoghurt in my single career-girl days. Life always seemed too short to cook.'

'Quite.' Tory gave the other woman a complicit smile.

'Of course, it's such an irony,' Caro ran on. 'There I was, doing features for this lifestyle magazine, full of cordon bleu recipes and articles on minimalist decor, and going home to cook beans on toast in a girl-sharing flat in Clapham with enough clutter to fill a builder's skip.'

Tory laughed at the image, before casting an appreciative glance round her present surrounds. The kitchen was large and light and airy, with up to date units and flooring in polished beech-wood.

'You have a lovely place now,' complimented Tory.

'Money,' Caro replied as she stirred a simmering pot. 'My husband's family have it.'

'Right.' Tory wasn't sure how to respond to such frankness.

Caro shrugged, dismissing it as an importance, beforc continuing, 'Anyway, I understand from Luc that you're also about to enter the bitch-eat-bitch world of the women's glossy.'

'I've already been through the initiation ceremony.' Grimacing, Tory relayed her brief meeting with the editorial board.

Caro's expression was sympathetic but hardly surprised. It seemed Amanda Villiers, the senior editor, was notorious in the business for savaging female staff.

Tory listened while Caro went through what her job had entailed when working for a very similar magazine to *Toi*. Obviously she couldn't teach Tory how to do the job. That required years of experience as well as talent. But she gave her enough pointers on how to *seem* to be doing the job to maintain her cover for a few days.

'You'll be fine,' Caro tried to boost Tory's flagging confidence, 'but if you do need advice, I'm available, nappy-changing permitting.'

There was a certain wistfulness in her voice that made Tory ask, 'When did you stop work?'

'The boys were about two, I think…' Caro cast her mind back '…so that's…what? Over a year ago. I was one of those having-it-all-mothers who suddenly woke up to the fact they were really having-absolutely-nothing but misery and stress.'

Tory gave an understanding murmur. 'It seems to be a trend—women re-evaluating their lives. Personally, I love my work but I don't think I could manage it all—home, family and a career.'

'You can for a while,' Caro responded, 'but then your energy levels go down while theirs go up and all of a sudden the crying babies became talkative two-year-olds well able to tell you they hate it every time you leave for work and your nanny informs you she wants to see the world, starting tomorrow, and your heart is desperate for another baby even though you're barely coping with the two you have. So it's crunch time…I was luckier than most, I suppose, because we didn't need my money.'

'Still, you must miss work,' Tory said in sympathetic tones.

'At times,' Caro admitted, shaking the contents of a pan, 'when the twins' squabbling reaches an all-time high—or possibly low—and the baby won't settle because she has a cold and the au pair has failed to return from a night out clubbing.'

'And total strangers turn up for dinner?' Tory suggested, her tone apologetic.

'Oh, I didn't mind that.'

'Really?'

'Well—' Caro pulled a face '—I wasn't too ecstatic when Luc called, but that's only because I thought you might be like his usual girlfriends—'

'I'm not his girlfriend.' A frown clouded Tory's features. 'Did he say—?'

'No, not at all,' Caro was quick to disclaim. 'Quite the opposite, in fact…'

Caro trailed off and left Tory wondering what Lucas had said about her that was quite the opposite of being his girlfriend.

'I just meant,' Caro tried again, 'that, on the few occasions Lucas has brought a woman to dinner, it has been a girlfriend and they tend to be…let's say, a certain type.'

Tory told herself she wasn't interested but, in the very next breath, asked, 'What type, exactly?'

Caro hesitated. 'Perhaps I've said enough.'

'All right.' Tory wasn't going to press her.

That was probably why Caro ran on, 'Well, it could be me, but I find them all unbearably superior. Admittedly, they're usually barristers or investment bankers or run their own PR companies and they're always clever and witty, and often fairly stunning in the looks department, too. Which is probably why they feel obliged to talk down to lesser mortals, as if we're one step up from the village idiot.'

Tory rolled her eyes in agreement. 'I know the type but I can't imagine they talk to Lucas that way.'

'Oh, goodness, no!' Caro exclaimed at the very idea. 'But that only makes it worse. They positively simper in Luc's presence, and gaze at him, all adoring eyes, like politicians' wives.'

Tory laughed as intended, before venturing, 'He probably loves it.'

Caro looked uncertain. 'Luc's never struck me as being that big an egotist,' she replied, 'although I suppose most men that gorgeous *do* have egos the size of a planet.'

'Too true,' Tory said with feeling.

Caro came back with, 'So you think he is, then?'

'What?'

'Gorgeous.'

Caro's grin made a joke of it.

Tory pulled a slight face, too. 'I didn't say that, exactly.'

'No, but he is,' Caro insisted as if it were a fact that couldn't be disputed.

Tory didn't try; she was acquainted with the phrase 'the lady doth protest too much'.

'I have wondered if it's a kind of protection,' the other woman continued in musing tones.

'Protection?' Tory had lost the thread. 'What is?'

'Going out with that kind of woman,' Caro volunteered. 'I mean, even allowing for other people's taste, no one, but no one, could have found his last girlfriend lovable. Smart, witty, classy, yes! Lovable, absolutely not.'

'What happened to her?'

'His relocation to Norwich, but I can't see that being an insurmountable problem. How far is it from London? Two hours?'

Having made the journey that day, Tory said, 'A little over.'

'No huge distance,' commented Caro, 'but that's the excuse he gave for the relationship petering out. I wondered if he'd met someone else. Any super-intelligent, arrogant, super-model types at Eastwich?'

'Not that I can think of.' Tory certainly didn't come into that category. At five-foot six, she was hardly a super-model type, was far from super-intelligent, and didn't see herself as arrogant in personality. That left her questioning whether Lucas Ryecart was stringing along some other woman besides herself.

'At any rate,' Caro resumed her original theme, 'I have this theory he dates women with whom he's in no danger of falling in love. As in, it's better *not* to love and *not* to lose, than ever love at all.'

'I always thought it was the other way round,' countered Tory.

'It is,' replied Caro, 'but, in Luc's case, he *has* loved and lost so maybe he doesn't want to go through it again.'

'I see.' Tory did see, too; she just wasn't entirely convinced.

Sensing her doubts, Caro confided in more sober tones, 'He was married once and she died.'

'Yes, I know.'

'Did he tell you?'

Tory nodded, recalling he had told her at one point.

Caro looked surprised. 'He doesn't usually talk about it—even among the family.'

The family? Tory didn't quite follow. Which family did she mean?

'Is Lucas related to you?' she finally asked Caro.

'Sort of. His wife was my sister-in-law. Or would have been, had she…' The other woman tailed off at Tory's expression and switched to asking, 'Is something wrong?'

Tory struggled to keep her emotions in check as the truth dawned. Lucas was an only child, while his late wife had one brother. There was no other link.

How could she have been so stupid? *Uncle Luc* really was Uncle Luc. She was in Charlie's, her ex fiancé's, house. She was talking to Charlie's wife, the girl who had so rapidly replaced her.

'You really don't look well.' Caro watched Tory's face become drawn with alarm.

'I… It's a bug,' Tory lied desperately. 'I thought I was better, but it seems not. I'll have to go back to the hotel.'

Tory picked up the pashmina she'd draped over a chair and her handbag, and started making for the door.

Caro followed. 'Yes, of course, I'll go and fetch Luc. He'll—'

'No!' Tory refused rather abruptly, then softened it with, 'Honestly, I don't want to drag him away. I can hail a taxi. I'm sorry to throw out your plans. It was lovely to meet you…'

Tory garbled on until she was in the front hall, poised for escape.

Caro obviously didn't feel she should be allowed to go on her own and looked relieved at the sound of a key in the front door.

'That'll be Charlie now. I could get him to run you back instead.'

Tory said nothing, did nothing. She felt trapped, caught like a rabbit in headlights. She watched the door push open. Her eyes went to the dark-suited man entering.

For a moment she almost thought she'd got it wrong and this wasn't Charlie. He wasn't as she remembered. Five years older, he had lost some of his boyish good looks and his hair. Her heart was beating hard out of panic but it didn't kick up any extra gears, even when she realised it was most definitely Charlie.

His glance first went to his wife, who'd launched into explanations of their guest's indisposition, before it encompassed Tory. Then any hopes that she'd also changed out of recognition faded rapidly.

Charlie was clearly shocked, opening and shutting his mouth as no words came, struggling to come to terms with her presence.

When Caro sought to introduce them, 'This is Tory, by the way,' he was already mouthing the name he'd known her by: Vicki.

Quickly, she shook her head at him, the slightest movement, but he picked it up.

When she said, 'Pleased to meet you,' he followed suit.

'Yes, hello,' he murmured, and let her continue.

'I'm sorry, but I have to go. I'm not feeling too great and I've left my medicine back at the hotel.'

She waited for him to play his part, say some farewell words, encourage her to leave, perhaps open the door, but he just stood stock-still staring at her.

It was Caro who insisted, 'Charlie will run you back. Won't you, Charlie?'

She seemed oblivious of undercurrents.

Tory anticipated Charlie making an excuse and was thrown by his acquiescent, 'Yes, of course. My car's outside.'

'See.' Caro was finally satisfied with the arrangements.

She escorted Tory down the steps while Charlie went ahead to unlock the car, then opened the passenger door and waited for Tory to be installed inside.

She said, warm as ever, 'You must come again for dinner. Let me know how you get on at *Toi*.'

'Yes, thanks.' Tory smiled at the other woman whom she

had really liked—still did like—knowing she would never meet her again if she could help it.

'I'll explain to Luc,' Caro called out as they drew away from the kerb.

Tory managed a weak wave and felt a measure of relief once they were out of sight.

But Charlie drove only as far as the end of the crescent, before parking in the first available space and turning in his seat to stare at her, as if he still couldn't believe his eyes.

'I'm sorry.' Tory felt she owed him an apology. 'I had no idea. He never said.'

'He?'

'Lucas.'

'You came with him?' Charlie caught up with events. 'Oh, you're the production assistant from Eastwich.'

She gave a nod.

'My wife called you by some other name.' He frowned, trying to remember.

'Tory,' she supplied. 'It was my mother's name for me when I was little. I went back to using it after…'

She left it hanging. What to say otherwise? *After you dumped me?*

It was true enough. She'd reverted to Tory in a desire to reinvent the person she was, but he'd been more catalyst than cause. She looked at him now and felt not a single ounce of passion. How strange.

'And you didn't realise who Luc was?' Charlie concluded.

'No, I did,' she admitted. 'I realised when he took over Eastwich. It was just that he offered to introduce me to someone who'd worked on a woman's magazine—Eastwich is doing this documentary—and it wasn't until five minutes ago that the penny dropped who Caro actually was.'

'Right.' Charlie absorbed this information while still gazing at her intently. '*You* haven't changed. Not at all.'

Tory pulled a face, trying to lighten things up. 'I'm not sure that's good.'

Charlie remained serious. 'You're just the same, just the way I imagine you.'

Tory felt no satisfaction at the wistful note of regret in Charlie's voice. The past was dead for her.

'Your wife's lovely,' she said quite genuinely.

'Thanks,' he replied but it was as if she'd complimented him on a new car, and he added with more feeling, 'She's not you.'

Tory couldn't misunderstand his meaning, not when it went along with the soulful look in his eyes. It was the look he'd worn during their long-ago courtship, when she'd imagined herself in love with him, and he with her. But now, from a distance, she could see it had all been illusion.

'No, she's not,' she agreed at length. 'She's the woman who gave you the children you always wanted.'

It was a pointed remark that hit its target as he winced. 'That was cruel.'

'Was it?' Tory didn't care as she stated, 'It's a cruel world.'

'You've grown harder, Vicki.' He looked troubled by the idea.

Tory wondered what he expected. 'Life does that to people.'

'Yes… Yes, it does. You have no idea how much I wish—'

She cut across him. 'Don't.'

'But you don't know what I'm going to say.' He reached for her hand.

She pulled it from his grasp. 'I don't want to know, Charlie. I think I'll get out here.'

'Please, Vicki,' he appealed, but she already had the door open and didn't stop even when he called out, 'You have to forgive me.'

She kept walking, wrapping her pashmina round her as the cool night air touched her bare shoulders. She didn't look back.

She didn't run. Charlie Wainwright didn't frighten her. In fact, he didn't do anything to her any more, except make her sorry for his wife.

It was a revelation. For years she had wondered if it was Charlie who had stopped her forming any other serious relationship. Always, at the back of her mind, had been the idea she might just still love him. And now? Nothing.

She couldn't even stay angry with him. As she walked the

Kensington streets, heading back towards the hotel, her anger switched to another man. A tall, blue-eyed, dark-haired American with a rather nasty sense of humour.

How else to explain what he'd done? It couldn't have been coincidence. It was too far a stretch

So what had it been? A social experiment to check how she'd react when face to face with her former fiancé?

Well, tough luck, he'd missed it, playing favourite uncle to Charlie's kids.

It was Caro she felt sorry for. Married to a husband who, at best, was a wimp, and deceived by a man whom she imagined loyal enough to make him her sons' godfather.

No one could be a real friend and engineer such a situation. Even if the plan had been to stir up things for Tory, there had always been a danger of hurting Caro along the way. He must have known that. He was no fool.

But that was what really got to Tory. She'd spent almost the whole day with Lucas Ryecart, her barriers against him slipping away. It was only now she acknowledged that she'd dressed for him this evening. Only now she admitted how jealous she'd been, seeing him with that other woman at the bar. And, in watching him with his godsons, listening to Caro talking about him with such fondness, she had been seduced into seeing him in a different light.

She supposed she should be grateful for the wake-up call, otherwise she might have been in real danger of falling for the bastard. Now anger was uppermost and kept her buoyant until she finally reached her hotel.

She hadn't eaten since lunch and the walk had given her an appetite, but it had also given her sore feet—her shoes had been new and high-heeled—and she decided to order room service. An elaborate variety of courses was on offer and she considered running up a huge bill, courtesy of Eastwich and Lucas Ryecart, but she eventually settled for a salad, omelette and a chilled bottle of white wine to calm her down. She took her meal, watching a documentary on cheating husbands. It seemed an appropriate choice of viewing for that evening.

She was getting ready for bed, mellowed somewhat by the

wine, when there was a knock on the hotel room door. She assumed it was room service although they'd already cleared her dinner. She tied the hotel's fluffy bathrobe tighter round the waist and checked she was decent before opening the door.

One glance and, registering the figure standing on the threshold, she shut it immediately before Lucas could even think to get a foot in the door.

She ignored his next knock and the several after it, and the repetitions of her name, 'Tory!' and the appeals to, 'Open up,' and 'We have to talk.'

Tory didn't see they had to talk at all. In fact, she'd already decided a resignation letter would do for their next communication. She'd been mentally composing it all through supper and preparing for bed. But she had no desire to deliver it in person.

'*Tory—*' his tone changed to barely restrained anger '—I don't want to have to do this, but you're leaving me no choice.'

Do what? Tory scowled at the door. It was thick and made of real wood. Did he imagine he could run at it and break it down? She almost wished he'd try.

'Tory!' Her name was called once more, followed by a determined, 'Right.'

She waited in anticipation for his next move. She didn't really expect him to do anything as crude as batter on the door and she was right. She heard the click of the electronic locking system and then he was in the room before she had a chance to react.

He shut the door behind him, but didn't come further into the room as he drawled, 'Don't look so panic-stricken. I'm not going to jump on you.'

'How did you get that?' She indicated the card key in his hand.

'I told them I'd lost mine,' he relayed. 'They handed another over once I'd proved I was the registered occupant of the room.'

'How low can you get?' She didn't hide her contempt.

'Lower than that,' he rejoined without apology.

'Well…?' She waited for him to state his business.

He seemed in no hurry. 'You could offer me a drink,' he said as if he were an invited guest.

'I could call Security,' she countered with a hard edge.

'You could,' he agreed. 'Go ahead, if you want.'

He leaned against the door and folded his arms. It didn't seem to bother him.

'You're so sure I won't.' Tory tried to sound threatening.

He was unimpressed. 'Not sure, no, but I don't think you like scenes. Otherwise you might have hung around at the Wainwrights.'

'I'm sorry if you feel cheated.' Her tone was derisive.

His brows drew together. 'You think I'd have liked to watch the grand reunion?'

'Why else did you stage it?' she rallied.

'Hold on a minute.' He abandoned his relaxed pose. 'I had no idea you had any connection with the Wainwrights until I came downstairs to find you gone and an agitated Charlie in your place.'

Tory wasn't convinced. 'You expect me to believe that?'

'I've pretty much given up expecting anything of you,' he said, 'but, yes, I'm telling you straight—I was as much in the dark as you.'

'All right.' It rang true. On his part, anyway. She, of course, hadn't totally been in the dark.

She must have looked guilty as the blue eyes were already studying her, narrowed.

'Or maybe even more so?' he asked astutely.

Tory suddenly found herself on the defensive. 'I did not realise who we were visiting until about a minute before Charlie came home.'

A statement of fact; he still saw behind her carefully chosen words. 'But you knew of my connection to the Wainwrights. You must have.'

Tory considered denying it. After all, he'd never actually mentioned his wife by name or his in-laws. But what would be the point?

'I did realise, yes,' she admitted, 'the first day we met.'

'No wonder you seemed familiar.' His eyes hardened with distrust. 'I must have seen a photograph or something, though I guess you've changed in…what? Five years, would it be?'

She nodded. 'My hair was longer and I wore glasses before I had contacts fitted.'

'Why didn't you say anything?' he added.

'What, exactly?' countered Tory. ' I was once engaged to your late wife's brother? Not quite the easiest of introductions to a new boss.'

'You had plenty of chances later… Do you honestly think I would have taken you to their house, if I'd been clued up?' His tone clearly told her he wouldn't.

It seemed she'd misjudged him, yet again, but rather than apologise she gave an uninterested shrug.

It was a gesture designed to annoy, and annoy it did as his mouth went into a tight line and he finally stepped away from the door to cross the room.

Misunderstanding his purpose, Tory retreated to the far corner. She felt a little foolish when he veered off towards the mini-bar.

He noted her jumpiness with a humourless smile. 'Relax. Right at the moment a drink is all I want.'

If it was meant to reassure, it didn't. His eyes lingered long enough to suggest that later he might want something else.

Tory took a deep, steadying breath and told herself to keep calm. He was playing games, that was all.

'Can I fix you one?' He bent to do a quick inventory of, 'Whisky, gin, vodka, beer…'

'No…thank you.' Tory had already had several glasses of wine earlier.

She watched as he took a couple of miniature whiskies from the cabinet and poured both in a glass, then eased his length onto the only chair.

As hotel bedrooms went, it had seemed quite spacious, but, with him in it, it suddenly felt overcrowded.

'So what happened between you and Charlie?' he asked, as if his interest was merely casual.

'Tonight?'

'No, we'll come to that. I meant before.'

Tory supposed she could have told him to mind his own business, but wasn't that making it a big deal? And it wasn't. Not really. Not any more.

'We met at college on the same media course,' she relayed, 'we went out, then became briefly engaged before having second thoughts.'

'Which one of you?'

'Which one of you what?'

'Had second thoughts?'

Both of them, Tory supposed was the truth.

She'd had second thoughts from the moment Charlie had proposed and pressed her for an immediate answer at the New Year's party they'd been attending. But she'd tried hard to ignore her doubts and let herself be caught up in Charlie's impulsiveness and sheer certainty about everything.

'Charlie,' she answered at length.

'That's not what I heard,' he drawled back at her.

Tory wasn't altogether surprised. It was Charlie who'd decided to call off the engagement but she'd left it up to him as to what story he gave people.

'I heard,' he continued at her silence, 'that all of a sudden the engagement was off and Charlie was devastated. Doesn't quite tally with the notion he was the one to back out, now, does it?'

'Who did you hear it from?' she retorted. 'His mother?'

'As I recall, yes.' He nodded. 'Charlie wasn't making much sense at the time. He just said he'd discovered something that made it impossible for you to go on together.'

That was true enough and she supposed she was glad that Charlie had been discreet, although it was questionable whether his intention had been to save her face or his own.

'I bet his mother couldn't contain her delight.' Tory knew she'd never been good enough for Diana Wainwright.

He raised a brow at her slightly acerbic tone before admitting, 'She did think you were unsuited, yes.'

'Not her sort at all.' Tory mimicked the other woman's posh way of talking.

'Yeah, okay, Diana can be a bit of a snob,' he conceded, 'but she was more concerned for Charlie and whether he'd ever get over you.'

There was a note of accusation in his voice. It seemed he'd cast her in the role of heartbreaker.

Tory resented the unfairness of it. 'Well, she was wrong, wasn't she? How long before he was married? A year, maybe?'

'And you'd prefer him to do what?' he grated back. 'Stay crying into his beer? Carry a torch for ever? Or maybe go crawling back to you?'

'I didn't want that,' Tory denied angrily.

'No?' He clearly didn't believe her.

'No!' she repeated, gritting her teeth.

He still didn't look satisfied as he muttered, 'Let's hope not.'

'Does it matter?' Tory wasn't enjoying this trip down memory lane. 'It's past, over, history.'

'Is it?'

Why was he looking at her like that?

'Yes, of course,' she declared adamantly. ' I haven't seen Charlie for five years.'

'But you saw him tonight,' he reminded her, 'and he saw you.'

What was he getting at? Obviously something, but she'd lost the plot.

'Yes,' she answered slowly.

'And?' He waited.

She still didn't know what he wanted her to say.

'And nothing,' she replied.

'He gave you a ride, you shook hands like nice polite English people do and said goodbye?' The mocking drawl in his voice was shot through with disbelief.

Colour seeped into Tory's cheeks even as she told herself he couldn't possibly know otherwise. He'd not been in the car with them and surely Charlie hadn't rushed off home to confess all.

'Something along those lines,' she finally murmured.

It was the wrong answer, evidently, as his lips curled with

contempt for her. Then he drained his whisky and set the glass down on a table with a cracking noise, before rising to his feet.

She watched him cross to the door, seemingly with the intention of leaving.

She should have been relieved but instead she found herself coming round the end of the bed, pursuing him as she claimed, 'Nothing happened between us, if that's what you're trying to imply.'

He paused mid-flight, hand on the lock, back rigid, then turned round to face her.

'Nothing happened?' he echoed, but there was a dangerous edge to his voice, and when she took a step backwards he reached out to catch her arm.

Unable to retreat, Tory stood shaking her head. 'I—I... No, nothing.'

'Liar.' The word was growled at her as he drew her closer. 'I just sat through dinner with a man who looked like a ghost had come back to haunt him. I spent most of it trying to distract his wife so she wouldn't notice how sappy he was acting, then afterwards had to listen while Charlie went on like a corny Country and Western song about the love of his life and how he'd lost her.'

And he blamed it all on her. Tory saw that in the scathing look he gave her.

'I'm not interested in Charlie,' she said in her own defence.

'And that makes it better?' It was a rhetorical question as he ran on, 'So why vamp him—to see if you could? Or a little revenge?'

'Vamp him?' Tory repeated, her own temper rising. 'Is that what Charlie said?'

'He didn't need to,' Lucas replied. 'It was obvious from the way he was behaving. Doesn't it mean anything to you, the fact he's married, has kids?'

She shook her head, denying that she'd done anything, but he chose to misunderstand, to believe the worst of her.

'Evidently not,' he concluded for himself. 'Well, I'm warning you now, go near Charlie again and I'll make sure you regret it.'

'Really?' The threat didn't scare Tory, it just made her madder. 'So how are you going to do that, Mr Ryecart? Let me guess? My P45 in the post.'

'P45?' The term didn't translate.

'P45, it's a tax form you get when you stop working for a company—' Tory switched to saying, 'Never mind. It doesn't matter. You can't sack me because I quit. As of now, this moment.'

It clearly took him by surprise as his brows arched together. Perhaps he'd imagined he was the only one who could call the shots.

'You can't quit!' he barked back.

'Oh, can't I?' Tory taunted, and tried to jerk her hands free.

He held them fast, long fingers circling her slender wrists. 'You're on contract and in the middle of an assignment. I thought you were the one who could keep work and their personal life separate?'

Tory recognised the claim she'd made that afternoon but didn't appreciate having it flung back at her.

'And this business with you and Charlie,' he continued heavily, 'has absolutely nothing to do with work, and everything to do with Caro and those three kids back there. You honestly want to wreck their lives just because Charlie was too spineless to marry you in the first place?'

Of course Tory didn't. No thought could be further from her mind, but his lecturing tone incensed her all the same.

'Why not?' she found herself saying. 'You don't expect anything better of me, do you? You imagine I'll sleep with anyone, after all… Well, anyone but you, that is,' she added with reckless intent.

She didn't regret it. Not then, anyway. She enjoyed wiping that superior look from his face.

It was replaced with a cloud of dark anger. 'You think I'd want to sleep with you now?'

His tone said he'd not touch her, but his eyes said something else, and Tory scoffed at him, 'Yes, actually, I do.'

She felt his hands tighten like bands round her arms, and waited for him to push her away.

But she had seriously miscalculated.

'Let's see, shall we?' he ground back, pulling her towards him.

At the last moment she tried to turn but it was too late. His hand was in her hair, holding her head steady. She saw his mouth curve into a humourless smile a second before it lowered on hers.

She meant to resist but she had forgotten how it felt to be kissed by this man. His lips moved against hers, warm and hard and persuasive, tongue tasting teeth until she opened to him, then thrusting inside to explore the warm, sweet intimacy of her mouth, making her breathing as ragged as his.

'You're right,' he murmured against her mouth. 'I still want you.'

It was the last they spoke, the last conscious thought formed as desire overwhelmed reason.

Afterwards Tory would try to tell herself it was down to the drink they'd both had. Afterwards she'd try to call it seduction but then she'd remember how it really had been. Too quick to be seduction. Too sweet to be force.

It was more compulsion as he began to touch her, a hand moving round, slipping inside her robe, pushing aside, seeking flesh, breasts swollen and heavy, fingering until she cried out for the mouth closing, sucking on her aching nipples. It was need and desperation as she fell with him on the bed and guided him down to the part of her that was already warm and wet and let him stroke her, deep and intimate, until desire kicked in her belly and she drew his hips to hers.

She was naked, he still clothed. Together they fumbled for his zip. Then they coupled in mutual need.

The first thrust and he filled her too completely. She moaned a little until his mouth covered hers in a sweet, drugging kiss. Then slowly he moved inside her and her body opened up as if it had always known his, and she rose and fell with him, grasping his shoulders, digging in at each shaft, panting and gasping, almost one being as they came together with wild, unrestrained pleasure.

They lay back on the bed, for a while suspended in time,

their bodies experiencing intense physical satisfaction—then gradually reality impinged and the mind took back control.

Tory remained paralysed in those first conscious moments, wondering what she had done. She'd never made love like that, with almost primitive urgency. She'd never felt like this, possessed to the core. She'd never wanted to let a man this close to her.

Every instinct told her to run. She'd nowhere to go but inside her head. So she retreated there as she slid off the bed and picked up the robe she'd been wearing and turned her back to him as she put it on.

Somehow Luc wasn't surprised by this reaction. He was more surprised by what had gone before.

He followed her up off the bed, straightening his clothes as he did so. He considered an apology but it would have been hypocrisy. He wasn't sorry for what he'd done. In fact, when he recalled her response, so warm and passionate, he wanted to do it all over again.

Her rigid stance, however, told him the cold war had resumed.

He restrained a desire to cross the room and take her back in his arms.

'You want me to go?' he surmised instead.

'Yes.' Tory didn't risk saying more.

He was equally laconic. 'Okay.'

But still Tory didn't imagine he would leave without another word, didn't believe it when she heard the door behind her open and shut.

She turned and found herself in an empty room. He was gone. Just like that.

But he couldn't be forgotten the same way. How could he be when he'd left his mark on her body, left a jagged tear on her heart?

She showered and tried to wash the smell of him, the taste of him, the touch of him from her body. She leaned against cool white tiles while hot tears of shame and rejection ran down her cheeks. She towelled her skin dry till it hurt and climbed into the crumpled bed and shut her eyes tight and prayed for sleep to come.

But it made no difference. When finally she slipped away, she found him chasing through her dreams.

It seemed as if she had opened a door that she couldn't close.

CHAPTER EIGHT

TORY woke, hoping it really had been a dream, but her eyes were drawn to the whisky glass on the table. This trace of Lucas's presence prompted vivid recall of what had happened last night.

She felt a measure of shame. She'd never indulged before in casual sex but what Lucas and she had done together could scarcely be described as anything else. And the worst part was the way he'd left her, as if he hadn't been able to wait to be gone.

She wondered how she could ever face him again. The easy option was not to. She could follow through her threat to quit her job. In the cool light of day, however, she knew such an action would damage her career as well as her finances.

And what else had she but work? It was the thing she did best, the thing that gave her life meaning and form. If she walked away from Eastwich now, how long might it be before she secured another post?

There was also a reasonable possibility that Lucas would no longer be a problem. Yes, he'd pursued her from the moment they'd met, but now he'd had her and used her and seemingly lost interest at once. Perhaps she was already history.

Tory visualised their next meeting. She'd be churned up inside while he would be his usual laid-back self. He might or might not allude to their one-night stand. If he did, it would be as a joke or a shrugged aside. No big deal. Couldn't she act the same way, regardless of how she felt inside?

Tory decided she could and would, and, driven by a mixture of pride and pragmatism, she got herself out of bed, showered and dressed and ready for her first day as an employee of *Toi.*

While she'd been nervous yesterday, she approached today very differently. She sailed into the offices with an almost reckless disregard as to whether she was found out or not, and straight away set up a meeting with her three assistants, listening as they explained the work in progress before making appropriate comments and suggesting approaches that might be taken for this or that article. She made it clear that they would have a fair degree of autonomy, and two of the young women seemed happy to accept her as their new boss. The third was Sam Hollier who'd been Acting Features Editor, and, not surprisingly, she was more hostile, although she stopped short of outright rebellion, and Tory decided she could probably handle her.

It was Amanda Villiers of whom she was most wary, but, to her relief, the lady in question failed to appear. Either she was too busy to bother or didn't really care whether Tory settled to the job or not.

Thus Tory survived the day with her credibility intact and actually stayed late, wading through some unsolicited articles sent by freelance writers. Most she earmarked for polite rejections, a couple were worth considering and one stood out as eminently printable. Unsure if she had the authority to commission the latter, she decided to play safe and placed a copy on Amanda's desk, requesting her opinion of it.

She returned to the hotel with some reluctance. Occupied throughout the day, she'd avoided thinking of Lucas Ryecart, but once back in her room she was unable to keep her mind off the events of last night. She felt she would have welcomed any distraction until Reception rang up to her room, informing her she had a visitor downstairs: Caro Wainwright.

Tory assumed it was a social call—perhaps Caro offering further work advice. Much as she'd liked her, Tory felt pursuing even the most tenuous relationship with her was inadvisable. But refusing to see her at all might prompt some suspicions in Caro's mind.

Tory resolved to go down and do her best to act normally. She greeted Caro with a polite smile and hid her surprise at the other woman's attire—an orange and black track suit over a running top.

'It's one of my gym nights,' explained Caro, 'but I decided at the last moment to come here…see how you were.'

'Much better,' Tory volunteered.

'That's good,' Caro murmured back.

Silence followed these pleasantries until Tory felt almost obliged to add, 'We could go for a drink in the lounge bar.'

Caro nodded even as she looked uncertain. 'Perhaps there's a dress code.'

Tory glanced towards a group of young men exiting the bar in question. They wore an array of scruffy denim jackets and tie-less shirts flapping loosely over jeans.

'Not from the look of that lot, there isn't,' she remarked on their dress.

Caro followed her gaze. 'Aren't they some pop group or other?'

'Possibly,' agreed Tory, before leading the way through the glass doors.

They gravitated towards a booth at the back. Tory insisted on buying the drinks and escaped to the bar. It gave her some precious minutes to compose herself.

When she returned, Caro took a good swig of the gin and tonic she'd requested.

It was Dutch courage, as she resumed, 'I'm not really sure what I want to say. I got myself riled up to come here but didn't think much further than that.'

Tory felt her stomach drop. It didn't take a genius to conclude from Caro's words, 'You know who I am, don't you?'

Caro nodded slowly.

'Lucas told you?' added Tory, a note of accusation creeping into her voice.

'When I asked him, he did,' relayed Caro, 'but not last night.'

Tory frowned, trying to sort out exactly what this meant.

Caro ran on, 'I knew there was something wrong at dinner. Charlie was acting really oddly but I thought it had something to do with work. Then, while I was making coffee, Luc changed his mind about staying and Charlie got very agitated at the idea that Luc had gone off to spend the night with you.'

'He didn't.' Tory could deny that at least.

'No, I know,' Caro stated. 'Luc told me he stayed with Chuck, his stepfather.'

So that was where he'd gone. Tory imagined the two men together, discussing Luc's latest acquisition—her! She just hoped she was being unduly paranoid.

'Anyway, Charlie thought otherwise,' Caro continued. 'In fact, to be honest, so did I. I made some joke about it—something about Luc meeting his match—and Charlie went ballistic. He made out he was upset because of his sister's memory, although he usually admired Luc for his success with women. It took me a while to figure out he minded for himself, not his sister…' Caro tailed off and her face reflected the pain she felt.

Tory wanted to say something. She just wasn't sure what. She was scared of making the situation worse.

Eventually she murmured, 'Charlie told you who I was.'

Caro shook her head. 'I guessed later, lying in bed, waiting for him to come up. I remembered your reaction to Charlie's name—your sudden bout of illness. It was obvious then that you knew him. I was just too stupid to realise it.'

'It's me that was stupid—' Tory sighed in response '—not realising who you were. I would never have gone to your house if I had.'

Caro's eyes rested on her, testing her sincerity, before she said, 'Well, it's too late to change things. The question is where we go from here.'

'I'm not sure I understand,' Tory replied carefully.

'Look, I know Charlie's rung you,' Caro informed her. 'I overheard him this morning, asking to speak to Victoria Lloyd. That's you, isn't it?'

Tory looked genuinely blank. 'I never received any calls.'

'He must have missed you,' Caro concluded, 'but that hardly matters. The fact that he's calling you at all is the issue.'

Tory could see that and ventured a possibility. 'Maybe he was calling to apologise. He *was* somewhat rude to me last night.'

'Rude?' Caro echoed in surprise.

'I'd say so. Claimed I'd grown very hard, ' Tory could relay quite truthfully, 'which is a bit of a cheek, coming from him. I mean, you know he dumped me, don't you?'

'Well, I...' Caro looked confused. 'I was never quite sure what had happened between you.'

'Not ready to commit.' Tory pulled a face. 'That's what he said. Rubbish, of course. I mean, he was ready enough when he met you a few months later; wasn't he?'

'I...um...yes, I suppose,' Caro agreed in apologetic tones.

'Well, you're welcome to him.' Tory gave a negligent shrug before reaching for her drink.

Over the rim she watched Caro's changing expressions. Having come here to warn Tory off or perhaps plead with her, Caro had not anticipated this outcome. She looked as if she couldn't quite believe things were going to be so easily resolved.

'God, jealousy does make fools of people. I really thought that you and him...' She trailed off and gave her a sheepish look. 'I wish now I'd listened to Luc.'

'Luc?' Tory repeated more sharply. 'What did he say?'

'I...' Caro hesitated, not wanting to commit another *faux pas*. 'Just that he didn't think you'd be interested in Charlie, that you had someone else.'

'When did he say this?'

'This morning when I phoned him on his mobile and started blubbering my suspicions.'

Tory's eyes darkened. She was beginning to form some suspicions of her own. What Luc and she had done last night, she'd put down to sexual urges and momentary impulses. She hadn't considered it a premeditated act on his part.

But what if it was? What if he'd slept with her entirely to discredit her in Charlie's eyes?

'He offered to tell Charlie as much—' Caro seemed to confirm the idea '—although he was convinced that I had the wrong end of the stick, which, of course, it appears I had... I really do feel a Class A Idiot.'

'That makes two of us.' Tory spoke her thoughts aloud.

'Two?' Caro raised a brow.

But Tory shook her head. Caro was never going to believe what a rat Lucas Ryecart had been to her.

'I've been making an idiot of myself all day,' Tory confided instead.

Caro was suitably distracted. 'The magazine, of course! How did it go?'

'You do not want to know.' Tory rolled her eyes, conveying disaster, and the two exchanged smiles.

It was a spontaneous reaction but the smiles soon faded. In other circumstances they could have been friends, but neither wished to risk it, Caro because her husband's ex-fiancée was prettier, smarter and a whole lot nicer than anyone in the family had led her to believe, and Tory, because Caro was too much like family to Lucas Ryecart.

So they finished their drinks, shook hands and parted company in the lobby.

Tory then went to the desk and, asking if there were any messages, collected several slips of paper.

There were four, three from Charlie, the last asking her to call him on his mobile. The message would have been easy to ignore but seemed safer to answer, and sooner rather than later.

Back in her bedroom, she dialled the mobile number given, and, when Charlie said his name, didn't give him much chance to say anything else. Spurred on by the sounds of children playing in the background, she told him straight. She didn't know why he'd been calling her, didn't want to know why unless it was to apologise for last night's rudeness, didn't want him to call again. If he did keep calling, then she would have to inform her rugby-playing boyfriend who would happily reconvey her message in person.

Charlie just managed to bluster out the words, 'Are you threatening me?' before Tory replied with a resounding, 'Yes,' and replaced the receiver with a decisive click.

Till that point she hadn't known she had such a ruthless streak. She rather liked it. In fact, it had felt positively liberating to say exactly what one thought.

She looked at the other message in her hand. She'd read it before her call to Charlie. It was brief enough:

'CALL ME. IT'S IMPORTANT. LUCAS.'

In fact, it couldn't be briefer. No one would have known they were lovers. Correction, *had* been lovers. Once. And that was one time too many.

Tory reached for the phone again and dialled an outside line, but that was as far as she got. Having vented her spleen on Charlie, she'd wasted precious reserves of anger and Lucas was nowhere near as easy to handle.

She returned the mouthpiece to its cradle. Silence was surely the best show of contempt. She limited herself to tearing the message into a hundred tiny pieces.

Tory realised, of course, that she couldn't avoid Luc for ever, not if he wanted to talk to her, but she gave it her best shot.

When her mobile rang the next day, displaying a number she didn't know, she switched it off rather than answer it, and when Lucas called the magazine's number directly, she was 'in conference' in the morning and 'out of the building' in the afternoon, lies happily relayed by the switchboard operator, Liz. The said Liz was a self-professed hater of men—having been recently dumped by one herself—and didn't need much persuasion to come up with varied excuses why Tory was perpetually unavailable.

Tory did, however, take a call from Alex.

He was ostensibly phoning to find out how she was doing, but, after some pretty token interest, launched into his own news. It seemed that Rita, his wife, had finally agreed to his coming up to Scotland to visit the children. Alex hoped to go that weekend, depending on whether he found a flat in the interim.

Tory saw where he was going and didn't wait for him to get there. Yes, he could stay another week. But only on condition that he did go to Scotland.

Alex assured her he would. In fact, he confided his intention to try and win back his wife's affections. Tory made encouraging noises although personally she felt he had more chance of winning the London marathon on crutches.

Then, almost as an afterthought, he said, 'By the way, you

have to phone Ryecart. There's been some new developments you should know about. I offered to pass on a message but he doesn't seem to trust me.'

'Snap.' He didn't trust Tory either.

Alex laughed briefly before advising, 'I'd do it soon,' and signing off with a, 'Good luck for the weekend.'

Tory was left wondering about the nature of these so-called new developments. Was it on the work front or the Wainwright business? If she could be sure it was the latter, then she'd ignore the royal command. But what if it were work—what if she were about to be exposed at *Toi* for the impostor she undoubtedly was?

She was still deliberating the matter at the end of the day and left the offices without calling him. She didn't feel ready to talk to Lucas, whatever the reason She went back to the hotel for another night and ordered room service.

She'd just finished her meal when the reception desk put through a call from an Alex Simpson.

'Alex, what now?' she asked with an impatient edge to her voice.

'Is that the way you normally talk to your boss?' a voice drawled back.

'You!' She almost spat the word down the line.

'Yes, me,' Lucas agreed and pre-empted her next move with, 'Don't hang up! Otherwise I'll keep calling all night.'

'I could ask Reception to block your calls,' she countered.

'My calls—or Alex's?' he threw back.

'I...' Tory asked herself why she was even having this conversation. 'Calls from anyone with an American accent,' she added at length.

'I can do British,' he replied and proceeded to prove the point with, 'I say, old bean, could I speak to Miss Lloyd, room two three five?'

'They'll know you're a fraud,' she retaliated. 'No one says ''old bean'' these days.'

'Old chap?' he supplanted.

Tory breathed heavily in response and, resigned, asked, 'What do you want?'

'Well, why don't we start with an apology?'

'An apology!'

'From me to you.'

'Oh.'

Tory waited.

'I shouldn't have sounded off about you and Charlie the other night.'

Tory waited another moment before saying, 'Is that it?'

'Pretty much,' he confirmed.

Tory's silence conveyed the fact that she was unimpressed.

'Unless you want it written in blood,' he suggested in a far from repentant tone.

'That would be a start,' she muttered back.

'Look,' he conceded, 'I'd apologise for the rest, only it would be hypocrisy. I'm *not* sorry we made love. In fact, I'd like to do it again, maybe a bit slower next time.'

Tory was glad he was at the other end of a phone line, although she should be used to his directness by now. His casual attitude to sex was no surprise, either, but it hurt all the same.

'And take pictures for Charlie, perhaps?' she finally ground back.

'What?'

'That's the idea, isn't it? To discredit me?'

'What?' he echoed with total incredulity. 'You think I slept with you so I could boast of the fact to Charlie?'

Did she think that? Tory wasn't sure any more. But she wasn't about to backtrack.

'I haven't said one word to Charlie,' he resumed through gritted teeth. 'It isn't me he's been calling.'

Tory didn't have to go looking for the accusing note in his voice.

'That's hardly my fault,' she retorted, 'and, for your information, I have told Charlie exactly how things stand. Check if you don't believe me. I have also reassured Caro that I have no designs on her husband.'

'You called Caro?'

'Correction, she called on me. Here at the hotel.'

'I told her not to do that.' He sighed heavily. 'What did you say to her?'

'Why don't you ask her?' suggested Tory.

'I will,' he countered.

He clearly didn't trust her. He still saw her as home-wrecker material. Forget the fact she was good enough for *him* to sleep with. Or perhaps bad enough was nearer the mark?

'So, if that's all—' Tory assumed they had no more to say to each other.

'I have a full diary the rest of the week,' he continued regardless, 'but we should meet up on Friday.'

'You and Caro?'

'No, you and I.'

Tory considered the prospect, before reminding them both, 'I'm off to the Derbyshire Dales doing outdoor activities.'

'I know,' he claimed.

It left Tory a little mystified. If he knew, then why…?

'How's it going at *Toi*, by the way?' he added, distracting her.

She'd thought he'd never ask. 'Easier than expected and more interesting.'

'Not considering defection, are we?'

'I wasn't, but now you mention it…'

He laughed. 'Are you sure—all those bitchy women?'

'You imagine they're any worse than Simon and Alex?' she countered without thinking.

The trouble was she kept forgetting Lucas Ryecart had two personae—careless, skirt-chasing ex-journalist and serious media boss who happened to own Eastwich.

'I didn't mean that,' she added quickly.

'Yes, you did,' he drawled back, 'but I'll forget you said it. I'll form my own opinion of those two in time, anyway.'

Tory assumed he already had.

'Meanwhile,' he continued, 'I thought you should know that I won't be broadcasting what happened between us the other night, in case that's of concern to you.'

It was, of course. Tory didn't want a reputation for sleeping with her boss, a reputation which might follow her round the industry.

'Thank you,' she said simply.

'Our business,' he replied with a quiet sincerity.

It was another trait of the man. As direct as he could be, he was also discreet.

'Quite,' she murmured back.

Both fell silent for a moment, aware of a rare accord. Tory half expected him to follow it up with another request for a date. She was debating her answer when he spoke again.

'In fact, next time we meet,' he suggested, 'let's pretend we don't know each other.'

'I...' Taken aback, Tory took moments to recover before she bristled with offence. 'Good idea!'

'Believe me, it will be,' he replied, tone cryptic.

It was as if he were up to something. But what?

Tory didn't get the chance to probe further as he signed off with the words, 'I'll be thinking about you till then.'

Tory was left holding a dead line. She stared at it, confused by the mixed messages he was sending. He wanted to forget about her *and* think about her. It didn't make sense.

Or maybe it did. She, too, wanted to forget what had happened between them. She didn't want to lie in bed, night after night, reliving his kiss, his touch, their coming together. But she did.

It was like having a film running continuously in her head. Each time she saw it, remarkably it seemed more real, more beautiful. Each time it left her shot with physical longing.

She felt like a voyeur, not recognising herself in the girl who twined her body with Lucas's and licked the sweat of his skin and spread her legs wide and drew him into her and moaned in pleasure as he penetrated her.

She wanted to destroy the film yet she kept viewing it. She tried to edit it, to have the girl reluctant, to make the man weak, inept, but she couldn't sublimate the truth, couldn't wipe out the image of Lucas as lover, strong and powerful, encountering no resistance as she accommodated his flesh and moved for him and rose to him and welcomed each thrust of pleasure until he finally took her, groaning her name as he staked his claim.

No one had ever possessed her like that. And somehow she knew no one else ever would. She didn't call it love. She *wouldn't* call it love. But whatever it was, it still frightened her witless.

Forget they'd ever met? If only she could.

CHAPTER NINE

'HE MUST be joking!' cried Amanda Villiers as they drew up beside a dirt track where the group from *Vitalis* was already waiting.

The co-ordinator from the outdoor activity centre had just announced that they were to walk the rest of the way, carrying their luggage.

Tory wasn't the only one hiding a smile as Amanda's designer suitcases were unloaded from the boot. They had been told to travel light—no more than a rucksack of essentials—but Amanda had chosen to disregard this instruction.

'How far is it?' someone asked.

'Not far.' The driver smiled briefly. 'Two miles, maybe.'

'Two miles!' shrieked Amanda with unfeigned horror. 'I can't carry these two miles.'

'No,' the co-ordinator agreed, but didn't offer any other comment.

Instead he began to explain that they were to proceed in pairs with an assigned member of the other group, leaving at three-minute intervals.

So Amanda directed at Tory, 'You'll have to take one of these.'

If she'd begged or even asked politely, Tory might have given it some consideration, but Amanda had been particularly bloody to her over the last two days and, now they'd left the offices of *Toi* behind, she no longer felt any need to go along with her.

'No, I won't,' she answered simply. 'You shouldn't have packed so much.'

'What?' Amanda obviously couldn't believe her ears.

'Didn't you read the booklet?' Tory ran on, positively enjoying her rebellion.

Amanda visibly fumed but to no avail. Tory's name was called out and she departed without a backward glance, accompanied by her 'twin' from the other team.

He introduced himself as Richard Lake, the features editor for *Vitalis*. It was the same role Tory was pretending to fill for *Toi*, and as they fell in step he wasted no time in quizzing her on her experience. When she revealed she'd worked at *Toi* just one short week, he initially looked cheered by the fact, then more pensive.

'Someone must rate you,' was his eventual comment. 'At *Vitalis* we've been told to limp on with the staff we have until M day.'

'M day?'

'Merger day.'

'You've been told, then,' Tory said somewhat foolishly.

It drew a sharp glance. 'Not for definite, no, but you obviously have.'

'I...' Tory tried to backtrack. 'Not really. Just speculation, that's all.'

He looked unconvinced and, with a resentful tightening of the lips, forged ahead of her.

Tory sensed the weekend was going to be somewhat tense if everyone shared the same paranoia. She supposed it would make for a better documentary although she was already having ethical reservations about spying on these people.

Not that it was being done surreptitiously. In the literature on the weekend, it had stated in the small print that much of the trip would be videoed and, when they'd disembarked from the minibus, there had been one of the centre workers, dressed in one of their distinctive green uniforms, wielding a camera in the background.

Tory was willing to guess it had been trained on a querulous Amanda but it was debatable whether Amanda had noticed it. Surely she wouldn't have behaved so pettishly if she had?

Tory wondered how Amanda was surviving the walk. It wasn't particularly rough terrain but, to someone unused to exercise, it could prove arduous.

Richard, Tory's own companion, had started off at a cracking pace but, after the first mile, showed definite signs of flagging. Tory, on the other hand, was more prepared through weekly aerobics classes, squash-playing and windsurfing.

'Let's stop for a moment,' Richard suggested as they came to a wooden stile.

'Why not?' Tory wasn't tired but she could see he was suffering. 'New boots?'

He glanced up from loosening his laces and decided she was being sympathetic rather than gloating as he admitted, 'Brand spanking new. Had to buy them because I had nothing else… Do you go walking?'

He regarded her scuffed boots with some envy.

'I spent a holiday, two summers ago, tramping round the Lake District with a friend.'

'Strictly a city man myself.' He made to take one boot off.

'I wouldn't unless you have plasters,' advised Tory. 'You may struggle to get it back on.'

'I suppose you're right,' he conceded. 'Best get going. Perhaps you'd set the pace.'

'Sure.' Tory climbed over the stile and started trudging up the next field, keeping a wary eye on some rather loudly mooing cattle.

She was relieved for a limping Richard when they reached the centre. A collection of old stone buildings, it was positioned on top of a hill. In its driveway were the two minibuses which had brought the groups from London.

There was a reception committee of uniformed staff waiting for them at the entrance. Tory didn't expect to recognise anyone and just stopped her jaw from dropping when she did.

Fortunately she was too shocked to speak and possibly betray them both.

Lucas Ryecart was totally composed, of course, but then *he* obviously expected to see *her*.

'I'm Luc.' He introduced himself in the same fashion as the others had. 'I'll be acting as an observer this weekend.'

'Pleased to meet you,' Richard murmured in polite return.

Tory didn't manage any greeting but her heart was beating so loudly she imagined the whole world could hear it. As well as shock, she'd felt a rush of pleasure at seeing him again. It seemed she wasn't cured at all.

A smile played on Lucas's mouth as he added, 'We'll speak later.'

He directed the comment to both of them, but his eyes dwelled on Tory, passing a silent message on.

Then a woman from the centre claimed their attention, leading them to their sleeping quarters. Tory followed on automatic pilot, nodding at the whereabouts of washing facilities and dining areas as they passed by on their way to the dormitories.

Assigned a bottom bunk in a room for six, Tory slumped down on it the moment the woman departed with Richard. She made no move to unpack her gear but sat hugging her knees and trying to come to terms with Lucas's sudden materialisation.

All week she'd worked hard to get him out of her head while every night he'd chased through her dreams and fantasies. Now here he was, large as life and irrepressible as ever.

It made sense now, of course, that last telephone conversation they'd shared. They were to pretend they didn't know each other next time they met. Next time being this time. He'd been preparing her.

But why? Why not tell her straight he'd be here, masquerading as one of the staff? Weren't they meant to be on the same side, working for the same aim?

The answer seemed obvious and any pleasure at seeing him again went sour. He didn't trust her. Not even on a professional level. He'd given her his pet project and then had second thoughts about her capabilities. She felt both hurt and angry.

Her face must have reflected this as another arrival was shown into the dormitory and asked, 'Are you all right?'

'Yes, fine,' Tory lied and began finally to unpack her rucksack.

'I'm not,' the woman continued. 'Bloody forced march! I'm Mel, by the way.'

'Tory,' offered Tory.

Mel looked disconcerted. 'Not especially. Why do you want to know?'

It took Tory a moment to realise they were talking at cross purposes. 'No, sorry, you've misunderstood. My name's Tory—short for Victoria.'

'Oh, right.' The other girl laughed at her mistake. 'I thought for a mad moment you were a recruiter for the Conservative Party. Can't abide politics, myself. Or politicians. Greasy bunch, the lot of them.'

Tory thought that a rather sweeping statement but smiled all the same.

'I take it you're with *Toi*,' enquired Mel.

'Yes, Features Editor.' Tory had said this so often she almost believed it herself.

'I'm Advertising Sales for *Vitalis*,' relayed Mel, 'or I was when we left the office.'

'You've been promoted?' Tory queried.

'I wish.' Mel pulled a face. 'No, I just reckon no one can count on being who they were before this weekend.'

'You think it's some kind of test.'

'What else?'

'A bonding exercise prior to *Toi* and *Vitalis* merging.'

The suggestion drew a sceptical look from Mel. 'You believe that?'

Tory shrugged rather than express another opinion. She wasn't there to stir things up.

'No, it's survival of the fittest,' ran on Mel, 'or maybe the sanest after a whole weekend of closed confinement. Still, there might be some compensations. Some pretty *fit* instructors, did you notice?'

'Not really.' Tory had been too busy noticing Lucas.

'Don't tell me—you're engaged, married or blind?' Mel bantered back.

Tory shook her head, joking back, 'Single but choosy.'

'*Very*,' agreed Mel, 'if Mr America didn't do anything for you.'

Tory might have known it. Of all the men at the centre over whom Mel could have drooled, it had to be Lucas that had caught her eye.

'You must have seen him,' she ran on. 'Dark hair. Sexy

mouth. Come-to-bed eyes. And when he spoke, oh, God, I swear I fell in love right then and there!'

Mel was exaggerating, of course. At least Tory assumed she was. But it didn't help Tory, knowing other women were just as susceptible to him.

'Yes, the weekend is definitely looking up,' Mel observed with a wicked smile.

Tory felt a great pang of jealousy. She looked at Mel, tall, blonde and more than passingly pretty, and wondered if she were his type. Probably.

Probably they all were. Every woman silly enough to fall for amused blue eyes and a handsome face.

'You're welcome to him!' she told Mel and nearly believed it herself.

'Girl, you don't know what you're missing. Still, I'm not complaining. The less competition, the better. What are the rest of your team like?'

Tory wasn't sure what Mel was asking—for a rundown of their personalities or their appearance. 'I don't know them that well. I only joined the magazine this week.'

'I see.' Mel gave her an appraising look. 'No point in asking pointers on how you put up with your cow of an editor-in-chief, then?'

'Not really, no.' Tory had no inclination to defend Amanda.

'Because I've heard she's the front runner to be El Supremo,' confided Mel, 'of the new hag mag.'

Hag mag? That was a new one on Tory as she speculated on how Amanda would cope with Mel's outspokenness. Not a relationship that promised much mileage, she thought.

'You could try laughing at her jokes,' suggested Tory, 'while practising the words, ''Yes, Amanda, no, Amanda, three bags full, Amanda''.'

'God, that bad?' Mel rolled her eyes. 'How do you put up with it.'

Tory shrugged, suggesting indifference. She could hardly explain how temporary her role in *Toi* was.

Mel continued to gaze at her curiously and Tory worried a little if here was someone smart enough to blow her cover.

Further conversation, however, was curtailed by the arrival of more course members. They came limping in at intervals, and talk revolved around sore feet, uncomfortable beds and pointless exercises. Tory hoped the bunk left unoccupied longest was for someone other than Amanda, but that hope was dashed when she eventually made an entrance, complaining bitterly at the ruination of her new designer boots and jeans. She made no mention of the scruffy old backpack she was carrying but it wasn't hard to work out that it was on loan from the centre, a condensed replacement for all the suitcases she'd packed.

Fortunately she moaned to Sam Hollier, Tory's erstwhile assistant, and contented herself with shooting Tory venomous looks until the dinner bell was rung.

The meal of pasta and salad was well cooked and put people in better spirits. It was still very much a case of them and us, however, with the staff from *Toi* seated round one bench table and *Vitalis* grouped round another.

At the end of the room sat the centre staff in their distinctive green sweatshirts. Tory risked a quick glance in their direction and saw Lucas engaged in conversation with an athletic-looking girl in her mid-twenties. Tory's mouth thinned. Trust him to home in on the prettiest member of staff.

She tore her eyes away and dragged her mind back to the task in hand. She wasn't here to monitor Lucas Ryecart's charm rating but to concentrate on the documentary-making potential of their situation.

There was certainly a general air of dissension about the weekend, some already refusing to go caving or climbing if either activity was suggested. All considered the course to be pointless.

Tory had doubts, too. She could see the theory behind it. If the magazines did merge, the staff from each would have to be integrated so meeting on neutral ground might help reduce suspicion and rivalry. Currently, however, it was serving to increase paranoia.

After the meal, they were all shepherded into a communal room for what Tom Mackintosh, the head of the centre, described as fun and games. Reactions were mixed. Participants either looked tense, regarding it as the start of 'testing', or feigned indifference.

For their first task, they were forbidden to talk before being given a piece of paper with a number, from one to twelve, on it, and blindfolded. They then had to arrange themselves in a line in ascending order from the platform to the back of the hall.

It sounded simple but wasn't. The only way of conveying a number was to tap it out on people's hands and, though one could quickly find a neighbouring number, it was some time before they devised a method of stamping feet to establish a way of ordering the line. By that time the fun element had kicked in and there was much stifled laughter as they tried to adhere to the silence rule while grasping hands and swapping about and half tripping over each other.

It took longer than they would have imagined but there was a definite sense of triumph when they finally established with hand-squeezing codes that they were in line.

It certainly broke the ice and they followed this exercise by giving, in turn, a brief account of themselves.

The majority talked of themselves in terms of work but a few concentrated on their life outside. Tory decided to avoid spinning any tales she couldn't support and gave out true personal details like her age, single status and interests.

Afterwards they were divided into three groups of four and sent to corners of the room to tackle their next assignment, involving a sedentary treasure hunt of cryptic clues and intricate Ordnance Survey maps. It demanded lateral thinking as well as map-reading, but the real object was to get them to co-operate as a team in order to solve the mystery first. As an added incentive, the prize was a chilled bottle of champagne in an otherwise alcohol-free zone.

Tory was in the same group as Richard, her opposite number on *Vitalis*. He'd mellowed since their earlier walk together and she discovered he was both smart and witty. She was smiling at his jokes even before she became aware of Lucas observing them from a discreet distance. After that she smiled that little bit harder while stopping just short of giving Richard any wrong ideas. Their table didn't win but came a close second and gave each other consolation hugs.

Tory was tidying maps, guard down, when Lucas finally approached. 'I'll show you where they go.'

Tory could hardly refuse the offer and fell in step with him as they walked to a store cupboard at the far end.

'Are you trying to make me jealous, by any chance?' he murmured when they were out of earshot.

Guilty as charged, Tory nevertheless snapped, 'Of course not!'

'Well, you're managing it anyway,' he drawled back.

Tory risked a glance in his direction. He didn't look in the least bit jealous. He looked what he always looked. Too laid-back and handsome for *her* own good.

She was thinking of a suitable put-down when Mel, the sales executive from *Vitalis*, appeared behind them. Tory could guess why.

'Let me take those.' Lucas emptied Tory's hands of the maps, before observing, 'You've dropped something.'

'No, I haven't,' Tory was quick to deny and slower to catch on as he indicated a folded piece of paper on the floor.

'Well, someone has.' Mel bent to pick it up. 'A note, I'd say.'

The penny finally dropped as Tory snatched it from Mel's hand. 'It is mine, actually.'

'Okay, okay.' Mel held her hands up in mock defence. 'I wasn't going to read it. I can guess who it's from, though.'

Tory looked alarmed.

Lucas, however, kept his cool and lifted an enquiring brow. 'You can?'

'Well, I could be wrong—' Mel directed a hugely flirtatious smile at him '—but I'd lay money on it being our Features Editor, Richard. She's definitely caught his eye, haven't you, Tory?'

Under normal circumstances Tory would have objected. She didn't like her name being falsely linked with men. But she left it, relieved that Mel hadn't guessed the true source of the note.

He was still smiling, relaxed as ever, and when Mel began to engage him in conversation Tory took the chance to walk away.

She didn't open the note immediately. She suspected its contents would make her mad and she wanted to be alone when she read it. She didn't get that chance for a while as Tom Mackintosh, the head of the centre, rounded up the day with a little pep talk about the rationale behind the centre's courses before they were served a variety of night-time drinks back in the canteen. This time seating was less polarised with the winners of the champagne remaining vociferously bonded.

It was late when they all trooped off to dormitories. The washing facilities were limited and they took turns. Tory volunteered to go last and was locked in a shower cubicle when she finally unfolded his missive.

She expected it to offer an explanation for his appearance but it was frustratingly brief: 'TRY TO SLIP AWAY. NEED TO TALK. ROOM 12. L.'

While she showered, she debated her next actions. She had only a vague idea where Room Twelve might be—the male and female dormitories were on two different sides of a rectangle with staff rooms on the short side connecting the two. What if she crept along to the end, only to be witnessed going into his room?

She could hear Lucas's voice in her head, saying, So what? And, of course, he was right. According to her research, assignations were not uncommon on these management bonding weekends. Why should anyone conclude their meeting was anything other than this?

She could go now or she could wait till everyone slept and go later. She weighed the options up and decided on now, while she had the alibi of showering to account for her absence from her dormitory.

She quickly towelled herself dry, put on a pair of passion-killing winceyette pyjamas and stuffed her clothes and toilet bag in a cupboard to be retrieved later.

She padded down the corridor, ready with an excuse about looking for a drink if necessary. She discovered Room Twelve to be on the corner. She presumed he'd be expecting her and slipped inside, unannounced.

He was there, but not quite expecting her as he turned to face her, naked but for a towel tied loosely round the waist. From his wet hair it was evident he'd just come out of a shower.

She'd never seen him undressed before. Her eyes went from broad shoulders to a chest matted with dark hair tapering to towel level, and, beyond that, lean, muscular legs. She wasn't conscious of staring until he lifted a mocking brow, seeking her approval.

She should have ducked out of the room at that point. She wanted to. But behaving like an outraged virgin seemed pathetic under the circumstances.

So she stood her ground and, in chilly tones, said, 'You wanted to talk.'

Always perceptive, Lucas observed, 'You're mad with me, right?'

Hopping. But Tory opted for disdain. 'Mad? Why should I be mad? If you want to waste your time, checking up on me, not to mention putting the whole project in jeopardy, that's your business.'

'Mmm, I was afraid you'd see it that way.'

'There's another way?'

He grimaced at her sarcasm before explaining, 'Wiseman Global intended sending an observer to evaluate the course but their man dropped out at the eleventh hour. Chuck asked if I'd go instead. Nothing to do with Eastwich Productions. I apologise, however, if you feel undermined,' he added, almost verging on contrite.

Tory wondered if he really expected her to swallow such rot.

'If that's the case, why didn't you tell me on Wednesday when you phoned? You knew then, didn't you? Hence the "let's pretend we don't know each other" speech,' she recalled, lips twisting.

'Yes, well, I suppose I could have said something,' he conceded. 'To be honest, I was afraid you might not show.'

He gave her a long, steady, sincere look that had Tory questioning if she had the word 'gullible' tattooed on her forehead.

'And Mr Wiseman had no one else he could send?' she retorted smartly.

He hesitated, debating his answer. 'All right, you've got me. I throw in the towel.'

Not literally, Tory hoped, glancing involuntarily to his makeshift loincloth.

He read her mind and grinned slightly before continuing, 'Bad choice of phrase… Still, I admit it. Chuck has a band of yes-men only too happy to go fish for him. I volunteered solely so I could see you again, but, trust me, it had nothing to do with your work at Eastwich,' he ended on an intent note.

He had no need to say more. Tory raised her eyes to his and his gaze said it all. Her face suffused with warmth.

Lucas did nothing to hide his feelings. He'd had her and wanted her again. He wanted her enough to put up with a weekend of hard bunks and tepid showers.

He started to close the gap between them and Tory backed against the door.

'I've got to go,' she garbled out, alarmed by the racing of her own heart. 'They'll be wondering where I am.'

'I expect so,' he agreed with a slight smile.

He made no move to stop her, no move at all, but continued to look at her as if looking were enough.

Tory knew that her own feelings were the real danger. She had to get out of here. She felt the door handle pressing at her back. She just had to reach behind her and turn it.

But it seemed her limbs were paralysed. Even when he raised a hand to cup her cheek, she stood stock-still. Even when the hand shifted to caress her neck, she did nothing. The truth was she wanted this, needed it.

He drew her to him and she went. He began to lower his head to hers and she waited. He covered her mouth with his and finally freed her from passivity.

Still she didn't fight him but, moaning, parted her lips to

accept his kiss, to kiss him back, to taste him as he tasted her, exploring each other's mouths while hands explored each other's bodies.

This time both were stone-cold sober and the heat between them was spontaneous. Her hands slid over his bare back already slick with sweat, twined round the nape of his neck, buried into thick, wet hair while he pulled at her clothes, tugging free buttons to slip inside her pyjama top, seeking the swollen weight of her breasts. A thumb began to stroke and rub her nipple into throbbing life. She groaned aloud. He tore his mouth from hers. She fell back against the door. He pushed her top upwards, and bent to lick and suck on one pink bud of flesh until it ached. She grasped handfuls of his hair, forcing his head away, but only to offer her other peaked nipple to feed his hunger and hers.

When he started to push down the waistband of her pyjama trousers, she let him. She reached for him, too. He was already naked, the towel dislodged. She touched the hard pulse of his manhood and he exhaled deeply. She stroked along the thick shaft and drew pleasure from him as he groaned aloud. He let her touch him until his control began to slip, then he curved his hands under her hips and began to lift her upwards.

It took Tory a second or two to realise he meant to enter her, there, against the door. It took her another to accept that she wanted it, too, wanted him inside her. She put her arms round his shoulders and braced herself for that first loving thrust of sex.

It didn't happen. Wrapped round him, wrapped up in him, Tory had ceased to be aware of the outside world when a loud, ear-splitting ringing suddenly rent the air.

Dazed and uncomprehending in the first instant, she opened wide, alarmed eyes to Luc.

He was already up to speed, swearing aloud, 'Jesus, a fire drill!' as reality rudely interrupted their lovemaking.

Then everything happened in hurried reverse as Luc set her back on her feet and helped her to pull her pyjamas back on while footsteps ran up and down the corridors outside and doors, including their own, were rapped and a voice shouted with some urgency, 'Everybody out! This is not a drill! Everybody out!'

It was hard not to panic but it helped that Luc didn't. He had her dressed, with a warm jumper pulled over her head and a hurried instruction of, 'Go straight out!' in moments before he kissed her hard on the lips and pushed her out of the door.

It closed behind her. She knew she should be following the fleeing mass round her and understood that Luc would be out in the matter of seconds it took him to dress. But she just stood there, waiting for him.

It was one of the centre workers who took her arm and shouted above the uproar, 'For God's sake, get moving!'

He didn't give her any choice as he forcibly dragged her along the corridor to the fire exit at the end. He led her away from the house to join the others already marshalling on the driveway outside. She stood aloof from the group, watching the exit doors, and, when Luc failed to appear, she started walking back towards the building. Someone detained her, a hand grasping her arm. She tried to wrestle free but gave up as a familiar figure finally emerged from the fire exit.

Now dressed in jeans and sweatshirt, he strolled calmly from the building.

In that first instant of relief, Tory wanted to run and throw her arms about him. Fortunately relief was closely followed by sanity as she realised they were surrounded by witnesses. God alone knew if someone had already spotted her emerging from his room.

She turned round instead and walked away, suddenly unable to face him. She knew it was absurd. Five minutes earlier and they'd been about to have sex. She wouldn't call it making love. She couldn't. That took two. But here she now was, acting like a love-struck teenager.

She sought safety in numbers and clung to the crowd as heads were counted and explanations sought and finally given some time later by Tom Mackintosh. It seemed somebody had sneaked back to the day room to have a cigarette and, on finishing, had dropped the butt into a metal bin where it had ignited some waste paper. There had been no real danger, the fire contained within the bin, but enough smoke had been produced to trigger the alarms.

This information was greeted less than enthusiastically by the crowd, most standing shivering in night-wear, and accusing eyes scrutinised faces in the hope of identifying the guilty party.

Tory kept her eyes fixed to ground rather than risk catching Luc's eyes and was taken aback when Amanda Villiers declared, 'Well, far be it from me to go around accusing people, but you were absent for some time, Victoria, darling, weren't you?'

The 'darling' was as poisonous as Amanda's tone and Tory assumed no one would give her any credence but a glance round the others' faces told her otherwise.

At least Tory had the wit to say, 'I don't smoke.'

'So you say.' Amanda clearly didn't take her word as proof.

Tory was formulating another protest when she caught Luc's eye over Amanda's shoulder.

He raised a brow and Tory understood immediately. If she wanted, he would wade in and tell the group she'd been otherwise occupied.

She shook her head in horror. Bad enough that he'd discovered she was a sex maniac. She didn't want the rest of the world knowing it.

She was considering another line of defence when Mel spoke up, 'I saw Tory coming out of the shower room when the alarm went.'

'Mmm.' A sceptical sound from Amanda but she could hardly continue arguing and no one wanted to pursue it anyway when the all clear was given, allowing them to troop back inside.

Tory fell in step with Mel and, when she got the chance, mouthed the word, 'Thanks.'

'No problem.' Mel grinned back at her. 'I did actually see you coming out of a room, just not that one.'

She nodded towards Lucas, a few steps ahead of them.

Tory's face fell and she felt only a little better when Mel promised, 'Fast work—but don't worry, my lips are sealed.'

Of course it had been too much to hope that she hadn't been spotted, emerging from Luc's room. She supposed she should be grateful that Mel thought it a case of casual sex rather than conspiracy which had led Tory to his door.

Later, lying sleepless in her bunk, she wondered if subconsciously it *had* been her real reason to go calling on him. Yes, she'd wanted to know what he was up to. And true, she had been incensed at the idea he was checking on her. But it hadn't taken much for her to suspend hostilities and re-enact their last encounter. And if the fire bell had saved her from going the whole way, she'd surely been willing.

She cringed now when she considered *how* willing. It was as if she'd turned into a different person. With other men, she'd been in control, choosing where and when and how they made love. With Lucas, no thinking or planning went into it. It seemed he just had to touch her and she wanted him. She didn't need words or tender gestures from him. She didn't care how he took her, as long as he did. Passion overwhelmed everything else.

And there was no point in saying she wouldn't let him next time, because she knew she would. No way of her dismissing it as 'just sex', because it wasn't. Ordinary sex, even loving sex with Charlie had never been like that.

It was a need, a hunger, a desperate thing. She still wanted him now. Only pride stopped her slipping out of the dormitory and walking the few yards down to his room.

Pride told her that, for him, she was simply a minor distraction. He was a man who worked hard and consequently played hard. Sex was sport to him, one he happened to be good at, perhaps through practice. Love was something else, quite unconnected.

And she had to give it to him. He never used the word love, never pretended. Right from the beginning, it had been a matter of sex. He hadn't wasted time wining or dining her, impressing her or persuading her. From week one he'd asked her to leave Alex and move in with him. But it had always been clear that sex was the driving force.

So why not go along for the ride? She asked herself that

now as she lay on her bunk, knees drawn up, trying to ignore the ache of longing inside her.

She didn't have to think too hard for the answer. She'd never used the word either. Love. But she'd thought it.

And what if the ache didn't go away? What if it got worse each time they made love? What if it consumed her?

CHAPTER TEN

THINGS were meant to look different in the morning and, yes, when Tory woke to the sound of Amanda grumbling, the previous night took on an air of unreality. She felt tired and irritable rather than frustrated or lovesick as she yawned herself awake and joined the lengthy queue for the centre's temperamental plumbing.

By the time she'd queued for breakfast, she was testy enough to resist any overture.

Not that Luc made any. Tory only knew he was present because, *en route* to her table, she'd briefly caught his eye. He looked as he always did—amused by something, or maybe just life. He certainly showed no signs of regret for his behaviour last night.

Tory looked away quickly and deliberately sat on a bench with her back to him. That was how she planned getting through the rest of the weekend. By ignoring him totally.

That wasn't so easy, of course. He was there ostensibly to observe, and observe he did. Every time she looked round, he seemed to be in view, smiling even when she blanked him.

She was just glad that she was reasonably fit and didn't end up a gasping, sobbing heap in the middle of the centre's assault course like Angela, the sales director from *Toi*. Or be as scared of heights as Sam, and be pressured into abseiling down a cliff-face, only to go catatonic halfway down and have to be rescued by centre staff.

In fact Tory acquitted herself reasonably well in such physical challenges but that hardly endeared her to Amanda who became increasingly vituperative. Tory was careful to react minimally. She wanted no suggestion that she'd encouraged Amanda's frothing at the mouth for the camera.

In fact, Tory was surprised how outspoken most of the

course members were, considering they knew they were being filmed. Even if Tom Mackintosh hadn't announced it at the beginning, the CCTV cameras were easy to spot. But it seemed, after some initial reticence, people just forgot about them.

They were more wary of Lucas himself, watching from the sidelines.

'Who do you think the KGB is working for, then?' speculated Jackie, *Vitalis*'s art director, during team games that evening.

'KGB?' was echoed by Mel.

Jackie nodded towards Luc. 'Killingly Gorgeous Bloke.'

It raised some laughter before Mel suggested, 'Ask Tory.'

Curious eyes fixed on Tory and she actually felt herself go red as she muttered back, 'How should I know?'

Mel grinned mischievously but didn't pursue it; perhaps she remembered Tory had helped her out twice that afternoon when they'd been doing daft things in canoes.

'He keeps watching you,' another girl put in. 'I noticed that when we were abseiling.'

'That's what he's here to do,' Tory pointed out.

'No, *you* specifically,' she added.

'Lucky thing,' rejoined Jackie. 'I certainly wouldn't kick him out of bed.'

Neither would Tory. That was the problem.

Listening to other opinions confirmed what Tory already suspected. Lucas was too popular for his own good—or for hers.

She shrugged, a pretence of indifference, and was relieved when they returned to the task, making a mock-up format for a new magazine. As ideas began to flow and rivalries were set aside, it proved an enjoyable exercise and there was much jubilation in the group when their creation was declared the winner.

They were sitting together later, toasting each other with their prize of champagne, when Lucas and some other staff came to sit alongside, offering them congratulations. By studiously staring into her glass, Tory gave him no openings to address her directly. She knew it might seem childish but she was scared of betraying any emotion.

He, of course, was as relaxed as ever. When Jackie specifically asked him if he worked for the centre or Wiseman Global, he stated neither and, without telling any explicit lies, gave the impression that he was an interested outsider, considering running his own management course.

'Well, darling,' Jackie continued in her flamboyant style, 'if you omit the assault course, abseiling and cold showers, and fill it with hunky, available men like yourself, we'll definitely sign up, won't we, girls?'

This was greeted with general laughter and agreement.

Tory remained aloof but a surreptitious glance confirmed that Lucas wasn't in the least bit disconcerted at being centre of attention.

'I'm honoured by the compliment, ladies,' he drawled back, 'though, the truth is, I'm no longer available.'

A mock groan went round the table while Tory's eyes flew involuntarily to his. He caught the surprise in them and slanted her a smile.

'You're married?' Jackie concluded.

He shook his head. 'Not yet.'

'But considering it?' she added.

He made a balancing motion with his right hand, as if marriage might or might not be on the agenda.

'Who is she, then?' asked Mel.

The same question was burning its way through Tory's brain. Not once had he hinted there was someone else in the background, someone he was serious about.

He glanced towards her once more and, catching the daggers look she was sending, answered circumspectly, 'I can't really say at the moment.'

Tory understood. He meant he didn't dare say. It made her even angrier. Did he imagine she had so little dignity she'd fight over him?

Jackie and the others remained intrigued. 'Is she married?'

'Not to my knowledge,' he replied.

'Someone famous?'

'A model?'

'On TV?'

The suggestions came thick and fast and he scotched them with a brief laugh. 'No, nothing like that. She's just a very private person who wouldn't appreciate me telling the world about her. Especially when I haven't worked up courage yet to tell her how I feel.'

This news was greeted with a collective sigh as the rest obviously viewed him as that increasingly rare type of man—a romantic.

Tory was left biting her tongue in preference to making a scene by denouncing him as the faithless cheat she now knew he was.

When someone asked him, 'What's she like, then?' Tory couldn't sit through any more. Scraping back her chair, she muttered to Mel about being tired and, before she could hear anything about Lucas's other girl, she walked away.

She took refuge in her dormitory and was lying on her bunk, trying and failing to concentrate on a novel, when Mel appeared.

'You okay?' Mel asked.

'Fine,' she answered shortly.

'I just wondered—' Mel hesitated before taking the plunge '—you seemed a little upset when Luc was talking about his girl.'

'Upset?' echoed Tory as if she'd never felt such an emotion in her life. 'Why should I be upset?'

'No reason,' Mel pacified, 'except that after last night—'

'Nothing happened last night!' denied Tory, as much to herself as Mel. 'You may have seen me coming out of his room—'

'No *may* about it.'

'But it was not what you think.'

'No?' Mel raised a sceptical brow.

'No!' denied Tory in resounding tones.

'So you won't mind hearing about his other girl, then?' Mel challenged.

Tory wondered why Mel was determined to twist the knife.

'I couldn't care less,' she claimed.

It wasn't true, of course. Half of her wanted to hear, the other half wanted to scream.

Mel continued determinedly, 'Apparently she's a bit younger than him. Quiet but strong-willed and fairly bright. Sporty. Not very glamorous. More your girl-next-door type. Lovely, though, with a really good complexion and large, soulful eyes.'

The description didn't strike any chords with Tory but why should it? He was hardly going to go out of his way to introduce one girlfriend to another.

Not that *she* was a girlfriend. From recollection he'd never even asked her out—asking her to sleep with him wasn't the same.

'Sound like anyone you know?' added Mel at her silence.

'Why should it?' Tory echoed aloud. 'I mean… I've just met the man.'

Mel looked at her in wide-eyed disbelief.

Tory suddenly wondered if she and Luc had been sussed.

But, no, Mel just went on to shake her head and mutter, 'A case of self-induced blindness, if you want my opinion.'

Tory gave her a quizzical look, as Mel grabbed a towel and wash bag to beat the rush to the shower room.

Later, when she should have been asleep, Tory dwelled over the attributes of Lucas's lady love, as relayed via Mel, and became increasingly convinced that he'd been making it all up as he'd gone along. She remembered the half-smile he'd been wearing when he'd begun his 'true confessions'. She knew that smile, had seen it before. It was the smile that said life was a joke.

And that, she suspected, was what he'd been playing on the others—spinning out a yarn about a fictitious girlfriend to keep them at a distance.

Or could it be the opposite? Tory recalled the women's faces at his tale of romantic love, their wistful expressions at this rare breed of man who was not only handsome and sexy, but true and faithful in character. Was Lucas astute enough to realise just how desirable that made him seem? Even as he'd claimed to be unavailable, had he been casting a net to see if he could land another gullible idiot like herself?

Because that was what she was. She could pretend to be experienced, even convince herself that she knew the score, but leave her alone with Lucas for a minute and she was as easy to take in as a schoolgirl.

She had to face it. A few tender looks from him, a passionate kiss or two, and her heart was racing as if it were true love, when it really was just sex. She only realised afterwards, but by then it was too late.

Best thing was to keep away from him altogether and she managed it at breakfast the next morning which was then followed by a briefing on the day's main event, a ten-mile-round hike and treasure hunt for real. But he was waiting his moment, catching her as she went down to collect some supplies from the kitchen.

'Look, Tory—' he brought her to a halt '—about the other night…'

Tory didn't want to listen. 'Someone's coming,' she hissed at him, simply to get free.

They heard footfalls, making her lie the truth, but he didn't react as she'd hoped. Instead he pulled her inside the nearest room, an empty office.

Tory wrested her arm away, complaining, 'You're going to blow my cover.'

'I don't care,' he dismissed. 'Sorting out things between us is more important.'

'Well, *I* care,' she retorted angrily, 'and I'm the one about to go on a ten-mile hike with these people. If anything happens, I want to be able to trust them.'

His eyes narrowed. 'What do you mean—if anything happens?'

Tory wasn't exactly sure. She just had a bad feeling about this particular exercise.

'Nothing,' she discounted at length. 'Look, I have to go. The minibus will be waiting to take us to the start point.'

She reached for the door handle and he put a hand on her arm once more. 'Meet me when you get back, then?'

'There won't be time,' she pointed out. 'After the debriefing, we have to drive back to London.'

'I could take you,' he offered.

Tory shook her head. 'I have to go on the minibus to get feedback.'

She was still taking this project seriously even if he clearly wasn't.

'Okay,' he conceded, 'so I'll follow you down and meet you off the bus.'

He was obviously determined and Tory was tired of arguing. She settled for saying, 'Won't *she* mind?'

'She?'

'The girl you were telling Mel and the others about.'

His blank look changed to a surprised, then amused one. 'Oh, that girl.'

For a man caught out, he showed no signs of guilt.

'Unless of course you made her up,' Tory suggested tartly.

He raised a quizzical brow. 'Why should I have done that?'

'Who knows?' She no longer did.

'Well, no, she's real enough,' he confessed, grinning slightly, 'but there's no reason to be jealous—'

'Jealous?' Tory cut across him, pride surfacing. 'Me? You think I'm jealous?'

'I didn't actually say that.' He raised his hands in a pacifying gesture.

But Tory didn't wish to be pacified. Much safer to be angry, disdainful.

'Why should I be jealous?' she challenged and, before he might actually answer, ran on rashly, 'I have Alex, remember?'

The words were out before she realised quite what she was saying.

Mr Laid-back suddenly turned into Mr Uptight, grating, 'Alex?'

'Yes.' It was too late to backtrack even if she wanted to.

His eyes narrowed to slits. 'So, tell me, do you happen to know where Alex is this weekend?'

Tory frowned at the question. She did know the answer. Alex was in Edinburgh, trying to patch things up with his wife. But why had Lucas asked such a thing?

Unless he knew, too.

'Do you?' she countered.

She watched his face, the changing expressions, and guessed he did. She waited for him to throw it in her face—that her live-in lover was with someone else.

He opened his mouth to speak, then closed it, shaking his head.

Tory understood. On the brink of exposing Alex, he had decided against it. But why?

Perhaps it suited him—that she maintain some kind of relationship with Alex. It would justify him playing the field in turn.

'Forget it.' He finally opened the door, allowing her to leave.

Tory escaped but with a heavy heart. Why had she mentioned Alex? It made all her other earlier denials seem so many lies.

Pride, she supposed. She hadn't wanted him to think her jealous. Forget that she was—achingly, gnawingly, spectacularly—at the idea of him with some other girl.

She felt like a schoolgirl again, in love for the first time. Only she never had been. Not with Charlie or anybody else. She finally understood that. Because love wasn't the warm, pleasant feeling she'd imagined it was.

She caught the drift of her thoughts and brought herself up sharply. She had to stop this. What she felt for Lucas wasn't love either. It couldn't be. She wouldn't let it be. It was desire, pure and simple, or maybe more accurately lust, less pure but just as simple.

So why didn't she let it burn itself out? Good question. Why didn't she just give way to sexual longing and climb into bed with Lucas the very next opportunity and stay there until the fire was out?

She knew the answer. She was scared, that was why. But she resisted analysing her fear.

She didn't get a chance, anyway, as she collected the supplies and headed for the bus to find her team already boarded and waiting.

Her team? Well, not quite hers. Or even a team. Five of them. Should have been six but it seemed Jessica Parnell, the senior editor from *Vitalis*, had woken up that morning and decided life was too short to scramble over hillsides to hold on to a job she had loathed for at least the last two years. Having had this revealing thunderbolt, she had shared it in no uncertain terms with Tom Mackintosh before calling a minicab to take her to the nearest railway station.

Mel shared it second-hand as they were driven to their drop-off point.

Amanda almost purred with satisfaction. Her dismissal of, 'Bloody prima donna,' however, was too much for Carl, their advertising sales director.

Normally an anything-for-a-quiet-life type, he actually commented aloud, 'Takes one to know one.'

'I beg your pardon,' demanded Amanda with an imperious look.

For once Carl wasn't quelled. 'You heard.'

She'd heard but evidently she didn't believe it. Amanda really wasn't used to opposition. It left her fuming with silent indignation.

To Tory, it was probably the most interesting aspect of the weekend. At the office Amanda ruled *Toi* with an iron fist in an iron glove and had expected to do so at the centre, too. But gradually, as various tasks challenged people's perceptions of themselves—or possibly fatigue and irritability set in—fewer and fewer of *Toi*'s staff were prepared to dance to Amanda's discordant tune. Tory was almost sorry she couldn't return to the office to see if this defiance would continue.

Amanda now complained loudly to Lucy, the somewhat sheepish make-up editor from *Vitalis*, going as far as suggesting that some people were in for a rude awakening on Monday morning, while Carl started to sing loudly and Mel grinned, seemingly enjoying the internecine strife.

So, no, they were not a team, which increased Tory's niggling worry as they were dumped in the middle of nowhere with basic supplies, a compass, one map and a series of clues as to what landmarks they had to capture with the digital camera they were issued.

They had practised map-reading, of course, and each team had a so-called expert. Carl was theirs and did seem to know what he was doing, although from their first step in what was hopefully the right direction Amanda tried to undermine him.

Despite this, they managed to follow the right track, finding the 'bridge over troubled water', a tiny footbridge over a fast hill stream, 'Stonehenge' or a mini version of stone slabs and columns, and 'the last resting place' which turned out to be a couple of wooden crosses in what had been the back garden of an old shepherd's hut on a hill. The names Rover and Robbie could faintly be seen, etched out of the wood. Dogs, they assumed.

They rested there for lunch: beans and sausage cooked over a Primus stove. Amanda, needless to say, slated such food but she still ate her share.

They were well over halfway and beginning to feel good about themselves when the rain started. At first it wasn't heavy and they walked on, quickening their pace slightly, but then it began to come straight down, almost in sheets. On open moorland, with nowhere to shelter, they pressed on. No bitching or complaining now. Breath was saved to battle the elements.

Even Amanda kept going, but she was clearly suffering, with chafing boots and tired legs, and when they were walking along the edge of a slight incline she tripped and rolled. She didn't have far to fall. Tory scrambled down after her in seconds. But Amanda's groans sounded genuine enough and she shrieked as Tory touched her leg, trying to find the source of her injuries.

It seemed she'd smashed her knee against rock as she'd tumbled. How serious, it was hard to tell. No one wanted to peel off clothing in this downpour. But their first attempt to support Amanda to her feet and walk warned them it wasn't a simple sprain.

It was Tory who said, 'We'll have to use the CB to call in.'

Carl was reluctant. 'We'll lose if we do that.'

Tory stared at him in disbelief. 'For God's sake, Carl. The game is over. She's really hurt!' she almost shouted the words at him.

He looked resentful but took out the CB handset from his bag. No amount of fiddling with bands and aerials, however, produced anything more than static. Either it was malfunctioning or the storm had broken up the signal.

Various suggestions followed and were rejected. They could sit and wait for rescue but Carl admitted he'd deviated from their suggested route, opting for a shorter but steeper path, and it could be hours until they were located. Hostile glares were sent in Carl's direction but no one commented aloud. They still had to rely on him to get them back.

Another attempt was made to shoulder Amanda's weight between Carl and Tory. With no alternative, Amanda gritted her teeth and tried to bear it, but the occasional sob still escaped from her. It was hard not to jar her leg and their progress was painfully slow.

Tory wasn't sure they should even be moving Amanda and was relieved when they finally came upon potential shelter. 'Over there in the rock.'

It was more an indentation than a cave, with barely space for two, but they carefully lowered Amanda to the ground while they took stock. It was decided that someone should stay with Amanda while the rest walked back to the centre.

Before anyone volunteered, Amanda spoke up. 'Victoria...I'd like Victoria to stay.'

Tory was taken aback. She'd imagined Amanda would prefer just about anyone else.

She glanced down at Amanda and was awarded an almost pleading look.

'Well?' Carl prompted her for a decision.

'Fine,' conceded Tory with good grace and joked weakly, 'as long as we get the rest of the chocolate.'

'You deserve it.' Mel gave her a commiserating smile and dug out a foil space blanket and torch to hand over before the rest of the party moved on.

Tory tried to make Amanda more comfortable, propping her against a makeshift pillow of their rucksacks before draping the blanket over her. They were already very wet and the wind whipped some of the rain into their shelter, but Tory did her best to shield Amanda from it.

They didn't talk much at first but Tory finally gave way to curiosity. 'Why did you want me to stay? I mean, we haven't exactly hit it off.'

Amanda pulled a face, conceding the point, then said by way of explanation, 'That Mel character loathes me and, as for Lucy, she's such a wimp.'

'So I'm it by default,' Tory concluded dryly.

'Perhaps,' admitted Amanda in a similar tone.

Well, it was honest. Tory had to give her that. She was also quite surprised by how well Amanda was behaving in the circumstances. She was clearly in pain yet now she had something real to complain about she was almost stoical.

'How long do you think before we're rescued?' was all she asked.

'Hard to say.' Tory didn't want to hold out any false promises.

'They may struggle to find us,' added Amanda.

That possibility had occurred to Tory but it seemed important to stay upbeat. 'I think Carl pretty much knows our location on the map.'

Amanda nodded, then commented, 'God, Jessica will be laughing her socks off when she hears about this.'

'Jessica?'

'Jessica Parnell—*Vitalis*'s senior editor. She was right. What the hell are we doing, playing girl scouts at our age?'

'You're not that old,' Tory protested automatically.

Of course she should have known the older woman would come back with, 'How old do you imagine I am?'

Thirty-eight was Tory's guess so she took off five years and said, 'Thirty-three.'

'I wish,' responded Amanda, obviously pleased. But not pleased enough to reveal her real age. Instead she said, 'I've been in the business more than twenty years. It really is true about time, you know, it flies.'

There was more than a hint of regret in Amanda's tone, even a suggestion of vulnerability, but Tory wondered if they weren't just products of their current situation.

'One moment you're the hottest thing in town,' continued Amanda, 'the next you're abseiling down a bloody cliff, just to survive…and what do you have to show for it?'

The question might have been rhetorical but Tory couldn't resist answering, 'A wardrobe full of designer clothes, the chicest of sports coupés and probably a garden flat in Hampstead.'

'Notting Hill, actually—' Amanda smiled briefly '—and, yes, I admit there are compensations… Just don't go thinking they're enough.'

It seemed like well-intentioned advice but Tory wasn't used to that from Amanda. 'Why are you telling me all this?'

Amanda caught her suspicious glance and read it astutely, 'You mean when I'm normally acting like the editor from hell?'

'Something like that.' Tory was surprised by the other woman's self-awareness.

'I'm not sure.' Amanda thought about it before coming up with, 'Maybe I see myself in you if I roll back the film fifteen years.'

Tory managed not to look horrified, although she couldn't imagine herself turning out like Amanda under any circumstances.

'In fact, I'm willing to bet we come from similar backgrounds,' Amanda went on. 'Raised by a single mother. High rise flat in inner-city London. State school. And a burning desire for something better.'

Tory could have denied it. It wasn't an exact blueprint of her early life. But it was close enough.

'Is that so wrong?' she said at length.

'Not at all,' Amanda replied, 'but knowing what you *don't* want out of life isn't the same as knowing what you do. And by the time you work it out, it might already be too late.'

'So what do *you* want?' Tory wasn't convinced Amanda was being genuine.

'In the short term, out of this hole,' Amanda said with a grimace. 'In the long term, what all us career girls really secretly desire—man, home, family.'

For a moment Tory didn't react. She was waiting for one of Amanda's biting, sarcastic laughs to follow. But nothing.

Instead she ran on, 'You can deny that, if you want. I certainly did for years, then one day you wake up and smell the roses. Only by that time, they've all gone—the nice young men who would have married you. And the bastards, the ones you really wanted, they've started to settle down, too, but with younger models,' she finished on a note more rueful than bitter.

Tory didn't know what to say. Not in a million years would she have suspected that an unhappy woman, frustrated by childlessness and loneliness, lay under Amanda's usual diamond-hard exterior. She felt an impulse to comfort but didn't think Amanda would accept it—not even in her current state.

Still, she felt the need to give something back, something of herself, as she finally responded, 'It's hard not to envy people sometimes. I had a boyfriend once—a fiancé, actually. It didn't work out and he went on to marry someone else and have kids. I met him again recently and I suppose I felt envy, but it turned out they weren't as happy as they seemed.'

'Most couples aren't happy,' Amanda observed in return. 'Not truly, deeply, deliriously. Not all the time. But maybe it's enough not to be *un*happy.'

Tory wasn't sure she agreed. 'I think being married and having kids for the sake of it would ultimately make a person more unhappy than being on their own.'

'So speaks a twenty-something-year-old,' Amanda opined. 'See how you feel at forty, assuming you're still alone.'

Tory heard the note of self-pity in Amanda's voice and did wonder if it would be any different for her.

Chances were she'd still be alone.

Not that she saw herself pining for Lucas Ryecart for the rest of her life. There would be other men. Perhaps not quite as attractive or smart. Nor as sexually exciting. But would she want another relationship that was both so intense and so basically shallow again?

Yet there was no point wanting it all—husband, children, home, happy-ever-afters. No point in wanting what she couldn't have.

Maybe she was luckier than Amanda, knowing it wasn't possible, knowing it would be crying for the moon.

She didn't feel lucky, however.

Didn't look it either as Amanda remarked, 'Well, now I've depressed the hell out of both of us, can you think of a way of passing another four hours?'

Intended to raise a smile, Tory managed a weak one before suggesting with irony, 'I-spy?'

'Riveting,' Amanda applauded. 'Bags I start.'

It was as good a way as any to pass time. They followed it with a game of name the film, twenty questions and their choice of desert island discs.

As time dragged and the storm failed to let up, they both began to shiver from cold and gradually lost any enthusiasm for anything but waiting.

An hour became two, then three and Amanda fell into an uneasy sleep, jerking with each inadvertent movement of her bad leg. Tory watched over her, growing concerned that they might have to spend a night outdoors. The rain had ceased some time ago but the temperature was still unseasonably low and she wondered how cold did it need to be before hypothermia set in.

She tried distracting herself from that possibility by planning her documentary of the weekend. She would splice between the staff's lectures and worthy intentions, and the reality of how much ''team-building'' and ''attitude-changing'' had been effected. Being lost on the moor would give it more dramatic impact, as proof of the centre's poor safety procedures and too exacting demands, but she would be reluctant to use it as a sign of retribution for Amanda, even if she had bitched her way through the weekend.

It was curious to think that underneath Amanda's tough exterior lay deep insecurities. Tory supposed it was the same for most people—a side they showed the world, and a side they kept secret.

Well, maybe not everyone. Involuntarily her thoughts went to Lucas. He seemed remarkably straightforward in his approach to life. He saw something he wanted, he went after it and made no apologies for the fact.

Tory wished in some ways she could emulate him. Be more ruthless, or at least more honest. After he'd tried—and pretty much succeeded—in seducing her on Friday, she'd cut him dead. Yet the truth was she'd loved it. She'd loved every second of those five desperate minutes with Luc. It had only been afterwards that she'd felt bad, seeing her easy surrender as weakness and resolving to resist the next time.

Now she wondered whether it would be simpler just to give in, to accept they were going to have a relationship and let it run its course. It would be brief. How could it be otherwise? Neither of them could commit. But if they both went into it with their eyes wide open, where was the harm?

Tory was still debating the issue when she heard it. A blessed sound. At first dismissed as imagination. How could she hear a car engine when there wasn't a road for miles? But that was what it was, or more precisely they were: four-by-fours, revving up and down gears as they tackled the terrain for which they were built.

Tory shook Amanda gently awake, then scrambled to her own feet, intending to go in the direction of the sound. Only hours of sheltering in one spot combined with wet clothing resulted in a debilitating cramp that had her collapsing back to the ground in agony.

They heard the engines cut and for an awful moment both women had visions of their rescuers searching in the wrong spot before abandoning them. It was with immense relief that they heard the voices drawing nearer.

Neither could now move but they could cry out, which they proceeded to do until they were hoarse from shouting and the first figure appeared through the clearing beyond them.

It was the abseiling coach from the centre, closely followed by three other men.

Tory had eyes for only one of them and he had eyes for only her as he dropped to his knees beside her. 'Are you all right?'

All right? She was absolutely marvellous. They had come. *He* had come.

'Your leg?' Lucas guessed.

Tory realised she was still massaging it. 'It's just cramp. Almost past. Amanda's hurt, though.'

'The medic's taking care of her.'

Tory glanced towards the little group round Amanda. A man she didn't recognise was already cutting off her trouser leg to examine the knee. Carl, their map-reader, had come, too, and was holding a folded stretcher.

'Can you walk?' Lucas added to her.

'I think so.' She let him put an arm round her shoulders and help her to her feet. Her calf muscle protested but she limped a couple of steps before finding herself being literally swept off her feet.

He told the others he was taking her back, then picked his way carefully over the rough terrain, easing them down a slight slope to where the two vehicles were.

He slid her into the rear bench seat. Her rucksack was on the floor. A pair of clean jeans, T-shirt and sweatshirt lay on the bench seat beside her.

'You'd better take off your wet clothes,' he instructed.

She nodded and shivered but didn't seem to have the energy.

He looked askance at her before saying, 'This isn't some clever plan to get you undressed, you know.'

'I know,' she echoed through shattering teeth. Reaction had set in and she felt cold to the bone.

'I'll get the heater on.' He went round to the driver's side to switch on the engine and heaters, before climbing into the back with her.

'Come on, trust me.' He unzipped her jacket. 'I promise I'll behave like a gentleman.'

Tory didn't need this reassurance. She didn't resist as he

slipped off her jacket, then outer layers of damp garments, before helping her into the dry clothes.

'You stay in the back—' he strapped her in '—and try to rest while I drive you home.'

Tory wasn't sure where he meant by home—the centre, the hotel in London or back to Norwich.

'Can we wait?' she asked as he slipped behind the driver's wheel. 'See if Amanda's all right.'

'Yes, okay,' he agreed with some reluctance. 'I'll just turn.'

It took several minutes to manoeuvre the vehicle to face the way he'd come and by that time the others had appeared, carrying Amanda on the stretcher.

Tory could see her knee had been bandaged and she watched as the men carefully eased her into the bench seat of the other off-roader.

'Where are they going to take her?' she asked Lucas as he waved a hand at the others and pulled away.

'Nearest hospital, I imagine. We can telephone the centre later,' he promised. 'For now, I suggest you hang on.'

Tory did just that as the vehicle bumped over the rough terrain and she was jolted to and fro.

It took them almost half an hour to reach what could be described as a road. Even then it was a minor one. Tory tried and failed to work out if they were going east to Norwich or south to London, but she didn't really care. The warmth of the car was lulling her into a state of drowsiness and she didn't fight it. She rested her head against the window and was asleep by the time they reached main roads.

London was her last waking thought but she was wrong.

When she woke, she was too disorientated to know where she was until Lucas came round to help her down to the street outside her flat in Norwich.

She was glad. She wasn't really injured but felt weak and shivery and home seemed the best place to recover.

He shouldered her rucksack, and, with a hand at her elbow, supported her up the steps to the front door. By chance she'd taken her house keys with her to Derby and he dug them out of one of the side pockets. He tried both keys before identifying the correct one, then used the other on her inner door.

Entering the flat, Tory was relieved to find the lights off, suggesting that Alex had yet to return. She could just about cope with this ncw solicitous Lucas but she suspected the old one was lurking somewhere, ready to emerge if Alex appeared.

As it was, Alex had left enough pointers to his presence. Tory felt tired just surveying the mess of take-away cartons, clothes and books.

'I take it you didn't leave the place like this,' Lucas concluded from her disgruntled expression. 'I'm amazed you put up with it.'

'And you're Mr Clean and Tidy, I suppose,' she snapped rather childishly, resenting the criticism.

'No, but I'm not a slob.' His gaze rested on a pair of male underpants actually lying on the sofa.

Tory wrinkled her nose, wondering if they were dirty or not, and resolved to give Alex his marching orders as soon as possible.

'Well, thanks for the lift,' she said before Lucas could make any further comment.

She imagined he'd be dying to get away to his nice clean room at Abbey Lodge.

He ignored her, however, saying, 'You can't have eaten since lunch. I'll make you something.'

'It's all right—' a surprised Tory turned down the offer '—I just want to rest.'

'You have to eat a little,' he insisted. 'Slip into bed and I'll bring you tea and toast.'

'I doubt there's any bread,' she countered dryly. 'Alex doesn't shop.'

She made the comment without thinking.

It almost begged a sarcastic reply. He didn't disappoint, drawling back, 'I wonder what Alex actually does do... On seconds thoughts, don't tell me.'

It could have been a joke but his eyes said not. They narrowed to a point.

'Please don't...' Tory didn't finish the appeal.

He understood, though, switching back to brisk concern. 'Okay, go rest and I'll forage in the kitchen.'

Tory hesitated. She didn't have the energy to keep arguing with him but neither did she have the energy for another bedroom scene with this man.

'Don't worry, you'll be safe.' He read her with irritating accuracy. 'Sharing another man's bed doesn't appeal to me.'

Tory felt her face go red. It was absurd because she had nothing to feel guilty or embarrassed about.

'Ten minutes—' he gave her a gentle push in the direction of the bedroom door '—and I'll expect you tucked up in bed with your teddy and a long-sleeved nightgown buttoned to the throat.'

This time he *was* joking but Tory picked up the underlying message. She had nothing to worry about.

She switched to asking, 'Could you phone the centre about Amanda?'

'Yeah, sure,' he agreed easily. 'Now go on.'

She went through to her bedroom and, with some relief, saw no sign of Alex in the room. At least he had respected her privacy this far.

She undressed quickly, choosing a nightie that, though short, was suitably unglamorous, and climbed into bed, all the time wondering if she should tell him the truth. That Alex did nothing, was nothing. But would he believe such an admission?

She worried the thought round in her head but came to no conclusion before her eyes became too heavy to keep open and she let it all go.

Lucas put the tray he brought down on a chest of drawers and sat for a while on a wicker chair, watching over her. She seemed much younger in sleep and more vulnerable, but he supposed it was an illusion. She certainly had proved herself one of the toughest on the weekend's course.

He recalled his reaction when her party had returned. He'd been waiting for them, of course—waiting for her. They'd been hours late. He'd already insisted the centre call up a search party when they'd finally trooped in, wet and miserable, one of the women breaking down in sobs.

He'd been furious when he'd heard their story. Having abandoned Tory and Amanda, they had lost their bearings for a while and even wasted half an hour taking shelter themselves before continuing. The girl called Mel had tried to reassure him that Tory was fine but it had made no difference. All he'd been able to think of was Tory, her unruly mop of hair plastered wet against a face pinched with cold and her slight figure, drenched and huddling somewhere out there in the dark. He'd joined the rescue mission in his own off-roader, meeting the centre's opposition with a threat to sue if any harm had come to Tory.

His reaction seemed over-dramatic now. She had been in no real danger. She'd kept her head and waited for rescue—exactly as she should have done. But he hadn't been thinking straight; what had been happening to Tory had somehow got mixed up in his head with the accident in which he'd lost Jessica, his first wife.

Not quite the same. Jessica had died in a car crash. There had been nothing anyone could have done, least of all him. He'd been on the other side of the world. But it had still felt like a rerun—as if he'd been going to next see Tory lying on some cold mortuary slab.

He shook his head, a dismissive gesture. He wasn't a man given to premonitions and if this had been one it was way off base. Nevertheless he recognised the emotion involved—a fear of loss.

Not that he had Tory to lose. Not yet, anyway.

CHAPTER ELEVEN

TORY woke in the night to find Lucas asleep on her wicker bedroom chair. She watched him for a while as he had watched her. It was odd: most people looked relaxed in sleep. Lucas was different—he was tense and restless, as if bad things were happening in his dreams.

She watched until she found she couldn't bear it any longer. She didn't consider her next action as she slid out of the bed and came round to his side. She knew not to waken him too suddenly. She put a gentle hand on the nape of his neck, the other on his hand and exerted the faintest pressure.

She thought he would gradually come awake but he reacted instantly, shuddering at her touch and issuing a brief startled cry.

Tory might have retreated but he caught her hand in a hard, almost convulsive grip. Only when he jerked his head back and opened his eyes to see what had woken him did he ease his hold.

Tory wasn't scared. She saw a range of emotions, dread, relief, shame, flitting across his handsome face before the usual mask slotted back in place.

'Bad dream. Sorry.' He finally managed a lazy smile behind which to hide.

But Tory wasn't fooled. 'You get them often, don't you?'

She didn't know how she knew this. She just did.

He shrugged. 'Not really.'

Tory took that as a yes.

'Things you've seen?'

'Partly.'

It was a brief admission. Tory didn't press him further. If he wanted to tell her more, he would.

'I should be going,' was what he said now.

But he made no move. Perhaps he couldn't. She was standing too close.

And Tory didn't want to take a step back because she'd finally accepted. This man was her fate, for good or ill. She was tired of running from it.

She looked at him with solemn, unswerving eyes. She wanted him to take her, cover her body with the hard heat of his, be gentle, be rough, control her, possess her, but ultimately love her. She longed for it even as she acknowledged that loving this man might destroy her—especially if he couldn't love her back.

Lucas held her gaze and understood. Not totally. But enough to know she'd surrendered herself to an inevitability he'd recognised from the beginning. Him and her. Together.

He took her hand and drew her gently down. He put an arm round her waist. She was soft and warm and yielding. His desire for her was immediate but this time he didn't want to rush things.

He waited for her to make the first move. She did so tentatively, a finger tracing the small scar that puckered the corner of an eyelid. Then, braving rejection, she cupped his face with her hands and put her mouth to his.

It was the lightest of kisses, her dry lips on his. Chaste but somehow sexy, too. He had to stop himself kissing her back.

Tory wasn't discouraged by his lack of response. She understood, too. This time she had to make the running, do the seducing.

It wasn't going to be hard. His hands had already left her waist to curve round her hips and his lower body shifted against her in arousal.

She threaded her fingers into his thick dark hair until she could pull back his head slightly and once more put her mouth to his, only this time she slid the tip of her tongue between his lips, moistening them. She withdrew immediately, however, when he began to kiss her back and nuzzled teasingly at his neck, twining her arms round, softly licking and tasting his skin, biting his earlobe with gentle savagery until she felt him draw several deep, unsteady breaths. Then she slid her mouth back to his and stole his breath and his reason as she kissed him with unfettered passion.

Lucas's resolve to take things slowly broke like glass shattering as he thrust his tongue inside her sweet, moist mouth and she twisted in his arms, small firm breasts against the wall of his chest, nightgown riding up, soft bare bottom against the hardness of his groin.

They explored each other's mouths with desperate thirst while their bodies strained to join, be one. All thought was lost in the heat of desire. His hands were everywhere, sliding up her back, round to her breasts, down to her buttocks, between her thighs. Then, still seated, they shifted until she was kneeling, her legs straddling his as he dragged her nightgown over her head and put his mouth to her breasts and began to suckle on her nipples with a hunger matched by the yearning noises she made.

When he finally entered her, it was with gentle, skilled fingers. She was already damp with desire and her body closed round him in spasm, then opened and shut like a flower as he pleasured her to the point of orgasm.

She moaned when he suddenly stopped and pushed her away slightly. Then she opened her eyes and realised.

Lucas had unzipped himself, taking out flesh that throbbed painfully in long denial. She made to touch him, to offer him the same satisfaction, but he caught her hand. He was ready to come and wanted, needed to be inside her.

Tory wanted it, too, shifting with him as he went to the edge of the seat, uncoiling her legs, tilting her hips until he was able to touch his swollen flesh against the soft, moist lips of hers. Then he lifted her slightly to push inside.

Tory didn't expect it. Not the first exquisite pain from the intrusion of his manhood, nor the pleasure that followed. She was gasping with it as he raised her to meet his thrust, bracing herself against his legs and arching back to accommodate him, crying aloud each time he pierced her to the core until they came together in a blend of agony and ecstasy.

She collapsed against him, naked in his arms, stifling a sob of fright that she could feel like this, riven yet complete, fractured yet whole.

He tried to soothe her with gentle kisses, hugging her to him, whispering, 'I've hurt you. I'm sorry. I didn't mean to.'

She shook her head against his shoulder rather than tell him that pleasure overwhelmed her, that love for him was her undoing.

'Shh. Shh. It's okay.' He half carried her to the bed, then lay down beside her, stroking the unruly hair back from her face, brushing a tear away with the back of his fingers. 'Do you want me to go?'

Tory shook her head again and looked at him with sad, dark eyes, unable to express her true feelings.

She wanted him to love her.

He did. After they'd lain together for a while, still on the bed, then wordlessly begun to touch, he loved her the way he knew so well. This time slowly, infinitely gently, undressing to feel the glide of her soft, curving body against the slick sweat of his, learning each part of the other, tasting fingers, toes, the most intimate places until pleasure was a long drawn sigh that left them too high to talk.

Yes, he loved her—if only with his body.

They slept and woke with the sun to make love again and lie, content, in each other's arms. That was how they were discovered.

By Alex.

They had ten seconds warning at most.

Tory heard the outer door opening, thought it imagination, then heard it shutting.

They both heard the tentative knocking on her bedroom door.

'Tory, are you back?' Alex called softly and, eliciting no response, stuck his head round the door.

They weren't caught in the act, but close enough. Tory had managed to sit up, grab a sheet and clutch it to her front. Lucas merely leaned back against the headboard, naked.

Alex took in the scene, too thunderstruck in the first instant to say a word.

When he eventually did, it was a somewhat anticlimactic, 'R-right.'

Tory frowned darkly. She didn't feel anything was right. Spending the night with Lucas wasn't something she'd intended sharing with Alex.

'Boss.' Alex actually nodded in Lucas's direction, before leaving with a 'Excuse me. I think I'll go make coffee.'

'Curious,' drawled Lucas when Alex finally bowed out the door, barely able to hide a grin. 'He took it amazingly well, wouldn't you say?'

'I…yes.' Tory supposed she should explain and turned to do so.

'Perhaps he's gone off searching for a loaded shotgun. What do you think?' Lucas lifted a brow in her direction.

'I think you know,' Tory countered.

'Know what?'

'That Alex was up in Edinburgh, hoping for a reconciliation with his wife.'

'But if *you* knew—' Lucas cut across his own question and, staring hard at her, answered for himself, 'You couldn't care less, could you? Which probably means one of two things—you and Alex are finished, or you and Alex never started.'

'The latter.' Tory didn't see any point in keeping up the pretence. She'd used Alex merely as protection against ending up in bed with Lucas—pretty ineffective protection as it turned out. 'He was broke and homeless so I took him in until he could find somewhere else.'

'Like a stray dog?' Lucas commented dryly.

'Quite,' Tory agreed, 'only a dog would probably be more house-trained.'

Lucas smiled at the acerbic comment. It wasn't directed at him, after all.

'So has he found somewhere?' Lucas was still not happy at the idea of Alex's proximity, however platonic the relationship.

'No, and I can hardly kick him out now.' She sighed in

exasperation. 'Not if we're going to get any sort of promise out of him to keep quiet.'

'About?'

'You and I. In bed. Together.'

She spelled it out for him although she didn't really think it necessary.

He astounded her by replying almost casually, 'Do we have to keep it quiet?'

'Yes, of course. I can't possibly go on working at Eastwich with everyone knowing that you and I are…' She searched for the right words.

'Are?' he prompted and when she didn't come up with anything, suggested, 'Living together?'

'We're not.'

'We could be.'

Tory stared at him in surprise. He'd asked her before but that was so she'd move out on Alex. Now that was hardly necessary.

'Why not?' he added simply, and, catching her chin with one hand, tried more effective persuasion.

The kiss quickly threatened to get out of control and Tory pulled away, shuffling to the other side of the bed to drag on a T-shirt and jogging bottoms. She didn't need sex clouding the issue.

He followed suit, dressing in his clothes from last night, but all the time talking her round. 'You could come stay with me. I've bought an apartment in town. You could keep this place and sublet it to Alex. You can always get the sanitation department in when he vacates,' he finished on a wry note.

'I don't know.' Tory wasn't averse to the idea. She wanted to be with Lucas. But it seemed a giant step. She'd never lived with a man before, not even her ex-fiancé.

He came round the bed to take her in his arms and, smiling down at her, ran on, 'I have nice clean habits, always replace the top on the toothpaste and put the toilet seat back down.'

It wasn't the most romantic of propositions but it made Tory smile and she nodded, thinking she could later change her mind.

She should have know better, of course. With Lucas things tended to happen yesterday.

'You finish dressing and I'll go speak to Alex,' he announced and padded out to the living room, still in his bare feet.

When she later emerged, feeling a little shy, it was to find the two men chatting over a breakfast of beer and corn chips—all that Alex had bought in—having already settled arrangements.

Tory scarcely believed it and remained much in the same state until four days later when she moved into Lucas's trendy loft apartment sited in a warehouse by the river.

For a while it continued to seem unreal to her, eating and sleeping and rising with Lucas before each going off in their separate cars to Eastwich, careful to maintain distance. That proved easier than she could have hoped, as Alex kept a discreet silence before eventually leaving for a new job with BBC Scotland, and his impressive replacement plus a new Lucas—appointed programmes director made contact unnecessary between her department and senior management. Given an almost free hand, she was increasingly confident about her documentary on the so-called bonding weekend and had followed it up by actually interviewing some of the participants—including Amanda who had chucked in her job to fulfil a long-held ambition to write a novel.

She still worked alongside Simon but he was deeply involved in his own project and, with Alex gone, had turned into a demon workaholic with no time to be curious about Tory's private life any more.

That life was something else. At home, they laughed a lot, Lucas and she, and talked endlessly, greedy to know each other, their thoughts, dreams, fears and failures. She learned what those occasional nightmares were about—sights witnessed, the dead and dying, bombs missed, the bullet that hit, during his time as a correspondent. She reciprocated with tales of her childhood—ordinary everyday horrors of maternal abandonment followed by reconciliation, good times with her mother's boyfriends, bad times with not so nice ones. She wasn't looking for sympathy and neither was he. They were explanations of how they had come to this point, the events that had shaped them before they had met.

He cooked and she ate. They shopped together. He fixed things and she tidied. Someone else cleaned. They went out at times but mostly stayed in. They made love, often.

In time it became normal life. She stopped analysing it and worrying there was no future in it and just lived it.

And was happy—deliriously, amazingly, joyfully happy for four wonderful months—until one day the sense of unreality returned.

Lucas noticed her distraction straight away, but wasn't sure if he wanted to discover the cause. He just knew that he'd made her happy all these months and suddenly she wasn't. She continued to make love and let him hold her when it was over and fall asleep in his arms, but when the day came she was restless and anxious and evasive, and, like a coward, he didn't ask why.

A week passed before Tory finally told him. She'd considered concealing it as long as possible but that seemed dishonest.

'There's something you should know,' she announced over the dinner table, then followed it with a lengthy pause.

She'd been rehearsing the words all day but getting them out was something else. She half expected him to comment, *That sounds ominous*, but instead he sat, eyes fathomless, mouth unsmiling. He couldn't already know, could he?

No, she was being fanciful. She decided to tell him the whole story in the hope he might understand and at least forgive.

'When I was a child,' she began quietly, 'I had leukaemia. I was ten and I was treated with a combination of chemotherapy and radiotherapy which—'

'What are you saying, Tor?' Lucas's face was ashen. 'The cancer's returned?'

'No. No, nothing like that. I'm completely cured of it,' Tory assured him hastily. 'I'm sorry. I'm telling this badly…' She took a deep unsteady breath before going off on another apparent tangent. 'Do you remember outside Charlie and Caro's, when I said I'd never have children?'

He nodded, blue eyes fixed intently on her.

'The thing is—' she licked dry lips '—such treatment for cancer has the side effect of making people infertile.'

She paused, giving that fact a chance to sink in. A range of emotions passed over his face, too quickly for her to really read, before he murmured, 'The way you said it, I thought it was a lifestyle choice.'

'I probably gave that impression,' she admitted, 'but, at the time, I didn't feel obliged to go into detail.'

'And since?' he challenged.

Tory hung her head a little. She'd had several chances to tell the truth but had ducked them. 'I was afraid you'd dump me.'

'Because you couldn't have children?' An angry edge had crept into his voice. 'You don't think much of me, do you?'

'Charlie Wainwright dumped me,' she said in her defence.

'That's why you broke up?'

'Pretty much.'

He frowned darkly. 'I suppose you kept it from him, too.'

She nodded. 'At first. But then I didn't see us as a long-term thing.'

'You became engaged,' he reminded her heavily.

'We were at a New Year's party at his parents'.' Tory wanted him to understand how it had been. 'Loads of people there and, out of the blue, Charlie proposes in front of them all. I should have said no, I accept that now.'

Lucas also knew her well enough. 'Only you didn't want to embarrass him?'

She gave a nod, before conceding, 'I guess I fancied it a little, too, the whole package. Up till then Charlie's mother had been pleasant enough to me and his father was really nice and there were so many of them, Wainwright cousins and uncles and aunts. You felt it was a real family, that you'd almost be part of a dynasty… Do you know what I mean?'

'I should.' Lucas gave a dry smile. 'I was an in-law for four years, remember.'

'Yes, of course.' Tory had momentarily forgotten his first wife had been Charlie's sister.

'I was similarly seduced,' he admitted, 'being also an only child from a single parent set-up. But the Wainwright clan can be claustrophobic after a while, and too dependent.'

Tory realised he was referring to his own experience with the Wainwrights and raised a questioning brow.

'When I married Jessica,' he went on to explain, 'I was earning a relatively modest salary as a correspondent. She couldn't manage to live on it, nor did she want to, and she couldn't see why we had to when her parents were willing and able to supplement it, not to mention my wealthy stepfather... Call it male pride but I didn't like taking handouts.'

A shrug dismissed it as any big deal but his tone had said something else. Like all marriages, his and Jessica Wainwright's had been less than perfect.

'I appreciate that,' Tory said supportively.

He gave her a brief smile. 'One of life's ironies, I suppose, that I eventually did make it, but at the time money was our greatest source of conflict.'

'But you were happy, by and large?' Tory asked.

'Mostly.' It was a measured response, qualified by, 'Not the way I've been with you... You know I'm in love you, don't you, Tor?'

It was the first time he'd used the word love. Another of life's ironies. A week ago she would have wept with joy at it.

'Don't, Luc!' She knew he might take it back all too soon. 'Not till I'm finished saying what I have to say.'

'I thought we had. You can't have children,' he stated baldly. 'I can live with that.'

It wasn't what Tory wanted to hear.

'I can't,' she replied quietly.

His eyes narrowed. 'I don't follow.'

'I...let me explain it all,' she ran on. 'So Charlie and I got engaged and I tell him the truth next day. I don't know what I expected. At any rate, *he* couldn't live with it. His branch of the Wainwright family depended on him, so I let him off the hook.'

Lucas saw her eyes reflect painful memories and reached across the table to cover her hand with his. 'Well, I for one am glad you did. Who needs kids?' He made a dismissive gesture.

It cut through Tory like a knife. She hadn't finished her story but she couldn't now. It was pointless, unfair even.

'So we haven't a problem?' He raised a hand to cup her cheek.

The tenderness in the gesture almost undid her. But he was right. *We* didn't have a problem. *She* did. Not his fault at all.

'No,' she agreed.

'We can go on as we are,' he added.

Tory could have nodded. So much easier to lie. But she suddenly felt sick to her stomach.

'Excuse me.' She rose to her feet as she realised she was actually going to be sick. 'I have to…'

She couldn't think of any invention so she just took to her heels down the corridor to the bathroom of steel and glass. She didn't bother locking the door. Making it to the bowl in time seemed more important.

When Lucas tracked her down, she was still leaning over the sink, the cold tap running as she washed her mouth out. She sensed him behind her and glanced into the mirror to catch his image.

'I can't say I've ever had that effect on a woman before.' Lucas hid his true feelings behind humour.

'It's not you.' She straightened and immediately felt dizzy.

He saw her sway and, catching her arm, led her to a window-seat. 'Just the prospect of continuing to live with me.'

She shook her head. 'I do love you,' she admitted softly. 'I just…just feel trapped.'

'You're lying,' he accused. 'Trapped doesn't come into it, not when you love someone.'

There was a bitter note to his voice that Tory had never heard before. Perhaps she deserved it but she really couldn't cope with acrimony in her current state.

Tears sprung to her eyes and slowly, soundlessly, slid down

her face. She didn't look at him but she heard his exasperated sigh.

'For God's sake, don't cry on me, Tor… Here.' He handed her a tissue from a box on the shelf.

She used it to wipe her tears but more just replaced them. It wasn't the first time in the last week that she'd been a helpless weeping mess—or the first time she'd thrown up.

'Look, I'm sorry—' he bent to kneel at her side '—but I've let down enough women gently to read the signs. I need you to be straight up and honest with me. Just say the words: I don't love you, Luc. Then one of us will pack a bag—me, for now—and we'll shake hands and wish each other well.'

He tipped her chin up so he could see her face. She tried really hard to make it easy on them both. Got as far as 'I don't lo…', then couldn't go on.

He must see the truth in her eyes, anyway. She adored him. Was absolutely, irrevocably, painfully in love with this man.

'Please don't…' She appealed for him to understand.

Lucas didn't but he still put his arms round her and held her and rocked her until her crying subsided.

Tory clung to him, her resolve weakened by his show of compassion. She couldn't leave him. Not today. Tomorrow, maybe. Or some time later. When it showed.

For now she wanted to go on loving him, making love to him as, tears dried, she turned her head and sought his mouth with hers.

Lucas let her kiss him. Began to kiss her back. Lifted her up and carried her to their bed. Sought oblivion in her sweet, slender body. Found it too for a few precious moments.

Then he lay there, watching her catch her breath, rediscovering for the hundredth time how beautiful she was to him, and said words he promised himself he wouldn't.

'Stay with me, Tor—' He just stopped short of begging. 'Give it another chance. I'll—'

Tory put a hand to his mouth, unable to bear it and finally used the truth as a weapon to stop him.

'I'm pregnant.'

She didn't add to it, didn't need to. It hung between them like an exploded bombshell that left silence in its wake.

This time the emotions crossing his face were all too readable. Shock. Disbelief. Anger.

'Run that past me again,' he demanded at length.

She repeated simply, 'I'm pregnant.'

'You can't be.' Not half an hour earlier she'd told him exactly that. He sat up away from her in the bed. He couldn't look at her and think straight.

Tory sat up, too, leaning back against the pillows.

'I know I can't be, but I am.' She'd found out this week, although her body had been showing the signs for months. 'The doctors were wrong all that time ago or maybe it was a chance in a million and I got lucky.'

'Lucky?' He glanced round to challenge her choice of word.

'Yes.' It was how she felt, even now when his, 'Who needs kids?' had told her how *he* would feel. 'I've spent half my life thinking I'd never have children and now this.'

'You're keeping it?' he added.

'Yes.' She'd never considered otherwise. 'I didn't plan it but now it's happened, I'll live with it. That's the reason I'm leaving. I can't and don't expect anything from you, Luc.'

They had once briefly discussed contraception. He'd offered to be responsible and she'd claimed to have it covered. The mistake had been hers.

He twisted round fully and misread the mute apology on her face. 'It's not mine, is it?'

Tory hadn't anticipated such a question. Wishful thinking? Or did he genuinely believe she'd been unfaithful to him?

She shrugged. 'If that's what you'd prefer.'

'Of course it isn't!' His voice rose with his temper.

But Tory felt too emotionally fragile for a slanging match. She shifted to the edge of the bed and, picking up his discarded shirt as a shield, stood up.

He followed, making no attempt to hide his nakedness. In fact, he took the shirt from her nerveless fingers and threw it on the bed. Then he stared at her, down at the slight curve of her belly.

Tory trembled at his intensity then actually flinched when he put the palm of his hand above the place where their baby was growing.

'It's mine now.' He stroked her flesh.

The most intimate of acts without being remotely sexual. 'I—I don't understand.'

'You're mine,' he told her, 'so it's mine. Simple. Just like I'm yours. What happened before we were together has no significance.'

Tory finally caught up. He thought she'd come to him already pregnant. And now, here he was, lying through his teeth—she knew fine he hated the idea of her with another man—so he could keep her.

'I do so love you, Lucas Ryecart.' She wanted him to know that. 'But it's not going to work. "Who needs kids?" Remember? That's what you said less than half an hour ago.'

His brow creased, as if he couldn't recall ever thinking such a thing, far less saying it, even as he admitted, 'Okay, I said it. But what do you expect? The girl I'm planning to marry has just told me she can't have children. So I tell her I want four? I don't think so.'

'Marry?' Tory repeated in a slight daze.

'The sooner, the better, don't you think?' he countered.

Tory still looked at him in disbelief. 'Isn't that rather conventional?'

He grimaced. 'These days conventional is: the man runs out on the women, leaving her holding the baby. I'm assuming that's what he's done.'

'Who?'

'Whoever.'

Tory could have been really mad with him but for the facts a) he was willing to look after her and the child, regardless, and b) she loved him, also regardless.

'My last lover was a sports commentator who worked for ITV,' she began to recount.

'I don't think I want to hear this.'

'Well, tough! Just listen. We had a brief, rather tepid affair that ended amicably when he went off for a month to cover the World Cup.'

'But that was a couple of years ago?'

'Quite, and I'm three months pregnant.'

He looked confused but Tory decided to wait until the penny dropped by itself and, feeling a bit absurd arguing naked, went to pick up her clothes from the floor.

Lucas watched her dressing, then dressed too, but on automatic pilot as the true situation dawned on him.

'It's my baby.' It was a statement this time.

Tory turned and awarded him a somewhat cheeky grin. ''Fraid so, but there's always plastic surgery.'

'It's not funny.' For once Lucas wanted a serious conversation.

But Tory felt skittish. He'd asked her to marry him! He'd asked her to marry him while thinking she was having someone else's baby! What other love token did a girl need?

'So why did you let me believe otherwise?' he demanded, trying to remain angry with her.

'Not guilty, your honour,' she threw back. 'I said, ''I'm pregnant.'' You said, ''It's not mine, is it?'' I rest my case… I'm starving. Fancy some supper?'

He looked ready to explode at the change of subject but Tory was too happy to care as she walked back through the living area to the kitchen beyond. All week she'd fretted over his reaction. She still wasn't sure precisely what it was but telling her he loved her was certainly an improvement on what she'd visualised.

He trailed her through, still arguing the toss. 'But why else keep it a secret? Why not tell me earlier? You knew days ago, didn't you?'

'I thought…' she paused to sort it out in her own head '…you'd imagine it was deliberate. That I'd got pregnant to trap you. I felt bad, too. You'd made it plain you weren't planning on children and I said I had it covered. I really did think it was impossible, you know?'

He nodded, accepting her word, and realised how each had

misread the other. 'In point of fact, kids were part of my five-year plan.'

'Five-year plan?'

'First year you live with me. Second year, I convince you to marry me. Third and fourth we consolidate. Fifth, we reproduce.'

He ticked each off with a finger and Tory was left wondering if he really could have thought that far ahead.

'I've wrecked that, then.' She grimaced in apology.

'So, things will happen a little quicker.' He shrugged and, coming round the side of the breakfast bar, put his arms round her waist from behind. 'And money isn't a problem so you can choose whether to take a career break or hire a good old British nanny or work part-time if the boss is amenable,' he ended on a wry note.

'And is he?'

'Very.'

It was banter but Tory added more seriously, 'Is he really? To fatherhood, I mean.'

'Hell, yes.' He grinned back. 'If I wait much longer, I'd be too old to swing a baseball bat.'

'Cricket bat, you mean,' she couldn't resist correcting. 'Anyway, it could be a girl.'

'Either one will suit,' he replied and Tory didn't have to see his face to know he was smiling.

She turned in his arms all the same and reached up to kiss him on the cheek and say, 'Thank you.'

He slanted her a quizzical look. 'What was that for?'

'Making it all right.' Tory still couldn't believe her luck.

'All right?' he echoed and laughed aloud. 'It's goddamn wonderful!'

And Tory finally trusted it was real, the life of happiness stretching before her, coloured vivid by the man at her side.

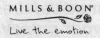

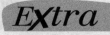

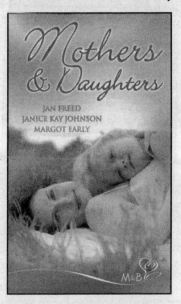